FIRE SONG

TANYA ANNE CROSBY

OLIVER HEBER BOOKS

Published by Oliver-Heber Books

© 2019 Cover Art by Cora Graphics

0 9 8 7 6 5 4 3 2 1

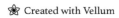 Created with Vellum

SERIES BIBLIOGRAPHY

A BRAND-NEW SERIES

DAUGHTERS OF AVALON

The King's Favorite

The Holly & the Ivy

A Winter's Rose

Fire Song

Rhiannon

ELEMENTAL MAGIK

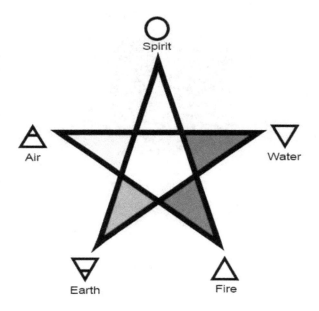

I have been a multitude of shapes before I assumed this form: I was a drop of rain in the air; I was the brightest of stars...

— *TALIESIN*

PROLOGUE

Moonlight shone off the oily contents of an ornately carved tub, making the substance darker under its silvery light.

From a dark corner of the foul-smelling room came a persistent *rap, tap, tap.* This was Bran—Morwen's familiar—though it was impossible to say what the filthy bird could be doing. There were no lamps lit to chase away the shadows, nor even a stingy taper, and it was perhaps to her mother's delight that her three youngest daughters sat shivering on a dirty bed in the darkness.

What in the name of the Goddess did she expect they would do? Burn down the inn?

For certes, any one of them could do so without a candle. But even as frightened as they were, they would never, ever endanger innocent lives. There were others in residence here at Darkwood.

Rap, tap. Rap, tap, rap. Rap. Tap.

Instinctively, the three sisters huddled closer. Soiled and greasy as the sheets must be, they daren't leave its sanctuary. Not only was the room cold and dark, but the scent of something pungent and disturbingly familiar filled Seren with a terrible foreboding. It was a feeling she couldn't ignore, for in itself, intuition was a form of *magik,* ancient as the world was old. According to their grandmamau all men, no matter their blood, had a sense for such things. At the moment, her own sense of intuition was like a mantle of gloom, dark and oppressive.

How wrong she had been about their mother— how very wrong. For so long Seren had convinced herself that, deep down, their mother must love them—as any mother should. She had convinced herself that once Morwen found herself a proper benefactor she would send for her daughters, and then, they would all live happily ever after. Only now she realized... that was a fool's dream... a child's desperate fantasy. Morwen's disdain for her children couldn't be more apparent. It was tangible, evidenced by the curl of her lip whenever she deigned to acknowledge them. And yet, the truth was difficult to bear: Their mother loathed them, and whatever plans she had for them now, they would suit Morwen and no other.

Rap, tap. Tap, tap, tap. Tap.... tap.

Silence met Bran's application—a silence so complete Seren couldn't even hear her sisters breathing.

Even if they were brave enough to attempt an escape, it would be impossible with those two burly guards posted outside their door. In the overwhelming gloom of this room, she couldn't even see her own hand in front of her face, much less a means for escape.

And... no matter that they were alone, save for that dreary old bird, Seren couldn't shake the awful feeling they were being watched...

Rap, tap. Tap, tap, tap. Tap.

"It's just a bird," she said aloud.

For her sisters' sakes, she refused to be cowed. They were Pendragons, descended of Welsh kings. But more, she and her sisters were the last living *dewines* born of the blood of Taliesin, the great Merlin of Britain. They were true daughters of Avalon, children of the Earth Mother and maidens pledged to the *hud*. And despite that their mother believed them without wit or will, they had skills, thanks to dear, defiant Rhiannon, who was led from their cottage last night with hands bound and a length of rope about her neck, like a bloody hound.

Much to their dismay, they hadn't seen her since. The very instant she was wheeled away, their mother ushered them into one of Ersinius' wagons and spirited them here, to this decrepit little inn surrounded by dark, twisty woods. And then, immediately upon arrival, their mother's sycophant, Mordecai, led them up the stairs, leaving Morwen downstairs to barter with the innkeeper.

Hours later, the shock of their ordeal was slowly subsiding, but uncertainty bridled their tongues, until finally, Arwyn dared to breach the silence. "Where do you think they will take her?"

There was no need to ask of whom she spoke... even without *mindspeaking*, they were thinking the same thing. "I know not," answered Rosalynde.

Seren rubbed her left arm, at the very spot where Mordecai's fingers had gripped her flesh so meanly. "I heard tell Blackwood."

"Blackwood?" asked both her sisters in unison.

Equally confused by the disclosure, Seren shrugged. Only Elspeth had ever seen their familial estate, built high in the Black Mountains. It was served now by a new lord—one of King Stephen's known assassins—but it was Elspeth, not Rhiannon, who had been promised to that lord.

Like Avalon, the castle and its lands were now lost to them forevermore because of their mother's greed, but evidently, Morwen had a plan to retrieve it.

"What kind of beast would accept a bride delivered by tumbril?" asked Rosalynde.

Arwyn retorted. "What kind of mother delivered her so?"

"A mean, greedy *witch*," answered Seren.

And, aye, she'd meant to use that word with all the disgust most commoners felt for it. *Witch.*

It was a very good thing Elspeth fled the priory when she did, else she might never have gone, and even now if she learned of Rhiannon's fate, Seren had little doubt her eldest sister would return. After all, Ellie had been more a mother to them than Morwen ever was, and she would never have left them if she had known what travesty would befall them.

On the other hand, Rhiannon must have known something. She had been so insistent that Elspeth leave, and once Elspeth was gone... *everything* changed.

As life happened, her sister claimed, nothing occurred without consequence. There was a price to be paid for every decision made. Seren's only consolation was that Rhiannon must have understood her fate. She must have known that she would be expected to take Ellie's place... but to what end?

It was only after the *rap, tap, tapping* began again that she realized they'd been blessed with an interval of silence—silence enough to allow her to think clearly.

But now the bird pecked more ardently at some unseen morsel, giving Seren a shiver as she listened.

It was a long, long time before Morwen returned, and when she did, she wore a smile as black as her heart.

Carrying a torch, Morwen waltzed into the room like a cat who'd swallowed a mouse, and it was only then, by the light of her flickering torch, that Seren saw what it was that Bran was pecking at... bits of raw flesh. Blood stained the floor where he pranced. Her stomach roiled, but she daren't look at her sisters for fear that one of them might sob.

For the moment, ignoring her daughters, Morwen gazed fondly at her hideous bird. "Has my sweet pet been entertaining you with his supper?" she crooned, more to the bird than to any one of her daughters. "My beautiful boy."

As the girls watched, she placed her torch into a cresset, and then, still smiling, she flicked open a small compartment on her ancient ring, then moved toward the tub, turning the contents into the dark liquid. Only then, once this was done, she met Seren's gaze, and like a lover tempting a man, she removed her gown. Convulsively, Seren swallowed, desperate to look away, only self-preservation kept her eyes affixed on her mother. Once bared, she slid her nubile body into the tub, wading into the glistening liquid, and then, sat, like a seductress bathing in oils.

But it was not oil, Seren realized belatedly.

It was blood.

Dark as a plum.

Horrified, she watched as Morwen painted her lips with the oily substance, then, thoroughly amused by Seren's expression, she giggled, and giggled... and giggled... and then she began to sing:

When thy father went a-hunting,
A spear on his shoulder, a club in his
　　hand,
He called the nimble hounds,
'Giff, Gaff; catch, catch, fetch, fetch!'

1

The skies were blue again, streaked with wispy, white clouds that were moving too fast to cluster.

With plenty of wind to fill the sails, the harbor was bustling with last-minute preparations—supplies being hauled onto ships, deckhands inquiring after work.

Adding to the mayhem, the Maritime Market was teeming, drawing merchants and customers to the Saturday Feria after more than a *sennight* of storms.

Considering his best course of action, Wilhelm Fitz Richard stood chewing on a length of straw. Tall as he was—six-feet-five and weighing more than sixteen stone—it had been teasing the pate of his head, and rather than move aside, he'd wrenched the offending tuft from the awning and slid it between his lips, hoping to deceive his brain into forgetting about his complaining belly.

By now he was ravenous, and to make matters worse, the scent of fowl roasting somewhere nearby was making his mouth water and his thoughts go astray. Truth to tell, he hadn't enjoyed a good repast since leaving Warkworth, but so much as he craved a fat, juicy bird leg, he wasn't about to leave his post... not yet. He had a feeling in his gut that time was growing as thin as those clouds.

Two months ago, Arwyn and Seren Pendragon fled the palace in London. Best as anyone could surmise, they'd slipped away during the wee hours, very likely on the day their sister Rosalynde stole his brother's horse.

Fate was such a trickster, twisting circumstances every which way and that. Inexplicably, they'd abandoned one Pendragon in London only to escort another one north. And then, after all was said and done, his brother forsook his intended, only to lose his heart to her sister.

Wilhelm couldn't blame Giles, not really. Somehow, despite his bitter loathing for their mother, Wilhelm himself had developed a soft spot for Rosalynde. That was why he was here, now, searching for her bloody sisters.

Thinking it only naturally the direction they would go, he'd wasted weeks searching north. Stephen controlled nearly every port save Bristol, and so it had surprised him to learn their trail wended south instead, ending here, then going as cold as a witch's tatty thereafter.

So, it seemed, the sisters were slippery as wet eels, and knowing Rosalynde so well as he did, he suspected Arwyn and Seren must be using *magik* to avoid capture—*magik* he didn't particularly comprehend, though he'd witnessed firsthand what it could do. God's truth, if aught plagued him more than the memory of his decimated kinsmen, it was the memory of the Shadow Beast they'd encountered a few months ago in the woodlot south of Whittlewood and Salcey.

To this very day he hadn't any clue how they'd defeated the hideous creature, and no matter how many times Rosalynde explained it, he couldn't wrap his brain about the doing of it—something about binding and transmutation, things he might never have dreamt of in his worst night terrors... leastways not before seeing it. Strange as it might seem, he owed his life to a slip of a girl, and God save him if he should ever encounter another.

Nipping at the straw, considering all the ships in the harbor, his best guess was this: If he were in their shoes, he might seek sanctuary with the Empress in Rouen. And, if this be the case, as a matter of conjecture, they must be aboard one of those larger cogs—the Whitshed perhaps.

Today, there were only three ships large enough to navigate the open sea—the Whitshed, the Achéron and the Cassiopé. The largest of these, the Whitshed, was owned by a known conspirator—a man who, though he remained suspect to the crown, was well protected by the Church, else his lands would have long been forfeit by now.

On the other hand, the captains of the other two vessels—the Achéron and Cassiopé—were fiercely loyal to the Crown. Even now, the Achéron harbored an emissary en route to St. Omer to bargain with Canterbury's exiled archbishop, Theobald of Bec. Perforce, Stephen would have Theobald crown his son though he still lived, though evidently, Theobald would rather keep his exile than put Eustace on England's throne. That was a good thing, because Wilhelm was like to commit treason if that fool was ever confirmed. As it was, it was all he could do not to take a torch to the royal palace and burn it to the ground.

Wasn't that what scripture ordained—an eye for an eye?

Aye, well... one day he still might.

One day he'd like to see every man and woman responsible for the slaughter of his kinsmen pay for their sins, and, aye, that included Rosalynde's wretched mother, Morwen Pendragon.

He bloody well wasn't afraid of her—or at least that's what he told himself every night before closing his eyes.

I'll see your skin turn black till it slips off your bones.

As it was with his loved ones.

All these months later, the memory threatened to purge his belly and ruin his appetite. God's truth, no matter how many years he lived, he would never forget... that stench... seared flesh. The eye-stinging smoke and ash that turned the landscape gray. Wilhelm had been the youngest of his father's sons, except for Giles, and in one fell swoop, he'd become the eldest, with two half-sisters gone, and an older brother as well. Only Wilhelm and Giles had survived, and only because neither were present at the time.

Pulling the straw between his teeth, he studied the Whitshed... he couldn't very well force his way aboard. If he tried, or even if he approached the situation with candor, and he was wrong about the captain's allegiance, it could very well alert the Crown of his intentions. Not only would he give away the sisters' location, it could bring undue attention to Warkworth —attention they could ill afford whilst Giles was busy conspiring with Matilda.

This was delicate business, but come what may, he'd sworn to find Rosalynde's sisters and see them safely returned to Warkworth and that's what he meant to do. Only he would need their trust. It would serve no one for him to go barging aboard that vessel to drag them away perforce.

Watching the deckhands trek from ship to ship, he thought perhaps he could inquire about work, perhaps ask to inspect the sleeping quarters... but, nay, that wouldn't do. There were more than enough willing and able bodies who didn't give a bloody damn about sleeping arrangements, so long as they had a belly full of victuals and a pocket full of coin. They were far more likely to turn him away.

But perhaps he could feign business with the captain...

He knew enough about Airard's history to know how to begin: As it so happened, his namesake and grandsire was the captain of the Mora, the flagship of The Conqueror's invading fleet, and judging by the simple fact that he'd followed in his father's and grandfather's footsteps (even despite that his own father also found his fate at the bottom of a salt-sea), meant that he was sure to be vain about his legacy. He could find a way to flatter the man, and then perhaps determine if the Pendragon sisters were aboard his ship. Alas, Wilhelm wasn't as sophisticated as Giles; lies tasted bitter to his tongue.

For the past two days he'd been watching the Whitshed's comings and goings. The only female he'd spotted was perhaps an elder sister of one of the deckhands. Arm in arm with a boy, she'd disembarked two hours past, although he didn't believe that could be Seren. He knew what she looked like and he couldn't imagine the sisters separating for any reason. Where one went, the other was sure to follow.

Unless...

He couldn't help but remember the morning they'd encountered Rosalynde in the thicket. She'd given herself what she called a *glamour*. The effect was hideous; it had been all Wilhelm could do not to look at her. Dressed as a nun, she'd fashioned herself in the most unappealing manner possible, with eyes crossed and a pocked face. How his brother had found the wherewithal to keep her on his mount was a mystery to Wilhelm.

To the contrary, it had been all Wilhelm could do not to gape at Seren when he'd met her in the King's Hall. She was easily the most stunning woman he'd ever beheld. Truly, even as lovely as Rosalynde might have turned out to be without the *glamour*, it was inconceivable to Wilhelm that any man—not even St. Giles—would rebuff Seren for want of another. Seren Pendragon was a paragon of beauty, rightfully earning her reputation as the Beauty of Blackwood. Even now, all these months later, and particularly whilst he'd been searching for her, it was much to his chagrin that he sometimes dreamt of the lady, even despite knowing she was not meant for him. And not only was she a coveted beauty, but she was an heir of the Pendragon line, a bastard child to Henry himself. All things considered, illegitimate or not, she was a valuable pawn in Stephen's game of Queen's Chess. Baseborn as he was, Wilhelm wasn't fit to kiss her slippers.

And by the by, if he couldn't win the hand of the daughter of a lowly baron, winning Seren would be hopeless.

Reminded of Ayleth of Bamburgh, Wilhelm's mood soured. With a grumble, he tossed down the tuft of straw, kicking it annoyedly, finally losing the battle of wills with his belly—he was famished, damn it all to hell.

Twenty minutes—that's all he needed. Those bloody ships wouldn't be going anywhere in the meantime. Merely twenty minutes, he reasoned, and then it was time to take more drastic measures.

Morwen Pendragon was due to be released from the Tower on the morrow, and she would immediately set out to accomplish what her minions could not. She would ferret out her daughters more easily than Wilhelm ever could, and judging by what that Shadow Beast had been capable of, its contemptible mistress was a force to be avoided at all cost.

No bloody wonder her daughters ensconced themselves like moles, never daring to peer out of their holes.

One way or another he was going to find a way aboard that ship... but first things first; it was time to silence the beast in his belly. His temper would be far less offensive if he shoveled something down his gob, and with that decided, he cast a last glance at the Whitshed, then made straight for the smoking brick building at the edge of the market, his nostrils flaring over the scent of freshly cooked fowl.

❧

AFTER ALL THESE MONTHS, Ellie and Rose must be worried sick. Seren was right; they couldn't depart England without sending news. But as the time neared to depart, Arwyn grew more and more anxious by the second.

Pacing relentlessly, she chewed at her nails.

Much as she loathed to confess it, she understood why Seren didn't wish for her to accompany them to the courier: Arwyn hadn't much composure, nor even a smattering of her sisters' *dewine* skills, but alas, she needn't have any *dewine* skills to sense impending doom.

Even now, safe in the bowels of this vessel, with so many of Matilda's allies surrounding her, she knew...

Something dreadful was looming, something she couldn't see or hear, but something she could feel... deep, down in her bones, like an ague.

Back and forth.

Back and forth, she paced.

The wooden floor was dry and full of splinters. Her slippers were ragged, catching every sliver as she passed. Muttering an oath, she took off her shoes and cast them away.

Ten long days they'd awaited opportune sailing weather—ten fear-filled days, wherein every second of every day they'd worried Morwen would find them. After all, Dover was no bastion, for Matilda and Stephen's guards were here in droves. It defied logic to be here at all, in the heart of Stephen's domain, but Seren, in her wisdom, had argued against doing what everyone expected them to do. Instead of fleeing north, they'd talked a fisherman into ferrying them east, traveling by night on the Thames all the way to Gravesend. Then, afoot they'd gone to Canterbury, where they sought shelter with the Church.

Fortunately, even after all these years, their Empress sister still had friends in high places. Escorted by Matilda's allies, they'd come south to Dover only to bide their time aboard this vessel. Now, very soon, after all the stories Elspeth told about Matilda, they would finally embrace their half-sister. And, so much as Rhiannon loved to begrudge Ellie's affection for their father's only true remaining heir, Matilda must not be so terrible as Rhi liked to believe—not if she so willingly offered her protection. By sundown, if everything went well, they would disembark in Calais.

From there, they would venture to Rouen—safe at last out of Morwen's grasp.

On her birthday, no less, they would finally depart England, and with a bit of luck and wind, Captain Airard assured them they could make the journey in less than three hours' time—only so long as Seren returned before the tide turned, and so long as their mother remained ignorant of the journey.

Faith, she commanded herself.

Have faith.

After all, it was faith that brought them to Dover.

Where are you, Seren?

By now, Arwyn's nails were spent to the quick, and regardless, she couldn't stop fretting.

What a heinous way to spend her birthday.

What if, after all, their mother should glean their intentions? All it would take to endanger the crossing would be for Morwen to have a small inkling they were traveling. Even from her tower prison, she could send a fog like the one she'd sent to doom the White Ship.

Look at the bright side, Arwyn...

There was no sign of Mordecai, nor any of her mother's minions. And despite that fact, with so much at stake, Arwyn could no more find peace in her heart than she could have remained in her mother's keeping. Perhaps, after all, she should have insisted on going with Seren...

"It'll be faster if you remain aboard ship," her sister maintained. "No one will be searching for a woman alone with a young boy. And besides, Arwyn, you'll attract undue attention."

"I would cast a glamour," she'd argued.

"Will you?" her sister had said, and Arwyn had blushed, because, nay, she could not. Her *glamour* spells were sorely deficient, and in the end, she was apt to move five freckles to one side of her face. Therefore, she'd relented—and here she remained, with sore fingers and a sulky mood.

Truth be told, the simple fact that they had avoided capture so long was more a testimony to Matilda's influence—none so much to their own ingenuity. Seren had no guile and Arwyn had no *magik*, but, thankfully, no matter that Arwyn and Seren had no true relationship with their Empress sister, they were bound by blood—and more, they were bound by a common purpose. More than anything, they would love to see Stephen deposed. Perhaps he wasn't as wicked as their mother, nor so greedy as his sour-faced wife, nor even as mean as his son, but he had nevertheless forsworn a sacred oath to their father, and his ignoble actions placed England at war—fourteen long years now. God help them all if Morwen should succeed in replacing father with son.

So much death.

So much destruction.

So much deceit.

All about her, the ship creaked like a bag of old bones. Arwyn could hear them trampling over deck with last-minute preparations. It was a continual reminder that she was alone amidst strangers—whether or not they be allies. After all, it would only take one traitor to reveal them, and it would be a terrible travesty if they were discovered so close to escape, when there was hope at last.

Seren is fine, she told herself.

It must be true, else she would know it. If aught should ever happen to *any* of her sisters, she would know it deep, deep down. They were connected, one to another, and each to the other. As *dewines*, they shared a very special bond, and she and Rose deeper yet because they were twins.

Somewhere up on deck, there came a dreadful thud, followed by a long interval of silence, and the heavy silence unnerved Arwyn even more than the preceding racket.

Irritated with herself—particularly, because this worrisome behavior was precisely why none of her sisters ever trusted her to comport herself accordingly —she reached into a hidden skirt pocket, and plucked out the shard of crystal she'd stolen from her mother's chamber.

She and her sister both had a piece of Merlin's Crystal. It was the last thing they did before leaving Westminster—shatter the scrying stone so Morwen couldn't seek them.

However, for much of the time since leaving London, Arwyn's shard had remained dark. At the instant it was flickering softly, and the light pulse managed to calm her nerves as words alone could not.

Fire was Arwyn's one true affinity, but though she liked to jest that Rosalynde had leached her powers in the womb, her lack of skill could simply be because their bloodline was no longer so pure. Her grandmother was not the first to wed a commoner. Long, long before Morgan Pendragon married a prince of Gwynedd, their great, great, great grandmother, Yissachar—the only daughter of Creirwy and Taliesin— married a Briton. She and her sisters were of a very noble and ancient bloodline, but little by little, their *dewine* legacy was dying... Like the shard in her hand, her *dewinefolk* were broken and scattered.

It was heart-wrenching to see what remained of such a venerable heirloom.

Mesmerized by the flickering in her hand, she sat

upon the bed, wondering idly if she would ever wed, and if her children would be more inclined to the Craft. Unlike Elspeth, Arwyn had no fear of the *hud* at all, and though she knew enough to respect it immensely, she desperately longed to wield it like their sister Rhiannon.

And perhaps she still might... they had the Book of Secrets after all. Once she was reunited with Ellie and Rose, she could apply herself to the Craft, study hard, and perhaps someday she would wield *magik* at least as well as Rose.

"Happy birthday, sweet Rose," she said fondly. Until this terrible travesty, she and her twin had never spent a day apart, much less a birth anniversary.

How she missed Rose. Rose understood her better than anyone, and though they couldn't be more different, her twin was everything Arwyn was not, and Arwyn was everything Rose was not. Together they were whole.

Above deck there came another boom, and the shard in her hand glowed a little brighter. Strange but... she was no longer afraid. Comforted by the crystalized flame in her palm, she wondered what the flickering meant. So often it seemed the shard was like the piece of a puzzle, showing bits and bobs. Betimes it was possible to put hers together with Seren's and more easily recognize a face, or a place. But it was impossible to say what *this* meant.

Turning the crystal, she studied it intently, in much the same manner she would, as a girl, sit for hours and stare into a hearth fire. No matter that she could never see what Rhiannon saw in those flames, she could still *feel* things. They'd had a maid called Isolde who'd claimed the world was born of fire and that someday it would be consumed by fire. Nothing about this prophecy frightened Arwyn. To the contrary, it intrigued her. Her soul was akin to fire and, even now, she could feel the intensity of her affinity simmering through her veins.

I am fire, fire becomes me.

Mollified by the glow in her hand, she marveled over what she held... the tiny shard, along with the Book of Secrets... they were all that remained of their *dewine* legacy. And yet for all that her name meant enlightenment, Arwyn herself was a testament to a dying breed. Sadly, the sons and daughters of Uther and Yissachar would be the last to bear Taliesin's blood, for it was one thing to be a Pendragon, and another to be a *dewine* born of the blood of Taliesin. These two things were not one of the other; they were each unto their own. Uther Pendragon was not a *dewine*, and neither was Taliesin a Pendragon. As a matter of due course, their *dewine* blood would continue to thin until not one drop remained, and no men or women were left who could conjure a mist, less remember the Promised Land.

Feeling a chill in the cabin, she tore her gaze away from the crystal and returned the shard to her pocket, focusing on the tinder in the brazier. There, ribbons gathered and converged into a point of light. Her *dewine* eyes could see what other folks might not—the twisting and turning of the *aether* as sparks ignited in the brazier. Encouraged by the ease of her *magik*, and only to try it—because she was thirsty—she laid out a palm, attempting to gather water from the *aether* as Rosalynde could do... Already, there were particles in the air, and her *dewine* senses could *feel* them, but unlike Rosalynde, she couldn't bring them together. It was no more a fantastical feat than to watch a lodestone draw metal, but it seemed that leaves could do a better job than she could, gathering dew by morn, whilst she accomplished naught.

Her palm remained dry as a bone and her tongue parched. She daren't go above deck without Seren, and she knew the men were all too busy to serve her.

Frowning, disgusted, because she understood very well how it all worked and simply couldn't perform the *magik*, she flicked another glance at the brazier.

By now, she had studied the Craft as dutifully as her sisters, and she kept her faith in the Old Ways, but for all that, she could only *mindspeak* with her twin, and draw a simple fire; that was all. She was a poor excuse for a witch.

Startled by the turn of the doorknob, Arwyn glanced up. The door creaked opened, revealing a black-hooded figure—a man she didn't recognize. Startled, she bounded up from the bed, her heart hammering over the look on his face.

"What is it?" she demanded. "Is it my sister? Where is Seren?"

The man's grin slowly unfurled. His dark eyes narrowed, and his canine teeth pressed ruthlessly over his lips. It was only then, as he glared at her, that she realized his black eyes held an unnatural gleam, and fear sidled down her spine. All the calm she'd managed to attain vanished in the blink of his eyes. Not once during the past ten days had she encountered this man aboard ship, neither below deck nor above.

"Who are you?" she demanded.

"Your sister will return soon," he said, smirking as he closed the door. He reached up to pull the bolt across to bar it.

Arwyn took a step backward, the tiny hairs on her nape prickling. "Who are you?" she asked again.

In answer, his grin spread wider, the pressure of his canines turning his lips bloodless.

"*Who* I am is of far less import than *who* sent me, my dear. Your mother is heartily aggrieved not to be able to celebrate your birth anniversary as she longs to."

Betrayed!

Arwyn opened her mouth to scream, but the instant she did so, her tongue grew fat in her mouth, choking her words as well as her breath. Her fingers flew to her throat as the man jiggled the door to make sure it was locked. Arwyn took another defensive step backward.

"Dear girl... you gave us a time," he scolded. "No matter how thoroughly we searched, we could simply not find you. We thought for certes you would fly north. But nay... here you are."

Clawing at her throat, Arwyn tried again to scream, but no sound squeezed through her tightened throat.

Clearly, this was her mother's servant—one of the many fanatics who bowed to Morwen's every whim.

Watching her face, smiling cruelly as she attempted to speak again, he said, "I am not so adept as your mother, but she taught me well." And with that revelation, he shoved back the hood of his cloak. "You see... we *have* met before," he said, introducing himself. "My name is Bran."

Arwyn's eyes widened with fright. She shook her head. *Nay!* It couldn't be. Bran was the name of her mother's familiar. Bran—the beady-eyed raven Morwen kept by her side.

Shivering with fear, recognizing the unholy light in the man's eyes, she nevertheless knew it to be true and she made a dash for the door. Bran caught her too easily, flying at her with his cloak unfurled and pushing her back onto the bed like a limp doll. "Where are your manners?" he scolded. "Nay, sweetling. We shall sit and wait for your pretty sister. And once she returns, we will *all* return to your mother."

Choking on her fear as much as her tongue, Arwyn scrambled backward on the bed, away from this unholy beast. Her gaze skittered across the room, from the door, over the walls, searching for something—*anything*, she could use to defend herself. But even as she searched, she knew... she knew... this man had come to her armed with her mother's *magik*... Arwyn had no *magik* at all.

She had but *one* tool at her disposal...

Only one.

Fire.

His smile stretched over those canines, widening so that his nose curved under like a beak. "I see you understand, my dear girl." And he cast a hand out. "Truly, there's naught to be done." His voice was ever-so calm. "Once your sister returns, my mission is complete. How pleased your mother will be."

Oh, nay! Nay! Nay!

It cannot end this way.

"More's the pity for you, she'll never underestimate you again."

Hot tears burned Arwyn's eyes. She wished so desperately to call for help, but even if she could have, she knew instinctively no one would hear. The surrounding silence was devoid of life.

Sweet fates! Had he murdered the captain and crew? Was that the sound she'd heard above deck? He leaned against the door now, his eyes smiling once he realized she understood the futility of her circumstances.

But... there *was* something she could do.

Until Seren returned, he had only her. Until Seren returned, her sister remained free. And, so long as one of them remained free, she would live to fight another day...

Like her mother, Bran was evil incarnate. Morwen *must* be stopped. At *all* cost her mother *must* be stopped. If no one stopped her she would doom England as surely as Cerridwen had once doomed Avalon. And if this man, in truth, was Bran, *shapeshifting* was *hud du* known to only one *dewine* in all creation: Cerridwen, the destroyer of realms.

Aye, 'tis she. You know what to do, sweet sister.

Rhiannon?

Trust your heart to the flame.

Somehow, it was as though Rhiannon herself came and embraced her, giving her strength in love, and in that instant, beyond all things earthly, Arwyn understood what must be done...

Bran constrained her words, but not her hands; that would be his undoing. One hot tear slid past her lashes, trickling onto her cheek as she reached into her pocket for the shard of Merlin's crystal, revealing it to Bran.

For an instant, her mother's minion tilted his face as though mesmerized. The shard ignited blue, and Rhiannon needn't speak again to say what she must do. Arwyn already knew. She was lost. Now that Bran had her in his grasp, he'd never set her free. He was far too canny to succumb to tricks. But Arwyn had no *magik*. And worse, she had no guile.

No one would come to rescue her—no one but Seren, and Seren was no match for this servant of darkness.

If they returned to their mother, their lives would be forfeit.

Sadness squeezed her heart, and her pupils reflected the blue firelight in her hand... else the fire in her eyes imbued the crystal...

The most tragic thing in the world for a flame burning bright was to become a harbinger of darkness.

Right now, this instant, Arwyn *was* the flame. She was born for this instant. No one could save her, but she could save Seren.

It was an instant too long before Bran understood what she held in her hand. The shard transmuted. The blue flame in her hand illumined the entire room. And before Bran could stop her, she hurled the crystal at the door where it burst into bright blue flames.

Excitement danced down Seren's spine.

Come nightfall she and Arwyn would be far, far from this nest of vipers, but at the instant, with the sun shining so brilliantly, she sorely regretted having left her cooped up aboard that ship—on her birthday no less.

After nearly a fortnight of raging storms, today was the Saturday Feria, and the entire affair reminded Seren of the merchant days at Llanthony, when Father Ersinius entertained his artisans. Naturally, that was always a crush, but nothing like this. The market affected an air of celebration, with jugglers and musicians in attendance and balladeers singing at the top of their lungs.

A wistful reed and a bullish lute vied for attention, even as the scent of Frankish perfumes competed with the aroma of smoked meats and the bright, inescapable hues of artisanal crafts.

Excited by the prospect of returning with a treat for Arwyn, she dug a hand into the pocket she'd sewn into her dress, searching for coins, and frowned when she encountered only loose bits of a philter for a glamour spell, and a shard of Merlin's Crystal—worthless to anyone who didn't know what it was. "Jack!" she called out, but he was already off around a corner, in a hurry to return to his father.

She quickened her pace.

Her escort this morning was a sweet lad, whose sense of duty was inarguable. Ignoring tarts and mouth-watering pastries, he hurried past fine, wooden boats with beautiful silk sails, but it was inconceivable to her that a boy could turn a blind eye to so many treasures.

There were desirables in every booth they passed, everything from intricate, wooden carvings inlaid with gold and beautiful, soft furs to sweets and strange, fire-colored fruits from faraway lands.

And, ye gods! If her nose spoke true, there must be every sort of bread to be had—biscuits, bloomers and barm cakes, walnut, fig, sourdough and rye. It was enough to make her mouth water and her eyes bulge with desire.

"Care t' try a boit?" asked a jolly looking fellow holding a morsel of pie. Seren shook her head, though regretfully. Jack was moving so swiftly now it was all she could do to keep up.

Sweet tarts. Oh, my!

"Jack!" she called again, reaching once more into her pocket, as though by sheer will alone she could alter their circumstances—and perhaps Rhiannon could, but Seren could not. Her *magik* was scarcely more puissant than Arwyn's, although at least Seren could keep a *glamour*, and failing that, she wasn't ter-rible with concealment spells, although at Jack's breakneck pace, a concealment spell wasn't necessary. They must be a blur to everyone's eyes.

Arwyn would love one of those tarts.

This year was the first year she and her sisters had

spent their birth anniversaries apart. After all they had already endured, Seren hadn't wished to remind Arwyn she was spending hers so far from Rose, but she was fooling herself if she believed Arwyn wasn't already lamenting the fact. From their very first breaths, and perhaps before, those two had shared an uncommon bond, as twins always must.

A tart would put a smile on her face, but, unless she could convince Jack to slow down and part with a copper or two, there wasn't any reason to linger.

She caught up to him at long last, and asked, "How long have you been sailing with your Papa, Jack?"

"Since I was a wee boy," he said.

Tall for his age, with sweet blue eyes and hair as yellow as the blossom of the broom, he mustn't be older than twelve.

Seren smiled at his choice of words. "You are still a boy," she said warmly, and he blushed fiercely.

Truly, it wasn't that she meant to disparage him, only that she wished to remind him that one day all-too-soon his opportunities to smash meat pies down his gob would be gone. He would be a man grown, with a man's duties, and if sweet tarts held any appeal at all, he would be honor-bound to spend his coin far more sensibly.

Without slowing, he lowered a hand to his knee cap, and said, with his odd accent, "Since I was here. Now, I am three and ten—hardly a boy." And he tossed her a backward glance, with want-to-be way-ward eyes.

Seren was all-too accustomed to such glances, but, alas, so it seemed, even thirteen-year-olds were not immune to her gifts. His gaze fell briefly upon her bosom, and quickly darted away. But he deepened his voice, and his cheeks turned rosy. "I have seen more than most," he said, straightening his spine, and Seren smiled, suspecting it could well be true, but she refrained from pointing out that he wasn't even born yet when Stephen stole her father's throne. Still and all, he seemed wise beyond his years, and he was responsible to a fault. Today, his Papa had tasked him with escorting Seren to the courier, and come what may, he hadn't been willing to deviate from that task, not even for the promise of a sweet tart.

Ah, well. There would be time enough for treats later. Matilda was sure to have bakers by the dozens.

"Do you think we will be in Calais by nightfall?" she said, getting excited again.

Jack cast her a backward glance, and said, sounding too much like a chiding Papa, "Not if we are haggling wi' every peddler we see."

Alas, point well taken.

Avoiding eye-contact a bit more dutifully, Seren kept her chin down, following her escort, and so it was that she missed the smoke curling up into the mid-morning sky... until they rounded a corner and emerged onto the Marine Parade. But even then, she thought little of the unfurling smoke, or even the congregation, until she overheard a snippet of conversation:

"Pity that... new ship."

"Can't see anybody's gonna make it out alive."

It was only then she peered up, her gaze focusing on the angry column of smoke that spewed upward into the bright, sunny sky—the ominous image so incongruous with the day that it momentarily confused her.

And then she looked closer... spotting a congress of ravens, flying altogether in a swell, and her heart constricted painfully... *Morwen.*

Jack gave a holler, pushing through the crowd, shoving men and women alike as he abandoned Seren to the crowd.

Fueled by something else, not only the desire to keep up, Seren hurried behind him, her heart hammering painfully, as she, too, pushed her way through a thickening crowd.

LESS THAN TWENTY MINUTES; that's all it took to ferret out his smoked bird, part with another copper and swallow his supper whole. Swiping the film of grease from his lips with his sleeve, Wilhelm re-emerged into the marketplace, feeling replete. There was naught like a belly-full to clear the head. But he stopped cold, catching sight of the thick column of smoke rising into the afternoon sky.

It was coming from the docks.

Something like dread shot through him, spurring him into movement. Cutting through the mob, he ran until he could see the smoke's origin, and there he froze again.

It was the Whitshed...

All ships were potential fire traps, but this one burned with a vengeance.

Even as he watched, a brilliant blue ball shot up from the ship's bowels, spitting yarns and yarns of blue flame, like a dragon spewing fire.

God's bones! Even at this distance he could hear the crackling of wood and the ocean hissing beneath the ship's burning belly. It was unlike anything he'd ever witnessed. From stem to stern, the Whitshed was a raging inferno.

A sick feeling curdled his gut—something like indigestion, only worse, though it had little to do with the greasy turkey leg he'd just consumed.

It was all he could do not to chug it up as he stood watching... remembering... the stink of burning flesh. "Sweet Mother of Christ," he said, under his breath.

Horrified, but drawn toward the flames, he moved slowly forward, pushing silently through the crowd, even despite that he stood heads taller than most men, and could see more than he wished to see.

The closer he came to the inferno, the hotter his face burned, until he could venture no closer.

There was only one thing he knew for certain: If the Pendragon sisters were aboard that ship, they were caught in a hell storm. It was not survivable—not even for witches.

Swallowing convulsively, his first thought was for his brother's wife. Already, Rosalynde had suffered more than enough heartache, and this was bound to devastate her. He'd made her a promise—to find and return her sisters. He'd begged her not to worry, and every day of these past few months he'd dedicated every waking moment to locating her sisters. Only, once he'd managed to find them, he'd taken his sweet time about retrieving them, utterly failing his mission.

Twenty minutes, he thought. *Twenty bloody minutes.*

The ship was a pyre. Two hundred tons, and twenty five meters of roaring tinder, and even as he stood watching, the masthead cracked, then buckled, toppling straight into the burning bowels of the Whitshed, even as another roaring ball of blue flame erupted from the ship's entrails.

Bits of material—God knew what else—rained down from the sky. The remembered stench sent his mind reeling and his stomach heaving. He leaned over, spewing his guts on the back of a spectator's boots, then wiped his hand across his mouth. The man wailed in complaint, fists curling by his sides as he turned, then froze as he faced Wilhelm... and then Wilhelm saw her.

Seren Pendragon.

She was unmistakable, with that rich mane of golden-red curls—a tumbling cascade not unlike the shade of a pale, cool flame. Shoving the sour-faced lout out of his way, he bolted in her direction.

SEREN STOOD FROZEN, her heart wrenching painfully as Jack bolted toward the fiery wreckage. Even as he ran, a host of men fell upon him, restraining him and he struggled in vain. "Papa!" he shouted. "Papa! Let me be! That's my Papa!"

There was another thunderous explosion. Seagulls shrieked as a roiling ball of blue flame catapulted sky-ward, spewing a shower of bright blue flames. Bits of blackened debris rained down on the crowd. Ash kissed her lips. Even from this distance, she could feel the heat on her face. But it was another flame she tried desperately to locate amidst the burning tinder... that of her sister's heart flame.

If you knew how to sense them, souls were as tangible as any part of a sanguine being—all the more so, for it was the essence of life itself, bound to the *aether*. But there was nothing remaining of her sister's life force... only how could she have passed so swiftly, so completely without Seren ever knowing—all the while her attention had been on tarts and treats? Sick to her belly and sick to her heart, she stood, wide eyed and frightened. "Arwyn," she cried softly.

"Come with me," demanded a stranger, his hand closing about her arm.

Seren resisted as he tried to drag her away. "Nay," she refused. "Nay!" Ducking under a man's arm, she freed herself and bounded toward the wreckage, shouting for Jack.

GOD'S BONES.

Wilhelm couldn't linger to see to that whelp.

Seren was his only concern at the moment, and if her sister was aboard that vessel, not even God could save her.

The conflagration was luring onlookers from the market and nearby streets. If he didn't get Seren away from this place, it would only be a matter of moments before the Guards swarmed the area and spotted her. All her months of eluding the king's guards would come to naught.

"Lady Seren," Wilhelm pleaded. "Please! Come!"

"Nay," she screamed. "Nay! I have to find my sister —Jack!"

Instinctively, Wilhelm tightened his grip on her arm, holding her steady as a black haze bracketed his vision and a wave of bile surged into his throat. Much as he wished to believe he was immune to it, the fire was taking a toll on him, body and soul. The burning at Warkworth was still too fresh in his memory, and the back of his knees and palms began to sweat.

Battling nausea, he held Seren's arm as a flash of memory assaulted him—fat and flesh sliding off bones. God have mercy, he remembered his terror as he'd stood counting Warkworth's dead—primal and alien to a man who'd spent his entire life training to look death in the face.

But this was something new—it wasn't only fear for himself. He was terrified for Seren, and he couldn't think while she was fighting him. Reacting instinctively, he battled through his nausea, lifting her up and hoisting her over his shoulder to carry her away.

RUDELY, and without warning, the stranger cast Seren over his shoulder like a worthless sack of grain. Screaming, struggling against his hold, she craned her head up, fixing her gaze on the burning ship, all the while pummeling his back and shouting for him to release her.

Not for an instant did she consider that she too might be in peril. Her only worry was for Arwyn. And when he did not release her, she screamed louder, though she knew it was done in vain; Arwyn was gone. She felt the loss acutely, like a limb ripped from her body, and she let out a low, keening sob, wilting in despair over her captor's back. And even as they fled the scene, she heard the thundering of iron-clad hooves and the shouts of men.

"Make way," they shouted. "Make way for the king's guard!"

3

Discouraged, Rosalynde thrust after her husband, missing again, striking the wooden post they'd erected only this morning—a pillar to mark the foundation of the new armory. With a clatter, the sword smacked the wood—so hard she felt the crack clear to the small bones of her hand. The impact left her hands aching, but the pillar scarcely trembled.

"Be damned," she exclaimed.

"Don't lunge," her husband said equably.

It was only one of a thousand rules he'd been boring into her skull—assess your surroundings, grip the sword properly, hold it steady, avoid stabbing, step away from the blade. Goddess only knew, there were too many moves and countermoves; she despaired to get any right. As it was, it had taken Rosalynde weeks and weeks of practice only to lift her new sword, and she still had a long way to go before she could wield it well enough to use it—not for lack of trying.

"Pay attention," her husband persisted.

"Goddess take your tongue, Giles! I am paying attention," she said plaintively—and she was. Alas, it was all she could do to swing the heavy steel, much less guide it properly to any given target. It wasn't nearly as easy as it appeared to be whilst watching her husband at his swordplay.

It didn't help matters overmuch that she didn't actually wish to strike Giles, not even with the flat of her blade. Now that it was her sword, not his, she feared the power it wielded, and she wished with all her heart that he would allow her to practice with someone else—someone more at her level and preferably, someone who wouldn't bleed.

Unfortunately, not his brother because Wilhelm had been gone now for weeks. Glancing up into clear blue sky, she longed for a messenger, thinking that surely, by now, Wilhelm must have learned something.

"Remember," said Giles. "I was ten before I could hold a blade upright."

Rosalynde scowled at him. "Do tell; is that supposed to make me feel better?" she asked. "Lest you forget I am twenty today, not ten." And that was another thing to sour her mood: Of the precisely twenty birthdays she'd celebrated in this mad world, she'd spent every last one with her twin. This was the first time in all her life she'd spent a birth anniversary apart from any of her sisters, much less Arwyn—and, by the by, what sort of celebration was this anyway? Prancing about a courtyard in leathers with a length of steel in her hand that she couldn't possibly control?

"Be damned," she said again.

Her husband grinned. "Shall we end for the day?"

"Nay," said Rosalynde, repositioning her sword as he'd taught her to do, then sidling about so she could once again swing the blade at him.

With scarcely any effort, Giles lifted his sword, but this time she heard the clash of steel and felt the impact—no less painful than her crack against the post.

Perhaps sensing her eagerness to advance, Giles

swung harder than usual. The impact sent Rosalynde scuttling backward, only to land on her rump.

"That was a good try," he said. "But you must anticipate my movements as I do yours. If you swing where I was, you will cut thin air, and your opponent will slice you in two."

Rosalynde's brows collided. Her tailbone felt as though it could be crushed. Her hands and both wrists felt trembly and numb. Her ears were ringing as well. And nevertheless, with as much dignity as she could muster, she found her feet, rising and thrusting the tip of Caledfwlch into the soil at her feet.

The bloody sword was nearly as tall as she was. "Why must you leave?" she asked petulantly. "I don't want you to go."

But even as she said it, she understood why. There was too much at stake for Giles to remain here at Warkworth. The king had yet to learn of their marriage, and the day was coming soon when he was meant to return to London to claim his betrothed— not that he would, mind you. His intent was to repudiate Seren, but there was other business to be dealt with at large. She simply must learn to wield this sword. Her husband didn't say anything, but his sympathetic look said everything. He held out his arms and she flung herself into his embrace, squeezing hard.

What would Seren do when she learned that Rosalynde had married her betrothed? Surely, her sister would understand—nor could she possibly care, but there was a wee part of Rose that felt guilty, nevertheless.

Very gently, her husband's fingers caressed her back, even as her own danced about the serpents on the hilt of the blade—a sword once gifted to Uther

Pendragon. Not even her husband could see what she saw—and felt—the faint, but endless writhing of the serpents beneath the pads of her fingers. It was this very sword that once felled the Dragon of the Isle, a formidable king of Briton.

As the story went, when Maelgwn ap Cadwallon reigned over Gwynedd, the Church tasked a Roman warrior by the name of Uther to smite the Dragon Lord. To ensure his victory, they enchanted this sword, Caledfwlch, with a powerful *magik* so that he who wielded it would never bleed, and he who suffered a scratch by it would perish, if not by violence, by disease. Rather than lose good men in battle, Uther devised a plan. He invited himself to Maelgwn's court under the pretense of friendship, and he gifted Caledfwlch to this king of Gwynedd, placing the enchanted blade into the man's upturned hands so that Maelgwn could admire the fine steel. While Maelgwn stood inspecting the sword, Uther drew it ever so slightly across the king's hands so that the metal stung Maelgwn's flesh. Soon thereafter, Maelgwn ap Cadwallon perished of the plague, and Uther took his castle, retrieving Caledfwlch for himself and designating himself as the new Pendragon. That sword, lost through the ages, was recently found in the unlikeliest of places: in her husband's armory. He gifted it to her the night they sealed their vows—a sacrifice only Rosalynde understood to its depths.

Unfortunately, only a Regnant priestess could unlock the full scope of the sword's *magik* to serve another, and Rosalynde was no Regnant priestess. Yay, the sword still glowed in the presence of evil, but that was the least of its enchantment. Unless imbued, she would bleed like anyone else.

But, for better or worse, it was hers—and so was

this beautiful man, who cherished her by day and by
night. They were bound to each other, if not by the
King's Law, then by the laws of Holy Church and the
laws of man—wed first by a priest, and later, after returning from Aldergh to Warkworth, they'd ex-
changed holy words ordained by the Goddess:

> Adiuro vos per amorem in perpetuum.
> Numquam Separari. Semper in
> fide.

> Bound in love, separated never. Always
> in faith.

She only wished all her sisters could share in her
joy; Arwyn in particular. As of yet, only Elspeth knew
they were wed, and they'd spent so little time at
Aldergh after their ceremony, because they'd had such
important matters to attend at home—namely the
restoration of Warkworth. Months later, the fortress
was now walled, with two sturdy towers guarding the
gate to their bailey. The keep itself was well underway,
and as a testament to the influence her husband
wielded, they had more than two-years' worth of ra-
tions stored in case of a siege. But this was where Rosalynde must rise to the occasion, because if Stephen
came calling with his armies, and Giles was not in residence, it would be up to Rosalynde to lead the garrison. With only days remaining before Giles was
scheduled to depart, she was ill prepared for him to
go, and she knew it. Merely because she was possessed
of a renowned sword did not mean she was prepared
to wield it.

Sensing her mood, Giles cupped her chin in a
hand, lifting her face, forcing her to look him in the

eyes—warm dark eyes that made Rosalynde's heart squeeze painfully.

"What troubles you, wife?"

"I miss my sisters," she said, without hesitation. Because it was true—and particularly today, she missed Arwyn more than words could say.

"I know," he said with a sigh. "I know. Fear not, my love. My brother will find them, and bring them home. I promise we'll find a way to recover Rhiannon as well."

But, nay. Infiltrating Blackwood was a fool's mission, and she knew it. Giles had never seen their ancestral estate and couldn't possibly understand how great a feat that must be. She doubted anyone could scale Blackwood's walls. Cael d'Lucy was bound to have mended any disrepair, and he had the land itself as his ally. If Rhiannon, with all her *magik*, couldn't escape the fortress, a thousand men in all their glory couldn't penetrate the bulwark to rescue her. Even so, she nodded, if only for Giles's sake. Her husband loved her truly, and his beautiful dark eyes were like a mirror, reflecting her joy and her sorrow as well.

"You've won my brother's affection," Giles persisted. "I vow he'll move mountains to keep his promise to you."

Rosalynde nodded, and this time, she said, with conviction, "I know." And she smiled, warmed by the truth of her husband's words and the unswerving loyalty of the gentle giant that was his bastard brother.

At first meeting, Wilhelm had been a curmudgeon. He'd scowled more than the Queen herself, but after their ordeal with that Shadow Beast, he'd come to respect Rosalynde. And then, when she gave all her gold marks for alms for Lady Ayleth's soul, he'd come to love her as well. She had no doubt that he would

bring home her sisters, or he would die trying. But
that was the crux of it all: It was entirely possible he
would die, and Wilhelm hadn't any true notion how
very dangerous her mother could be, even despite
their tangle with that Shadow Beast. Alas, it was only
a small taste of what Morwen was capable of.

Allowing her thoughts to wander, she considered
the night she and her sisters had spent at Darkwood
and shuddered. A full year later, it still gave her night
terrors.

"Let us be done" said Giles, turning her about and
putting an arm around her waist, gently leading her
back to the marquee. "'Tis long past time to celebrate
and I have a small gift to give you."

"Another?" Rosalynde asked glibly, stretching her
hand back and plucking her sword from the ground to
take it with her.

"Aye," he said. "Another. But this one will tickle
your tongue and then later, I will tickle you with
mine."

Rosalynde giggled. "You are such an unrepentant
lecher," she said, jesting, but she reveled in the promise. For all that her husband was a servant of his
Church, he was as lusty a lover as ever was born, and
she was discovering day by day how to please him in
return. If she kept it up, soon he might give up all resolve to leave her, and she would lock him away in
their chamber, to tempt him day and night. The
thought lifted her mood, but her joy turned to dust in
her mouth. Without warning she felt as though she
might swoon. The world wrenched itself from beneath
her feet and her stomach heaved violently. It was a
feeling unlike any she'd ever experienced before, but
she understood what it was, because she'd feared this
moment nearly every second of every minute of her

life. And now... she knew... she *knew* precisely what it felt like to lose one of her sisters, and the feeling was... debilitating.

Clutching her breast, she fell to her knees. The pain was so intense that for an interminable moment she lied to herself, assuring herself it couldn't be true.

But, yes, it was... she felt the loss acutely, like her very heart was being carved from her breast.

Fire turned to raining ash before her eyes, and just that swiftly Arwyn was... *gone.*

"Arwyn," she cried, and she would have spilled into a hapless puddle on the ground, but Giles swept her up into his arms. Her eyes stung as she blinked away tears and peered into her husband's worried gaze. "Arwyn," she said softly. "My sister... she is dead."

4

I t was done.

An old crow sat perched in the window, peering within.

Only moments ago, the sun had shone brightly. Now there was a pall cast over the day... a long shadow of gloom. It was impossible to say whether it could be storms... or whether Rhiannon herself summoned the brume.

For the first time since finding herself behind bars, she wept openly, daring her captor to speak a word to her. By the blessed cauldron, if he had come here to gloat or to hound her again, she would not be held responsible for the things she would do.

Hot tears burned her pale cheeks.

To his credit, Cael d'Lucy stood quietly, listening to her sobs from afar. Regardless that her gaol had only one small window, and there were none in the hall, she knew it was him because she recognized his boots, illumined by the golden light spilling out from her cell.

Choking on her grief, she couldn't speak to demand her tormentor leave, but she needn't say a thing because, after a moment, Cael d'Lucy turned about and walked away, the sound of his footfalls ebbing as he retreated—clearly more intimidated by her grief than he ever was by her threats. Perhaps he understood her better now: Rhiannon would never act imprudently. No matter what she liked to believe, no matter what her threats might be, she was ultimately responsible for everything she did. Every decision brought consequences, and if she needed more proof that she was naught more than a pawn in life's cruel game, today she had confirmation.

Arwyn. Sweet Arwyn...

Her sister had never once spoken an unkind word to anyone. Elder born by only minutes, she had lived contentedly in Rosalynde's shadow, never regretting her lot for a single moment. If it pleased her sisters, Arwyn would be happy, and her sacrifice came as no surprise to Rhiannon.

She was gone... on her birthday, no less.

None of them would ever again have the chance to embrace her or tell her how much they loved her. How mean the fates could be—how cruel.

Anger surged through her veins, bursting forth from her lungs with a terrifying shriek that she hoped would cut fear into the hearts of d'Lucy's minions.

Just as her own heart was shattering, her sisters' hearts must be crushed as well. But, unlike Elspeth, Seren and Rosalynde, Rhiannon had always known this would happen, and there was naught she could have done to divert the hand of fate. She had lived every day of this past year knowing what end would come of her decisions, and *any* other choice made would have led to something worse—and regardless, Rhiannon was only master of her own fate. All she could do was make suggestions, and no one must heed them perforce. Free will was a gift from the gods and she was not her sisters' keeper. No matter what encouragement she ever gave them, their choices must remain their own.

If Elspeth hadn't fled Llanthony with Malcom, she would have found herself wed to Cael d'Lucy instead, and worse, Malcom would have betrothed himself to Dominique Beauchamp. More importantly, if Elspeth hadn't escaped to Aldergh, she would never become an ally for Matilda. Rosalynde herself would never have found sanctuary after leaving with the *grimoire,* and Rosalynde's affiliation with Giles now gave her possession of Caledfwlch, the only weapon of consequence that could return Cerridwen to her watery grave. All was as it should be, and no matter that Rhiannon wished she could take her sister's place; that was simply not an option. To arrive at this place and time there was no other path to be taken, and if dearest Arwyn had not sacrificed her life to destroy Bran... Seren would not live to see another day. Somehow, though she didn't know why, she sensed Seren's life was more important than hers, but unfortunately, there was no way to be certain Arwyn had responded quickly enough. She was gone, truly, but there was no way to know for certain if Bran had survived her fiery retribution. Gods only knew, her sister might have died in vain. Glimpsing now at the fire burning in her brazier, tears blurred Rhiannon's vision, and though she sought confirmation from the Goddess in the dancing flame, nothing was revealed to her.

"Sweet Goddess," she whispered brokenly, sliding from her bed to her knees, then clasping her fingers in prayer—but not a prayer meant to be heard by the Goddess alone. Rhiannon would appeal to any who would listen.

"Mary, mother of Christ; mother of Light, Oh,

Wise One, for whom I am named... intervene if you please... *please, please*... lend my sisters strength—lend *me* your strength."

There was still so much to be done... the way would be long and perilous for Seren, and there were obstacles to overcome...

"Please," she begged.

I will wed the fool if it be your will.

I will do what must be done.

"Anything," she swore.

I will do anything.

"PLEASE. I MEAN YOU NO HARM," said the stranger. In an impossibly fluid maneuver for a man his size, he slid down from his saddle, swung the horse about, then dragged Seren down onto her own two feet, releasing her at once. "I am Wilhelm Fitz Richard," he explained.

Heartsore, confused, Seren stumbled backward.

Fire. The Whitshed was on fire!

Even now she could taste the smoke clinging to her lips. She felt a sting in her eyes—though it could be tears. They were safely away from the harbor, perhaps, but grief clogged her throat, stealing her breath as surely as did the viscid, black smoke.

"M'lady," the man entreated. And then, when she would not respond, he said more softly, "Lady Seren..."

"I must go back," she said.

He shook his head very sadly. "Your sister is gone," he said, and in the heat of that moment, Seren's tears evaporated. Her baby sister, her sweet darling, who'd never once inflicted her will upon others... *gone*?

Sweet fates! If only she had said *yes* when Arwyn asked to accompany her to the courier—*if only!*

If only.

If only.

If only!

But nay. She'd left her alone on that ship, and now she was dead. The realization made her long to empty her belly. Tears scalded the rims of her eyes.

"I'm so sorry," he said.

"Nay," she spat, lunging at him and clutching his *sherte*. "Take me back! You must take me back!"

"She is gone," he said again, and every time he spoke those grotesque little words so calmly, Seren longed to scratch out his eyes. For every day of her past twenty-one years, she had been the gracious one, always reasonable, always serene, the peacekeeper in all things. At the instant, nothing Seren was feeling was vaguely familiar. She was a glowing ball of rage, burning as hot as the firestorm she'd left in the harbor, growing stronger with every word this man spoke.

He caught her wrists and held them away, as though he meant to cast her away, but he did not. His dark eyes were a mirror to her anguish, and he said very firmly, but calmly. "I cannot allow it."

"*You* cannot *allow* it?" Seren raged. "Who are *you* to *allow* aught? I *will* go back. With, or without you."

She *needed* to see that ship again—needed to be sure her sister wasn't out there, frightened and alone, seeking help. "Arwyn," she sobbed, because she knew in her heart it wasn't true. She could sense her sister's absence down to her marrow. Once more, she probed the *aether*, and knew beyond a doubt. *Arwyn was gone.*

Forevermore, the world would be deprived of her sister's sweet smile—her quiet wisdom and endless fervor. All these things were turned to ash—*and why?*

What happened?

What in the name of the Goddess happened?

What could possibly have happened?

She asked herself these questions over and over, but even as she did so, she suspected the answer... *Morwen*.

Somehow, inexplicably, her mother must've discovered their plans—but, nay... wouldn't she simply take Arwyn away? Why would she kill Arwyn? Would she truly have been so heartless to have murdered her own flesh and blood?

Seren's eyes burned with unshed tears; rage frizzled them away—rage against her mother, rage against herself, rage against this rude beast who'd wrenched her away from the harbor. Without a by your leave, he'd seized her away from the docks, flinging her over his saddle, and for all she knew, *he* could have been the one to set that fire.

"I will not go with you," she said. "You cannot make me."

"I can, and will."

"NAY! YOU'LL NOT," Seren said, flying at him again.

He caught her and held her firm, and if she glared at him with ill-repressed fury, Wilhelm more than anyone understood how she felt.

He knew because he'd stood in her shoes... except for the fact that he hadn't had the luxury to stand there, raging against fates. Perforce, he had been the one to march into those ruins in search of their dead. And yet, more than he could bear, Seren's sorrow and pain was his sorrow and pain, and even now, all these months later, he hadn't properly mourned. The unrepressed grief and

anger so apparent on her face was a mirror to
his own.

Like a torrent, the sound of rushing blood deaf-
ened his ears. His heart pounded against the cage of
his ribs, and he wanted desperately to shout back at
her that she *must* listen. But he swallowed his words,
constraining himself, holding her steady when he felt
her knees might buckle.

But even then, her fingers wrenched at his *sherte*,
clutching him desperately. Tears stung his eyes as her
pale eyes beseeched him. It was that piteous look that
nearly unmanned him. "Please," she begged, and he
was nearly undone.

He hadn't wept that day while burying their dead,
nor any day since, but he longed to weep with her
now. His own grief throttled his words, and he swallowed with difficulty, assaulted by the image of Ayleth
of Bamburgh's body lying scorched before him. But
this was *not* Lady Ayleth weeping. This was Seren Pendragon. Nor was she dead. She was alive. She was only
broken as Wilhelm was broken.

In that instant Wilhelm felt a communion with
Seren unlike any he'd ever experienced with anyone
—not even with Lady Ayleth of Bamburgh. He'd
pitied Lady Ayleth, in truth, much as he pitied Seren
Pendragon, but this was *not* what rendered him
speechless as he gazed into Seren's shimmering blue
eyes—eyes that were so pale a shade they reminded
him of the silvery hue of a winter sea.

And... unlike Lady Ayleth, who's fingers were so
rigid in death that he'd had to break them to rest them
in repose, Seren Pendragon's hands were clutching
him in desperation, pleading with him to return her to
the harbor... but he couldn't. *No, he wouldn't.*

For the longest time, she clung to him—or perhaps Wilhelm clung to her. He didn't know, precisely. But he swore in that instant he would do all in his power to aid her—not only because he'd promised her sister. He would champion Seren Pendragon because they were one and the same. He would protect her, not because she was his sweet lady's sister, but because there was a small boy inside him longing to do what she was doing right now... a boy as lost to the world as she was lost. "Shhhh," he said. "Only think," he begged. "Wouldst your sister wish you to put yourself at risk?"

WRENCHING HERSELF AWAY, Seren shoved at his chest. "What can you possibly know of my sister?"

What in the name of the Goddess could he know about anything?

Her face twisted with anger, and in that moment, she couldn't have cared less if she looked like a demon possessed. If, in truth, men wept with longing o'er her beauty, there was naught in her countenance now that would lend truth to this tale. She felt as hideous as Morfran of legend—Morfran whose countenance was so hideous that his mother had pledged herself to the worst *hud du*. Filled with anguish, Seren let loose a scream at the top of her lungs.

"Seren," he said softly. "Seren, please listen to me." He gripped her by the shoulders and shook her gently. "It was your sister who sent me."

Confused, Seren blinked at him. "Arwyn?"

"Nay, your sister Rosalynde. I am Wilhelm Fitz Rich—"

It was so cruel to give hope, only to rip it away. *So cruel!* Once again, she flew at him, this time pounding his chest with all her fury. "I heard you the first time, my lord!"

A flash of irritation ignited behind his dark eyes as he caught her wrists once again, saving himself from the assault. Bewildered, Seren stilled, only because she was too confused to do aught else.

Who was this man? What was she supposed to do? Where should she go? *Arwyn—oh, Arwyn, oh, nay.*

"I'm no lord," he explained. "I am baseborn son to Richard de Vere."

De Vere?

De Vere!

"Giles?" she said, blinking with sudden comprehension.

He nodded. "Your betrothed," he said, and when she did not respond at once, he prompted again, "Lady Seren?"

Seren's jaw went slack. After everything that had transpired now, Giles de Vere would still force her to wed? Sweet mercy, in the wake of her sister's death, marriage was the least of her concerns. Words failed her; grief caught in her throat like a sticky pit. And once again she wrenched herself away, this time, rubbing at her wrists. "He is *not* my intended," she professed. "I repudiate him!"

The man coughed, looking askance, then scratching the back of his head. "Aye, well," he said. "As to that... whatever lies between you and my brother lies between you and my brother. 'Tis none of my concern. Rather, I was tasked to find you and return you safely to Warkworth and this I will do."

He lifted his face to Seren's and for an instant she was lost in his dark, fathomless gaze—eyes that were so profound they left her confused. But there was something in his expression that calmed her, because even despite that she was still furious with him, he was looking at her as though he somehow understood... and more... as though he felt her pain. For a long, long instant, she couldn't avert her gaze.

Baseborn, so he'd claimed. Giles was his brother. Wide-shouldered, brawny and swarthy, Seren had little trouble believing the man could be lowborn. But something in her expression must have revealed misgivings, because he said, "Hold me in contempt, if you will... I am only here to help."

Normally, Seren was not an angry soul. If the truth be known, she had the least temper of all her sisters, but it was so much easier to be angry with this behemoth—this beast of a man who seemed so intent upon forcing her to acknowledge the truth. "How can you help me?" she asked, lifting her chin defiantly. "Can you resurrect my sister?"

His jaw grew taut, and he pursed his lips, displacing a long, dark curl from his forehead as he shook his head. At one time, his hair might have been shorn in the Norman fashion, but it was overgrown now, and disheveled. His beard was sorely unkempt. "I am sorry," he said. "Your sister cannot possibly have survived the blaze. She is gone, Seren, and you must return to Warkworth with me."

Crying out in pain, Seren pressed her hands to her ears, refusing to hear, even knowing he spoke true. She simply could not accept it. Arwyn died on her birth anniversary, no less—alone!

Goddess, please, she begged.

Let it not be true.

How could she face Rose and Elspeth?

How could she look her sisters in the eyes and confess how miserably she'd failed Arwyn?

Perhaps sensing her distress, Wilhelm stepped forward, and all Seren's years of careful aplomb shattered like Merlin's Stone. White hot intensity surged through her veins, and she felt a tempest rising in her soul, manifesting a wind that spun between them and eddied into the tree tops, shivering the boughs. *Witchwind.* It seemed as though all her twenty-one years of careful restraint loosed at once, and the potency of it changed the weather.

Seren herself might have been startled, except that fury held her in its throes. She surrendered to the feeling, allowing her spirit to unfurl into the *aether*, hoping for the first time in all her life that her demeanor could be frightening.

She wanted to frighten this man. She wanted to scream. She wanted to send trees toppling. She wanted to shout obscenities at the heavens and drive a silver blade into her palm to cast the most hideous *hud du*. For the first time in all her living days she welcomed rage, and intuitively understood how the feeling could drive her mother to dark *magik*.

Fury, hot and savage twisted through her like a maelstrom, and something deep inside her snapped, like a twig. Something broke. Something Seren was sorely afraid she could never repair.

Somehow, she managed to recover herself, crossing her arms to keep from trembling, and after a long, long moment, the *witchwind* settled, but she could spy through the treetops that the sky was no longer blue. The storms that had plagued the city for more than a *sennight* had returned, and the air held a new chill.

5

S*he* was doing *this*.

Somehow, she was causing the change in the weather.

It took Wilhelm a full moment to realize what precisely was transpiring, and if he hadn't understood intrinsically *who* and *what* she was... he might never have believed what he was witnessing. His skin prickled as he watched storm clouds form overhead. In scant seconds the air went from balmy to blustery, and every tree without substantial girth shivered against the onslaught. The occurrence was enough to make a grown man piss his breeches, and nevertheless, he wasn't afraid. He understood intuitively what she was going through. She was taking refuge in her anger—as had he. No matter what he'd wished to believe of the lady his brother was once betrothed to, he recognized a gentle soul when he met one, and realizing he was only making matters worse, he stepped back, giving her space to breathe.

The wind calmed when she calmed, but Wilhelm was more ashamed than he was relieved. He'd never once manhandled a woman, and if she still had eyes to see, Lady Ayleth would have been mortified by his rudeness. He took meager comfort in the fact that if he'd not taken Seren out of that city, she too would be lying six feet under, like Ayleth.

For his own part, the scent of smoke clinging to his leathers was enough to make him empty his guts, but he swallowed the bile that rose again and held his aplomb for the lady's sake. Desperate to have her heed him, he said very gently, "M'lady?"

Seren peered up, blinking.

Her face, though filled with outrage, was as beautiful as he remembered. But, as livid as she might be, he recognized the sorrow nestled in her wintry eyes, and God's bones... the sight of her suddenly discomfited him, because, in contrast, he was nothing more than a lumbering beast.

Even as far as Warkworth, he'd heard tales of men who were driven to duel over the Beauty of Blackwood, and he could easily see why. It was this aspect of her that he'd been so afraid would blind his brother. He'd been sorely afraid Giles would turn his heart against Warkworth and against vengeance if only for the grace of her smile, because, in truth, hers was a face that could inspire men to war.

Standing here, now, regarding her, he couldn't help but remember the day they'd arrived in London so Giles could claim her as his bride—*was that only three months ago?* On that day Wilhelm had vowed to keep Lady Seren as far away from Warkworth as humanly possible. He'd called her a witch and he'd promised to thwart Giles at every turn, certain as he was that she was a spy for the king. And for all that ado about nothing, he stood here now, fully prepared to see the lady home. Only now that he'd witnessed her untempered emotion, he knew in his heart that she was innocent of her mother's treachery. These sisters were all blameless, and one had lost her life to prove it.

Seren, too, might have met that fate. Now it was his duty to keep her safe. And yet, what a tricky web they'd spun. For, even now, he was certain King Stephen had no inkling his brother had forsaken Seren to wed her younger sister; and he doubted Seren knew it either.

How could she possibly? Rosalynde and Giles were wed in secret, and even if their vassals suspected, none would defy their lord to divulge it. For better or worse, Seren must still believe she was betrothed to Giles, and Wilhelm wasn't sure how much to reveal. "M'lady," he said when she was calm enough to listen. "I swore an oath to find you and return you to Warkworth; this is what I *must* do."

Her brows slanted. "To my intended?" she asked, and it took Wilhelm a full moment to respond. Though, in the end he decided it would be best if she thought he acted with authority.

"Aye," he said gravely. "To your... *intended*." But he cursed even the sound of that lie on his lips.

Seren's brows collided.

On the day her sister quit London, she and Arwyn had spied Rosalynde in their mother's crystal traveling with two men. She was so certain it was Giles de Vere, and some part of her had dared to believe Giles must be her sister's champion. But it would seem Lord Giles still intended to honor his vows. But what if, after Seren denied him, he would feel compelled to return her to her mother? Or, worse. What if *he* were the very one her mother had sent to retrieve her?

Plainly, Giles couldn't care one whit about her, else

he'd have come to find her himself, instead of sending his bastard brother in his stead.

But, of course, he must have delivered Rose to Aldergh. Her sister would *never* have trusted him. Rosalynde would have kept her *glamour* spell and she would have allowed the king's lackeys to continue believing her a hapless nun. Only then could she have avoided their lechery and rest assured of their compliance. Men were generally faithless, were they not? Even her own father had discarded them so easily. But she remembered the undisguised look of hatred on Giles's face as he'd regarded her mother in the King's Hall and hope flared in her breast. "You said you were sent by my sister, Rose? Where is she?"

He made some frustrated sound, then, once again scratched at the back of his neck. "Warkworth," he said, and, before Seren could speak another word to question him, he reached out to place a hand on her shoulder, looking her straight in the eyes. It was impossible to think clearly while he gazed at her so compassionately, and to make matters worse, she found his voice, soft as a whisper, equally as disconcerting. Perhaps under different circumstances, Seren might have even considered him handsome, except for that razor-thin scar that parted his left brow.

"As God is my witness," he said. "I am your servant."

When she said naught, he continued. "I will see you safely to Warkworth. And once there, reunited with Rosalynde, you may decide for yourself where else you might go. I warrant my brother will not keep you against your will."

Seren lifted a brow. It was not her experience that any man should ever behave so honorably. In fact, over the past year she'd endured much at the hands of "honorable men"—a grope as she passed in the hall, a wandering eye, a crude gesture when it was certain no one was looking. Even Father Ersinius had cornered her inside the chapel at Llanthony, where God's eyes were said to keep their keenest vigil. And yet, her sister Elspeth had, indeed, found herself a champion. If there was one, perhaps there could be two... and where there were two, might there be three?

It was as though Wilhelm read her mind. "There is no love lost betwixt my brother and your mother," Wilhelm said.

Seren considered the verity of his words. "What about you?"

A hint of a cruel smile turned his lips. "I cannot lie. I wouldst put my hands around her throat if ever I could," he confessed.

Seren sensed he spoke true, and if she'd also sensed he understood her grief, she now remembered why. He, too, had suffered a devastating loss—perhaps, even worse than hers, if only by measure, because his entire family was burned alive. And yet... she could not bring herself to trust him so blindly—nor was she prepared to dismiss his initial rudeness, tossing her willy-nilly over his horse.

Unfortunately, he was thrice her size. He didn't have to win her consent. Nor, by the same token, must he say sweet things to sway her, she realized. If he were so inclined, there was naught she could do to prevent him from sweeping her away—not even *magik* could stop him. It didn't work quite that way, and considering how little time she'd had to study the *grimoire*, the *witchwind* had come as a surprise.

Reminded of that, she peered up into the sky, noting the darkened horizon—lingering evidence of her temper. But, truly, never before in her life had she experienced such a tempest. She only knew about such things after reading the Book of Secrets. Tied to emotions, a *witchwind* was essentially the inspiration of the world, inexorably linked to the soul of a witch. Just as some *dewines* could use fire or water, a *stormwitch* could harness the wind, making use of its energies in much the same manner some *dewines* used crystals, sunlight or moonlight. It was a powerful tool she had never anticipated using, and be that as it may, she didn't know how to control it. And now that it was gone, *he* was still here... waiting patiently for her to speak.

"What say you? Will you come willingly?"

Willingly?

Nay. But neither would she fight him. Seren could scarce consider anything at the moment, much less where to go or what to do. As for Warkworth and its odious *lord*, she had no intention of wedding that poppet, but the closer she ventured to Aldergh, the easier would be her journey to Aldergh. And, perhaps after all, if Wilhelm spoke true, Giles might be persuaded to escort her a little further north.

With canny eyes, she studied the giant who'd spirited her out of the harbor. Wilhelm Fitz Richard was easily the brawniest fellow she'd ever laid eyes upon, and yet for all his size, he hadn't actually harmed her, nor did she sense he was inclined to. His face, scarred though it might be, betrayed not a trace of enmity or even disgust for her witchery, and now that they were away from the harbor and she was calmer, he made no additional attempt to restrain her. Alas, she wouldn't call him a champion, but in the end he might do. And yet, be that as it may, she couldn't leave Jack in that city, not when she knew he hadn't any place to go. His mother lived in

Calais; and thanks to her mother, his father was dead.

"Aye," she said. "I will go." And the tension in the warrior's shoulders seemed to ease before her eyes. However, before he could rest too easily, she added, "I'll not leave without Jack."

His head cocked backward. "Jack?"

"Captain Airard's son."

WILHELM FROWNED.

She would have him return to the city?

Now?

Even as they'd fled, the king's guard had come rushing into the vicinity. By now, every last soul in the city was bound to be watching that ship burn to its bowels. It was the last place he should take Seren. He didn't even have to think about it; he shook his head. "'Tis unwise to return, m'lady."

"And will you endeavor to stop me?"

As he sometimes felt with Giles, Wilhelm felt cowed by the marked intelligence in her gaze. And nevertheless, despite that he'd never learned to read like his brother, he could read people well enough, and he knew her question was a trick. If he answered nay, she would test him, and then he would be forced to stop her for her own good. If he said aye, her ire would no doubt return—and so might the storm.

By God, he'd suffered enough witchery these past few months to know he didn't wish to challenge another Pendragon. That witch storm alone was alarming. He scratched his head, again, for it seemed there was no proper answer. And still he tried, answering her question with a question of his own. "Wouldst you truly have me betray an oath to your sister?"

"Rosalynde?" she asked, and when he nodded, she narrowed her gaze. "How much has she told you?"

"About what?"

She thrust her hands against her hips, eyes red-rimmed—hardly as serene as he remembered her from their first encounter in London, and yet... even in her anger and grief she was far lovelier than he remembered. Wilhelm held her bright silver gaze. "Everything," he confessed. And then he repeated, lest she mistake him. "*Everything.*"

She lifted her chin, clearly doubting him. "And?"

"And what?"

She lifted her hands, turning up her palms. "For example?"

"Aye, well..." He peered into the treetops. "I know enough to know that sudden change in weather was no act of God."

Clearly it was the wrong thing to say, because once again, she sought refuge in anger. "Not *your* god, perhaps," she said.

"M'lady," he argued, trying desperately to reason with her. "The king's guards are still seeking you. Wouldst you have me leave you to walk straight into their arms? Wouldst you not be better off with my brother and your sister?"

No doubt his question annoyed her; he could tell by her vexed expression. She peered down at the ground, tears brimming at the corners of her eyes, and he felt a swell of pity for her. Then and there, he resigned himself to rise above whatever stones she might throw his way. Whatever Seren needed to get through this, he would allow it—except for that boy. He was firm in that decision, until she began to cry. "I... I c-can't leave him," she said despondently. "He has no one. Please, Wilhelm, please!"

6

I t was all Seren could do not to collapse into a puddle and weep over his boots. *Arwyn*, she thought, tears scalding her eyes. *Oh, Arwyn!*

"He's old enough to find his own way," her dubious champion contended, arms akimbo. "If the truth be known, he's like to have more friends than you and certainly more than me." He spoke matter-of-factly, not cruelly, and nevertheless, it gave Seren a fit of rancor.

But, of course, it would be true; he was a sour-faced lout and Jack's father had friends in high places —namely, her sister Matilda—but Jack was still just a boy, and his father was dead. The lack of sympathy in this man's tone was no less than infuriating. Along with her sweet sister, that boy's father had perished aboard the Whitshed, and this behemoth expected her to sit idly by and allow a young man to fend for himself in the face of this tragedy? "You expect me to do nothing?"

"I expect you to live to see another day. That is *not* nothing."

Seren lifted her chin, curling her fingers into fists, only daring him to deny her. Perhaps there was naught she could do for Arwyn, but Jack was alive, and he needed help.

"I'll *not* leave this city without that boy," she said stubbornly. "And if you'll not return to help him, I will."

She narrowed her eyes in warning, tipping her chin skyward to remind him of the *witchwind* she'd conjured. It didn't matter that she didn't know how to use it, she would summon it if need be, along with the wrath of the Goddess herself. "If, in truth, you know *who* I am, you know *what* I am capable of, and I will do my worst if you stand in my way."

For the most part it was a bluff. How could he—or anyone else—know what she was capable of if Seren didn't even know herself? And yet if Morwen's sorcery was any indication, she had a very good sense there was quite a lot she and her sisters had yet to learn. And, regardless, Wilhelm already knew what her mother could do; let him wonder if she could do the same.

And still, he wasn't afraid, judging by the look on his face. But he was certainly flummoxed, and once again, he scratched the back of his head, perhaps considering what more to say. Seren longed to weep. She was already worn to bits, emotionally and physically, and this was only the beginning.

"M'lady," he argued. "You mustn't believe I would leave you undefended? And neither can you return to the harbor." His voice held a note of compassion coupled with frustration. "What you ask is untenable."

Glaring at him, she found a wellspring of stubbornness she hadn't previously realized she possessed. "I'll not go without Jack," she maintained. "He has no one in England, and I will see him returned to his mother in Calais."

"Warkworth is not Calais," he argued. "Calais lies in the opposite direction."

"And how will he get there without money?"

"How do you know he has no money?"

"How do you know he does?"

Seren placed her hands akimbo as he had, stubbornly refusing to give up. If naught else, his refusal would provide her a good reason to resent him, and sweet fates, she needed her anger as a balm. If she couldn't help her sister, at least she should endeavor to help Jack.

They stood, at odds, both frowning at each other, and, at long last, he cast his hands up, and said, "Bloody hell! You cannot go, you cannot stay; what makes you believe that *eegit* will trust my word? Do I look like a man to be taken in confidence?"

"He's no *eegit*," Seren said. "He's well learned and even knows how to read." Forcing herself to meet his gaze, she studied her would-be champion.

In truth, he did *not* appear very amiable, and certainly not while in that confrontational stance. To make matters worse, that hideous scar across his brow put her in mind to a demon.

So, this was where they were? She must travel north, perforce, with a man she scarcely knew while her sister's ashes drifted on the wind and a young lad starved on the streets in Dover? An overwhelming surge of emotion choked her again, and she said softly, swallowing a knot of grief. "Arwyn..."

"God's bones! Putting yourself at risk will not bring your sister back," he said, and Seren's gaze snapped up to meet his. It struck her once more how tall he was.

"I know this, you dolt."

She needed time to think... if only he would leave her be for a while... she could consider her best course of action—if, indeed, she did not seek a quiet place in the woods to hide beneath a pile of bracken and sleep for a hundred years.

For all she knew Rosalynde was at Aldergh, not Warkworth, and perhaps he was only telling her what she wished to hear in order to ensure her compliance. It could be that he intended to return her to his brother by hook or by crook—and then what? As conniving as it might seem, her best course might be to insist he go after Jack, then steal away while he was gone.

By all rights she should be petrified of this man and concerned for her own safety. But, in fact, Seren was too grief-stricken to care what happened to her. And anyway, even if she did slip away, could she possibly make it all the way to Aldergh, alone—without Arwyn?

The very thought made her eyes swim, because, in truth, she wouldn't be so constrained. Her sister's lack of *ability* had left them both disadvantaged.

Even so, Aldergh was a long way away, and, at the instant, she had no silver or gold. She wasn't even sure poor Jack had a copper to his name. Whatever coins she herself had possessed were lost with her sister, and young as the boy was, she was certain his father wouldn't have given his son bait for thieves. There had been no reason to believe that ship wouldn't be there, awaiting their return... except that it wasn't. And, for certes, Seren would be as horrid a person as her mother if she abandoned Jack to the city without a coin to his name. She'd heard terrible stories of what happened to young boys on their own. His voice might be breaking now, but he was by no means a man.

"You leave me no choice," Wilhelm said. "If I

abandon you here... alone... you'll be as vulnerable as your sister. We know how that turned out?"

There was genuine frustration in the man's tone, but he was far too plainspoken, and his proclamation was ill-timed. Seren glared up at him. "Need you remind me?" she rebuked, thinking him daft. Clearly, he knew naught of subtleties or manners, blurting whatever came first to his tongue. Fresh as it was, she was hardly in danger of forgetting her sister was dead.

Goddess lend me strength.

Thankfully, he had the good graces to blush, but then, he stood silent, mulling over the options, much as Seren was doing, and she was grateful for the silence—even if she knew he was bound to be forming another argument.

Indecision tormented her; truly, even if he relented and went after poor Jack, she couldn't abandon that boy to this man's keeping. Wilhelm would dispense of him the instant he could. And neither did she sense he would allow her to leave in peace. He'd come all this way, searching for her, and it wasn't likely he would leave now that he'd found her.

And still... if she accompanied this man to Warkworth and all his lovely assurances proved false... or if Rosalynde wasn't there waiting for her... and if somehow Giles was allied with her mother... what if he forced her into wedlock? Then what? Her best opportunity to escape was... *here and now.*

What should I do, Rhiannon? she inquired of the *aether.*

Her sister didn't respond—or perhaps couldn't. So far as anyone knew, *mindspeaking* was not possible outside proximity, and it must be true, because if anyone could do it, Rhiannon could. The situation seemed hopeless. Not in all her days had Seren felt so utterly bereft. She was nearly twenty-two now, and not a single day during the course of her life had she not had at least one of her sisters by her side. Till very recently, she'd been blessed to have them all.

Sometimes, she wished she could turn back time, return to a bright, sunny day in their garden at Llanthony... back, before Morwen remembered she had five daughters...

And now there were four.

Once again, the pain of Arwyn's loss made her long to prostrate herself and weep, but tears wouldn't come. The heat of her anger diminished them before they could form. By all that was sacred, if it was the last thing she did before closing her eyes, she would see that Morwen paid for her crimes.

If ever Seren had believed her mother could be redeemed, she now knew that wasn't true. Morwen was a fiend of the worse degree—she was a monster willing to murder her own kin. There was no other explanation for that fire. Seren knew it wasn't natural. That pure-blue flame could only have been conjured by *witchfire*—something she now understood to be real, for if *witchwind* existed, so too did *witchfire* and *witchwater*. But if only Rhiannon could advise her...

His voice was gruff, filled with torment. "Lady Seren?"

Seren longed to send him away.

Ambivalence ruled her emotions. After all, she did need his help, and she must believe he was Goddess-sent. His presence here must not be a coincidence, and yet, if she believed in fate, she must also consider that Arwyn was meant to die, and this was simply detestable. How could the Goddess forsake her sister that way?

How could the most innocent of lives be squashed like a fly?

"Have you..." Again, Wilhelm Fitz Richard scratched at his head. Seren was coming to realize this was a nervous habit. "Perchance you know... some... spell?"

He fluttered his fingers at her, and Seren's heart skipped a beat. "Spell?"

He rolled his hand in the air. "Aye. What is you call that... a *glamour*?"

Seren blinked.

He knew about glamours?

"Your sister... when we met... she was wearing some mask, or so she claimed—can you cast this spell?"

Sweet fates! Was he truly asking her this so openly? Dare she answer? Could she trust this man?

Inexplicably, despite that his presence disturbed her, she did long to trust him.

"Aye," she said, with no small measure of trep-idation.

Never in her life had she spoken so freely of the Craft to anyone but her sisters. And yet, he clearly un-derstood a bit of what a *glamour* was already. It was a chimera, like maquillage, only drawn by the *aether*. Rosalynde must have enlightened him.

"I could do it, but I have no philter," she lamented. "The little I had was in a pouch aboard the Whitshed."

Tears pricking her eyes again, she reached into her pocket to dig out a few oddments—not nearly enough for a spell, and still she saved what remained, drop-ping the fragments back into her pocket. She knew better than to discard even the smallest seed.

He blew out a sigh, sounding resigned. "I've no idea what that means, but never mind." He turned and went for his saddlebag, lifting up the flap, dipping his hand inside, and fishing out a thin, black woolen cloak of the sort that her mother's minions sometimes wore. Returning to Seren, he offered the garment to her. "Wear it," he said, and it was a command.

Mother's mercy! He was contrite and ready to serve one minute, arrogant as a king the next. What must she make of this man? Aggrieved as she was, she accepted his cloak. "Does this mean you intend to take me with you?"

"Aye," he said crossly, then muttered something unintelligible beneath his breath.

"What did you say?"

"Naught, damn it all! If you'll not leave without that boy, and I cannot truss you up like a goat ready for slaughter, so it seems you must accompany me back into the city, after all."

Trussed like a goat for slaughter?

The image incensed Seren, but she suspected he might be needling her, and so she tossed his cloak over her shoulders and said, drolly, "How good of you, *my lord.*"

He didn't bother to turn to speak to her. "I have already said, I am no lord, though if you mean to mock me, enjoy it, *m'lady.*"

Seren blushed, because, in truth, she had forgotten. Despite all his poor-mouthing, it was simply impossible to think of him as aught less than a man of authority, dressed as he was in those sigil-embossed leathers. He wore them only too well, she noted, with shoulders high and straight, and his bearing more attuned to that of a king or a duke. His aura and presence were undeniable. The entire woodlands seemed filled by him. Sweet Goddess have mercy, even his trews were dwarfed by his size, and to the contrary, the cloak he'd lent her swallowed her whole. When she lifted up the hood to conceal her plaited hair, she couldn't even see beyond its folds. And so it was that when she neared his horse, he swept her up without warning—yet again—only this time putting her neatly in the saddle.

She yelped in surprise. But he didn't give her time to protest. He mounted behind her, putting his spurs to the horse.

It never occurred to her until they were well away that she hadn't even considered balking. Every thought of escape had vanished the very instant he'd said she could accompany him. And now, it was all she could do not to turn and sob against his shoulder as his arms enfolded her.

He is not comforting you, pea brain, she reminded herself. *He is performing a duty to his lord, keeping you safe until you may stand before your betrothed.*

And nevertheless, the urge to unburden herself was unbearable. She caught her sob before it formed, and stiffened when he touched her, drawing away from him and making herself as small as she could in the cage of his arms.

7

No friend ever served me,
no enemy ever wronged me,
whom I have not repaid in full.
—*Sulla*

I have been called many names:
The Dark Goddess, the Shadow Crone, the Shapeshifter of Legend. I am the Mother of Avalon, Keeper of the Cauldron, Defender of the Grail. I am, and ever shall be, the most gifted dewine to walk the realms of men. But for love of a man, I found myself in a watery grave...

Pity me not.

Pity yourself.

My heart is basalt, forged by the fires of vengeance and rage.

Today I will be released from my shackles, and whatever traitor has betrayed my weakness to this metal, I will repay him in kind.

Biding my time, I brush a finger across the inscription so delicately etched into the silver-infused metal —hallowed words imbued, but not by the *hud* or *hud du*, only by holy writ. The rough edges catch the light like tiny diamonds. Untrained eyes might see glitter against the light, but I do not need light to read these words; I know what they say:

> Hic est Draco,
> Ex undis,
> Tenetur in argenteas
> A capite ad calcem, tace, et sile

Only one woman I know could have prescribed these words, and she suffered the consequences only to spite me... my mortal mother, Morgan Pendragon, she who birthed my body, but not my soul, and if aught remains of her inside me, I will suffocate her until she turns blue.

> Here be the dragon,
> From the waves of the sea,
> Bound in silver,
> From head to toe, silent and still

Silent and still.

Upon the high window, seven of my ravens sit, peering within, eyes black and shining.

There are no bars mounted here, for the window is too high and only winged creatures may come and go.

I could go, too... but for these shackles.

Soon, I think. Soon.

Resting my head back on the wooden chair... I wait... silent and still... like a fat bellied spider... remembering the moment of my mother's demise.

Little more than twenty years ago, they burned that bitch on a stake while she wore these very shackles—bindings she conspired to create. And perhaps she breathed her last on that pyre, hoping that someday I, too, would don them as she did. I offered her up as a sacrifice, and in the end, it was she who was destroyed... and all because she forgot a woman's most seductive *glamour*: I spread my legs for a king, whelped him a litter of bastards, and so of course, who was he to believe? But for that look upon her face, it was worth the loss of my most precious possession...

Blackwood, Blackwood... there she remains...

Oh, but I cherish that day... her flesh shriveled on brittle bones, the scent of death wafting on the breeze like a rancid perfume. Vivid as the memory remains, I inhale deeply, ignoring the dankness of the *donjon*, for even now my mother's burnt flesh is a bouquet I long to inspire...

Ah, yes, even now, I hear wee Elspeth whimpering beside me... I see her tiny fist rising up to wipe her runny nose... and all the while her grandmamau burns.

Burn, witch, burn!

By the Cauldron, I will slay her again, and her granddaughters, as well... except for these shackles.

For weeks they have been my burden, leaving me wasted of *magik* and challenged by even the smallest of tasks. And yet... now that I know them... now that I know what power they possess... I will put them to my own good use. One fine day, I will clasp these bracelets on my daughter's wrist, and I will devise a retribution, fit for a traitor.

As for that other bitch, Matilda... I do have plans for the woman whose piety was ever the bane of my existence.

It was not enough she turned her nose at me as a willful child, not enough that she begrudged me all I earned... not enough that she accused me of murdering her self-righteous mother, or that she disdained five sisters of her own true blood, only because they were born to me. But even after all this she revealed me as a heretic, and if you must know why I murdered her father when I could... it was for fathering a monster... and then for aligning her to the Holy Church, by whose very dictum I am dispossessed.

All those cold, dark years spent dreaming at the bottom of the Sea... all my delight over returning to my holiest of Grails—all for naught, because that pinch-nosed bitch deprived me of Blackwood. And yet... though I have been thwarted, Blackwood's cauldron belongs to me—a relic of my Avalon—and I will restore myself as its keeper.

Morgan Pendragon be damned.

Matilda be damned.

Kings and queens be damned.

All will grovel before me.

"It won't be long now," announces the guard, offering a wink and a smile. I wink back, grateful for his succor. Despite that he would not defy his king by removing these accursed shackles, he brings me soft, warm blankets and clean water to drink. Every now and again, he retrieves my philters—else, I'd never have kept my *glamour* so long.

Beauty is the finest weapon. Rot and curse Seren for wasting hers so ignorantly. She's been gifted that for which I now must strive, against the laws of nature. For love of beauty men will do anything—anything—and the price for the unlovely is repulsion.

Poor, poor Morfran.

I tried to avenge you, my son.

I longed to give you but a trace of what your sister possessed—Creirwy, who married your Nemesis only to crush me. She was ever your father's favorite, and to me, whilst I carried you in my womb, he gave naught but grief. He filled me with loathing, and you were my odium manifest. You were the face of envy, bitterness, and jealousy.

Morfran, oh, Morfran.

Tegid, I will see your blood expunged from this world—vanished, like your hair—plucked painfully from this realm until none remain. I could have loved you, you ungrateful fool; I could have loved my daughters, as well. And I could have taught them so much...

But nay.

I smile now, closing my eyes, satisfied with the dealings of the day. Bran is lost to me, but it was worth it.

One down, four to go.

I will smite you all as you smote Morfran. I will destroy you as you destroyed my Avalon.

After a while, my guard returns, and this time he brandishes a key, his face split with a toothy grin—and of course should be pleased. I have promised him more than silver and gold. I have promised him immortality... for a price.

He jingles his chain, and asks, "Art ready, *my* lady?"

I lift my chin to the unnatural glow, for it is not the key to my cell he holds. Iron bars could never contain me, and if not for greed, no *dewine* would ever suffer this sorcery. Like these shackles locked about my wrists and the Palatine swords imbued by Taliesin, this key was forged from blooms of steel containing a special consecrated alloy that glows in my presence.

"I was born ready," I reassure the man, and I rise from the pillow that softens the seat of my chair, crossing the measure of carpet, far quicker than he can unlatch my door. Eagerly, I offer my wrists, only waiting.

He uses one dull key to unlock the cell, and it is all I can do to maintain patience, waiting for him to employ the key to unlock my shackles.

"The king bids you join him in his apartments. But, first, a warm bath has been ordered to your chambers, along with a bit of supper. He wouldst see you refreshed before your meeting, and he begs pardon for the judgment you were wrongly given."

The ensorcelled key glows brighter as it stretches toward me and I twist my shackled wrists to reveal the small aperture—a perfect fit for the tongue and grooves.

For barely an instant the scratch of metal is unbearable to hear, and then I catch the click, and the air itself sighs as the manacles unclasp, releasing my long-imprisoned flesh. Only there, where the alloy resisted my *glamour*, my skin appears bruised and paper thin, peppered with liver spots. I quickly rub them in relief and the damage is healed before my gaoler can blink. "I hope the *vin* is better than the *vin* served here," I say, as I slide past my dutiful servant. And now, as I abandon my plush little prison, I reassure him. "Come to me later to claim your prize, my pet."

"I will, *my* lady. I will."

And I leave him to the joys of his trade, as my ravens delight upon the sill and sing to me in chorus.

Caw! Caw! Caw! Caw, caw!

8

D ressed in leathers, fresh from practice, Rosalynde stood in the bailey, arms crossed, waiting as they lifted the iron portcullis to admit her sister's cavalcade.

Heavy as it was, it took half a dozen men to lift the heavy, bolted iron, but closing it wasn't nearly so much of an ordeal. Taking their lessons from Aldergh's construction, Giles employed pulleys to lift the gate more effectively, but instead of cutting and wasting lengths of rope, a clasp was designed so that the gate would release with the turn of a latch. Little by little, the castle was coming to completion—a bulwark that wouldn't so easily be vanquished, should Eustace decide to return.

At long last, the gate was open, and Elspeth rode in with an escort of seven well-armed men. She slid down from her mare the instant she spied Rosalynde and came rushing with arms open wide. Tears in her eyes, Rosalynde welcomed her eldest sister, embracing her joyfully.

"Rose," said Elspeth, returning the embrace, and Rosalynde buried her fingers into the soft velvety folds of her sister's cloak, grateful for her company.

"Elspeth," she cried. "What are we to do?"

She held her sister tighter, afraid to let go, and for the longest interval, the two stood embracing, unwilling to part for fear of the void they would suffer—not so acute for Elspeth as it was for Rosalynde, because she and Arwyn had shared a womb. In her absence Rosalynde felt bereft. It was all she could do not to weep inconsolably, and her throat grew too thick to speak as she hugged Elspeth, but thankfully, they had no need to command well-trained men to do their jobs.

Warkworth's aides moved to assist with the horses. Elspeth's retainers did the same, giving up their reins and conferring with Rosalynde's men-at-arms. It was as somber an occasion as any they'd met over the past twenty years, and there were none present who did not understand the loss the sisters had incurred.

Dry though they were at the instant, Elspeth's eyes were red-rimmed from weeping—as Rosalynde's must be, as Seren's must be as well. *Poor Seren,* Rosalynde thought.

Poor, poor Seren.

At least she and Elspeth had each other. Seren was out there... somewhere, alone in the world. There was simply no way to know if Wilhelm had found her. Every day, Rosalynde feared the worst—that Morwen encountered both her sisters together and even now Seren was being held in London. If that should be the case, Giles would know it soon. And in the meantime, she was sick with worry and anguish.

She didn't worry so much for Rhiannon as she did for Seren. If there was one thing she knew about Rhiannon, it was that Rhi could fend for herself.

"No word yet?" Elspeth asked, releasing Rose, but reluctantly.

They couldn't stand in the middle of the open bailey, weeping like babies. They had attendants to see to and men and women who looked to them for direction.

"No word at all," Rosalynde said, dabbing a finger to the corner of her left eye to stem the stubborn flow of her tears. "Not yet." And then, realizing her sister had arrived without a wet-nurse and her babes, she peered up in surprise. "Where are the babes?"

Elspeth shook her head somberly. "I daren't bring them. So much as it pained me to leave them, they are safer at home. We could not be certain Morwen would not set upon us as Mordecai did with you in the woodlot."

Rosalynde nodded, understanding. A few months ago she and her husband and his half-brother encountered a Shadow Beast in the woodlot south of Whittlewood and Salcey. Although Morwen herself never appeared, if her manservant could *shapeshift* as no *dewine* they knew ever could, what more could her mother do? Sadly, Elspeth was right to leave the boys at home. Grown as he might be, it gave her a shiver to think of Giles in her mother's proximity.

Stubbornly pushing away the thought, she hooked her arm about her sister's and said, "Come inside. You may tell me everything whilst we dine. The lot of you must be famished."

"I am not," said Elspeth, peering back at her escorts, and then her gaze scanned the premises. "I... I have not been hungry since..."

Arwyn.

Rosalynde, too, had felt sick to her belly since the *perception.* Food was the very last thing on her mind, and despite that, she forced herself to sup when she could, because what good would she be to her people if she wasted away to naught.

"Where is your *donjon*?" Elspeth asked, her tone full of surprise.

Rosalynde smiled gently. "No *donjon* yet. For now, we have a marquee."

Her sister turned about, examining the immediate surroundings with furrowed brow, Her gaze returned to Rosalynde, inspecting her leathers with a troubled expression. Instinctively, Rosalynde understood her sister's concern. She and her eldest sister might not be twins, but she knew Elspeth only too well. "Worry not, Ellie. The *donjon* will be finished soon. In the meantime, we are safe here. Where is Malcom?" she asked, changing the subject.

There was misery in her sister's voice, but not a trace of bitterness. "Where he e'er is of late—in council with David. For better or worse, he has made his decision. He will nevermore bend the knee to Stephen, nor raise a sword for the glory of England. But, I fear it pains him to turn his back on a man he once loved. Alas, to make matters worse, there are many who oppose his return to David's council."

Rosalynde nodded with comprehension. Few understood the role Malcom Scott had played for England, all to aid her sister in her flight from Llanthony, but it was no piddling matter. He was once a member of the king's elite Rex Militum, a powerful but secret guard assigned to protect the king's interests—and, so Malcom had once believed, the welfare of the realm itself. For those whose loyalty remained fast to Scotland—as most Scots doubtless would be—they were bound to be offended by the return of a prodigal son.

In fact, Malcom's own father, a powerful laird, disowned him for a good many years; thankfully he was also the first to embrace his son's return.

Unfortunately, these were fickle, fickle times, and the barons—particularly the border lords—remained suspicious for a reason. Words of fealty were far too easy to speak; it was what a man did in times of war that mattered most. Too many waffled in their allegiance, one minute siding with Matilda, the next with Stephen.

But come what may, Malcom's fealty was sealed. Already once, despite Malcom's initial defection, and in spite of some of the counsel, David mac Maíl Choluim rode to Aldergh's defense, even though he'd been called upon by an unlikely ally... Elspeth herself. After all, it was David of Scotia who so long ago put forth the indictment against their grandmamau. It was his actions that sealed Morgan Pendragon's fate and sent her to the Inquisition, where, by their own half-sister's intervention the lady of Blackwood was dispossessed and dragged through the streets of London to be burned at the stake as a heretic. The Empress's own husband sentenced her to death, and though Matilda might have believed she was spiting her father's mistress, in the process they'd murdered one of the kindest souls that ever took a breath. And yet, somehow, Elspeth still blamed David for their grandmamau's death, never Matilda. That was the bone Rhiannon always wished to pick with Elspeth—and Rosalynde, as well.

But, no matter; this world was rife with unlikely alliances—not the least of which included her own marriage, for she, a *dewine*, a daughter of Avalon, was now wed to an executioner for the Church.

Nothing was simple anymore; so Rosalynde said nothing. She listened quietly, squeezing her sister's arm when words might be expected but wouldn't serve.

Elspeth told her briefly about the Scot king's visit some weeks ago, about his generous gift of armored soldiers—a gesture meant to appease Malcom since her husband was constantly en route to Carlisle. But at least Aldergh was well defended. There was not an inch of the fortress that wasn't manned by guards, and what was more, Elspeth had installed a powerful warding spell only to be certain.

Rosalynde expressed her disappointment not to be able to hug her sweet nephews, because their presence alone was like a shining light, but she assured Elspeth that she understood. A mother must do what was best for her babes.

Elspeth patted her hand and said, "Oh! I brought the book."

The Book of Secrets.

"Good," said Rosalynde, with no small measure of relief, because if there was one thing they needed right now it was the words of their *dewine* forebears. Somewhere in that ancient tome there must be some means to defeat Morwen—and if not defeat her, per se, then perhaps disarm her.

But what a wonder it was that Elspeth was so willing to exploit the secrets the grimoire contained, when little more than a year ago her eldest sister would have gone to great lengths to deny their *dewine* heritage.

Rhiannon would be amazed.

9

The brume Seren conjured near Dover doggedly pursued them, showering them with a fine, cold mist that never quite soaked them, but left them immersed in a discomforting cocoon of dampness.

As a matter of expediency, they dared travel by road, avoiding travelers whenever they must.

Although it was impossible to say whether anyone knew that she and her sister had been hiding aboard the Whitshed, there was no immediate sign of pursuit, and so, concealed beneath Wilhelm's immense, brown cloak, a glamour spell wasn't necessary. Albeit, dressed as she was, Seren couldn't help but feel like an oversized sack of meal.

Chafing beneath the crude hood, her hair teased loose from her braid, clinging damply to her cheeks. Now and again, she swept the wayward strands beneath her hood, and dared not complain. It was her own doing, after all, and the best she could hope for was to ride out of the brume.

Considering the circumstances, Wilhelm was sober as he should be. Jack was hard-pressed to keep his eyes from welling with tears. All afternoon, the mood remained grim.

Then again, Seren couldn't have borne it had there been gaiety or laughter. No one could possibly have any reason to laugh. She felt grief-stricken, and still couldn't weep.

Silence ensued as she contemplated her losses—her sister, foremost, but that certainly wasn't all. Along with Arwyn, Seren had lost her one true chance to escape England. Now she was well and duly caught amidst the *politikal* machinations of would-be kings and queens.

Women like her were little more than pawns to be played.

What would be her fate once her *intended* got hold of her?

Would he do as he'd sworn to do and marry her, all the while bending the knee to an unworthy sovereign?

But, of course, he had too much to lose to break faith with the crown. Naturally, he would honor their betrothal. The king's son had burned his castle once already. Stephen had all but threatened to do it again. But sweet fates, if he was aligned with Stephen, then for certes he would be aligned with her mother, and to be within her mother's grasp would be a fate worse than death.

Arwyn, she thought. *Poor, poor Arwyn.*

By the time they'd returned to the harbor, the entire area was aswarm with guards. It was fortunate enough she'd been wearing Wilhelm's cloak, or they may have recognized her, though, in truth, fugitives though they were, it didn't appear anyone knew that Arwyn Pendragon was aboard the vessel when it burned. Her sister's name was not bandied once, and, in truth, there was no one who even bothered to wonder what had happened to the captain's son.

Nary a survivor emerged from the wreckage. *Not one.* Her sister was well and truly gone. Whatever had set that ship aflame had done so with great expediency and violence. Barely a cinder remained; and what little survived, sank to the bottom of the harbor. Captain Airard, so it seemed, came from a cursed lineage. After two generations had found their graves amidst shallow seas, she hoped Jack would be smart enough not to follow in his father's shoes.

Each mulling over their own part in the day's tragedy, the trio journeyed in silence, with no one quite certain how to breach the ever-expanding chasm.

After all, how did one comport oneself after the loss of a loved one when there wasn't time for grief or tears?

Danger lurked in every passing shadow. Any moment Morwen could pounce upon them, and there was little to be done more than persevere.

There was no time for tantrums or tears.

No time for regrets or self-recrimination.

No time at all for suspicions or doubts.

And nay, she didn't like Wilhelm overmuch—he was brusque and unbending—but at least he seemed dutiful, and she had a sense he was honor-bound to defend her—Jack, as well, if only because she'd begged.

But for all that Seren sensed he was acutely aware of them—every muscle taut and ready to defend—he scarcely looked at her. Betimes he rode ahead, betimes to the rear, but never beside them, always keeping to himself.

In the meantime, she and Jack rode together in companionable silence, near enough that she could, now and again, reach out and take him by the hand.

As much as he could be, he was the opposite of their surly protector—as fair as Wilhelm was dark, sweet as Wilhelm was sour, and truly far more considerate.

Even so, the youth she'd walked with only this morn was hardly the same boy she rode with now. Like Seren, he was sorrowful to his soul, and who could blame him. During the course of a single day his entire life was changed.

Late afternoon they slipped into the woods to avoid a small band of bawdy travelers and re-emerged onto the North Road at twilight, when Seren was certain the bells must be ringing for vespers. Presently, they arrived at a rotting signpost, and she stopped to push her hood back and read the plaques—two nailed to the post, one newer, one older, judging by the condition and the paint. The elder sign read Ramsgate, the newest, with letters deeply etched and painted in white, read Canterbury.

"Canter...bry," said Jack, struggling with his letters.

Arwyn would have been proud. As their trade for passage, the boy's father had enlisted them to instruct Jack so he could learn how to chart and read the captain's log. But the job was mostly Arwyn's, to keep her from growing bored. Seren was content enough to sit and listen.

"Aye," said Seren, mustering an approving smile.

Wilhelm didn't bother to stop. Without a by-your-leave, he trotted past as Jack attempted to read the other sign.

"*Where* are you going?" she asked in surprise.

"Home," he said irascibly.

"Nay, my lord—not lest you mean to go by boat, and you'll not put me on another after what I have witnessed. You would have to bind me, and 'tis not likely I would stand still to allow it."

"I am *not* your lord," he said again. "I am no man's lord." And he kept riding, without bothering to turn back.

Seren cast Jack a bewildered glance.

The boy shrugged.

It was her habit, she supposed, to call every man of consequence lord. Somehow, it seemed better to give deference, but clearly, Wilhelm did not like it, despite that he behaved like a willful lord, doing whatsoever he pleased, keeping whatever pace he saw fit, and never bothering to ask what Seren would like to do.

Hadn't he said he was here to help?

"Wait," she said to Jack, and spurred her mare to catch up with the sour-faced lout. "I do not mean to disparage you," she confessed. "'Tis only that you seem more a lord to me than most lords do."

He grunted in answer, but kept going, and Seren frowned. How was she supposed to travel with this man, who seemed so intent upon ignoring her? Since retrieving Jack he hadn't said much of anything.

"What in the name of St. Afan would you have me call you if not lord?"

"Wilhelm," he replied. "And since when do Pendragons swear by the name of saints?"

Seren lifted her chin. "I lived most of my life in a priory," she informed him. And then she leaned over to whisper. "I cannot very well swear by the Goddess, can I? Else Jack would wonder."

"Well," he said. "This is your fault. Had you left that boy in Dover you wouldn't have to pretend you are someone you are not."

Seren bristled. "Can you, please, stop! Please?" She reined in her horse, peering back at Jack, who was still waiting where she'd left him, far enough away now that he couldn't overhear their discourse.

"Nay," he replied, without turning.

Seren sighed, moving forward again, entirely frustrated. Her horse nickered, prancing impatiently, none too pleased with her indecision. "*Where* in the name of the Goddess are you going?"

"Home, I said."

Seren furrowed her brow. "You are not going home. Did you not read that sign? You are going to Ramsgate, returning to the ocean, and, once again, I remind you that lest you have a ship, or you and your horse would like to have a good swim, the road to Canterbury is the road best traveled."

Finally, he stopped, turning back to look at her, and his cheeks appeared to bloom. He scowled then, and without a word, spun his mare about, trotting back toward Jack. He passed the boy by, never sparing Jack or the signpost a glance.

He couldn't read, she realized, in a moment of blinding insight.

She dropped her reins over the revelation.

He hadn't read the sign, because he *couldn't* read.

What was more, if he hadn't come by way of Canterbury en route to Dover, he would be judging his direction by the sun, traveling due north. Unless he'd done as she and Arwyn did, traveling straight from Canterbury to Dover, he would have no inkling that he would run straight into the sea where the ocean flowed into the Thames.

In fact, they would be hard-pressed to avoid London's proximity when skirting the city, and she was already fretting about how they would do it. She wouldn't feel safe until they were well north of the Wash.

Sadly, these were not areas that supported her sister Matilda. Matilda had fewer allies in the south than she did in the north, and infinitely fewer in the southeast than she did in the west.

Wilhelm trotted on, leaving the boy to wait for Seren, and if Seren didn't know better—know he'd come so far only to help her—she might think he didn't care one whit where she ended. Frowning, she turned to follow, calming the horse with a hand to its withers.

WILHELM REALIZED he was sorely lacking in manners.

He was hardly well versed in social decorum. Certainly, he didn't know how to read. But he didn't need some haughty witch reminding him of these truths— nor did he appreciate that Seren kept calling him *lord*. It was a grating reminder that he was lacking in every possible way.

To be sure, he was naught more than a servant with a sword, and if his sire had loved him well enough to keep him and train him, he'd never once mistaken him for an heir.

And neither had Wilhelm ever dared aspire to such heights. For the most part, he'd accepted his lot in life, and there was only one time in all his given days that he'd lamented his station. That was when he'd believed he was ill-equipped to keep his brother and people safe.

God's truth, not even his desire for Lady Ayleth ever made him rue his birth. But there again, he found himself wallowing in envy—why?

For some slip of a girl.

From the moment they'd met, he'd recognized disdain in Seren's beautiful blue eyes.

To make matters worse, that boy—that stupid boy from the harbor—could read better than he could.

He hadn't stopped to ask what the sign post said for one reason alone: He lived his life by his wits, and he knew the way home by the turn of the sun. But he did not like himself overmuch for disparaging a grieving child, no matter that he'd not spoken his vitriol aloud.

Consequently, his mood soured by the minute, and it didn't help that he'd been on his toes for weeks now, deprived of sustenance and ale, deprived of his bed, deprived of companionship and the people he most cared for.

Instead, here he was—with *her*—and she couldn't care less how much effort he'd already put into helping her.

Of course, he understood she was grieving, too, but when he'd tried so hard to reassure her that he well understood what she was going through, she hadn't bothered to ask how he knew.

What was more, in her presence, he felt for the first time in all his days as though he were being judged.

No one had ever done this to him—no one among the people he loved. Every day of his life his father had treated him with respect. His elder brother Roger had treated him more like a brother. His sweet sisters had loved him truly. And his mother—God rest her lovely soul—whilst she lived, she'd doted upon him.

He didn't like it that Seren Pendragon made him question himself.

Not even Giles with all his fancy learnings ever made him feel so much a lesser man.

But none of that was the true reason he was so ill-tempered. This was it: Even despite Seren's grief, she had smiles aplenty for that *eegit* boy, and none at all for him.

And there it was—the rotten egg in his coop.

He was envious of a boy, for the love of God!

He was envious of those gentle smiles she gifted him, and the patience she bestowed, when all she had for him was querulousness.

Wilhelm only longed for some small acknowledgment for all he'd endured on her behalf—not to mention all the silver he'd spent. He'd fully anticipated having to spend good coin for horses for both Pendragon sisters. He hadn't felt it appropriate to bring mounts, because they would have slowed him down, but he'd brought along plenty of coin to buy each sister a healthy mount. But the truth of the matter was that he didn't enjoy putting out so many shillings for a horse only to serve a horny boy who, even in his grief, couldn't keep his eyes off Lady Seren's bosom.

And by the by, Jack hadn't bothered to thank him either, and some part of him longed to chide them both, but he felt like a sorehead, because their grief was entirely too fresh.

How else should he expect them to behave?

How dare he lament feeling unworthy when she had so recently suffered such a devastating loss—so had the boy, for that matter. But for all Wilhelm's own demons, he was poorly equipped to comfort them, when even now the lingering scent of smoke made him long for a dark corner in which to sob like a wee girl.

God's truth, his eyes burned even now, so far from the city, and he could no longer blame it on the reek of smoke. He was a man full grown, bigger than most, and he felt like a child, longing for the solace of his mother's embrace. Some called him the Hammer of Warkworth, and he had scars aplenty to show for his trials—the most hideous of all delivered by Seren's own mother.

Wilhelm was no blubbering boy, but, of late, his emotions had bubbled to the surface, and he loathed the weakness in himself and begrudged Seren her mettle, because it made him feel so much less a man.

If, only once, she would cast herself at his feet to weep, if only he could lift her up and smooth a hand o'er the silk of her hair and whisper, "There, there," maybe then he could feel like a man worth his weight.

But nay, he was left wanting by a pretty little boy— a skinny child who could read, while he could not.

And, in the end, he had no right to any of these feelings. It was a bitter pill to swallow knowing he could not rise to the occasion and be a better man.

He wanted to be a better man—*she* made him long to be a better man—but he simply wasn't. He was baseborn—a babe born in the rushes to a mother who was never even tended by a midwife. She spat him out and returned to her duties, and as much as she had been enjoyed by his sire, and perhaps even loved by him, she, like Wilhelm, was never worthy enough to carry de Vere's name. He was Wilhelm Fitz Richard, no more, no less—bastard son of a dead lord.

And here was the worst of it: Once upon a time, he'd loved a girl who was too highborn to love him in return, and never once did Ayleth of Bamburgh admire him, not even after his brother left for the seminary—not even after Wilhelm gifted her that beautiful cross she'd worn about her neck, a cross that cost Wilhelm five years' worth of his earnings.

For years, he'd loved Lady Ayleth from afar, but what scared him now was this: So much as he'd fancied himself in love with that lady, it was naught at all compared to the attraction he felt for Lady Seren.

Wilhelm didn't *want* to want her. He knew in his heart of hearts that it was a sin to consider such a union. He was unworthy of even her lowest glance... and still, despite the grim occasion, he was blue in the balls and hard-pressed to keep his mind on the task he'd been given.

How in God's name was he going to help anyone if he couldn't think beyond the haze of lust she invoked in him... with nothing so much as a glance.

Wilhelm was furious at himself for his weakness to her. She was a bloody enchantress, and if he didn't know better, he would think she'd cast a spell on him.

But nay, because long before Seren Pendragon ever deigned to acknowledge him, he was already bound to do her will. She needn't *try* to sway him, and what was more, he had every sense that this woman he was traveling with hadn't the first inkling of her power over men. How Giles ever walked away from her he didn't know.

And, aye, while it was so close to the surface, it was time to confess the bitter truth: From the very day he'd set eyes on her—that day in the King's Hall—he'd been grateful she was not meant for him, because he, himself, would have forsaken everything he ever held true only to lie with her once.

So there you have it; that, above all, was the crux of his problem: He didn't want to want anything so much that he was in danger of betraying his honor or his oaths—including the oath he'd sworn to himself. *To see Morwen pay for the death of his kin.*

It didn't matter much that he knew there was no love lost betwixt that witch and her daughters. Inevitably, they shared the same blood. Seren was a witch, as well, and there, too, he suffered a bucketful of ambivalence, because so was Rosalynde, and a finer lady than Rose Wilhelm had never met.

Mulling it all over, he rode in silence, wondering how the hell they were going to get around London without being discovered. Seren could cast herself a *glamour*, but she likely couldn't mask them all. And, even if she could, how in the hell was she going to do aught with her *magik* whilst in the company of that annoying boy?

No, he mustn't be jealous of a child, he decided. It couldn't be that. He simply resented being saddled with another mouth to feed, and keeping the two of them safe could prove to be an impossible feat.

Alas, deep down... he knew... he was jealous, and jealousy did not become him.

10

Rhiannon sensed they were coming before they arrived—a crackle of energy in the *aether*. She awoke, shivering away the stupor of slumber and sat on the bed, throwing her legs over the edge to wait...

It was still dark out. The fire in her brazier burned low.

She shivered again, this time not because she was cold. Much as she loathed to confess it, some small part of her thrilled over the fact that Cael d'Lucy was returning so soon, but the new lord of Blackwood was not amidst his guards when they arrived.

Coward.

So, then, he meant to avoid her after their latest discourse?

She frowned, wondering where he could be, wishing so much that she could find a way to convince the fool to ally himself properly. Deep down, she believed Cael had a good heart, even if he wasn't a good man. It was merely that he was enthralled by a demon, and so it seemed, like the entire realm, he was blind to Morwen's evil as well. It didn't help matters any that he was ambitious and bitter—why she'd yet to discover, but she was coming so close to the truth.

Coward, she thought again.

Thrusting a palm across her sleepy face, she yawned into her hand and crossed her arms as she waited to see what his lackeys wanted this time.

Without a word, one of the guards slid a now familiar turnkey into her lock, rotating it with a vicious twist, then pushing the cell door open. The very instant the door came open, in rushed two guards, and before Rhiannon could guess their intent, they'd pounced upon her, grabbing her by the arms. "What in the name of the Mother?"

"Silence!" screamed a stranger, his tone full of venom, as his men used undue force, despite that she'd never once fought them, not from the instant they'd tossed her in the tumbril.

The night before leaving Llanthony, she'd had a vision from the Goddess to show her what destiny she must seek, and she'd come to this place willingly.

Why this? Why now?

"What does it appear we're doing?" snarled the man, as he entered, dangling a pair of shackles and Rhiannon laughed ruefully. Little by little, she was learning to master her *dewine* skills. If she so wished, she could shed those silly manacles; and therefore, she allowed their pageantry, leaving the guards to do what they must, despite the fury welling inside her. She was ever only kind to these imbeciles, and despite the bitter words they'd shared yesterday evening, she was ever only guileless to their lord.

Cael d'Lucy was originally intended to wed her sister, but Elspeth was now well and duly wed to the lord of Aldergh—a traitor to the Crown, so Stephen had proclaimed. Now, the king wished for Cael to marry Rhiannon, but despite a fine bunch of carrots dangled by their king, d'Lucy had yet to agree to commit himself to any but Henry's favored daughter. To a man, the Welsh sorely despised Stephen, more so than they had Henry, but at least Henry had treated the Welsh lords with some measure of accord. The moment Stephen stole his uncle's throne, the Welsh revolted. Little doubt Elspeth herself was needed to bring peace to these lands, for she was not only elder-born, and blood to a king, she was also the rightful heir to Black-wood, and Cael was wise enough to know that if he was going to keep his entitlement in the face of so much opposition, he would need to wed the heir of Blackwood—something Rhiannon would never be so long as Elspeth lived.

As for her own druthers, she had none. Cael d'Lucy was like any other man—as unpleasant in demeanor as he was blessed in countenance. One marriage shackle was as loathsome as another. "Where is your lord?" she asked, spitting the question like an oath.

"Gone," said the man dangling her new silver bracelets.

Rhiannon didn't recognize the odious fool. The other two must have come along with him from whatever infernal hole they'd crawled from, but, alas, they were only doing Cael's bidding. It was not their fault their lord was a traitor to the realm.

But never mind, because she was biding her time.

Day by day her powers were growing stronger, and little by little she was learning what tricks she could wield against her captors. She wanted to crow that their puny bracelet would never bind her, but before she could wonder why they'd approached her in the wee hours of the morn, and with such expediency, when all her senses were dull and drowsy, the shackles were on her wrists and locked. But at least her hands were in her lap, not strapped behind her back.

The man smiled as he stepped back, inclining his head in a gesture of mock deference. "William Martel at your service," he said, and Rhiannon narrowed her eyes.

William Martel? The man her mother would have Seren wed? The betrayer who'd poisoned one king already, and who stood ready to murder another?

"The king's steward?" she asked, surprised.

His smile was too smug, and Rhiannon would have enjoyed wiping it from his face, except... she moved her arms and felt... *weaker*.

Confused, she furrowed her brow.

It was only a sense, she supposed, but in a matter of seconds she felt inordinately lethargic—as though she'd gone too long without supping and left wasted.

"What is this?" she asked, confused, weaker by the second. Far too late, she realized... it was... the shackles...

The metal stung her flesh wherever they touched her, and it was the strangest, most uncanny feeling, but even the *aether* surrounding her was somehow depleted.

"A gift from your mother," Martel said, then snapped his fingers before Rhiannon could recover herself well enough to respond—it was almost as though she were drunk now, impaired. The guards were long gone before she could speak another word, and darkness enfolded her in their absence. Little by little, the fire in her brazier grew dimmer.

Rhiannon struggled to put her thoughts into the *aether* to seek help from her sisters—a thing she would never have done had she not had such a terrible sense of danger. It was too dangerous to *mind-*

speak outside proximity because all thoughts put into the firmament were left vulnerable to all who might seek them—including their mother.

It was far too late when she understood what Morwen had done... and not until her room grew uncomfortably cold and she could not bolster the fire in her brazier...

She was bound, not only by the iron shackles, but by *magik*. The shackles were enchanted, she realized, and if they were enchanted, it meant... not only was she well and truly alone, powerless to do aught... her sisters were on their own as well.

Elspeth! Seren! Rose!

"Cael," she called weakly, but this time, there came no reply from the shadows. Cael was truly gone. Her answer was a silence so complete that it left her shivering in its void, and for the first time in all Rhiannon's entire life, she was afraid. Not since the time before time in her mother's womb had she sensed such bewildering darkness... helpless... only waiting, waiting. But this time, not to be born... to *die*.

11

A chill fog drifted along the woodlands, eddying so high that cool air tickled Seren's feet. It reminded her of that mist they'd conjured on the night Elspeth had fled the priory. It was the first time she and her sisters had ever dared perform a rite of such magnitude. To aid Elspeth's escape, they'd conjured a mist that climbed out from their cauldron and stole out the door. Elspeth used the cloak of mist to elude the dogs and guards Ersinius sent to retrieve her. But words like those were never to be uttered lightly; they could never be evoked without consequence. And yet, it was an impressive feat. And later, after their mother arrived, Seren couldn't help but note a certain gleam in Morwen's eyes. No doubt she'd been furious with them, but she was proud as well. That was the first time in Seren's entire life she'd ever experienced the warm glow of a mother's pride, short-lived though it was. Immediately thereafter, Morwen had tossed Rhiannon into a tumbril to be carted away, like some animal, bound and leashed. Even now, Seren could feel her sister's warning gaze. *Be silent, be still. Be silent, be still.* But the look in her eyes as they'd dragged Rhi away had broken Seren's heart, and she had never imagined she could be more broken-hearted than she was that day... until now.

Grief was a fourth companion, ever with them, pursuing them like the shadow of a hound. But so long as Jack held back his tears, Seren felt duty-bound to hold back her own. Together, they would endure—with or without Wilhelm's help. But truth be told, it wasn't only Seren and Jack grieving; Wilhelm wore his own grief like a mantle of sorrow. She could feel it as surely as she felt her own.

"E's not too friendly, eh?"

"Surly, to be sure," she said, her gaze boring into Wilhelm Fitz Richard's back. His entire demeanor had changed the instant they'd retrieved Jack. Before then, he'd practically begged to serve her, and now, he appeared for all the world to be a man ruing his circumstances.

"I ain't ne'er seen so big a fellow," said Jack, with an unmistakable note of appreciation in his voice—and, of course, he would note such a thing. He was at an age when his own virility must be foremost in his thoughts. Even struggling with his own grief, she couldn't help but note the solicitous way he remained by her side, like a self-appointed guardian angel.

"Aye," she said. "He is."

And it was true. It wasn't very likely that anyone could overlook the man, no matter how quiet or unassuming he appeared to be. And yet Seren had a sense that there was more to Wilhelm Fitz Richard than met the eye. His aura was bold and unmistakable, but confusing.

Much like the glow of a flame, all creatures radiated shades of color that revealed more than words alone could say. Like her sister Elspeth, so long as Seren remained within proximity, she could read them. In fact, she was quite proficient at determining the nature of a person's temperament based on emanations. After a year at court she had good practice, and it was rare that she was ever wrong, even though the truth disappointed her. She wanted desperately to think better of people, but so often they failed to live up to their potentials.

Wilhelm's colors were perplexing, to be sure...

His most predominant shade was a vivid, angry orange, mixed with intense coils of red. More oft than not this combination revealed a kindly, honest disposition, even if betimes he might be quick to raise a temper—already, they'd suffered glimpses of that. But, these colors also implied immense loyalty; whatever this man set his heart to, that's where it would remain unto his dying breath.

Alas, these shades were interwoven with shades of brown and gray, and those were the colors that thoroughly bemused her, because his demeanor belied what they implied. You see, brown was the color of uncertainty, or it could mean he somehow lacked confidence. But there was naught in Wilhelm Fitz Richard's demeanor that gave truth to this interpretation. What was more, he had darker shades of brown and gray that indicated selfish tendencies, negativity, or a predilection toward deception. Even more alarming, betimes these threads bordered on black, which was a far, far worse implication. Black, you see, was the color of hatred, and she knew this only too well, because Morwen drifted through Westminster's halls enshrouded in a blue-black aura, much like a bruise on the *aether*.

Fortunately, Wilhelm's aura was nothing like Morwen's.

Day to day, her mother's essence remained predominately black, with coils of blue and furls of red; this was perhaps the most dangerous aura to be encountered. The red bespoke her passion—and she was, indeed, very passionate. She was rabidly so, and there was little that could dissuade Morwen Pendragon from her schemes. The blue, on the other hand, was an indication of supreme intelligence and a given ability to influence the masses. To Seren's horror, her mother could charm folks with a bat of her lashes, and lest you understood what it was she was doing to you, you might be fooled until it was too late to extricate yourself from her dangerous web.

Inevitably, all her mother's minions ended up with a similar aura, sans the blue, and Seren could sense these creatures from leagues away.

But though Wilhelm's was not at all like that at all, he was nevertheless no man to be trifled with, and neither was it the least bit likely anyone would consider him easy prey. For certes, they would be safe traveling with this man, but she had yet to determine... were they safe *from* him?

Seren thought, perhaps, the answer to that question must be yes, though she couldn't be certain—and yet, somehow, she was driven to vex him. Why, she hadn't any clue.

Or perhaps she did suspect why and didn't wish to acknowledge the truth, because Wilhelm had the dubious misfortune of appearing in her life at the most inopportune time. He'd kept her from going after Arwyn, and despite the fact that, in retrospect, she knew there was naught she could have done to save her sister, some small part of her begged the question: What if she had responded sooner? What if she had cast away her fear and gone after Arwyn?

What if... what if... what if...

The endless questions bedeviled her. Wilhelm was an easy target for her fury—an emotion she had never in her life dared to nurture. What must her own aura be now?

It simply wasn't possible to see it for herself, but, according to Elspeth, it used to be a shimmering shade of silvery—the mark of the serenely gifted, but with the palest hint of blue, which was also a distinction for peacekeepers. Elspeth had often likened her aura to the wintry color of her eyes, and Seren had taken much pride in Elspeth's interpretation, because there were far worse things in this world than to be a peace-monger. Only now... she must be awash in deepest reds. What was worse, she felt shades of black coiling up from the depths of her soul, tendrils of loathing sprouting from the silvery ash of her grief.

Arwyn's death was transformative.

Whereas previously Seren had only feared Morwen, now she despised her with every fiber of her being. Given the opportunity—like Wilhelm—she would snuff her mother's heart flame as easily as she would snuff a candle, and she would do that to the woman who gave her life.

True hatred was all consuming, she feared, because she could feel it growing, intensifying, wending its way through her veins, black as the wings of her mother's treacherous birds.

It was all so perplexing—nearly as much so as the man she'd now pursued throughout the night, mile after mile, hour after hour, into woodlands and out. Glaring at his back again, she wished he would turn and face her... *only why?*

So, she could complain about how long they'd traveled? Goddess knew, he was like to be as weary as they were and still, he persevered. And, forsooth, it wasn't as though he was doing this for his own pleasure. He was ushering them back to safety... so why, oh why, did she long so much to smack him upside the head?

Perhaps because he wore that perpetual frown on his face, putting her in mind to those hideous stone *gargouilles* installed at the palace, with their immense twisted, grotesque mouths. In the foulest of weathers they were terrifying, with rain lashing down and bolts of lightning silhouetting their forms. One day, a few weeks before Rosalynde stole the *grimoire*, she and Seren were caught in a downpour out in the castle yard. Together, they'd witnessed the *gargouilles* at their intended purpose. Built to gutter rainwater, they'd spewed a torrent at their feet, muddying their dresses. They'd returned to the apartment, sopping wet, and filthy besides. Arwyn was worried, even though they were gone little more than an hour. That was all the time they'd dared to spare in order to scope the area and make plans... plans for Rosalynde to steal the Book of Secrets.

The memory enveloped Seren in a cloud of misery, because Arwyn hadn't gone with them that day for the same reason Seren had left her aboard the Whitshed... because her *magik* was weak, because she didn't know how to lie, because she couldn't conceal her presence or her purpose from Morwen. They had coddled her to save her life, and, in the end, their coddling was Arwyn's ruin.

White-hot fury bubbled up from the depths of her, and her silvery gaze returned to Wilhelm Fitz Richard. She focused her anger on him in the absence of her mother.

"Do you... think... it 'urt?" Jack asked, intruding on her reverie.

Seren blinked back tears, knowing instinctively what he was asking by the unhappy look on his face. Sweet fates, She needn't read his mind or his aura to know he was fretting over his father. So far as Seren was concerned, she couldn't imagine a worse way to die, but she didn't wish to say so. She could scarcely bear to consider Arwyn's final moments, but she did so now perforce... suffering anguish anew over how much she may have suffered. And yet, judging by the swiftness of Arwyn's departure—the rending of her soul from this plane of existence—she thought perhaps that wasn't true. "I don't know," she confessed.

Once, when Seren was fifteen, Llanthony suffered the loss of one of their aviaries. The structure ignited sometime after Matins, and by Lauds, there was naught left, but wisps of smoke and piles of ash. It took hours and hours for that edifice to burn, and she and her sisters had carried bucket after bucket of water from their hatchery to douse those flames—all night long, until their arms and legs ached from the effort. Back in those days, the aviary had been no more than a tiny structure far from the main buildings, and even so, the flames had lit the night till morn.

In contrast, the Whitshed vanished behind a veil of blue so intensely hot that Seren could still feel a fever burning in her cheeks.

"I'm tired," Jack complained, sliding a hand to his middle in a gesture of hunger, peering up at Seren, looking more like a small child than a man. They had been traveling so long now. It was no wonder the boy was hungry and tired.

She peered back instinctively, spying only trees and a long dusty road behind them. Dover was long in their wake and dawn was breaking. They'd ridden all night long without stopping, and if no one complained until now, it wasn't because they weren't bone weary.

Certainly, she understood why they'd set such a grueling pace—all for her sake, but seeing the strain on Jack's face, she realized it was only a matter of time before he tumbled from his saddle. Meanwhile, twenty paces ahead, Wilhelm's horse let loose a pile of dung without so much as bothering to pause for the duty, swishing its tail in annoyance, sour-tempered as its master.

Deciding they'd had quite enough, she spurred her mount forward to trot beside the bastard son of Richard de Vere.

It was a long, long moment before she worked up the nerve to speak. But then she said, "We've been traveling overlong. I understand why, but Jack is tired and by now the horses must be fatigued as well. We must rest, if only for a few hours."

His dark gaze swiveled to meet hers, cutting in its intensity. "We'll stop soon," he said, averting his gaze, looking into the sunrise, so that his face was lit by a golden hue that made the strands of silver in his beard glitter fiercely.

No "THANK YOUS," no praise for his efforts, no warmth from this rare, beauteous flower of Blackwood—and there it was, he supposed: She was as distant and unapproachable as he'd surmised she would be, with that lovely golden-red hair, those flawlessly arched brows and pale, luminous skin.

Her cheeks were bright pink, either from exertion or from exposure to the Whitshed's flames. She looked sad to her soul, and Wilhelm longed to comfort her, but something in her expression left him cold.

For all that she appeared so delicate, she reminded him of a ghost orchid he once encountered, with its leafless spine pointed high and straight and its milky blossoms with soft blushing spots. He'd been so afraid to pluck it in the presence of his brother, and he'd resolved to do so upon returning so he could gift it to Lady Ayleth. Regretfully, that flower was gone when they returned, and it didn't reappear for another four years—in an entirely different location. By then, Giles was long gone to the seminary, and Ayleth's heart was well and duly broken. She'd scarcely looked at his gift, much less thanked him for it, and he'd found himself wholly embarrassed for the effort.

Seren Pendragon gave him that same pause.

She was far too lovely for the likes of a beast like him, and even so, who in the hell longed to curl up with an icicle?

More than aught else, she seemed angry over the turn of events, and he had yet to see her weep a single tear. She was an ice princess, to be sure.

"Jack is hungry," she persisted, as though her first complaint hadn't moved him well enough. "So am I. And—"

"And what?" he snapped, forcing himself to meet her gaze, loathing the way his heart struck a discordant beat over the haunted look in her eyes.

She peered down at the reins in her hand, her impossibly dark lashes fanning her toasted cheeks and God help his rotten soul, some foolish part of him longed to reach out and caress her fire-roasted skin. In his mind's eye, he allowed himself to kiss it ever-so sweetly, and to his utter dismay, his cock hardened over the imagery, straining against his well-worn leathers. He growled audibly in disgust.

"Are you always so pettish, my lord?"

Wilhelm ignored her use of a title, weary of correcting her. "Pettish?"

"Aye, Pettish."

He frowned. "Pettish is what ladies should be. Pettish is for wayward children. Alas, if my mood does not strike you as genial, Lady Seren, you may call me bad-tempered to your heart's content, but you should at least thank me within the same breath, because I have come a long way only to help you." He sat quietly a moment, and when she did not respond, he added, "That I did not do so before your sister's death is not my fault any more than it is yours."

SEREN'S HEART SQUEEZED PAINFULLY.

Well and duly chastised, she cast her gaze into the passing trees, swallowing the painful lump that rose to choke her.

She daren't weep now, because if she began, her tears might never end. She would sob puddles and puddles, and perhaps add *witchwater* to the *witchwind*, because she sensed that same bewildering intensity rising in the aether, leaving her to wonder if her serenity was but a matter of self-defense. Deep down she must have sensed everything she was capable of.

Witchwater.

Surveilling the woodlands, she sensed more than saw the glittering dew drops shivering on the leaves of trees, and like a lodestone, she drew them, feeling small droplets splash against her cheeks.

But, nay, she was not weeping.

It was witchwater... she was certain.

But how is that possible?

"We have a long way to go," he said. "Please do me the inestimable favor of at least appreciating that I, too, have gone the whole night without resting, as I have done so for you."

It was true, Seren acknowledged, and not for the first time. He'd arrived like a delivering angel, plucking her up, willy-nilly, from the harbor. Against her will though it might have been, he'd nevertheless sheltered her from harm. More than she had, he'd had his wits about him enough to know that the king's men would be arriving soon. Were it not for him, she would be on her way to gaol, or worse.

If she were less of an ingrate, she might thank him...

"I am not your gaoler," he said, "I swore to keep you safe, and to do so, I must get you and that boy as far away from London as possible, so bear with me, if you please."

At his chiding tone, Seren felt chagrined, though anger pricked at her heart. She felt like an ungrateful wretch, and still, she couldn't bring herself to apologize. Her pride simply wouldn't allow it, so she fell back again to ride with Jack. She and the boy shared a glance, but she daren't hold Jack's gaze—or anyone else's for that matter. Fat tears welled in her eyes. *Don't cry,* she demanded of herself. *Don't cry.*

Don't cry. Don't cry. Don't cry.

A light drizzle accompanied them... until finally she dried her tears.

12

I t was impossible for Elspeth to concentrate.

No matter what Rosalynde claimed, it was disheartening to see how little protection her sister had here at Warkworth, with only a handful of tents for housing, and her *donjon* still in the midst of being constructed. Oh, how her sister expounded over the design and details, but all Elspeth saw was a pile of rocks, and this was not meant to be disparaging. Rather, it filled her heart with dread.

A quick breeze ruffled the heavy canvas, causing the marquee's faded blue walls to billow like waves. Inside, *all* the tapers trembled, their flames dancing along unseen currents. Certainly, as tents went, the marquee was quite sumptuous, boasting a lovely curtained-bed heavily veiled in the prettiest shades of blues, from the palest hue that brought to mind Seren's wintry eyes, to the richest cerulean blue Elspeth had ever spied. A sturdy, ornately carved table sat to one side of the marquee, bare as a bone, as though all schemes and blueprints had been hidden away before the lord's departure. Elspeth could easily imagine this would be the lord's table, where Giles de Vere made all his cloak and dagger plans. As for the remainder of the space, it was far plusher than any room Elspeth had at Aldergh, with many brightly colored embroidered cushions, all bearing exotic designs that put Elspeth in mind to the Saracens. But, despite all this luxury, it was only a tent, vulnerable to the elements—and worse, vulnerable to the likes of Morwen. All it would take for the entire edifice to erupt in flames was for someone to topple a candle.

Frowning, she said, "I must say you would be safer at Aldergh, Rose. Please, come home with me; we can send word to Giles in London. I know he will understand. He loves you."

Rosalynde glanced up from the *grimoire*, regarding Elspeth with heavy lidded eyes. Elspeth knew Rose wanted her to stop bedeviling her, but she couldn't. She was a mother now; it only served to bring out her maternal instincts all the more. Under the guidance of a constant stream of nursemaids, she'd raised all four of her sisters— including Rhiannon, no matter what Rhiannon would like to claim. Rhi had been such a willful child. From the time she could walk and talk— earlier than all the rest—it took all her efforts to keep her sister out of harm's way.

Morwen herself was never a proper mother. For love of the Goddess, she was hardly a proper human being. But for all Elspeth's cautions, betimes, her sisters were impetuous and reckless, and so far as Elspeth was concerned, this was one of those times.

"Nay," Rosalynde said willfully. "I cannot."

"Cannot or will not?"

Her young sister sighed, her attention returning stubbornly to the *grimoire*, one finger traveling the ancient page as she perused the text. "Both," she said quietly, but Elspeth heard the iron-will in her voice.

She cast a hand up in frustration. "For the life of

me, Rose, I cannot comprehend why your husband would allow you to remain here with so little protection."

"To the contrary, Elspeth, I am well defended. Giles took every precaution before he left, and our gate is nearly impenetrable."

"Nearly?"

"Completely," Rosalynde demurred. "I warrant, 'tis as much so as yours. We took the design from Aldergh, after all."

Elspeth tilted her youngest sister a dubious look. She waved a hand in a gesture to indicate the entirety of their surroundings. "What about this? Do you think *this* will stop *her* if she manages to find a way through your *impenetrable* gate? Your entire garrison, armed to the teeth, will be hard-pressed to protect you—and by the way, those leathers of yours, they are laughable in defense against our mother."

"I have a very good suit of armor, fashioned to precise dimensions."

"But, of course," said Elspeth, hating her chafing tone, but unable to stop herself.

"Please, Elspeth. Stop worrying. Now that you've brought the Book, we'll find a proper warding spell. Please, stop. I'll not go," Rosalynde said, more firmly. "I am needed here, and you, above all should understand why."

Elspeth frowned. "Why?"

Rosalynde gave her an exasperated glance. "Because, as I have said. This is where Matilda plans to mount her campaign into England." When Elspeth said naught, she lifted her brows. "You remember Matilda, do you not? You championed her all those years, and now wouldst you have me turn my back on our sister when she needs us most?"

"Half-sister," Elspeth corrected. "And since when do you concern yourself with Matilda?"

"Since now." Rosalynde said, her gaze flicking up to meet Elspeth's, incensed. "Truly, Elspeth?"

"Do not mistake me, Rose. I realize how critical it is for Matilda to take her rightful place on England's throne, but you are my true-blood sister, and I'll not risk you, not even for such a noble cause."

"I will not fail my lord husband. Nor will I betray *our cause,*" she said, dismissing Elspeth's complaints.

Mother's mercy! Everything for the cause.

Elspeth more than anyone understood the importance of deposing the Usurper, but to leave another of her sisters vulnerable was unthinkable—not even to support Matilda.

Already, they'd lost Arwyn. Elspeth could not bear to lose Rosalynde as well, not even for the sake of the realm. Their sister Matilda had more than enough men to defend her, and proof of that was plain to see... if not, Morwen would have already found a way to kill her long ago—which was, in itself, heartening, because if Morwen could not destroy the one person she most loathed in this realm, there must, indeed, be some way to stop her—some way that did not involve losing yet another sister.

Months ago she'd taken to picking at her thumbnail. Now it was raw. Really, so much as it pleased her to see Rosalynde rallying behind Matilda, and so much as it relieved her to see that something was being done about the current *politikal* clime, she absolutely loathed the thought of putting any of her sisters in danger. At one point, she herself had been prepared to lay down her life for *the cause*, but now that she had two sweet babes, she must reconsider. If she died, what then would happen to Lachlan and Broc?

Nay, there was only one reason in the entire world she would ever leave them... and that was to aid her sisters. But considering Giles de Vere's occupation, she had come here thinking Rosalynde would be very well defended. That did not appear to be the case, and they would be better off scheming at Aldergh, with three times the number of men, and a well-fortified castle and *donjon* filled with loyal stewards who would all die to defend them.

But here they were...

With a vengeance, Elspeth flicked her thumbnail, aggravating the flesh beneath.

What about Seren—where was she?

What about Rhiannon?

In the direst of moments, both she and Rosalynde always managed to hear from Rhi. For Elspeth, through *mindspeaking*. For Rosalynde, *mindspeaking* and dream visitation. But no matter how many times they engaged her now, Rhiannon remained eternally silent. The *aether* was as devoid of her presence as it was of Arwyn's... except that Rhiannon's absence was more like a closed door. Arwyn's was a terrible, empty void.

With a weary sigh, she gave up the fight for the moment, thinking that so long as Rosalynde's sword was not glowing, she must take comfort in that. And yet, no matter that it lay so quietly beside them, she couldn't keep her eyes off the shining metal blade, with its intricately crafted serpents. She couldn't believe all the things Rosalynde told her...

A gift from her husband, the sword was crafted by one forebear to give to another; it was the same weapon that once belonged to a son of Uther, by all accounts, as fine a warrior as ever did live. When the time came to choose his allegiance, he chose, not his mother's kinsmen, but the people of Wales. And yet, the troubadours had this story wrong: Avalon was gone before Arthur ever took his first breath. He was only blessed by Avalon by virtue of his association with Taliesin, and though he was half-brother to the first Morgan Pendragon, those two siblings never produced a son. Moreover, Arthur's sister was not responsible for his death. What the troubadours did have correct was this: With that sword Rosalynde now possessed, Arthur slew hordes of Saxons, and eventually, he and his armies caused the Romans to flee Wales. But how ironic it was that the very men he vanquished were the very men who'd, somehow, not only come to possess his sword, but were also the ones Matilda now called in defense of the realm—the Romans with their Paladins. Even now, Elspeth could hardly believe Giles was a member of the Papal Guard—defenders of the realm, so 'twas said, but huntsmen nevertheless. They were the ones who'd carried out her grandmamau's sentencing—a fact Elspeth was still coming to grips over.

Sighing ruefully, she watched her sister pore over the ancient tome. The Book of Secrets was ancient and irreplaceable. There was no other of its kind. Within its hallowed pages were hundreds of untold mysteries, alchemic prescriptions and long-forgotten spells. To the wrong eyes, it could be infinitely dangerous, and therefore, the Book was bound by blood *magik*; only a *dewine's* blood could reveal its true nature. To keep it safe, Rosalynde had risked her life to steal it north, and if Morwen ever retrieved it... well, then, the realms of men should hide beneath their beds.

Embossed upon the aged volume were endless, ever-changing symbols emerging and receding into the leather surface—a wonder to be sure, and she marveled that not so long ago she would have considered this utterly impossible. And yet, here they were, and there was Rosalynde—wife to a huntsman— reading the Book of Secrets in plain sight.

Truly, it was a marvel, and Elspeth was glad to be a witness to it, even if she missed her babes so much it hurt. Even now, her nipples were sore from having suckled them so long after the wet-nurse advised her to wean them. Her body remembered their weight at her bosom, and her nipples throbbed with the desperation to feed them. But, alas, dwelling on that served no one right now, and if she kept it up, she would ruin yet another gown.

Pushing her sweet boys out of her head, she peered down at the *grimoire*. For hours now they'd been searching for a good protection spell, and there were many, but none powerful enough to wield the way Elspeth had wielded that spell on the battlements the eve of their mother's attack. *That* spell was not in this book, for it had come directly from the Mother Goddess, fully formed as it sprang to her lips.

And yet, so much as she appreciated the divine intervention, that night was a blight on her memory.

That night, whilst their mother had waited in a tent—not unlike this very tent—outside proximity of Aldergh's missiles, she'd sent an angry swarm of ravens. Thousands upon thousands of black birds descended upon her home, and Elspeth had not known what to do.

On the one hand, she hadn't believed she could do anything at all. On the other hand, she was mortified to reveal herself as a witch—no less before the very souls she'd hoped to impress. But in that instant, spurred by the memory of something Rhiannon had said to Malcom, she'd lifted her hand and cast a warding spell unlike any she'd ever heard.

But that was the thing about *grimoires*; not everything was perfectly recorded; some spells were Goddess sent. And still, it was easier to imagine what could be done if only one knew what had been done —and this, no doubt, was the reason their mother would not allow them to open the book.

That, and Elspeth had a burning suspicion there was something else hidden amidst these pages... something Morwen didn't want anyone to see... something Elspeth had yet to discover...

"What about the warding spell you said you cast at Aldergh?"

"The one before I left... or the other?"

"The one you cast before you left."

"Nay," said Elspeth. "That was not precisely a protection spell. Rather, it only fortifies the spell I cast on the battlements. It would not serve you here."

"What about this one?" Rosalynde asked, tapping a finger on the page.

Elspeth leaned closer, reading the words below her sister's fingertip.

"Sacred Water?"

"Aye," Rosalynde said . "It might not protect us from the firmament, but it could keep Morwen and her minions from crossing the *motte*. We could divert the river, fill the ditch, then bless the *motte* with this spell." She tapped the book again.

Elspeth lifted a brow. "What *motte*?"

Rosalynde sighed. "We do have a *motte*," she persisted. "You must know, it takes time to rebuild, and truth be told, this is why I cannot leave. There is too much to be done, and I will not abandon Warkworth."

"What about Edmond? Is he not your steward?"

"Newly appointed," Rosalynde said. "He knows little."

"Little as you?"

Arching her brow again, in much the same way Elspeth was wont to do, Rosalynde countered, in a high-handed voice. "As little as you when you came to be lady of Aldergh?"

"Point well made," Elspeth relented, because that was true. Until she'd applied herself to the task, she hadn't had the first clue how to run a castle. She still wouldn't know how to lead a garrison, nor command a workforce. But these were tasks better left to her lord husband, and nevertheless Rosalynde was here prancing about in men's leathers, trying to wield a hefty sword that was more than twice her size. It befuddled Elspeth, and she didn't see a woman grown when she looked at her baby sister.

"And yet you flourished." Rosalynde persisted.

When Elspeth pursed her lips in answer, Rosalynde continued, "Do not gainsay me, Elspeth. I have been to your home. You are an excellent *chatelaine*, sister mine, and so, too, will I be with time."

Elspeth pouted, because that was, precisely, what she was afraid of; she didn't know how much time they had. Any given moment their mother could arrive with the king's army, and Eustace had already demolished Warkworth once, burning the entire castle, with its lord and lady asleep in their beds. By the cauldron. She had never heard a more horrific tale. Any man who could rise above this, to help Morwen's daughter, was a saint.

And truly, if, indeed, he so wished to exact revenge, agreeing to help Seren would be the perfect way to do it. He could strangle her in her sleep, and no one would be there to stop him. And why wouldn't he?

Wilhelm and Giles—half-brothers by blood—were the only survivors of a once noble family, but only because neither was present at the time of the burning. Wilhelm, so she'd been told, arrived in the wee hours, with the castle and fields still smoking and the stench of death wafting in the air, only to discover that his entire family—father, brother, sisters, and sister by law, the latter pregnant with her firstborn child—burnt in their beds. If that could be the fate of a *donjon* built of wood, a marquee was entirely too vulnerable.

"I have a well-equipped garrison at my command," Rosalynde said, laying a hand atop Elspeth's arm to assuage her. "Moreover, my husband left his best warriors at my command."

"*His best*?"

Rosalynde sighed. "Stop arguing, Elspeth. I grow weary. It helps not at all."

Elspeth sighed as well, blinking back tears as she glanced down at the page... at the warding spell her sister had proposed—and then suddenly recalling a trick her grandmamau taught her. She bent close, blowing softly over the vellum, searching for hidden script.

She frowned when she noted the shimmering symbol that materialized—a downturned triangular mark.

This was the arcane symbol for water, but it lay encircled, which was the mark of the divine. "Rosalynde... to cast this spell you need *witchwater*," she explained. "That is not a thing you can make, nor summon if you've not the power to do so. 'Tis not the same as water you bless." She met her sister's shimmering blue eyes—eyes that were so like her own. "To my knowledge *none* of us have ever summoned elements in this fashion—not *witchwater*, *witchwind* nor *witchfire*. Not even Rhiannon."

"Aye, well... perhaps that is not entirely true," said Rosalynde. Elspeth blinked and Rosalynde shrugged. "I believe Arwyn could summon *witchfire*," she said.

Elspeth screwed her face.

"'Tis true. I saw her do it once, perhaps twice, though she did not understand what it was, nor did I at the time. 'Tis only now that I've had the opportunity to read through the *grimoire* that I understand what I saw. It was *witchfire*, no doubt. I know it by its color—that odd, blue flame."

"Hmm," said Elspeth, remembering a time at Llanthony when Arwyn scorched Father Ersinius' opulent robe that lay drying in the yard. She'd been washing the garment when that cantankerous old fool approached her to scold her, bidding Arwyn to watch what she was doing, lest she ruin the material. Later, when no one was looking, while that gown lay drying in the sun with its gold threads shimmering, Arwyn consumed the cloth with a strange blue flame that burned so swiftly and intensely the robe was reduced to ash in the blink of an eye. "I do remember," she said. "But keep in mind that you cannot fill a *motte* with *witchwater*, if you do not have a *motte* or if you cannot summon *witchwater*. Neither you, nor I, can summon *witchwater*." She swallowed, heard. "Arwyn is dead."

Rosalynde frowned.

"Well," Elspeth challenged. "Can you?"

Rosalynde shook her head, looking discouraged. Both sisters fought tears. But, sad as the case might be, they hadn't the luxury of underestimating their mother, or all would be lost. Now that Elspeth had her babes, she understood precisely what it meant to rise to this task. If she were to lose one child, she couldn't simply lie down and allow the other to perish. This was a time for strength. "We shall keep looking," she said. "Do not fret; we will discover a way."

Nodding, Rosalynde turned the page, then flipped the book to read a scribbled note in the margin. "There are so many notations here... this is an interesting one: "Did you realize the Mark of the Mother —" The crossed eyes that denoted a Regnant— "Are not always evident at birth?"

"Nay," said Elspeth. "What does it say?"

"Well, there is an entry here under Mark of the Mother—perhaps in our grandmamau's hand. It says, carnelian at birth, be apprised, by pubertas, a mark of the wise."

"How curious," agreed Elspeth. "Though I do not remember a time when Rhiannon's eyes were not afflicted."

Rosalynde shrugged. "Aye, well, neither do I, but this is what it says." She put the book down again, and turned another page.

"Keep looking," said Elspeth. "Somewhere in those pages lies something Mother doesn't want us to see."

13

Dawn broke with a bruised sky that mirrored the bruises in Seren's heart. But at least she didn't have to remind Wilhelm to keep watch for Morwen's birds. Instinctively, he seemed to understand the threat, surveilling the skies as carefully as he did their surroundings. But, of course, she needn't wonder why he knew to do it; surely Rosalynde had advised him. After all, they'd spent much time before Rosalynde's departure from London, worrying about their mother's birds—those odious white-necked ravens born and bred to serve one master. Like most rooks, they could be taught the king's tongue, and while messenger pigeons returned only to the location of their birth, these abominations were drawn to Morwen, making her entirely indispensable to Stephen. After all, since all her little spies were controlled by her, and spoke only to her, it was only natural she should become such a valuable resource to England's sovereign, intercepting messages from all over the realm.

Point in case: When Duke Henry defied his mother to attack Wiltshire two years ago, it was Morwen's ravens that warned Stephen of the invasion.

Stephen's army was already waiting to oust him when he arrived.

Seren didn't know precisely how it worked. She suspected the *magik* involved was somehow connected to Merlin's Crystal. This was why they couldn't leave London without destroying the scrying stone. But, of course, Rose could have had no inkling what they'd done. She would have worried all the way north. But fortunately, without that scrying stone, Morwen couldn't spy on anyone anymore, save through her minions and remaining birds, diminished as they must be. Thousands upon thousands of ravens were slain at Aldergh. Even in their solitude, they'd heard rumors. The court was atwitter over it all, whispering in the halls. "I knew they were witches," she'd overheard one woman say.

Then, from her gossipmongers:

"But, of course! Have you never seen the way she defies *him*?"

She being Morwen. Him, being the king.

"With nary a word of reprimand," hissed another.

"If anyone ever dared such things as Morwen dares, they would find themselves drawn and quartered, entrails ripped from their bowels."

"But not her."

"Of course not. Because she's a witch. Can you imagine entertaining such a lover in front of your Queen? How can she bear such insult?"

She, being Maude—the king's greedy, pinched-nose wife.

"Alas, 'tis one thing to have a nice, discreet paramour, but, nay. There's no telling how many men have sampled her wares. She's been with Henry, Stephen, now Eustace, and I rather imagine Cael d'Lucy is no less a bedfellow."

"Eustace is a mean little—"

"Hush now... do not speak treason. I am told 'tis only a matter of time before he convinces the archbishop to confirm that wretch and Eustace will be our rightful king before long."

The first woman crossed herself, whispering, "God forbid."

But nay, Seren thought. These past fourteen years, God and his saints had all abandoned them. Better that each man and woman look to their hearts and seek the truth, for the realm was filled with prevaricators, who'd much rather entertain a beautiful lie than know a terrible truth.

And, in the meantime, her mother was a master of legerdemain. With such careful slights of hand, she twisted *truth* as easily as a court jester shuffled cups and balls.

Her mother would have everyone believe Elspeth was being held against her will by the traitor Malcom Scott. But the truth was more likely that Elspeth had aligned herself with him, and Malcom had defected of his own accord. After all, wasn't he Scots-born? Surely, he must have found some cause to return to the troth of his birth. And, if, in truth Elspeth remained at Aldergh, perhaps she was there because she loved the man. Like Rosalynde, Seren preferred to believe that, for love's sake, her eldest sister had summoned the most powerful *magik*—*magik* borne of love. And it made sense, knowing Elspeth—how little love she had for the Craft. Only true love could ever have forced her to acknowledge her *dewine* legacy. And nevertheless, despite this, Elspeth's *magik* was not enough to save them. Scotia's king had intervened, arriving at Aldergh with more than three thousand warriors, forcing Eustace's army into retreat.

Only now, in hindsight, Seren wondered if Elspeth could have had a hand in that as well, because David owed them, and Elspeth was not above demanding recompense. And considering all that, she wondered why Rosalynde would abandon Aldergh for Warkworth. Could she have gone anticipating Seren's arrival?

But nay, that didn't make sense.

Why should Rosalynde wish to remain in the company of Seren's betrothed when she could have remained with Elspeth? If, in truth, Giles de Vere still meant to wed Seren, her sister was not born to be anyone's mistress. Rosalynde was far too proud to allow herself to be used so meanly, and Seren knew Rosalynde well enough to know she would never seduce another woman's betrothed. Nor would she ever be content to be a courtesan.

Nay. Rosalynde was too smart, and too spirited.

And yet, Wilhelm had clearly said she was waiting at Warkworth for Seren, and if he was to be believed, there must be a reason for that—what was it?

Had Rosalynde quarreled with Elspeth?

That was entirely possible. Rosalynde and Rhiannon both often took umbrage over Elspeth's officious manner.

And still, the question thickened her throat, for even now, were the bonds of sisterhood unraveling, only to leave her and her sisters lonesome and vulnerable?

Goddess only knew, their mother would love that. Aside from killing Matilda, there could be little more satisfying to Morwen Pendragon than to see her daughters estranged and alone.

Poor, poor Arwyn.

But at least her baby sister would suffer no longer.

She was at peace now, loved and protected by the Goddess. Morwen would never again harm her.

Grief made her swallow with difficulty. There was so much she wished to ask Wilhelm of Warkworth, but so far, they hadn't had much accord, and it wasn't so much that she was afraid of him. Rather, she didn't know *what* to ask, nor was he very forthcoming.

Later, she decided.

Later, when they were settled, after Jack was asleep... then she would inquire.

❧

LATER CAME SOONER THAN ANTICIPATED.

About an hour after the sun rose, Jack slumped over his horse's withers.

Without a word, Wilhelm seized the boy's reins. He led them into the woods, ferreting out a secluded spot within a thicket of hickory, elm and ash. Nearby, though not precisely within sight, Seren could hear the gurgling of a brook, and it seemed entirely probable he had been there before.

It made sense not to sleep so close to the brook in order to avoid travelers, but it was close enough to hear the trickling—a sound that until yesterday had been comforting. Now, it reminded her of Arwyn. Night after night, she and her sister had slept together in that cot, listening to the sound of water outside the ship's hull, and she had dared believe they were safe. Tears stung her eyes as she tethered the horse, and once the mounts were secure, Wilhelm left, again without a word, presumably to hunt for their supper —or, rather, to break the fast, as the case should be. Seren only guessed as much because he'd grabbed a quiver and a bow before leaving.

In the meantime, she encouraged Jack to find himself a comfortable spot to lay down. She helped him relocate a few rocks, gave him a pillow of bracken to lay beneath his head... and just for good measure, she used a bit of *magik* to fluff the leaves. He would never know.

"I'll wake you when it's time to sup," she said gently, as she threw his blanket over him. Weary as he was, it didn't take long; he closed his eyes at once and was snoring within an instant.

As she knelt there, watching him sleep, the sliver of crystal in her pocket hummed. She ferreted it out, examining the shard. It glowed faintly though without imagery, but she thought she spied a golden eye peering back at her—odd. It wasn't a vision... more like a reflection, but her eyes were not amber. Rhiannon's eyes were amber. Like their grandmamau, her sister bore the Mark of the Mother—the crossed, amber-lit eyes that distinguished her as a Regnant Priestess. What was the shard trying to tell her?

Frowning, she returned the shard to her pocket, wandering over to inspect her saddlebag only to discover how attentive Wilhelm had been to detail.

Already, she'd found there was a blanket for each of them, strapped to the backs of their mounts, but inside her own bag, she discovered a few bites to eat, which made her complaining all the more unreasonable, though surely, he could have said so. How obnoxious to keep silent, save that she might have responded the same if faced with an ungrateful companion—which, of course, she knew she was. It simply hadn't occurred to her to look.

There were a few more surprises; most notably a change of clothes—not one, but two—and a lightweight cloak, making her wonder why he'd allowed her to wear his crude brown cloak for so long. She also discovered a comb in the bag, and a thin, blue ribbon to plait her hair—small gestures, but each considerate beyond measure, and this from a man who, until now, had seemed entirely disagreeable.

So, it seemed; Wilhelm Fitz Richard was even more a conundrum than she'd suspected him to be.

Unfortunately, there wasn't time to explore that thought. There was too much to be done, and she didn't particularly feel like forgiving him, not yet. Before he returned, she must draw herself a pentacle large enough to protect them tonight, and she must do so without Wilhelm or Jack realizing what it was she was doing. She wouldn't feel comfortable sleeping without warding the premises, but despite that Wilhelm seemed to understand who and what she was, she still didn't feel comfortable performing the Craft in his presence.

Nor did Jack have any inkling who she was. So far as the boy was concerned, she and her sisters were merely passengers aboard his father's ship, awaiting their time to set sail. It could well be that he would rise above prejudgment, but it was more likely he would fear her for what he couldn't possibly understand.

Breaking off a piece of the *pan*, she tasted it, surprised by the subtle flavor of salt. In truth, salt was an extravagance available only to the wealthy, and even then, it was never wasted on *pan*, since *pan* didn't need preservation.

"Fascinating," she said, and resolved not to waste it. She swallowed hastily, shed herself of Wilhelm's cloak, folded it neatly, put it in his saddlebag, and then considered what she presently knew about pentacles —nothing much, until Rosalynde decided to flee with the Book. Her sister had been so sure she could travel inconspicuously, aided by no more than a *glamour* and warding spell. So, for weeks before she left London, they'd practiced spells together, and studied the diagrams until Seren could now draw pentacles in her sleep. She might not have the *grimoire* in her possession at the instant, but the incantations were etched in her brain.

As a matter of practice, the pentacle was only intended to harness *magik* within a specific area. Though certainly a warding spell could be cast without it—proof of that was in the spell Elspeth cast at Aldergh—the boundary offered added protection.

Deciding she must draw one large enough so no one could discern it at a glance, she searched for a proper stick to etch with, and while she was at it, she gathered enough tinder for a small fire. Piling the tinder near sleeping Jack, she studied the perimeter, because, truly, it was a complicated matter and she still had matters to resolve.

Most notably, no single diagram could serve every situation. There were many, many things to consider. No two *dewines* were alike, and the Craft was specific to every individual. She and her sisters each had their own predominant skills: For Elspeth this was her ability to read auras, and Elspeth also had a certain charm for animals. Seren, too, had this calling to the natural world, but her métier was more healing and all things apothecary while Rosalynde had a very good feel for elemental *magik*. Rhiannon, of course, could do all they could do and more. But regardless of their skills, she and her sisters each had an affinity to one element, from whence all powers manifested; and this is where Seren found a quandary.

You see, altogether, there were four main elements, plus a fifth element called the *quintessence*. Only a *dewine* with a primary to the *aether* could ever hope to master all five. Her sister Rhiannon was such a *dewine*, but one needn't be a priestess to be aligned to *aether*. But the *quintessence* was a divine element. It contained in itself the essence of life, the very matter from which all else was born. If Seren, too, were aligned to *aether* it might explain why the *witchwind* had appeared so belatedly. She had always assumed hers was a gentler form of *magik*, but what if, in truth, it only appeared to be gentle because, like Arwyn, she'd had trouble conjuring it?

Clearly, Arwyn's element was fire. That was the only *magik* she'd ever possessed. Rosalynde was aligned to water. And, after much discussion, they'd surmised Elspeth must be aligned to Earth, but it was impossible to say for certes, because Seren doubted even Elspeth knew it herself. For so long, their eldest sister wouldn't even speak of their legacy, much less practice the Craft. So, then, it made sense that for so long Seren would believe her own affinity must be air, because, after all, what were the odds of having two blood sisters aligned to *aether*?

Amidst five siblings, it was far more reasonable that all would be aligned to one single element, rather than to have even one aligned to *aether*. The *quintessence* was that rare.

But here again was Seren's dilemma: The *witchwind* she'd conjured yesterday might, indeed, attest to an affinity with air, but although it never materialized, she'd also had a very strong sense of *witchwater* as well. These two conjurations were impossible for a *dewine* aligned to air.

It was easier to explain when looking at a fully drawn pentacle, with all the elements properly placed, because there was naught accidental about their positioning. So here... she drew out a small pentacle for good measure.

If, in fact, Seren were aligned to air, then water would be her divergent—no *witchwater* there.

If, instead, she were aligned to *aether*, it should be fire. She tapped the ground where the fire symbol would go.

Witchwater was, indeed, quite possible with a fire affinity, but here was the case: If she were aligned to air, as she'd so long believed, she would also be aligned to *aether* and earth, but *not* to water, making *witchwater* an impossible feat.

On the other hand, if she were aligned to *aether*, with a bit of practice, all elements could be hers to manipulate, including fire and water, but, in truth, she'd never had much luck with fire. And this is why that was important: A pentacle must *always* be drawn precisely to one's own affinity—precisely. If she drew it wrong, and made the mistake of choosing the wrong element to place at the vertex, it would leave them defenseless. The pentacle would be useless.

To make matters even more complicated, there were two types of spells to be cast: All things were either summoned or banished, accepted or denied, created or destroyed, transformed or reformed. A protection spell was in essence a banishing spell, meant to repel. Therefore, she must begin drawing with her divergent at her southernmost point, and end with her true element at the vertex, always with the properly drawn symbol. For a summoning spell, it would be exactly the opposite, and she would begin drawing at her vertex, ending with her divergent, always leaving her most vulnerable ingress at her feet.

After all, she could play it safe and choose the

affinity Rhiannon had claimed was hers, but Rhiannon was hardly infallible. She was flesh and blood, like anyone else. She could be mistaken. And, if Seren chose air, when her affinity was *aether*... well, then... these two might seem similar, but they were entirely different.

She took the stick and erased her drawing, still contemplating...

She didn't know how to explain the feeling she'd had... it wasn't like anything she'd ever experienced in all her life. It felt... *strange*—as though if she merely let herself go, if she'd allowed the first tear in a moment of fervor...

Well, she might never know, because it didn't happen, and still, she had a feeling that she, like Rhiannon, was aligned to *aether*.

Could it be? Was it possible? Could two blood sisters be aligned to the quintessence?

Inhaling a breath, Seren decided upon *aether* as her primary and began drawing the pentacle precisely as she remembered, murmuring softly as she worked.

> Goddess of light shield us tonight.
> Ye who would harm, ye who would
>   maim,
> Proceed and face the same.

A band of light burst at the edges of her diagram, thrumming softly, then vanishing, and she exhaled in relief, never realizing she'd been holding her breath. *Aether*, it must be. If she were doing this wrong, there would be no power in her words. Encouraged, she continued again, murmuring softly, so as not to disturb Jack.

With cloth and cord of darkest night, I
    shroud my soul.
Light is the weapon I wield to keep us
    whole.

By all on high and law of three,
This is my will, so mote it be.

14

Wilhelm held back, reluctant to disturb.

After their encounter with the Shadow Beast, her sister had insisted upon casting that very same warding spell every night before sleeping; he recognized the strange motions Seren was making with her stick.

Doubting the power of *magik* wasn't an option. The alternative was far worse. God only knew, he'd witnessed the unbridled power of evil with his own two eyes, and if *magik* couldn't protect them, Wilhelm would never sleep again.

His gaze drifted to Jack. Somehow, the boy was fast asleep under his blanket in the middle of her rendering, completely unaware of the protection spell Seren was summoning—oh, to be so innocent. Clearly, he trusted his elders to keep him safe. Poor boy, he couldn't possibly understand what menace surrounded them, and if Wilhelm could spare him that truth, he would. As annoyed as he'd been over having to bring the lad into their fold, he was coming to admire him. His father had taught him well. He was polite, intelligent, respectful, and if he had a wandering eye for Lady Seren's breasts... well, then... Wilhelm hadn't any stones to throw. He was hard-pressed not to look himself. But, more and more, he was coming to see that whatever beauty Seren possessed on the outside, she possessed it threefold within. For all that she was angry over her sister's fate, and for all that she seemed to need to blame Wilhelm, she took good care of the boy, willing to challenge even Wilhelm over the child's wellbeing.

And, in truth, had Wilhelm not been so ill-humored, he would have jumped to her bidding. Helping that boy was the right thing to do.

He bided his time, watching her work...

Before meeting Rosalynde, he'd never believed a word of those rumors. He was not a believer in witches; the very word was but an epithet for women the likes of Morwen Pendragon. But now he was a believer. There was no denying the things he'd witnessed over these past months. And he still couldn't conceive it, but his weedy little brother, the boy who wouldn't put down his books to consider a sword, was a Paladin for the Church—a huntsman Rosalynde called him.

Huntsman... executioner... headsman...

God only knew, there was so much about Giles Wilhelm still didn't know—and to think he'd once doubted his brother's prowess with a blade.

Never again.

If the Black Knight of legend was a master swordsman, Giles was something *other*, expertly wielding his weapon with incredible feats of physicality. Much as he'd feared that Shadow Beast, some part of him would go back and do it again, if only to see his brother in action—standing atop his mount and pirouetting his weapon like a spintop.

Shifting his burden from one hand to another, he

waited for Seren to finish, his heart squeezing over the way she looked at the boy—her gaze so full of tenderness. To his chagrin, it still gave him a small tweak of envy, even as it warmed the cockles of his heart.

How might it be to have her look at him with so much affection? Only for him with the heat of desire.

She is grieving, fool. Get your head out of your breeches. And what makes you think she would think of you this way? Only look at her, and then look at yourself.

She looked tired, he thought, bedraggled even, though her long, pale red hair was no longer escaping her thick plait. That's precisely why he'd bought her the new ribbon, and he was pleased to see she'd found it and used it. It gave him a strange feeling down in the pit of his gut...

Pleasure? Pride? Satisfaction?

As much as he tried to understand, he couldn't fathom how his brother could turn his back on the lady. She was nothing at all what Wilhelm had supposed... she, too, was something *other*... And yet, so much as he'd feared she would seduce Giles, she was seducing him without even trying. And perhaps that was the greatest source of his unease... because if he chanced to misjudge her... if she was more like her mother...

Here we go, again.

Cursing himself for a fool, he shifted the cony yet again, feeling the slow drip of warm blood glide down the butt of his palm. It was early yet. If he had his druthers, they would eat, nap briefly, then return without delay to the road. The sooner they returned to Warkworth, the better.

By now, Giles would have left to attend Stephen in London. Wilhelm had promised to hurry back, to watch over Rosalynde. Much as he loathed the thought, there was a good chance his brother might not return. Rosalynde had no inkling of this, else she might never have let him go, and there was little wonder Giles gave her his sword. Evidently, he feared as Wilhelm feared, that the instant he repudiated Seren and refused to kneel before Stephen... well... he shouldn't dwell on that right now.

Giles was his own man and Wilhelm trusted him to do the right thing. And if doing the right thing got his neck in a rope or his entrails fed to Morwen's birds... well, there was little he could do about that.

Right now, his main concern—his only concern—should be Seren. Come what may, he would deliver the lady safely to Warkworth... or die trying.

As for that boy... he didn't know what to do with Jack. Perhaps his brother's affiliations would better determine his fate. In slumber, the lad seemed so bloody innocent, and Wilhelm's heart swelled with pity for the loss he'd endured. Even as a man grown, Wilhelm had wept blood tears to look upon his own sire's burnt carcass, and even now, the memory wedged a meaty lump in his throat.

In contrast, even despite her own grief, and soft as she appeared, Seren had been a pillar of strength.

Wilhelm was slowly but surely coming to admire her as well.

All night long they'd traveled in silence, stopping only when necessary, and unless she was caring for the boy, she scarcely spoke, much less sniveled or mewled. So much as he loathed to confess the truth, he, himself, had been far more whingey than she. It took Wilhelm a while, but he was over his pique at having been judged and found wanting. So he wasn't a scholar, like Giles. Never once had he aspired to be one. He was a warrior to the bone, and the sword in his belt was deadlier than any pen. And this time, given the opportunity, he would use it with deadly force.

Impatient now, he fidgeted yet again, feeling guilty for spying. But he sensed she felt ill-at-ease performing her sorcery in front of others, so it was only after she was finished with her incantation and then had a chance to sprinkle handfuls of leaves over the edges of her diagram that he stepped forward from the shadows.

GASPING IN STARTLE, Seren raised a hand to her throat. She had scarcely completed her ritual when Wilhelm appeared. Without a word, he emerged from the trees, stepping gingerly over the pile of leaves she'd put down.

"Forgive me," he said. "I didn't wish to intrude."

Was it her imagination, or was his tone a little gentler?

"Hungry?" he asked, and when she frowned at the poor, dead beast she spied in his hand, he put the cony down and divested himself of the quiver on his back, emptying the contents. Out spilled his arrows, along with a stash of mushrooms, berries and truffles.

"A peace offering," he said, with a tiny smile.

"For me?"

He inclined his head, giving her a nod, and his full lips tipped higher at the corners, his lips parting enough to give her a glimpse of straight, white teeth. The sight of his smile made Seren's heart thump.

"Pax?"

Seren nodded eagerly. "Pax," she agreed, and came forward to admire the wealth of his foraging. Amidst the lot, she recognized a horse mushroom, along with wood-ears, and grisettes, but she also spied a suspicious one, and plucked it up. "This is not edible," she said, plucking off a piece, and showing it to him. "It looks like the others, but when you bruise it, it turns yellow."

He nodded, his gaze shifting from Seren to the mushroom, then back. Standing so close, it was impossible to ignore his gargantuan size, and she wondered idly what he'd eaten as a child to make him sprout to such great heights.

Smiling, she said, "It won't kill you, but..." She winked. "You might wish it had."

It would seem more natural for Elspeth, as an Earth Child, to excel at herbs, but Seren's natural affinity was akin to an apothecary's. She was quite well versed in *medicinals*. The yellow-staining mushroom might fill his belly, but it would empty it in minutes.

He nodded, and she blushed, feeling oddly embarrassed about discussing these matters with him. To cover her nervousness, she lifted up the horse mushroom, tasting it gingerly. Clearly, he'd put so much effort into hunting for sustenance in order to please everyone. Jack would be grateful for the rabbit, but, she would be quite content with whatever he'd foraged. Whilst living at the priory, their meals had rarely consisted of animal flesh. Betimes they ate a bit of fish, but Seren preferred to harvest what could be grown in their garden.

In London, there had been no dearth of carrion on the table, but it was not appetizing in the least to ogle a carcass made to look as though it could still be alive, complete with head and eyes. Thankfully, their mother rarely invited them to sup. Mostly, their meals had been consumed in the privacy of their own quarters. And, fortunately for them, Rosalynde was a handy little thief, so she'd quite oft ventured down into the kitchens to pilfer whatever could be found. Whilst on the road with Arwyn, they'd eaten nothing but bread—so much *pan* that Seren now felt like a fat loaf herself.

This was a nice surprise.

"Thank you," she said.

He cast a backward glance at Jack, snuggled comfortably underneath the blanket, and shrugged. "Your sister did eat some cony, but it seemed to me she preferred not to. I thought perhaps you might feel the same."

"Thank you," she said again, surprised by his thoughtfulness, dropping the poisonous mushroom and crushing it beneath her slipper so Jack wouldn't find it and mistakenly eat it. Then, wiping her fingers on her skirt, she wondered what else Wilhelm knew— and moreover, whether he'd spied her at her casting. There was that about his expression that made her feel maybe he had, and she tilted him a glance. "Did you see me?"

"I did," he confessed, blushing, then averting his gaze, and turning toward the horses. Once again, he stepped over the leaves, and she knew beyond a shadow of doubt it was not a coincidence. Withdrawing something small from his saddlebag, he returned, once again taking care to avoid her pentacle lines. He knelt by the kindling, picking a stick. "Thank you," he said, waving it at her.

"For what?"

"For gathering wood."

Seren smoothed her skirts. "Well... it was the least I could do," she said, feeling self-conscious. And then he peered up, surprising her with a question. "It was never my forte," he confessed, pointing at the tinder.

"Before I go making a clod of myself, I don't suppose you can..."

Seren's brows collided. "Kindle the fire?"

Wilhelm nodded, and she blinked, surprised that he would ask—not that she wouldn't happily do it, if she could, but it surprised her they were speaking so frankly about the unspeakable. Her grandmamau was executed only because Elspeth had breathed a word of *magik*. How times had changed.

She thought perhaps Wilhelm was trying to make the point that he was okay with witchery. But, alas, she couldn't do it. "I've never been good with fire," she said, shaking her head.

Wilhelm nodded, then shrugged. Resigned, he struck his fire-steel to the pile of tinder as she knelt to watch, thinking that, after all, it might be a good time to broach the unbroachable. "So... you know?"

Two more times he struck his fire-steel to the kindling, then cursed. "Aye."

Seren inhaled sharply, then exhaled. "You are not afeared?

He peered up then, his dark brows furrowing. "What gave you that stupid idea?"

Seren frowned. "Well... because... you don't appear to be afraid."

He tilted his head, and said with certainty, "You are wrong. I am terrified."

And with that declaration, Seren's heart sank.

15

Wilhelm realized he must have disappointed her with his answer, but he was unaccustomed to speaking aught but truth. He wasn't afraid of Seren, per se, but he was, indeed, afraid of everything she represented.

And more, he was afraid unto death that he would fail her—and this man-boy as well—just as he'd failed his kinsmen on the eve of Warkworth's burning.

As he'd failed her sister the night in the woodlot.

If there was one thing he'd learned that day it was that there were forces at work outside his dominion that he was powerless to control, much less defeat.

That day, he'd been little more than a raging beast himself, brandishing his weapon against a creature that could not bleed—least ways not the way mortal men bled.

That strange amalgamation of smoke and shifting flesh had put the fear of God into him. Alone, he had been powerless to stop it. It descended from the heavens like a winged serpent, with a wingspan longer than Wilhelm was tall and a tail that could have sliced his flesh to the bone. Both appendages had put him on his arse faster than he could blink, and it was Rosalynde and Giles who'd discovered a way to defeat the creature—if, indeed, it was dead.

Somehow, Rosalynde's incantation gave it form, and the instant Giles severed its head, it shifted again, metamorphosing into the shape of a man, then into a rush of foul-smelling smoke that vanished into a bauble.

God's truth, he didn't know where that reliquary was now, but he hoped with all his heart to never to encounter it again. Harmless though it might be, the very thought of it gave him a shiver, and truth be told, he wasn't over the ordeal any more than he was over the burning at Warkworth. Admittedly, he'd experienced a jolt of fear when Seren ran toward that burning ship to save her sister, and he was still suffering the consequences—physically. He had a bellyache that could only be attributed to the greasy turkey leg he'd consumed in the market—that, or the ungodly knot of fear she'd inspired in the pit of his gut.

And by the by, it didn't help matters overmuch that she'd felt the need to enlighten him about the mushroom. Of course, he didn't eat any, but he needn't eat a bad mushroom to suffer the ill effects she was warning him about, and it was as though somehow she knew... as her sister seemed to know so much. These *dewine* sisters were canny in a way that gave Wilhelm pause. In fact, he wasn't even all that tempted by the cony he intended to cook. He knew the boy would be famished, and he wanted Seren to have her choice of sustenance, but, for his part, he would have been content enough with the *pan* in his saddlebag, and little of that besides.

He frowned. To be sure, they had this much in common: He couldn't start a fire to save his life. Cursing beneath his breath, frustrated by his lack of skill, he struck the fire-steel half a dozen more times, until finally, a spark ignited. Very quickly, he settled the flame over the thin, dry end of a twig and was immensely relieved when the flame took, spreading swiftly over the brittle stick.

Watching him intently on the other side of the fire, Seren sank to her bottom, no doubt trying to think of more words to speak, although it seemed to him that perhaps she thought better of it, because she said nothing more. She was still holding a small bit of mushroom.

"Eat," he demanded. "Then rest. We won't be here long."

"How long?"

"Not long," he said curtly, and Seren huffed a sigh of frustration, the flames bending against her breath —in much the same way he longed to bend as well.

God's truth, he bloody well didn't like the way he felt—or maybe he did—but never in his life had he felt so much like a poppet. If only she would smile at him one more time, as she had when he'd revealed the mushrooms, he would prostrate himself at her feet. If there was aught of witchery at play this morning, it was her smile. She was irresistible and yet, he must resist, for this was no time for foolery and flirtation.

What in God's name was he thinking?

Hadn't he learned his lessons already? Loving a lady who could not love him back? What a halfwit he must be.

Seren Pendragon is not meant for the likes of you.

"Why are you so ill-tempered?"

He flicked her a glance, his cheeks warming to his chagrin. *Because I can't stop thinking about you, woman.* Because I yearn for something I cannot have.

She sighed. "So much for our peace."

Dispirited perhaps, her gaze fell upon the fire, and Wilhelm felt heartsore, because he wanted so desperately to be different. He wanted to sit here beside her, as Giles had done with Rosalynde, and banter wittily. He wanted to learn more about Seren and her sisters. He wanted to tell her about his own life. He wanted to know what she loved, what she despised. He wanted to reassure her that in some ways they weren't very different—and perhaps share their losses.

But, alas, it wasn't only Seren who'd judged him and found him wanting. He imagined himself through the eyes of a lady of her caliber, and saw only a fool of a man who would like to be something more. But that was the trouble... she made him long to be what he wasn't. So, then, if he was, indeed, ill-tempered, it was all because of her. The way he felt about her was like a gaping hole in his leathers, leaving him vulnerable in a way he might never have anticipated.

She is not for you, he reprimanded himself again.

Whether she be witch, or a *dewine*—or whatever the hell Rosalynde called her sort—she was still a highborn lady, true-blood daughter to a dead king. Illegitimate or nay, Seren Pendragon was meant for a better man than he. But though Giles didn't want her, Wilhelm did, and the longer he spent in her company, the more he wondered about the softness of her skin and the sweetness of her lips...

Even now, he felt his loins stirring, and he would like to have smacked his cock limp.

Annoyed by the turn of his thoughts, he waved her away. "Don't you have some spell to cast, or something of the ilk?"

"Spell?"

"Whatever," he said, waving her away.

Her eyes narrowed again, looking as stormy as

they had when she'd cast that witchy wind over Dover.

God's blood, that's all he needed right now was to say the wrong thing and spur her ire. She would whip him into a tempest and cast him away, and he might well deserve it.

At any rate, he had a very good sense that whatever that was back there—that startling wind—it was only a fraction of the power this flower of Blackwood could harness. The simple fact that she seemed equally surprised by the conjuration was no comfort at all. It only left it all the more ill at ease.

"Nay," she said, eyes glittering fiercely. "I have no *spells* to cast, but I'd very much like to turn you into a toad."

That did the trick; she got up, abandoning Wilhelm to his dark, brooding thoughts. But he watched her walk away, wondering: Could she do that? Turn him into toad? Nay. It couldn't be possible.

And yet... that beast in the woodlot had shifted shapes...

Every nerve in his body warned him to stay clear of Seren Pendragon, and nevertheless, he was never more aware of another human being in all his days— and that included Ayleth of Bamburgh.

Ayleth was not for you, he told himself.

Seren is not for you.

Good God, man—get hold of yourself.

16

Fixing her gaze on his back, Seren willed the man to feel her outrage. So much for their truce, so much for peace. He was a sour-faced lout, and she didn't know why she'd even considered his offer of *pax*.

Dwarfed by his size, his mare didn't appear as though she could comfortably carry him, and even so, like most women, that poor beast managed to be stronger than people imagined. For certes, Seren was discovering her own strength, and though she still didn't comprehend what happened to the Whitshed, she knew in her heart that her sister would want her to carry on.

She still had three living sisters, and together they must find a way to stop Morwen, else there would be more blood shed over this land than the last fourteen years of war combined.

Later, she would allow herself to mourn—later, when she was reunited with Rosalynde, and until then, she would continue to fantasize over ways to torture Wilhelm Fitz Richard.

For one, she would like to tie his ankles together

and hang him like a bundle of herbs from the bough of a tree, then call bees to harass him.

Or mayhap charm a polecat and let the foul beast spray him so thoroughly he'd have good reason to scowl.

Only then, she recalled all his thoughtful gestures: the effort he'd taken to forage for her, the ribbon he'd bought in Dover, the satchel full of provisions, and the fact that he'd returned to help Jack, even against his will, and her anger dissipated.

Reaching back to finger the silk ribbon in her hair, smoothing it between her fingers, she decided that everything about this man confused her.

Three days had gone by since Dover, and so it seemed, he was still determined to ignore them. Mother's mercy! He reminded her of those silly guards outside the King's Hall—silent, long-suffering, and ever ready to serve, only pretending to look straight through them. But if you dared attempt to enter the King's Hall, they planted their lances in your face quicker than you could blink.

Truly, in all her days, she had never been in the company of a man so intent upon dismissing her. She considered that a long moment, releasing the ribbon as her lips twisted wryly.

Elspeth so oft said her charm was a gift, like a *glamour*, irresistible and inescapable. But if that be the case, Wilhelm was hardly fazed at all. Riding beside her, Jack remained mopey. Long-faced, he chewed his left cheek and no doubt he was worried about finding his way home. For his sake, she realized that the worst thing she could do right now was to give in to her grief. "Do you have family in England?" she asked conversationally.

"Nay," he said, shaking his head. "And you?"

Seren nodded. "I have four—" she swallowed suddenly and painfully. "Three... three sisters."

"They are waiting for you?"

She sighed. "Only one... my sister Rosalynde."

"Where are the rest?"

Seren sighed. "One sister in Wales, the other somewhere near Scotia."

"Oh," he said, and then went back to chewing his cheek.

Like a lodestone, her gaze returned to their rueful champion. He wasn't unkind, not at all. Nor was he contemptuous; that wasn't the problem. Rather, he was unapproachable and uncommunicative. And despite this, he still managed to be incredibly solicitous, looking after their every need—not only hers, but Jack's, as well. Three full days they'd been on the road, and, aside from that first day, she'd not had to harry him once over stopping to see to their needs. Considering that, it seemed ungrateful to complain. If Seren was lonely, she had Jack to keep her company, and anyway, she was accustomed to silence. Much of their time at Llanthony had been spent in prayer, mostly because Ersinius was ever intent upon saving their heathen souls.

For the most part, Morwen had never bothered with her daughters. From the very instant they'd left court as wee ones, to the instant they'd returned as women-grown, their mother appeared to have forgotten she had daughters altogether, only rousing herself to do aught for them when it suited her purposes.

All those new dresses this past fall? Only because their appearance embarrassed Morwen—and particularly so when their "competition" was dressed to the teeth in the finest of Flemish cloths.

Invitations to sup? Only when their mother wished

to remind King Stephen that she had daughters to wed to his endless list of new men—hundreds and hundreds of oath-breakers, whose only recommendation was that they were in the right place at the right time to serve.

As for Seren, Morwen had a particularly hideous beast in mind—one William Martel, who espoused loyalties to his sovereign, but was ever-prepared to betray him, as he'd once betrayed her father.

So they said, lampreys killed Henry, but Seren didn't believe it for an instant. Eels' blood was poisonous, and a small amount could, indeed, kill a man, which was why no one should eat them raw. But in such cases, the manner of death should be swift and painful. By all accounts, Henry had been hale that day, and though his death might, indeed, have been painful, he'd lingered overlong with fever and took his last breath with his "loyal" steward by his side—suspicious to say the least. And, according to Morwen, it was Martel who'd administered the poison, and if you asked Seren, her father made a far deadlier mistake than eating lampreys that day in Saint-Denis-en-Lyons; he'd made the mistake of inviting his vicious, deceitful mistress to the hunt.

But, of course, Seren couldn't prove it. Neither was she present at her father's deathbed, but she'd heard more than enough accounts of her father's passing to know it was as suspicious as Wilhelm's mood.

Something was niggling that man... something she couldn't put her finger on. And yet if he was still piqued over having to go back for Jack, he never once took it out on the boy.

It must be something else.

To be sure, she didn't have any sense he was resentful of his assignment. Rather, she had the feeling he took this task quite seriously, and more, he held Rosalynde in very high regard. He hadn't said so, precisely, but whenever he mentioned Rose, there was a curious softening to his dark eyes. *Could it be those two were... entangled?*

Could this be why Rosalynde eschewed Aldergh for Warkworth?

Curious, indeed.

That made more sense than anything else Seren devised. And, it would also explain why Wilhelm was so intent upon ignoring her... perhaps he meant to be true to Rose?

At least it was something to think about, and if she ever found the nerve to pry, she would endeavor to ask.

Only, now, having considered it, she couldn't get the possibility out of her mind...

She couldn't blame Rosalynde for being drawn to Wilhelm. Even despite his sour disposition, there was something about him... She had a good sense that he was precisely who he was, and there would never be any pretense. And, to Seren, he was more attractive than his brother.

Of course he was also less refined, but whatever he lacked in social graces, he made up for in countenance. Giles was far too erudite for Seren's taste, and she was much more attracted to Wilhelm's strength—more's the pity for her if her sister had already claimed him for herself.

Only why would you wish to claim that man?

Why would you pine for someone who doesn't want you?

Only because he doesn't treat you like everyone else?

She had a sense that he was only hiding behind his aloofness, because she felt his regard, as though he had eyes in the back of his head.

Unbidden, she thought about his hands... If his finesse with that blade was any indication, she believed he could be a gentle lover. But that thought burned her cheeks, because a lady wasn't supposed to consider such things. And yet, betimes, when she lay abed and the room was quiet and dark... silvery moonlight peeking in... she imagined herself lying with a man, and her body burned nearly as hot as her cheeks.

Oh, she did, indeed, understand what transpired betwixt men and women. They were *dewines*, after all, and her people did not believe a woman's body was a temple to be worshipped. Rather they worshipped the Goddess with their gifts. She was no different from a flower—and if one understood a flower as a *dewine* understood a flower and could sense life and the pursuit of it, it was easy to see how it bent to the sun... how it titillated over the puff of a warm breath... how the small hairs on its stem shivered in delight to a touch.

"E's got a bee up his bum," said Jack, interrupting her reverie, and Seren gasped, lifting a hand to her lips, trying not to laugh.

Jack shrugged. "This is what my papa used to say when I was ill-tempered."

Indeed, boys were such plainspoken creatures. But though Seren would never have suggested such a thing herself, Wilhelm did seem to have a bee up his bum. She smiled at Jack, rewarding him with a smile —their first light-hearted banter since leaving Dover.

"I am sorry about your sister," he said.

"I'm sorry about your papa."

His voice was sad. "I keep thinking it is not true."

So did Seren, but, alas, it was.

She couldn't feel her sister's heart flame anymore. Arwyn was long gone to wherever spirits were borne.

Tears pricked her eyes anew. Only by night did she shed them, and only when everyone was fast asleep.

The boy's lower lip fattened. "Me mum said he was too mean to die; I really believed her."

"Well," Seren said, with a lingering note of sorrow. "Everybody dies, Jack. Fortunately, you still have your mother, and..." She looked at him, wondering what else she could say to assuage him. "You know, my grandmamau said death was naught more than the shedding of flesh and bones."

He lifted a shoulder. "What is left?"

"Spirit," she answered brightly, and she gave him a nod, when he tilted her a questioning look. "'Tis true."

"You mean, like souls?"

"Aye," she said. "Precisely so."

Seren smiled at him fondly, hoping he wouldn't see past her facade. All she felt now was emptiness where her sister was concerned, and if there was, indeed, another plane of existence, she couldn't feel it right now. "According to my grandmamau," she expounded, "there are five components to the spirit. The first wouldst be the name you are given at birth. So long as your name is remembered by anyone at all, you remain in this world. This is why, if you do great deeds, your memory endures. It is also why sometimes names are etched upon tombstones."

"Only lords have tombstones."

"Mayhap, though you don't need a tombstone to be remembered; I know the names of many men who have gone from this world."

He lifted his chin. "Like who?"

"King Arthur, for one."

Jack frowned. "I don't know this man."

Well, of course he wouldn't know a Welshman. Seren tried again. "What about your grandsire? He captained the Mora, did he not?"

The boy nodded, peering up hopefully.

Seren smiled. "You know, The Conqueror is my grandsire."

"'Tis true, then; your papa is King Henry?"

Seren nodded, then shrugged. There was so little of her father's presence in her upbringing, even despite that they'd spent their early years wandering his halls. Alas, Henry was but the stallion who'd sired her, and despite that England might never forget him, she had no inkling of him at all. He was but a shadow from her past. And, perhaps Elspeth knew him better, but, in Seren's estimation, barely more than she did. Her sister, for all that she was Goddess sent, was a beautiful dreamer. She was a *fantast*, who imagined the Empress cared about her bastard siblings, and so much as Seren would like to believe it as well, she supposed now she would never know for sure. Whatever opportunity she'd had to meet Matilda was gone, along with the Whitshed. And it was just as well; that part of their journey had meant more to Arwyn than it ever did to Seren. If the truth be known, she was glad to be seeking her true sisters instead of Matilda.

"I don't believe in witches," Jack said proudly, without any prompting. "My papa says people love to talk, and I should ignore them."

Seren peered down at the boy, puzzled for an instant, only to realize that he and his papa must have been discussing them. No doubt some rabble-rouser had warned Captain Airard about harboring witches. Was that what led to his death?

Indeed, Seren suspected there was foul play, but so much as she wished to believe it must be Morwen, perhaps there was another reason for the burning. More's the pity, one way or another, she had the sense Captain Airard would still be alive were it not for her and her sister, and Jack might not blame her, but she did blame herself, and now more than ever, she was duty-bound to do right by the boy.

"What is the second part?"

"Second part? Oh!" Troubled as she was by her glum thoughts, she had nearly forgotten what they were discussing. She pointed to the shadow of their horses lumbering before them. "Shadows," she said. "They contain a piece of our essence, and so long as we live, our shadows follow wherever we go."

And, though it was hardly a thing to share with an innocent boy, shadow lore was a discipline of black *magik*.

"But shadows are gone when we are gone, no?"

Seren nodded, though it wasn't entirely true. Essentially, shadows also remained after the casting of shadow *magik*. It was like sucking nectar from a fruit; all that remained afterward was naught but a rind. But with shadow *magik*, so long as the essence remained tethered to its host, the flesh survived in perpetuity. Only once severed, the body withered, and the essence was loosed into the world without a receptacle. These were something like ghosts.

But only their mother would ever dare to challenge the laws of nature, and, if they doubted that was true, they needed only remember the blood bath she'd wallowed in at Darkwood. *Virgin's blood,* so she'd claimed. And once again, that memory left her sick to her gut.

The tinny scent in their room... the putrid stench

of death. The sight of Morwen's grisly little pet hiding in the corner, pecking at the remnants of her victim.

How could they ever vanquish such evil?

Morwen would do whatever she wished, whenever she wished, whatever it took, to serve her will. She would murder innocents, eat their....

"And the third part?"

Seren shuddered, shaking away the gruesome memory. "Heart," she said, masking her distaste. "This is where the spirit lies." And that, inevitably, was why her mother consumed it... to steal the very essence of her victim.

Seren swallowed the bile that rose in her throat, wishing with all her soul that she could be free of the memory of Darkwood.

Listening to her talk, Wilhelm slowed his canter. Her voice was soft as velvet, and he was glad Jack prodded her to continue, but not only so he could hear the musical lilt of her voice. He was curious as well. He wanted to know more about Seren Pendragon.

Who were her people? Whence did they come? How was it they were able to conduct sorcery? Was witchery truly an abomination of nature, or was it something holier?

How could anyone as lovely and pure as Seren Pendragon be anything but good and true?

In fact, hadn't Giles claimed his sword glowed only in the presence of evil? If that were true it never once glowed in Rosalynde's presence when Wilhelm was near, nor should she be able to wield it. And yet, she did.

"The last of the five are *ysbryd* and *morâl*. *Morâl* would be akin to character; all that makes you unique —like how brave you are."

He turned to see that she winked at Jack, and Wilhelm slowed to ride beside them, watching as Jack sat straighter in his saddle, his smile stretching, like a flower blooming beneath the warmth of the sun. In fact, the boy's entire body seemed to lean toward Seren—as Wilhelm was seeking her as well.

"*Ysbryd*, at long last, is the spark within us that distinguishes life from death." And then, once again, her voice sobered. "Some call it the Heart Flame." She was quiet a moment, then offered, "This is how I knew my sister was gone."

"How?"

It was a long, long moment before she responded, and then she swallowed audibly before speaking. "Because I can feel it," she said. "As you might have felt your papa. It is an essence we sense with our hearts, particularly with loved ones... like... for example... have you never sat alone in a room with your back to a door, and suddenly, without turning to see who has arrived, you know who it is?"

The boy nodded, and Wilhelm fell behind the pair, to better listen to their discourse unheeded. He knew exactly what she was talking about, but that wasn't only reserved for loved ones. He remembered very well the morning he'd returned to Warkworth... while he'd been hauling out their dead... that strange feeling came over him... a sense that someone was out there, watching.

And then he'd felt *her* again in the King's Hall: Morwen Pendragon.

He'd also had a sense of it the day his mother died.

Whilst the lord's physician had tended her, he was sent away to keep himself occupied. But there was little he could do to keep her off his mind. He'd sat on a bench, watching the blacksmith pound at a hunk of metal on the anvil—the *clang, clang, clang*, in time to the quickened beat of his heart. Any moment, he'd hoped they would summon him, and he would return to his mother's bedside to discover her awake, eyes wide... He was nine when she died—a wee, dirty little boy, whose good fortune it was to have an honorable sire. It was his brother, Roger, who'd arrived with a glum face to tell Wilhelm the news. But somehow, Wilhelm had already known. As he'd sat there, staring at the sparks flying from that anvil, he'd sensed his mother's heart flame extinguish, and it was only curious that he'd never truly realized until this very instant what that was.

Why was it you sensed some folks, not others? He didn't remember having any sense of Lady Ayleth's parting—not until he saw her ravaged body.

More to the point, why did he feel so connected to this woman, when there was little doubt Seren was not meant for him.

For a long while, he lost himself amidst these thoughts, turning a deaf ear to their conversation, until he heard Jack's whistle. "S'blood! Di' you see that bird?" he said, excitedly.

Wilhelm and Seren both peered up to spot a black and white magpie, chattering noisily on a nearby branch.

When Jack spurred his horse in the bird's direction, Wilhelm spurred his own horse to sidle up beside Seren, thinking it high time to put her mind at ease. He'd asked for a truce between them and it was time he behaved like a man.

No one saw that *other* bird that held Jack's attention, with its telltale neck. It stepped sideways on a branch as though to conceal itself behind a cluster of leaves, opening its shining beak to shriek as the boy passed beneath. Then it flew away.

17

"She was a fairy, a sylph, I don't know what she was—
anything no one ever saw...
everything that everybody ever wanted."
—*Charles Dickens*

"Have you need of a bath, m'lady?"

"Nay." Removing my gloves, I snap them together, tucking the shining-black leather underneath my arm. "I won't be long."

"Very well, m'lady."

The innkeeper bows, a humble gesture meant to honor his betters; I brush past him, because, tis only my due.

More's the pity, this realm is not my realm and I am no longer welcome amidst my people. But, here and now, I tell you true. Forget everything you know.

Eons past, when gods walked amidst men, I was here then—a maiden true, not this withered crone I have become, whose *glamour* depends on the contents of a vial and the callowness of men. I am but a shade of myself.

But, in those days, my heart sang for a man, a prince with eyes so blue as the sea. And though he was said to be cruel, I gave him all—my heart, my home, body and soul.

He courted me long, singing sweetly from his keel and named me his lady of the lake. For a time, I was a queen and my Avalon was like paradise, with a palace and courtyard so fine, it lit a spark of greed in the hearts of men. But, alas, my land was no man's land, forbidden to all but gods and demigods. Enshrouded by an enchanted mist, my isle was, indeed, such a hallowed place that the waters of the River Dee, passing through on its way to the sea, never stopped to mingle with my own, but still, fishermen longed to cast their nets near my shores, because there lived the pearl-scaled *gwyniad*, native only to my seas.

My fields? Scattered with poppies so far as the eye could see. My woods? Filled with *fae folk*, whose home was my home, whose blood was half my blood as well.

I was, you see, a child of the *aether*, born with knowledge of all that was and all that shall ever be. My Sylph-kind are sky speakers, able to commune with creatures of the air. And, like the Sylph, themselves, Avalon was a bit of a mirage... here one instant, gone the next.

But this is where my tale forsakes me:

I was heaven-sent to watch o'er the tricksy *fae*, who were created to beguile the realms of men—because, of course, even gods must grow bored. But tricksy they are, and tricksy even with me—but now, I digress.

Whilst I remained Sylph, I was pure and elegant, coveted by men across the realm, like my precious, inviolable Avalon—and, yet, it *was* violated, no less by me.

You see, I had everything... truly, and yet, my

Sylph eyes wandered o'er the kingdoms of the Welsh... to a mortal king who was said to be a giant among men.

Tegid Foel.

Even now, his name fills me with ambivalence, for I cannot vanquish my sweeter memories, and they must endure eternally with loathing.

Tegid, oh Tegid... strong, wise, and as handsome as the Sylph were pure. But mostly the man was powerful, and there is a manner of seduction in power.

The longer I watched this king; the more I loved him, and for love of him, I conspired with the *fae* to consign myself to mortal form—beguiled by the very beings born to beguile. *Imagine that.*

Alas, there is little across the realms more powerful than love, and there is nothing even a God wouldn't do in pursuit of it. So, I offered my new prince the keys to my city and to my heart as well. But, Tegid squandered this, poisoning my Avalon with avarice, desire and hubris, until, black and putrid, like cancer, it seeped into the soul of my lands. After a while, that which was pure began to wither, including my own flesh, and day by day he turned me into a bitter crone, until naught was left of my Sylph-self, and all that endured was jealousy and loathing. Until finally, Tegid stole our beauteous daughter, leaving me to care for our son, whose heart was fair, but whose countenance was not. Because of his face, Tegid renounced our sweet boy, and he called me a pythoness. Lusting after his own daughter, he stole my first-born —all that remained as proof of my Sylph beauty. He crushed my soul, and still, with a shred of my spirit, I swore to avenge my son. One year and one day I toiled over a potion to give my son the greatest gift a god can give to man—enlightenment.

I imagined my Morfran a poet laureate—beguiling his own father with the heartrending beauty of his words.

I saw his name so renowned that he would be sought far and wide. After all, this would be the power of my potion—and yay, I know, how fitting my daughter's end should be so... illuminating.

Arwyn, my dear, you were always meant to die that way. I saw your death the day you were torn from my womb, squealing and eager to suckle at my breast.

What I didn't know was that the tricksy fae had sent me a tricksy little boy... Gwion Bach ap Gwreang. He stole my Arwyn potion. And, later, when he was reborn as Taliesin, my husband, my betrayer, offered him our daughter to wed. I raged, and raged, and raged, and raged. I raged so far and wide that I brought down the wrath of the gods. Not only did they take away my beloved Avalon, they exiled me to the sea, imprisoning me by the one barrier a Sylph may not pass any more than the River Dee may pass into Avalon... *water.*

Gone.

My Island.

Vanished.

Drowned like they drowned me.

The *fae* folk were set free to roam this earth, and to this day, on a moonless night, if you stand upon the banks of Bala in Gwynedd, you will still spy my courtyard shimmering 'neath the silvery billows—a ghost of a city, gone forevermore.

As you can imagine... the blood in my veins turned black with my hatred, spreading to every fiber of my body. Where once I was beauty incarnate, I am frightful now, a creature born of all that is vile. All that was good in me is lost. Love, after all, is the purest of essences, and no trace of this remains in my soul.

So, there you have it: my story. Pitiful, as it should be, but you must rest assured I am not defeated. I am stronger for the absence of my weakness, and I will never again be brought low by this debility called love.

Love, love, love—even a mother's love is forgotten, gone the instant my son breathed his last.

Sighing as I reach my suite, I peer within.

"You should find everything to your specifications," says the guard at the top of the stairs.

"Leave me," I say.

Inside, the candles have been lit... twenty at least. Shoved to one side sits a beautiful, ornate, but empty tub, and a bed shoved to another. In the center of the room lies a rather large cauldron, iron-built, with rust tears staining it from rim to belly. But though it has served me well enough these past years, it is not my cauldron from Blackwood.

If you have not guessed by now, my true name is Cerridwen. Creirwy, Morfran and Taliesin are children of my blood. I took this body, thinking it would serve me, but I chose wrongly. I chose the sister, not the brother. Those two scarcely knew what mysteries they would reveal... but I thank them, even so. *Emrys. Poor Emrys.* Would he have lain with his sister had I not inhabited her body? I think not. And Morgan? How did she know?

Alas, I suppose... a mother *always* knows.

Stealing over to the cauldron, I peer inside. Empty at the moment, but there is residue and I reach down to taste the blend. *I need more coltsfoot, I think. And, of course, blood...*

Mentally, I pore over the faces I saw in the tavern ... a man and a woman traveling together, a trader and a thief. These are my choices, and perhaps I will have them all...

Incidentally, do you how the *fae* were created?

Cauldron born to serve the Sylph.

So, you see... my daughters are gifted with *fae* blood, but I am born of the essence from which they draw. They are whispers of the wind from which I am formed. They are breeze-kissed whilst I am the storm. They are sparks, I am the flame. They are demigods, like the *fae*. But I... I am a Goddess, and once the light of this world is extinguished like the flames of a thousand dying stars, and the hearts of men are stillborn in a cradle of night... here, I will remain.

Stupid fools.

Kill me?

I'd like to see you try.

I may not see my Avalon again as it is not in my power to resurrect paradise, but I will not rest till I see the blood of my betrayers expunged from this realm. Yay, I know my *daughters* believe I live to defy an Empress, and no doubt, I will snuff that bitch's Heart Flame before I am done, but nay. I will avenge *all* I have lost.

"You will not have died in vain, Bran," I promise.

Taking my time, I fill the cauldron... water, the elixir of life. Lavender. Catnip. Milk of the poppy. The petals of a blood red rose. A wee bit of coltsfoot—all that I have remaining. Perhaps that will do. And finally, a pinch of my most prized receipt, complete with newts, moon snails and a pinch of human remains. One day, I will use this very philter to create an army of *meirw byw*, whose hearts will beat in their breasts, but whose loyalties belong to me. Once that day arrives, I will sweep through these lands like an avenging flame. And, in the meantime... I remove the divine athame from its scabbard, then slash the ancient blade across my open palm, holding it above the steaming cauldron.

One. Two. Three. Four. Five.

One drop of blood for every facet of the human spirit I wish to vanquish. Then, I return my blade to its sheath, all the while lapping the remaining blood from my flesh, wiggling my tongue into the fresh wound, taking pleasure in the sting as I watch my blood come alive, swirling in silver rivulets inside the cauldron, spreading, spreading... until the surface appears mercurial, and finally, once I have enjoyed the anticipation long enough, I whisper...

> Blessed flame, shining bright,
> Aid me now in my fight.
> Unveil to all another self,
> Liken me to Elspeth herself.

> Power of three, let them see, let them
>   see, let them see.
> Power of three, let them see, let them
>   see, let them see.
> Power of...

Ah, now. Tis done. My face is *her* face. My eyes, *her* eyes. My chin, *her* chin, willful and defiant. Smiling, I wave at the visage of my eldest living daughter.

"Good day to you, Lady Aldergh. How lovely you are. But is it any wonder? You were born of me."

18

S eren cast Wilhelm another glance. Leaning against a tree, he stood carving a point into his stick, all the while watching Jack, and she wondered how he managed to save his fingers from the blade when he never once stopped to look down to see what he was whittling.

By now, this was becoming a routine. She knew precisely how long she had before Jack returned. It was one thing to perform the Craft in front of Wilhelm, who understood who and what she was, but she daren't draw pentacles or cast spells in front of an unsuspecting boy, no matter how much Jack appeared to like and respect her. She simply couldn't bear it if he ever looked at her the way some folks did—as though she were an abomination of nature.

Once they learned who she was, it was impossible to miss the whispers and backward glances. She and her sisters were aberrations, merely curiosities to divert the court.

Somehow, Wilhelm was different. No matter what he claimed, there was no fear or revulsion in his gaze when he watched her, merely curiosity... and perhaps something more—something that never failed to make her heart quicken a beat. She was unfailingly aware of the man, and he seemed equally mindful of her, but she couldn't account for it. Nor was it remotely appropriate considering his association with Rosalynde.

Were they affianced?

Was she his lover?

For the first time in all her life she felt a stab of envy that her sister had encountered Wilhelm first, and yet, she was never a jealous spirit, so envy was not a feeling she cared to explore. Putting her dark thoughts out of her head, she picked out a new stick to draw with, and gave Wilhelm a nod.

Against all odds, he had become her conspirator, sending Jack after firewood, then keeping watch while the boy foraged. Fortunately, Jack needn't go very far, only far enough that he couldn't spy Seren at work. And, naturally, as boys were wont to do, his task became a veritable adventure: He gathered two sticks, picked up a stone, then hurled it at some imaginary foe, before returning to his chore. A task that should have taken him only fifteen minutes oft took thirty. At the instant, she could hear him talking to himself all the while he played, and meanwhile, she drew her pentacle, then cast a hasty warding spell, and when she was done, she gave Wilhelm another nod, after which he returned to his stump to fix dinner, watching between thick lashes as Seren studied her artwork.

So far as she could tell, her warding spells appeared to be working, though it was impossible to say for sure unless they were tested. Unfortunately, the only true test was the continued absence of her mother and minions, and if Morwen should ever appear, Seren would know her casting was wrong. Only then it would be too late. Her warding spell was not the same sort of spell Elspeth had cast from her ramparts. Judging by all those dead birds, her sister's spell had had a defensive property to it, though its source and words were a mystery to Seren. She wouldn't know how to do that. Rather, a warding spell of the sort she was casting was more like a *glamour*—a suggestion by the Goddess to passersby that there was no one abiding within her circle. It was no more than a trick of the eyes. And regardless, she considered the weaving threads a positive sign—the bright striations and smoky coils evoked by her words were in fact evidence of her manipulation of the *aether*.

Matter—even the smallest, most ethereal particles —could not be rearranged without evidence.

While Jack remained otherwise occupied, Seren took time to cover the periphery with leaves so he wouldn't discern her diagram, and finally, she let it be. It wasn't the best crafting, but it was the best she could do under the circumstances. Later, when everyone was abed, she would do what she could to fix her lines again. Casting another glance at Wilhelm to find him staring, she blushed hotly, averting her gaze.

"If tis any comfort," he said, "I do not think he would judge you." Regarding her still, he held the evening's meal firmly positioned between his thighs. "*I* do not."

The warmth in his gaze made Seren's cheeks burn. "Mayhap," she said, "but, believe me, I have seen the way folks regard those who are different, and it would destroy me to see him look at me this way."

Or, you, she added silently.

He nodded again, retrieving his knife, slashing a few judicious slices across the carcass, severing muscle, she presumed. Afterward, the pelt came off easier.

Dropping his knife again, he tugged the remainder

of the fur off the rabbit without much effort, and, for an instant, as she watched, Seren was beguiled by the sinew of his arms—every muscle dancing.

What are you doing, Seren? Pining after a man already taken? Censuring herself, she tossed her stick into the flames, marveling over the fact that Wilhelm took so much care with their pit, surrounding it with field-stones, very much the same way her pentacle was meant to work for protection. He might not have much skill with fire-kindling, but he was a custodian of nature no less than she was. Her *dewinefolk* fancied themselves guardians of nature, and *magik* was only a tool, Goddess-given, to accomplish good works, each according to his way. The Craft of the Wise was simply a practical study of the *hud*, and *dewinity* wasn't so much about what skills one possessed; it was a philosophy of being. Her people believed all things were connected, living or dead. All told, there was very little difference between her and Wilhelm, save for the tools they wielded.

Seren was coming to understand him better. To be sure, he had a servant's heart in that burly breast, even if his demeanor was far from subservient.

In fact, she wondered how those Warkworth brothers fared when together. As well as she could remember Giles, she didn't believe he was all too forbearing, and she had a vision of them coming to fists quite oft. Men were like that, she supposed, simply because they could be. No matter what circumstances they met, she and her sisters hadn't the luxury to quarrel about who should be in command. They might not always agree about what path should be taken, but all together they discussed it, giving every argument equal merit. *Dewinefolk* were not so concerned with kings or queens, nor earls or barons. According to their tenets, all men and women were created equal, and even Rhiannon would not presume to command them.

For a while, there was a priest in residence at Llanthony—one Father Cabot. For the most part, he'd been a kindly soul, but Seren could see that he had his own plan for the priory, one that didn't align itself with Father Ersinius' plan. Those two had argued and often, and soon it became apparent that two such strong-willed men could never preside under the same roof. So, Father Cabot departed one day, and Ersinius was inordinately pleased by the fact though betimes, Seren wondered where the man had gone, mainly because on the day he departed no one came to call for him, nor did he take a priory wagon or a horse from the stables. He simply vanished. Though, of course, it was entirely possible he took the Rhiw Pyscod afoot to Llangorse, no word ever arrived to corroborate that fact. It was also possible that he went to Abbey Dore, but that didn't seem likely either since Llanthony was Augustinian and Abbey Dore was Cistercian.

Perhaps it should seem a small matter for men who all claimed to follow the word of the same God, but it was not. This was, in truth, much the source of Father Cabot's dissent. He was a true Augustinian by nature, which was to say he interpreted scripture quite severely. He'd believed in living in silence, eating and drinking sparingly. Manual labor did not suit him. To his manner of thought, men and women should spend *all* their time contemplating God in prayer, and while he was never precisely unkind to Seren and her sisters, he never condoned their presence at Llanthony—not merely because they were women, but because they were presumed to be *witches*.

Seren loathed that word for all it implied. To be sure, no one ever called her or her sisters witches with a smile. Even Ersinius, who'd vehemently argued the need for their asylum, had treated them rather poorly. Overall, though he'd claimed to answer to the Rule of St. Augustine and the Austin Friars, he was more Cistercian in nature, turning Llanthony into a flourishing center of trade. If not by word, by deed, he was of the mind that everyone should do their part, and he was more concerned with how to make their God-given lands a service to God, hence the hatchery and the aviary. Moreover, he was inclined to seek grants to apply his "works" though a true Augustinian would no more put expensive German *waldglas* in a vestibule —three times no less—than he would ever approve of having Morwen's witchy daughters on the premises, only for the sake of gold.

As for the Vale of Ewyas over which the priory presided, it was no more God-given than it was modeled after St. Augustine's rule. Those lands, along with the majority of the Black Mountains, were stolen from her people, snatched perforce and by royal decree from men who would never call that English Usurper king. But, so long as Stephen of Blois sat on her father's throne, Wales would never come to heel. Even now, it made her smile to think of that defiant child who'd smashed the chapel's windows—not once, but twice.

"We should be another three or four days before arriving at Neasham," Wilhelm said, interrupting her reverie.

He was impaling his cony on a skewer, and though Seren was growing accustomed to the sight of depilated hare, she held her gaze aloft of the poor beast.

"Neasham?"

"Abbey," he explained. "If you'd like to, we can stay overnight. I know the prioress well enough to beg a favor."

Seren nodded, rubbing her arms absently. She knew those nuns, too. They were dressmakers for the Crown, and they were nice enough, to be sure, but not so much after learning they were Morwen's daughters. However, unless Sister Emma had returned to their fold, they wouldn't recognize Seren, and she hoped Wilhelm would keep that bit of information to himself. "Yay," she said, looking up into the canopy of shimmering green. "I think it could be nice; thank you, please." She would desperately love a bath, and a change of clothes. She could have donned one of the dresses Wilhelm bought her long before now, but it seemed abominable to do so when she smelled like the Thames.

"I suppose I should say... it was your sister Rosalynde who earned that lady's good will. She offered Mother Helewys five gold marks for alms."

"Five gold marks?"

"Aye," he said. "I know. She said it was all she had." And he smiled very fondly. "Your sister is—" He paused, seemingly unable to find the proper words to describe Rose, and his cheeks flushed so brightly. Seren presumed it was because he was trying and finding it difficult to tell her he loved Rosalynde, but it was clear enough by his words and his actions. Once again, she felt a stab of envy. "You care for her, do you not?"

He lifted his gaze from the cony. "Rosalynde?"

Seren nodded.

"Aye," he confessed. "I do. And, if you ask me, the world needs more ladies like her, and fewer pious fools. I am so sorry about your grandmamau."

Seren blinked in surprise. He knew about that, too?

Sweet fates, what didn't he know? Clearly, Rosalynde had confided all, and Seren felt yet another inexplicable stab of jealousy, though she had never envied her sisters aught.

In truth, it was Seren who was blessed with the most good fortune, and it was about time the Mother Goddess blessed someone else, but... well... she didn't wish to entertain those thoughts either.

Sighing very wistfully, she wished she could read Wilhelm's thoughts as Rhiannon or Elspeth could do. Much like his face, his aura suddenly turned scarlet, and she assumed it was because he was thinking of Rosalynde. Red, after all, was the color of passion.

It was also the color of fury, but there was naught about Wilhelm's demeanor that betrayed the latter. Aside from his surliness, she'd come to see that he was as placid a man as his sort could ever possibly be, taking immense pleasure in the task he'd been given —namely sheltering her and returning her to safety. She only wished she could do something to repay him.

"Wilhelm... I was thinking... mayhap I could teach you," she said, regarding him across dancing flames.

Overhead, the rising moon was a smile upon the twilight sky.

"Teach me... what?"

"To... read... letters."

His brows twitched, and then he frowned.

"That was our price for passage aboard the Whitshed. When Captain Airard realized we didn't have fare for Calais, he asked we teach his son to read."

Wilhelm's gaze narrowed and he maintained his silence, his blush only heightening. Heartily afraid that she'd offended, Seren said, "Tis hardly a sin not to be able to read."

"And nevertheless, you and your sisters, and Jack—"

"His trade demands it," Seren explained gently. "As for me, and my sisters... we were locked away in a priory, with little more to do but garden and learn letters."

He lifted a dark brow. "And cast spells?"

Seren blinked, surprised to find that his lips had turned at the corners and his near-ebony eyes had caught flames in both pupils. The smile transformed his face, stealing Seren's breath. He was teasing her, she realized, sensing a glint of humor, and she blinked once more in surprise. "Yay, I suppose," she said. And then, "Well, at least, I did. Arwyn tried. But Rhiannon never needed any practice, nor did Rosalynde."

"What about your eldest sister, Elspeth?"

"Aye, well, for so long Elspeth was afeared of the Craft." Seren narrowed her gaze at Wilhelm, putting him on the spot. "But regardless of what you have said it seems to me you are not."

Wilhelm shrugged. "You mistook my meaning, I think. I did not say I was afraid of you, Seren. Verily, there are worse things in this world than witchery."

"We are not—"

"Witches, yay I know. So, Rosalynde said." He tipped his chin to indicate the boy, who'd only just returned and was dumping an armload of tinder into a pile near the horses.

"Bones o' the saints, lad. Did you leave any rock unturned?"

Even dirtier now than he was before he left, Jack scratched at the top of his head, leaving a few greasy strands standing on end. "But ye said—"

"I know what I said, whelp. That was an hour ago. What have you been doing so long?"

Seren giggled to hear their banter—so familial. The lighthearted chatter reminded her of her sisters—until Jack's next words gave her a fright.

"I was out speaking to a bird," he said, and when Wilhelm tilted his head, he added, "I am not lying!"

Fingers of dread squeezing Seren's heart. She met Wilhelm's gaze, swallowing convulsively as she then cast her gaze into the trees. They were in the Royal Forest of Kesteven only days north of London. "Was it a raven?" she asked.

Jack shrugged. "I don't know what it was, it was big."

Wilhelm asked, "And... you say you *spoke* to it?"

Jack shrugged again. "I don't know." He scratched nervously at the hair above his ear, tousling more greasy locks. "I thought I heard my name, like this: Jaaack! Jaaaack! But when I tried to make it speak again, it would not."

Seren's heart thumped painfully against the cage of her ribs, and with a gob in her throat, she cast another glance at Wilhelm, who instinctively seemed to comprehend what it was she was thinking. Very, very casually, he dropped the skewered cony onto the spit, and said, "I'll be back."

"I can come too?" asked Jack.

"Nay," barked Wilhelm. "I've no need of an audience to piss. Stay here, and see to your lady. Eat your dinner."

There was no question about disobeying his command. Disappointed though he must have been, Jack stayed, coming into the circle to sit beside Seren.

"Cony again," he grumbled, sounding disappointed. "I wish it were *bacoun*." And then, with Wilhelm's departure forgotten, he asked her, "'Ave you never tasted *bacoun,* Lady Seren? Me and my papa 'ad it first time this Yule."

Seren's gaze shifted from the woodlands where Wilhelm had gone, and then to the cony and then to Jack's face, shaking her head, distracted.

He sounded sad now. "We were supposed to save some for me mum. But we didn't, and I was mad when he ate it, but now I am not." He reached out to gently turn the spit in Wilhelm's stead. "'E said it was the best *bacoun* 'e ever ate, and now I do not suppose I'll eat it again."

"Aye, you will," Seren promised, hoping Morwen wasn't out there. If, in truth, he had been speaking to one of her birds, her mother couldn't be far. "Once we arrive at Warkworth, I will see to it you get to carry some home to your mum."

And she only hoped it was a promise she could keep.

19

Giles had no sooner stabled his mount and entered the palace when the king's steward intercepted him. At once, he was ushered into a private meeting, where Stephen acknowledged his entrance with a nod—so much for washing the dirt from his travels before addressing the king.

He soon discerned why: It was an emergency meeting of the Rex Militum—a secret league, known only to a few. It was perhaps similar to the Papal Guard, only licensed to enforce the King's Law, by sway, or by sword. Giles was one of eleven men present today, including William d'Aubigny, the Earl of Arundel and Cael d'Lucy, the newly appointed Earl of Blackwood. In attendance, as well, was the Queen Consort of England, and though she was not seated precisely at table, her attendance could hardly be mistaken. Whatever lack of affection she and her husband shared in the bedroom clearly it did not extend itself to his court. Giles had always suspected her to be a driving force in her husband's *politiks*, but now he knew it for certes. It was uncommon to see any woman in such a venerable position, and Henry himself, though he'd raised up his daughter to be his heir, never granted such liberties to either of his wives, nor to Matilda.

Adeliza of Louvain had been a quiet lady, with grace beyond her years. She would never have presumed to advise Henry. And though Henry had worshipped his first wife, she, too, would never presume to advise him as Maude did with Stephen. In fact, so far as the Empress was concerned, it came as little surprise that Stephen could so easily rouse the barons against her when even her own father never took her seriously.

Nor, in truth, had the Vatican ever considered bowing to a woman's sovereignty. The instant Matilda's first husband died she'd had to cede the Empire to her husband's successor. Her crowns, such as they were, were only adornments now, and no matter how proudly she wore them (or how stubbornly), she would never wear them on her father's throne. After all was said and done, Duke Henry was their only true chance to restore the realm to Beauclerc's blood.

Curious about the agenda, Giles remained silent, listening.

He was not a member of this cloak and dagger company, and he only knew of its existence because one of the members was also a spy for the Papal Guard—of which no doubt, Stephen had already surmised Giles was a constituent. Even as he took his seat, the mood in the chamber turned grimmer and the men sat on tenterhooks. The candle flames stilled over the hush of the room.

King Stephen held a small taper before him, with a wick that had burned so long it nearly consumed itself. He spoke gravely, "Tis no' enough he insults my wife—his blood—forswearing her right to be my queen. My spies tell me he intends to seize York, and

I'll not sit idly by whilst David mac Maíl Choluim robs me of another bishopric."

Remembering a conversation he'd had only months ago with the king of Scotland, Giles wondered how Stephen discovered the plot. So, it seemed, he still had spies at large—not Malcom, for certes. From what he knew of Malcom Scott, he was not a vacillator. He'd turned his back on kith and kin once before, and Giles doubted he would return to the Scots' fold only to play them false. At any rate, one did not rouse entire armies, with thousands upon thousands of warriors, only to act as though on the stage of a play. Nay. It was not Malcom, though he had his suspicions over who it might be...

The silence was deafening, until Stephen spoke again. "You'd think it was enough to have Carlisle —bastard."

"Your Grace, I did warn that it was a mistake not to challenge him all those years ago," said one of his counselors. "He has established himself well enough that England will be hard-pressed to ever see his lands or levies again."

The king's gaze slid to the man speaking—tall and lean, with dark hair that was shorn to the nubs. His face sported a number of scars. And judging by the mirror image of the face of the man seated beside him, those two must be the Beaumont twins, Waleran and Robert. In reward for their services, Stephen had already awarded them Worcester, Leicester, Hereford, Warwick and Pembroke. Now that Robert of Gloucester was dead, the Beaumont twins might well be the most well-appointed men in the realm.

"Your Grace, I am also hearing rumors to the effect that Duke Henry is bargaining with Ranulf to give up his claims to Carlisle in return for the Honour of Lancaster."

The king twisted his lips. "De Gernon?"

"Aye, Your Grace, de Gernon."

"You should never have trusted the faithless bastard," interjected D'Lucy, with an ease and familiarity regarded only to a man of his station. "I warrant de Gernon has flipped more times than a gambler's coin."

Someone else interjected. "I believe that is true, Your Grace. We are fortunate enough to have discovered his intentions in Wales, or we would still be mired in disputation."

Cael d'Lucy rested his face between his thumb and forefinger, regarding the speaker pointedly. "Are we not still mired in disputation? Pray tell, know you something I do not?"

"If there is disputation, perhaps you should look to yourself. You had Elspeth Pendragon at your whim, and yet you tarried so long she made you a fool. Now, you will tarry with her sister, until—"

The king waved a hand in dismissal. "God's bones! That is a matter for another time," he said. "The matter for discussion is Carlisle, and Carlisle is not Ranulf's to bargain with."

"And, nevertheless, if David agrees to the terms, de Gernon will give homage to David and Duke Henry both, and with the backing of the Scots, they will surely turn their heads toward York."

"Why? Why should David give up Carlisle when he has clamored for that seat so long as he's had hair on his balls?"

"For the glory of York, Your Grace."

"He would, for York," agreed another.

Giles watched the king's men—head gestures and subtle hand signals... Clearly, there were spies in

David's court and spies in the Earl of Chester's retinue... all these men were well connected... none more so than Cael d'Lucy.

The two regarded each other with an air of affected boredom, but there was underlying tension burning beneath the surface. Giles was the first to look away.

"Father," said Eustace—that fresh-faced bastard responsible for the burning at Warkworth. "Send *me* north with *my* army," demanded the nineteen-year-old scissorbill.

My army, not yours—as though he already possessed them.

The bloody wretch had a title he didn't deserve, and somehow, his father would still advocate to place him on the throne. The very truth of that was deplorable. Eustace was naught but a stupid little boy with an ego as immense as his head, and his villainy would someday be his undoing.

It wasn't enough he was said to abuse his own wife, an esteemed princess of the House of Capet; he was a brutal liegeman as well. If Giles were the lady's sire, he would gut the muckspout from belly to throat, and it was all he could do to look at him now.

The very fact that they could put Giles in a room with Eustace was dangerous—but nay, the simple fact that he could sit here at arm's length, across table, without shoving his blade down the boy's throat was a testament to his years of careful training. But here and now, he sensed a test...

"Nay," said the king, with a glance toward Giles. "You've cost me too much already. You will remain here, learn the true value of patience."

"What, then, would you have us do?" ventured D'Lucy.

Once again, the king slid a glance toward Giles, and when he spoke, he spoke not to the high commander of his Rex Militum, but to Giles himself. "Indeed, I will send an army north, but I leave you and the Earl of Warkworth—" A pointed reminder of the title Giles had been awarded. "—in command. I shall have you ride north with one thousand men, and if you need more, send word via raven."

So, then, the witch was still alive.

The king's gaze was direct, his eyes changeable, betimes blue, betimes grey, depending on the light in the room. Right now, they were steely and dark, but with a flicker of gold from the candle turning before him.

Indeed, it was a test.

Giles tensed. If there was one thing he could not do it was intervene at York. He'd given his solemn oath to David of Scotland—and more, he'd promised his brother by law that he would abstain from the battles to come. For this promise, he was awarded yards and yards of stone—stone he was now using to fortify the fortress Eustace had burned.

By the bloody cross, even if he did not, in fact, loathe Eustace—which he did—he was a man of his word. Clearly, the king already knew what David was planning, but still Giles would not betray his confidences by revealing his own intelligence. Whatever his response, he must remain circumspect, because, while he no longer intended to take a bride of Stephen's choosing, he could not presently repudiate the man or his throne—not without consequence.

He said nothing for a long moment, merely regarded D'Lucy. The two men shared another meaningful glance.

D'Lucy said, "It would be my honor, Your Grace. I

am quite certain the Earl of Warkworth understands the privilege you bestow upon him."

From the back of the room came another voice, that of Maude's. "As you must know, my lords, we have suffered a loss in his majesty's Guard."

Her quick-blue eyes flirted with Giles, though it was a dark flirtation, not one that could be remotely confused with matters of the flesh. She gave him a thin smile, and Giles was quick to catch her intimation.

"So, then... with Malcom Scott gone... are you saying you would like me to join your... Guard?"

"Aye," said Maude. "How astute, my lord."

Giles de Vere's dark eyes glinted, though he'd slid a veil over them the instant he'd walked into the room. Only now and again, something like a glimmer of loathing slipped past, like a glimpse of morning light through heavy drapery, and she wondered if there could be truth to the rumors she'd heard about this man—that he was a member of the Papal Guard, a Paladin for God. Named for the twelve knights of Charlemagne's court, over whom Count Palatine had first been in command, the Guard had been recommissioned to the Vatican, in exchange for indulgences. But, if this were, in fact, true, why in God's name would Giles de Vere leave an ambitious position to return to a northern province with so little promise? Moreover, why would the Church allow him to go? She wanted to know how far they could trust him, and his response would speak volumes.

"Alas," he said. "I cannot."

"Cannot? Or will not?" asked the king, and Maude frowned, annoyed, because Stephen's ego was such that he could not fathom she had the guile to outwit a man—else he was far too stupid to realize what she was trying to do.

"I cannot," answered Giles, and, then, dismissing Maude, he turned to address the king directly, and said, "Would you have me break an oath to God?"

Stephen frowned.

"In essence that is what you would be asking of me," Giles said, and Stephen shoved his candlestick aside, his steely eyes darker now, unyielding. "And yet you have sworn to kneel. Are you telling me now that you will not do so?"

A muscle ticked at de Vere's jawline, and Maude watched it, fascinated. "I considered you a man of your word," raged Stephen. "As am I. But mark me, de Vere, if you have lied to me, I'll not only return my men to Warkworth, as I have promised to do, but you will not live to see it burn a second time. If I do not take your head, I will lock you in the tower, and your Papal Guard be damned. By God, I have been called many, many things, but never once have I been called a liar, and I'll not tolerate a liar in my company."

Maude tried not to roll her eyes. But, of course, that wasn't true. After all, her husband told the grandest lie of all. He'd knelt before his uncle with such a radiant smile, and he'd sworn his allegiance to their cousin, only to rescind his vow the instant Henry gave up his ghost. Usurper they called him now— some to his back, some to his face.

Feeble. Ineffectual. Weak.

These were more of the things her husband was reputed to be, and most of these things were true.

Stephen of Blois had no spine at all when it came to disciplining those who deserved it. It was likely that, in the very near future, Eustace would need pay another visit to Warkworth because his father didn't have the constitution to do what was necessary to ensure their son's ascent to the throne. This was the one true cause she and Morwen Pendragon shared in common, and for all her annoyances, the Welsh witch was a necessary evil. If Maude ever hoped to see her son crowned in place of Duke Henry, she must endure. Alas, Morwen was not in residence today; Maude was, and if she had her druthers, she would see to it David of Scotland never succeeded in taking York. It pained her immensely that her mother's brother would cast her away in favor of his *other* niece—the one with whom Maude shared a name and to whom her uncle would so readily bow.

Saints abide! All her life she'd been forced to share what she held dear—her name with a cousin she despised and her husband with his mistresses. But it wasn't King Henry's daughter whose arse was planted on the throne; it was hers. And it was not Duke Henry who would triumph in the end, it was Eustace, even despite that the stupid fool seemed so ill-prepared to receive it.

Affecting an air of serenity and grace, as befitted her station, Maude sat patiently, studying the exchange between the king and subjects, considering the man who'd supposedly come to bend his knee... Giles de Vere was seething, like a teapot over a low flame. And yet, the look in his black eyes was never so canny and he chose his words carefully.

"I, too, am a man of my word, Your Grace. I will, indeed, kneel for my lands and I will fight for my country, but I cannot join your *Guard*."

She did not miss the look he cast Cael d'Lucy.

Curious that...

"In fact," he continued. "It is your right to send an

army north to secure York, and, of course, you must do so. You may rest assured the Vatican has no more desire for David mac Maíl Choluim to take this bishopric than you do."

"And you know this, how?"

Here it was, at last; Maude scooted to the edge of her seat, anticipating Giles's response. No man had ever revealed an association with the legendary Papal Guard, for which her husband had modeled his own cloak and dagger company.

Giles smiled, though barely. "Alas, Your Grace, this you must know I cannot reveal. But I can tell you this: In the matter of York, my sword and my fealty are not in disagreement."

Stephen narrowed his gaze. "So, then, you *will* kneel for me *today*?"

The lord of Warkworth's dark eyes glinted with cunning. He paused overlong, Maude believed, but there was little she could say over the matter when he nodded assent, and said, "I will, Your Grace."

Upon his agreement, the gloom of the room immediately lifted. Thirteen sighs blew and the candles on the tables shivered in relief. Still, she not did not join them in their solace, because she couldn't help but feel there was something she was missing... something that called to her woman's intuition. She simply could not fathom how any man could see his house burn to the bedrock, knowing full well her son was responsible, and not still entertain some manner of vengeance. Morwen, when she returned, must get to the bottom of it.

20

Wilhelm searched, but found no sign of those birds. If, in truth, Jack saw one, it had fled, and good riddance.

Cunning little creatures. Once, as a child, he'd watched a raven solve what was essentially a cunning puzzle, learning to pick a warehouse lock by trial and error only to get at the grain within. And this, after mimicking the sound of a woman's shriek in order to rid itself of the guard.

Fascinated by its machinations, he'd watched from his perch in a nearby tree, leaving the raven to its machinations all the while he'd trimmed cock feathers for fletching.

But these ravens were not those ravens.

These ravens were Morwen's ravens—uncanny was more the like. Immediately discernible by the patch of white on their napes, these birds had thickset bills, short tails, and ebony feathers that bore a deep purple sheen. More the size of a goshawk, they were rather enormous birds, with four-foot wingspans. He could scarcely imagine what a sight they'd presented with thousands of them bearing down on Aldergh. The image alone gave him a shudder. Insofar as he knew these particular ravens were not native to Briton. Where they came from was anyone's guess. Perhaps Morwen had summoned them from her cauldron. But this much he knew: By that witch's design they'd gifted one of those infernal birds to nearly every household throughout the realm. The simple fact that Warkworth escaped having one was only due to the fact that the king's son had burned down their demesne.

Bloody bastard.

One day, he would see justice done for his kinsmen—his father, brother, sisters, and aye, Lady Ayleth, as well, even despite that he could no longer recall the lady's face. It had been replaced now by the bewitching countenance of a sorceress whose beauty was the least of her *magik*.

Aye, he must confess it; Seren Pendragon occupied his every waking thought. He didn't care who her mother was. Like Rosalynde, she was innocent of Morwen's sins. He was wrong about her, and, some-how, despite the grim occasion, in her presence he was like a seed, unfurling and reaching for the brilliance of the sun. Her smile, little occasion as they'd had for it to appear, was fleeting, but exquisite, nonetheless.

So, it seemed, he was guilty of everything he'd ac-cused his brother of—being swayed by a lovely face, so much so that he was willing to risk everything for her cause.

It left him with a strange ambivalence, but none at all when it came to keeping the lady safe. If he'd en-countered one of those birds he would have twisted its neck till it was dead and left it to be devoured by dung beetles.

Simply to be sure, he searched for hours. By the time he returned to camp, he had a grumble in his belly that threatened to wake the dead. Fortunately, Seren and the boy were already asleep. He took every care to step over her pentagram, stooping first by the boy's side to tug the blanket up, over his chin. Tired as he must have been, he never once stirred. And neither did Seren when he moved to her side, falling to one knee to gaze into her face.

So beautiful.

So still.

A sudden thought occurred to him and his heart thumped—what if Morwen's minions found them whilst he was out searching? God help him if he'd failed her—as he'd failed her sister.

His breath caught in his throat as Seren's bosom lifted, straining against the bodice of her gown, and he swallowed with relief, cursing himself silently for the stirring in his loins. Without a moment's hesitation, he reached down, resetting her blanket so it covered her entirely, sheltering her from his greedy eyes.

God's truth, never in his life had he felt so protective over any living soul—not even Lady Ayleth, truth be known.

SEREN HAD WATCHED as Wilhelm tended Jack and the sweetness of his gesture stole the breath from her lungs.

He lifted the boy's blanket, tucking him in, and by the firelight she could see the look of compassion on his face. It tugged at the iron laces of her heart, dismantling her shield.

By firelight, his face was swarthy, the gold on his dark hair giving the long ends a burnished shade that complemented the hue of his skin. Long, and disheveled though it might be, his hair was a glorious mane, cast behind his shoulder like a shining velvet cloak. The slant of his brows gave the appearance that he was deep in thought. And his lips, generous and full, were no longer so full of disdain, but half turned with a tender smile.

Sweet fates, he might not have relished the thought of taking charge of Jack, but he'd done so nonetheless, and not for an instant had he taken those duties lightly.

How in the name of the Goddess he had managed to remain so vigilant all day long, and scarcely sleep by night, Seren couldn't fathom, but the strain was beginning to show. There were bruises forming beneath his eyes.

Unheeded, she allowed her gaze to travel his wide shoulders... long, muscled arms... his thighs as he sat on his haunches... Aye, he was a beautiful specimen of a man... more than she'd realized when she'd first set eyes upon him... more than his brother. This man— well, he was a man, well-built and gentle despite his brawn.

Not for the first time she felt a terrible twinge of regret that she hadn't met Wilhelm before Rosalynde did, and her envy was her undoing, because if there was one person who should never begrudge her sisters aught, it was Seren.

Throughout her life, she had been overly blessed —or cursed—with more than her share of attention. And yet, not only did she envy Rose, she despised the thought of her own betrothal to Giles. Giles was *not* the man in her dreams.

Giles was *not* the man she longed to kiss.

And more and more... it seemed to her that Wilhelm shared her inclination—she could spy desire in his eyes... and in his aura—that, too, was beginning to weigh heavily upon her. It was not enough that she must lose one sister to the Great Beyond. Now, must she yearn to betray another and lose Rosalynde as well? It was unthinkable, and yet... and yet... she couldn't tear her gaze away from Wilhelm. *Was it merely because she couldn't have him? Was she so vain?*

But nay, it was not that... during these past weeks Wilhelm had been her rock, her strength. He'd made her feel for the first time in all her life as though she were... *normal.*

He did not revile her for her *witchery*, even if he did not agree with it. He was a man who did not shy away from his duty, nor did he long to be something he was not.

He lifted his gaze, staring into the darkened woods, and in profile his face was achingly beautiful... his nose wide, but suited to his face... his brow imperfect, with that terrible scar, but arched so that his narrowed eyes gave her gooseflesh, despite that it was trained elsewhere.

His jaw, thick and masculine, was shaded by a fortnight's whiskers, and she wondered what it might feel like to press her lips so gently against the nubs of his beard.

He rose suddenly from his haunches, and Seren closed her eyes. She held her breath as he moved toward her, unable to bear the mortification of being caught spying. But then she sensed him, gazing down at her, his regard as tangible as the soft warm stream of his breath... and her heart thumped mercilessly at the cage of her ribs.

Mother Goddess... something inexplicable stirred inside her... something warm and titillating. It filled her with a longing so deep that it gave her a pang in her womb. The very sense of him made her yearn to lift her nose and follow his distinct male scent... sweat, sunshine... and something else...

Don't notice I am awake, she thought. *Don't see me.*

She longed to whisper words of concealment, but she had a true sense that they would never work against Wilhelm Fitz Richard. She had a strong sense he saw her more clearly than she saw herself. *But how could that be?*

For a long, long moment Seren held her breath... praying that he would go away... but then she heard his sharp intake of breath, felt a tug on her blanket and opened her eyes to meet his dark, brooding gaze.

Black pupils glinted against the firelight and her lips parted to speak, but her voice faltered. His whisper somehow managed to be silky, yet deep as the night. "Did I wake you?"

Seren shook her head.

He huffed a sigh. "I found no sign of that raven," he said, lifting a hand to his chin to scruff it with his fingers. "Tis possible it was there and fled."

Seren should have felt only relief to know her mother's birds were not spying on them, but she could scarcely think with Wilhelm hovering so near. "It seems to me they've a good sense for peril," she whispered.

He nodded, as though he understood, and agreed. "How is Jack?" Something about the concern etched upon his face should have triggered a question, but Seren couldn't remember what that question should be.

"None the wiser, I think. If he puzzled over why you were gone so long, he never said. He ate his supper, then went to bed. He and I tended the spit as you taught us, removing the cony when it was done."

"Did you eat as well?"

"A little, but we left the majority for you." She smiled, admiring the hard lines of his jaw... he had a small cleft in his chin, very, very tiny, but there, nonetheless. "A growing man must have his sustenance, after all."

He chuckled softly. "More's the pity; I need do no more growing, Lady Seren, but alas, I thank you regardless."

He made to rise then, and Seren reached out impulsively to stop him. "Wilhelm?" Her hand fell upon his forearm, hardly so noticeable as a butterfly's touch, yet it held him firm.

"Aye?"

"I... I am sorry."

"For what, m'lady?"

There was so much she wished she could do all over again—so much she wished she had never said. "For not thanking you properly before now. You've... well... you've been... a godsend."

His lips spread into a warm smile. "Your sister would make no bones about it; she would have said goddess sent."

He winked at her.

Seren averted her gaze at the mention of Rosalynde, but he mistook her gesture. "Worry not; you are thanking me now. All is well that ends well. Is that not so?"

"And will it?" Seren asked, clutching at her breast as though to still the beating of her heart. "End well?"

The question seemed to sober him, and his smile fled.

"Wilhelm," she said, again. "I do not know what we would have done without you. I am so grateful for your succor. I only wish..." She averted her gaze, tears pricking her eyes, and Wilhelm heaved a burdensome sigh, and then fell back upon his rump.

Seren sat as well, pulling up her blanket up to wrap it about her shoulders, shivering a bit, though not because she was cold. It would have been easy enough to cast a simple warming spell, but there was no remedy for what she truly felt.

"I am sorry," he said, his turn for apologies. He plucked up a pebble. "If only I'd not wasted so much time..."

"As you have said, my sister's death is *not* your fault," Seren reassured, and for a moment, Wilhelm wouldn't look at her. He tossed his pebble into the darkness. She heard it smack a tree somewhere in the depths of shadows.

"I suppose tis no one's fault."

"Aye, but it *is* someone's fault," Seren argued as the fire crackled behind her. "Tis my mother's fault. She is the one responsible for my sister's death—not you."

Silence.

"Wilhelm," she said again, in part because she liked saying his name. "I fear, if we do not stop her... England could be lost."

He stared at her intently. "Lady Seren... even without your mother's intervention, England may still be lost. Eustace is not Stephen, and Stephen is not Henry."

Now, more than ever, hearing the affection in his voice, Seren wished she'd known her father better. So many of his barons seemed to hold him in such high regard—why then, had they allowed Stephen to steal his crown?

Oh, but she knew why, even as she wondered... Morwen. Although Matilda had not won herself any devotees, so much of this was Morwen's fault, and she and her sisters had been naught but pawns in her un-holy war against this realm.

If Wilhelm only knew half her story, he might abandon her, here and now. "Alas, there is so much I would say—so much you do not know."

"I know enough," Wilhelm said, pulling up a knee, and wrapping an arm lazily about it. Seren longed for that embrace to be hers. "I know enough to have judged you when I should not have," he confessed.

"Aye, well... so did I—judge you—do not fret."

He lifted his brows at her confession. The gesture only accentuated his scar, and a hint of his smile re-turned. It made her heartbeat falter and her pulses scatter.

"You are not as I once supposed," she said shyly.

His full lips turned a little more. "Neither are you."

Bracing herself for truth, Seren wrapped her blanket tighter against the cool night air. "So, what is it you thought about me... before?"

He tilted her a look. "Alas, m'lady, I should not say, but I will. I thought you vain, selfish and self-impor-tant, for what else could such a beautiful lady of your caliber be, but all these things and more?"

Seren blinked. She had expected him to speak of her witchery, but the confession startled her. The smoky look in his dark eyes, and the spread of his deep red aura warmed her more than any fire could, and she was suddenly acutely aware of the boy sleeping not more than five feet away. She blew out the breath she forgot to exhale.

He thought her beautiful?

The thought was so arresting that the rest of his assumptions about her vanity didn't faze her. Goddess only knew why this should excite her so much when he was not the first man to say it was beyond her.

Somehow, none of those other professions seemed to matter one whit. Only Wilhelm's.

She swallowed now, uncertain how to respond. "My sister Rosalynde is beautiful," she said, discomfited, trying to remember all the reasons she could not have this man—primarily, he was already bound to her sister and who was she to come betwixt them?

"Aye," he said, staring hard. "So she is." And, somehow, though guilt should have tainted his admission, he said it without the least bit of compunction, as though it should be perfectly acceptable to covet two women at once—sisters, nonetheless.

Men were insouciant creatures. That fact sobered her. "*All* my sisters are beautiful," Seren added, finding some small comfort in annoyance. "Each in her own way."

"I have only met Rosalynde," he said conversationally. "But I know Giles made the acquaintance of your elder sister."

"Elspeth?"

He nodded. "When he took Rosalynde to Aldergh."

"But you did not go with them?"

He shook his head.

Seren flicked her gaze away. "I was surprised to learn she did not remain at Aldergh."

There was a wistful smile in his voice when he said, "True love, I suppose. It makes us do the oddest things. But, I must confess, she would have been safer at Aldergh. But you know your sister; she insisted upon returning with Giles."

For Wilhelm, Seren presumed. "For love?"

"For love," he said, smiling a devastating smile.

Seren turned away again, peering into the firelight, swallowing as she glimpsed Arwyn's face.

Sadly, she was beginning to fear she might never again look into a fire and not remember the Whitshed aflame. It was still so painful to think about.

She swallowed convulsively, taking comfort in the golden-red color of the flame.

"Seren... there is something I should confess..."

Blinking away tears, Seren lifted her gaze to Wilhelm's, loving that her name came so intimately to his lips. "What is it?"

The look in his eyes was so full of ... *something* she couldn't name. Was he finally going to declare his affection for Rosalynde? Did he mean to speak the unspeakable—confess her this... this bond they were forming? But, then, even as she considered that possibility the red in his aura shrank back, giving way to shades of brown and black.

"I feel I must tell you... *everything*."

"What do you mean, *everything*?"

He shrugged. "About what transpired with Rosalynde."

Seren swallowed yet again, preparing herself for the worst. And yet what he disclosed wasn't at all what she'd feared; it was so much worse...

He told her about the battle in the woodlot en route to Neasham—how Mordecai descended from the skies like a demon, shifting shapes, so he was one instant a bird of prey, the next a serpent and, somehow, the next, both.

A shadow beast?

"It was Rose and Giles who defeated it. She spoke words to bind it so my brother could take its head." He lifted a second leg, wrapping both arms about his knees, turning his face so she couldn't see the shame in his eyes. "And me... well, I sat on my arse like a knot on a log, too stupid to do aught but gape. My brother swooped in on his mare—like a delivering angel—smote the beast with his Palatine blade."

Seren sat dumbfounded, uncertain what to say.

Shapeshifting was not a thing *dewines* were inclined to, much less a common man such as Mordecai. "Art certain he *shapeshifted*?"

"Quite. Until your sister spoke those words, he was no more solidly formed than..." He waved a hand in the air. "Mist," he said. "The man was a changeling in the manner of smoke, ebbing and flowing like the wind."

"A shadow beast," she whispered aloud.

There were references to such things in her grandmother's *grimoire*, though only in the manner of stories—no incantations. Cerridwen herself was a *shapeshifter*, but there was a difference between these two types of *magik*. The *shapeshifter* was never insubstantial, not at all like smoke. But only a very, very powerful *dewine* could ever perform shadow *magik*. No proof of it existed in written form so far as she knew. Her grandmamau had said all knowledge of these darker arts—if ever they'd existed—passed away with the fall of Avalon. But then again... she blinked, realizing what more he'd said. "Palatine?"

Wilhelm gave her a meaningful nod. "So it seems... my brother is a Paladin."

Seren gasped aloud, her brows colliding. "A huntsman?"

The Church gave them one name, but, like the king's Rex Militum, they were naught but a company of assassins—executioners for a cause. It so happened that one of their causes was the slaying of witches. From time immemorial the Church had been determined to vanquish all enemies of its doctrine, whether or not they were enemies in truth.

Wilhelm lifted a shoulder, then his hand. "Paladin, huntsman. Aye, whatever name you must give them."

But, nay, it could not be true...

"Do you know who they are, Wilhelm?"

He nodded soberly. "I do."

"And yet you left my sister alone with that man?"

Wilhelm gave her an odd smile. And his explanation in no manner assuaged her. "You mean your betrothed?"

Seren frowned at him.

"Rest easy, m'lady. My brother is no longer at Warkworth, I would presume, but I promise you he would never harm your sister."

"And you? Are you—"

"A Paladin?" He shook his head. "I am but a simple man."

Hardly, Seren thought, but she pinched her blanket together, peering over at Jack, realizing only this instant how much danger she'd placed him in. If only she'd left him in Dover, he would have been safer there.

There simply hadn't been time to inquire after help, and even if she'd had time aplenty, she knew the boy had no one there to give him shelter. And, besides, if she'd raised suspicion for herself, they might all be locked away in a tower—Wilhelm, too, for abetting her, and Jack, as well.

But how would she bear it if Morwen slew them?

"I did not realize *shapeshifting* was possible," she said after a moment. "We are not witches of the sort men so long have conceived, who turn men into toads at will. This is but an old wives' tale, Wilhelm—a tale of the sort mothers tell young children to frighten them into behaving."

"I know," he said gently. "I know. Your sister explained it all to me. I know who you are, Seren." And once again, her name, whispered so gently on his lips, made her heart skip another beat. Only it affected her more deeply this time. It brought a new sting of tears, because there was not only acceptance in his tone, but a note of affection as well. He understood who she was, and still, he cared.

"Remember that day... in the King's Hall... I must confess, I saw only your mother. My heart was so filled with vengeance—how dare Stephen ply my brother with riches and beauty, I thought to myself: How could Giles possibly have any hope to defy you, if in truth your mother would send you to Warkworth as her emissary—this is what I believed. It was only later... once I met you that I realized how fortunate my brother was to have been offered you to wed."

Seren choked on her emotion over his confession. She opened her mouth to speak, but he wasn't through yet. He held a hand up to silence her.

"Alas, men such as I are simply not fit to kiss your feet. We are fortunate to wed at all, much less wed a bride of our choosing." Seren wanted to argue, but she could not. Men of his station were never so fortunate. He was bound to his lord in ways even a simple farmer might not be. If he married at all, he would marry whom his lord decreed, and since he was blood-kin to her betrothed, Giles de Vere would no doubt wish him to marry to strengthen alliances.

But... she was sister to Rosalynde. If, indeed, he was free to wed Rose, he should certainly be free to wed her—*but, nay, Seren. Nay! What are you thinking?*

If Wilhelm was promised to Rosalynde, who was she to turn his heart? She was no wanton, nor was she a siren, luring men to their doom.

So, this was the thing her sisters had so oft teased

her about. Her beauty *was* a curse, because she could, indeed, turn men's hearts with a glance, but if she should ever inspire them to sin against their beloveds... how was she any better than her mother?

And anyway, theirs wasn't true affection, she apprised herself—at least not on Wilhelm's part. If aught, it was lust. And though Seren was beginning to feel something akin to affection for this man, what Wilhelm felt for Rose was bound to be more sincere.

Sweet fates. At the moment, she wished so much she could be as ugly as Morfran, because then, folks might love her for her soul, or not at all. They would not tempt her with glances like the one Wilhelm was tempting her with now... as though he could, in truth, be fond of her.

Groaning inwardly, she averted her gaze, and she was thankful when he changed the subject entirely. "I must confess, I fear for that boy," he said. "I worry for you, as well, but if you can do half of what your sister can do..." There was a note of admiration in his tone. "Well... let us say you might be saving me. Jack, however..."

The very implication tightened her shoulders. "Oh, nay! We couldn't leave him."

"Not here," Wilhelm agreed. "I meant Neasham. The sisters there are kind and they would keep him safe until such time as we can arrange for his return to Calais."

Seren lifted a thumbnail to her lips, nipping at it. "Neasham?"

"Aye." He nodded. "Your sister saw to it they would be forever in our debt."

Our debt, he'd said.

And he'd smiled yet again, very fondly, at mention of Rosalynde. Much as it pained her, Seren resigned herself to their love, even as she found new cause to fear her own fate. How could she wed a member of the Palatine Guard? Those murderers were tasked with the execution of her grandmamau. Only how, in the name of the Goddess had her sister found it in her heart to accompany that odious man anywhere once she'd learned the truth?

Giles was a Paladin?

A Paladin!

"Seren," Wilhelm entreated again, perhaps thinking her reticent. "If, indeed, the boy saw one of your mother's ravens, I'd not put him at risk any more than we must. After what I have witnessed, I fear for the lad. He would be much safer at Neasham. Without you, he would be of no concern to your mother."

It was impossible to argue. He was right. Jack was in far more danger traveling with them. And though she thanked Wilhelm for not mentioning the fact, she knew very well that the journey would be quicker as well. So much as she would love to linger in perpetuity with Wilhelm, she knew it was folly. He was not hers, and he would never be hers. But, in truth, her mother would kill them all if she found them, and how would Seren feel, if she were responsible for the deaths of both Wilhelm and the boy?

She peered once more at Jack, sleeping so peacefully, weary from travel, then nodded. "Very well."

"We are agreed, then?"

"Aye," she said. "We are agreed. We will leave him at Neasham."

As for her heart, she apprised herself, she should abandon that as well. It would serve no one at all if she pined for this man, and neither could she encourage his attention. Until they arrived at Warkworth, she must harden her heart.

21

"Man's mind is so formed ...
it is more susceptible
to falsehood than truth."
— *Erasmus*

Patchwork stone, blackened by age, ravaged by the elements, the very sight of Aldergh fills me with boundless rage.

Simply for your part in the killing of my birds, someday I will turn you stone by stone, until naught remains but rubble and ash.

Even now, Elspeth's warding spell weaves boundary lines upon the *aether*, leaving me at the mercy of her gatekeepers, and nevertheless, if they wonder why their mistress returned, riding a stranger's horse, they do not presume to ask. On sight, they raise the portcullis, but then, when, at last, the gate is open wide, I still cannot pass. Such is the nature of *magik*. I cannot not enter this place until I am bidden to do so—a small matter, to be sure.

I lift a hand to my brow as though to swoon.

"M'lady, art unwell?"

I do not answer. I waver a bit in the saddle.

"Go! Hurry! Get Cora!" the man shouts, and he disappears from the ramparts, scrambling down to the aid of his mistress. It comes as little surprise to me when he appears by my side.

"I am but weary," I say in the sweetest of voices. "I rode all night long."

"M'lady," he says gravely. "My Lord Aldergh will be vexed. "Come," he demands, as he steals the reins from my hands to lead my horse within. "At once, we will send word to Carlisle."

"Nay," I say. "Please, do not."

I scarce can hide my joy. Aldergh's lord is not in residence—but of course, he would never allow my daughter to travel without his protection. My sojourn here will go all the easier, and, with the lord and lady both absent, the courtyard is uncannily quiet, though the instant I enter, an elder woman flies out to greet me. "M'lady," she shouts. "I had no inkling ye'd be returning so soon. Fie on ye," she exclaims. "You're e'en more stubborn than my daughters."

"Don't worry, Cora; I am fine," I say, realizing this must be the woman Aldergh's guard sought to bring to my aid. "I merely forgot... *something*."

The elder woman gives me a toothy grin, one that feels entirely too familiar, and her voice softens when she speaks. "I ken what ye forgot," she says coyly, and it is all I can do not to slap the impudent smirk from her face.

I force a smile and a singsong tone. "Do you?"

"Aye, m'lady," she says. "But dinna fash yourself. I've spoilt them good and well."

She's a Scotswoman, I presume, perhaps long gone from her motherland. Her accent is soft, only with but a hint of English.

"Spoilt?" I ask.

The Scotswoman laughs softly. "Aye," she says. "Well, ye ken how they be. I canna hold one without rousing the other, so, then, I've had Ellyn help me when she can."

"Sweet, sweet Ellyn," I say, and I wonder what in the name of the cauldron this woman is prattling about—babies? *Could it be, babies? Why didn't I know?*

"I thought for certes I would have them all to my-self for at least another fortnight yet," she says. "But I should ha'e known." She waggled a finger, smiling still. "I should ha'e known."

Yes, of course, it *must* be babies, and tis no surprise my eldest bore her husband twins. They are a curse to my blood. I myself suffered more than one, and judging by the manner in which I have been treated, I should have murdered them all before they took their first breaths. I laugh softly, reaching out to grab the lady's arm for support as I dismount.

At once, a groomsman moves forward to take my horse to the stables. "Saddle a fresh one for me, please," I command. And then I turn to Cora to say, "I should see them at once."

I know this is what my daughter would wish, and I would give this wench no reason to see through my *glamour*. Fortunately, mine is more powerful than most. But this woman is entirely too familiar, threading her arm through mine, and I am outraged by how far my eldest has fallen—consorting with her servants. The woman prattles on and on and on, leading me inside, telling me about kitchens and rushes and servants and suppers. I conceal a yawn, following along. And when she turns to tilt me a questioning glance, I say, "I am so sorry, Cora. I am but weary."

"Ah, well, dinna fash yourself, Mistress. Only tell me how I may serve you."

"Well, there is something I must retrieve, and then I must return to Warkworth. If you will do me any favors it is only to keep this news from my husband."

I brace myself for questions. As familiar as this woman appears, I fear she will ask me what is so crucial that I would return and leave with such haste. But she does not, and I am relieved. "Very well," she says. "But I must say, my lord Malcom will hear of this, no doubt. You should take another retinue when you go, or I vow he'll return in a rage."

"Nay," I say, firmly. "We need all the men we can keep. Aldergh's garrison is too lean as it is."

"M'lady," she protests. "I—"

"I will travel more swiftly alone."

"But—"

"But naught," I say. "I am here in one piece, can't you see. You mustn't worry for me, Cora. I have my ways, as you know." I wink then, when she looks at me, and her smile returns.

"Ah, yay, m'lady. Very well. Only please, will you sup before you go?"

"Perhaps," I tell her. "But I have vittles in my pack, and I prefer not to travel by night."

"Very well," she says with a sigh, and the pout in her voice reminds me of my long-dead mother—Morgan, whose incessant needling ever drove me to distraction.

At least, she harried me until she learned who I am—*not her daughter.*

Morgan, do you see me now?

Are you turning in your grave?

But nay, I think, with a slow grin. *There is naught of you left but ashes, all scattered to the winds.*

"Cora," I say. "I hope you do not mind, but I prefer to see to the babes on my own. Also if you, please, apprise the cook to provide me a treat for the saddle."

"Oh," she says, sounding dismayed. "Yay, of course. I'll see to it at once, m'lady." And she leaves me standing at the foot of Aldergh's stairwell, relieved that she is gone.

I do not know this castle, nor its occupants, but I should take care in that lady's presence. It is not the way of *magik* to know everything, for I must know a question before the *aether* provides an answer. But I do not need Cora to guide me; given time alone, I will sniff out my reliquary. It calls to me, even now.

Babies, I think, as I climb.

Twins.

My, oh my.

⌣

THE VELLUM'S surface shifted beneath Rosalynde's fingertips, as though resisting with musculature. It was like a willful creature, bent upon making its point, every so oft turning pages of its own accord. It did so once again, settling once more on a page scribbled heavily with notes.

"I cannot read if you keep turning those pages," complained Elspeth.

"I am not turning pages," argued Rosalynde. "I do believe *it* means for us to read this page."

"It?" Elspeth asked, lifting a brow.

"I don't know. 'Tis the Goddess, I suppose. How

can I know? I only know I am not the one turning the pages, and it always returns to this one."

Showing Elspeth the page in question, she splayed the book as wide as it would go, and urged Elspeth to peer over her shoulder. The entry was titled: The Duality of *Witchwater* With Arcane Properties.

So, it appeared, you could, indeed, simulate elemental *witchwater*. It could be created with the help of certain mushrooms, and there were a number of rare forms conducive to the transformation. And therefore, they could, indeed, finish the *motte* and fill it with *witchwater*, only not the form of *witchwater* that was summoned from the *aether*. Rather, transformed *witchwater* had somewhat different properties. Instead of calling upon arcane forces, the transformed water was like a strange brew to be used for transmutation. For example, if a priest fell into a mixture, he might become a bandit. Or, if a stone fell into it, it could become a fish. However, if created in just such a manner, the results could be milder. For example, those who waded into the *motte* might simply become confused and forget themselves, so they forgot they were even fighting a battle. But, this brew was impossible to make as it was, because it called for items Rosalynde had never heard of before—like the scales of a fish called a *gwyniad*, which was said to be native to the waters of Avalon.

Well, Avalon was long gone, so how was she supposed to acquire this *gwyniad*? Or, barring the use of *gwyniad,* she could use something called a "puffer fish." But then, they would need finely crushed moon dust—and where by the love of night was she going to find moon dust? Also, to her complete horror, it called for a measure of human remains.

"What is this?" asked Elspeth, inquiring over a short verse that was scribbled sideways on the page—not in Morwen's writing, and probably not their grandmother's either. Bewitched and spellbound, this particular tome had been in existence for at least a thousand years.

"Only true love's tears will save the newborn prophet," Rosalynde read. "What do you suppose it means?"

Elspeth furrowed her brow. "How are we to know? Not even grandmamau allowed me to read the book without supervision. She claimed the words written therein were too dangerous. Misinterpreted they could lead to unintended consequences."

"Unintended consequences?"

Elspeth nodded. "She would not say precisely what or how or why, but I suspect our mother was transfigured by something within that book."

She tugged the book out of Rosalynde's hands and into her own lap, turning to another page. And, once again, like it had more than half a dozen times before, the *grimoire* quivered, and the page returned to The Duality of *Witchwater* With Arcane Properties.

"I cannot help but think this book somehow wishes for us to glean something new from this page, because it cannot be the transmutation of *witchwater*. Avalon does not exist, and who in this world has ever seen a moon rock to crush into dust?"

"Indeed," said Elspeth. "And what is a puffer fish?"

The words on the page seemed to ripple then glow, and Elspeth was compelled to reread the words: "Only true love's tears will save the newborn prophet." She shook her head, confused. "I cannot fathom what it means, but... somehow... I feel... moved by these words."

"Moved?"

Elspeth frowned. "Yay," she said. "Almost as though there is something I should do... or something I should know."

22

Well-rested and bathed after a night at Neasham, Seren nevertheless left the abbey in a pique. Wilhelm hadn't lied to her, not precisely, but she was vexed that he had disdained to reveal the entire truth: He was *not* affianced to her sister. And furthermore, Rosalynde was already wed to Giles de Vere—none other than her own betrothed!

Of course, it was no secret at all that Seren didn't actually wish to wed Giles. He was not the man she pined for. And even so, Wilhelm had led her to believe that his brother meant to honor their betrothal, and that he, as a matter of due course, was honor-bound to return her to Giles—all this time he'd perpetrated a lie.

Never had she felt so muddled—relieved one moment, infuriated the other. And despite everything, she should be pleased beyond measure, because, now, she wouldn't have to wed Giles. And truly, aside from Wilhelm's lie, at the instant, there was little she should find to complain about, considering the circumstances: She was still breathing. Her belly was full. Jack was safe. She was clean and no longer dressed in foul smelling clothes. And, according to the nuns at

Neasham, her sister was happily wed to the lord of Warkworth.

There was more they had to say, of course, and though none of it was particularly unpleasant, it made Seren long to pull out every strand of Wilhelm's beautiful hair—and aye, it was beautiful. Long and thick, it shone like ebony silk. If she were a cruel sort of *witch* of the sort folks gossipmongers like to fie on, she might give his horse a fright, then watch him tumble to the ground, muddying his clothes and hair. But she was not, and neither would she treat an animal so cruelly. But so far as Wilhelm was concerned—a pox on him!

And, by the by, the next time he considered eating a poisonous mushroom, she should let him. It would serve the deceiver right to spend every waking moment moaning and groaning on a pot.

Fie on him!

She muttered crossly beneath her breath, her appetite soured, despite that the sisters at Neasham had loaded their satchels with victuals aplenty for the journey. She settled a hand beneath her breast, grimacing over a burn in her breast.

"Art unwell, Seren?"

He'd said it with such concern that her anger wilted, if only slightly. She lifted a brow, and slid him a furious glance, then quickly averted her gaze, discomfited by her anger. "I am well," she said. "Never better," she lied.

How could she be? One sister was dead, the other imprisoned in Wales. Elspeth was wed to a stranger, and now she'd learned—not from Wilhelm, mind you, but from strangers—that Rosalynde was married as well, and to none other than a huntsman for the Church.

"You don't seem well," he said.

"Oh, but I am," she snapped. But, truly, she couldn't restrain herself any longer. "Why did you not advise me my sister was lady of Warkworth? I had to hear it from strangers."

Never mind the fact that for all intents and purposes, Wilhelm was a stranger, too. It was only that, after traveling so long in his company, Seren feared he must know enough about her now to never want her for himself. Whatever beauty she possessed could never vie with all her many faults. Ever since leaving Dover, he'd seen her at her worst—hair disheveled, sleep-dust forming in the corners of her eyes. And, to make matters worse, to her utter mortification, he'd listened to her relieve herself on occasion, and then whilst they were still at Neasham, he'd accidentally walked into her bath, only to fly away the instant he saw her.

He did not stand there, gawking at her with a flame of longing burning in his eyes, nor did he linger in the doorway. He'd turned and *fled*—as though she were a viper he'd discovered coiled amidst the dust beneath his bed.

It was mortifying. Seren only wanted to be clean so she could wear one of the lovely dresses he'd procured for her. She longed desperately for him to look at her again as he had that night before arriving at Neasham, despite that, considering the circumstances, appealing to a lowborn bastard was the last thing that should be on her mind.

For Creirwy's sake, her sister was dead—or had she forgotten so easily?

But nay, she had not.

It was just that... Wilhelm made her feel... what? *Not so lonely? Admired? Cherished?*

All these things and more.

And nevertheless, he was *not* courting her, she had to remind herself much too frequently. He was only escorting her to her sister—not even to Giles.

And still, though she longed desperately to take offense over his motives, not once during the long hours they'd spent together had he once behaved inappropriately. Unlike most of the lords she'd encountered at court, Wilhelm Fitz Richard had treated her with utmost respect—and, no, it wasn't as though she wanted him to kiss her. She only wanted him to want to. It was all so confusing.

Winding the excess length of reins in her hand, she gave him another narrow-eyed glance.

Wilhelm had the good graces to look away, and she watched as his aura shifted from red to brown—good, then, let him be discomfited. For certes, she herself had never felt more a fool, and she could not say it was all his fault, because she was the one who'd tormented herself with thoughts of a man she could never have.

And, lo, now that she realized it was perfectly possible all along—that he wasn't betrothed to her sister —mayhap she shouldn't want him, but she did. But clearly, he didn't want her, and it was becoming quite apparent that the red in his aura was not desire at all; it was something else.

Finally, he turned to look at her, his lips twisted ruefully. "Take it as you will, Lady Seren; I did not believe you would agree to accompany me if I did not say it was to return you to your betrothed."

Fie! So now he would return to formalities? *Lady Seren, Lady Seren, Lady Seren!* For the love of night, she was no more a lady than he was a lord. "And yet you might have told me it was my sister who'd commanded you to find me—she's your mistress, after all."

He lifted a shoulder. "So to speak."

"So to speak," Seren railed, feeling her *witchwind* rising yet again with her anger. "So to speak!"

The tops of the trees shimmied with fright, and the poplar leaves tinkled like warning bells.

"You speak in riddles, Wilhelm de Vere. If Rosalynde is not your mistress, then say so. If she is, speak true."

His voice was taut. "I am not de Vere," he corrected. "I am Fitz—"

"Richard, yay, I know. What does it matter? Amidst my own *dewinefolk*, we are kindred no matter whether we are conceived in the rushes or in a fine-feathered bed."

He said naught.

"I do not understand your English sensibilities."

His cheeks were flushed. "I am sorry," he said, and then he hung his head, looking too much like a sweet young boy, save that there was nothing so small about him, nor could she mistake him for a boy.

Furiously, Seren coiled the reins tighter, trying desperately to master her emotions.

This was all too much.

For months now she'd been fleeing her mother's wrath—all to no avail, because her sweet sister was dead. She had allowed herself to trust this man. And that was not all. Yay, it was true; she must confess it all: Her heart fluttered each and every time Wilhelm came near enough for her to smell his male scent. All it ever took to make her nipples taut was to hear him speak her name so intimately. For Creirwy's bloody sake, she was like a lute to be played at his whim—an instrument of desire that remained finely in tune to his every sigh. It was disgusting. Maddening. Embarrassing.

"Seren," he said, the timbre of his voice low and husky, and once again, it spoke to some secret part of her she had never even known existed.

"Fie on you, Wilhelm! I'd not hear you speak my name ever again," she said irrationally.

He grumbled, then asked, "What would you have me call you?"

In truth, Seren didn't know. She might be daughter to a long-dead king, but she was no more high-born than Wilhelm was, even despite having been appointed a title. She couldn't bring herself to ask him to address her as a lady, because she most certainly wasn't a lady. And regardless, her true kinsmen had no need for such formalities. She was Seren to those who knew her best, and Seren to those who knew her least. And even so, she did not wish to hear Wilhelm speak that name again so intimately... as though in itself the word could be a caress.

Fie on him.

Fie on Giles.

Fie on her mother.

Fie on Rose, too! Though why Rosalynde, Seren didn't precisely know. Her poor sister had had naught at all to do with any of this. If Rosalynde was guilty of anything at all it was only that she hadn't insisted this stiff-necked behemoth reveal the entire truth to her the minute he met her.

And nevertheless, knowing Rosalynde, her sister would never have suggested he lie—she would no more have done so than she would have... what?

Lain with another woman's betrothed?

Ye gods, Seren was so confused.

"I am sorry," he offered again, and then he left her to ruminate in silence and rage.

.   .   .

Sensing her witchy wind rise again, Wilhelm fell silent.

God's truth, when most women got in a temper, they roused an altogether different sort of tempest. When Seren Pendragon grew angry, she bestirred a wind that shook the very tree-tops. It was unsettling to say the least.

And still, he couldn't say for certes whether she even realized what it was she was doing. Watching her expression as she surveyed the shivering woods, he could easily believe she was as startled by the revelation as he.

She peered at him through long, thick lashes, lowering her gaze so that her lashes fanned her rosy cheeks, but not before he spotted the torment stirring in those beautiful, stormy eyes. It made him long to put his arms about her and offer solace, though it was quite clear to him she would never accept it—least ways, not right now.

Thereafter, three things occurred to Wilhelm all at once: the first, no matter how vexed Seren might be with him, she was somehow more embarrassed by her tantrum and the tempest it roused—which gave rise to the second revelation; two, she wasn't particularly savvy about *magik*, because it seemed to him that she was as clueless as he was about the power she wielded; and three, she was sorely affronted by him and the choices he'd made. If he dared speak another word to her in her present mood, she would raise a storm that would rip out the trees by their roots. Therefore, he fell silent, giving her all the time and space she needed. But, in truth, he felt sick to his gut over the mood his actions engendered, and even so, if her anger gave her the strength to endure, he would endeavor to take comfort in that, because, even now, he felt a persistent sense of danger... a *knowing* in his gut that had little to do with her mood, nor even the threat of her witchy wind.

It was more like a shadow of doom.

Bones of the saints, not even her sister could tug at his heartstrings the way Seren did. Whereas Rosalynde was as fierce as a lion, Seren's demeanor was gentler. He could see she was disarmed by her own anger—no doubt for more reasons than for its physical manifestation. She was a kind soul, not unlike Lady Ayleth, but unlike Lady Ayleth, he sensed in her a spirit and devotion that rivaled her sister's.

She hid her passions well; he would give her that —which only made him wonder... *would she be equally passionate between the sheets?*

To his utter disgust, his cock hardened over that thought, and he let fly a string of oaths. In her presence, he was naught but a beardless youth, with so little mastery over his manhood that a good, stiff wind could rouse him hard as stone. And it didn't help matters very much that after spying her at her bath, he now had a vision of her to burn over—skin so pale and perfect it appeared translucent, hair so rich and coppery it illumined her skin like the soft glow of a warm fire, eyes as silver and sparkling as the water she lay in.

Admittedly, he hadn't seen very much of her, but he'd seen quite enough—those pale, perfect moons rising above the glittering water, the darker tips of her areolas tempting him just beneath the surface, like a siren singing her song beneath the waves.

For certes, Seren was a Siren, and his physical response to her was instantaneous and incontrovertible. He'd fled her presence before he could unman himself.

God have mercy, even now, he was wholly undone by the memory, and despite that they remained in danger, he wished to God she were his wife so he could coax her down from that mount and find some secluded spot to rut together like mindless beasts.

Perhaps he could rouse in her a different sort of passion...

He might not be a rich man, nor even entirely couth, but he was born with a talent for pleasing women. For all that he'd pined for the untouchable Lady Ayleth, he'd never actually burned for her in his bed. He hadn't had much need to burn. No matter how wide a berth he gave temptation, there were many a morn he'd awakened to a sweet mouth pulling his cock, or a warm, wet flower opening to greet him.

And yet... with Seren—he looked at her now, tugging at her reins with a vengeance—it was different.

It wasn't a rutting he yearned for... he wanted to show her what mysteries her body concealed. He wanted to know the taste of her mouth, and drink of her sweet flower until he was drunk with desire... until his cock throbbed so hard that his eyes rolled back in his head.

He could well imagine her nipples pebbling beneath his palm, and he longed to slip his tongue between her ripe lips, and elicit moans from her that would silence the world.

Even now, as he watched her hips sway in time with the horse's canter, he could imagine her nude and riding him with abandon—her lithe body undulating and her glorious mane unbound and tickling her soft, beautiful breasts.

God help him. From the moment he awoke, it was all he could think about, even as her *witchy* wind roused, and he wished to God in heaven above that he didn't feel so concerned about leaving her alone, because they would both be better served if he could find himself five minutes alone so he could strangle his cock.

How the hell was he going to keep her safe if he couldn't stop thinking about the beast in his breeches?

Growling with dissatisfaction, Wilhelm surreptitiously adjusted himself so that the horse's gait wouldn't offer more pain.

In retrospect, he should have told her everything. From the very beginning, he should have sat her down and explained all he knew. And still, in his defense, he'd had more than a few confusing feelings of his own to muddle through—for one, she represented everything Wilhelm could never have, and yet she was everything he could ever want.

And then there was this: He hadn't appreciated the shrewish tone of her voice, nor her lack of enthusiasm for his aid. He'd traveled a long, long way to help her, and he was risking life and limb, even now. If they should happen to encounter another Shadow Beast, there was little he could do to save them, and he would die with certain regrets.

And, so much as he loathed the events that transpired before his arrival, it also wasn't his fault her sister was dead, nor had he wished to embroil himself in her family's troubles. They had enough troubles at Warkworth, and he'd been dragged into this kicking and screaming, because why in damnation should he agree to aid the daughter of the very woman who murdered his kinsmen?

Aye, despite knowing it wasn't Seren's fault, it took Wilhelm time to reconcile that fact—not to mention that she'd saddled him with another poor soul to see to, and despite all Wilhelm's objections, he'd come to care for Jack—well enough to part with yet another gold mark for the boy's care, and the horse as well.

The sisters at Neasham were pleased enough to take his coin and his horse, and so much as he'd believed they would remember his generosity and refuse any more gold, they took everything he offered, and more. And, then, after taking his hard-earned coin, they'd gone and filled Seren's ears with tittle-tattle.

They ought to add that to their tombstones: Servants of God, celebrated seamstresses and gossipmongers. Every last one. And particularly Mother Helewys, who'd filled his own ears with whispers about Giles and Rosalynde—whispers he ought never have heard.

Evidently, the abbess didn't condone bathing. She'd bent his ears for over an hour over that sin. And then, Wilhelm made the mistake of revealing that Rosalynde and Seren were sisters, and once revealed, Mother Helewys had rebuked him, telling him to never darken her doors again with Morwen's offspring. Not that she didn't believe Seren a perfectly lovely young woman, she'd said. She simply didn't wish to court trouble, and trouble was all the Pendragons ever wrought.

For his own part, he couldn't disagree. He had his own demons to excise over that, but now that he'd gotten to know both Seren and Rosalynde, he presumed her other sisters should be as sweet and lovely as they were. They but had the grave misfortune of sharing Morwen's blood—and consequently, it was a good thing Mother Helewys didn't ask him to negate the rumors of sorcery, because Wilhelm was a poor liar. He wouldn't have been able to gainsay them, and, if that be the case, they would have put Jack out on his ear. As it was, he'd promised to retrieve the boy the instant he could, because they didn't wish to involve themselves in *politikal* intrigue.

Hoping against hope that Seren's mood would improve, Wilhelm amused himself with his own thoughts, never for one instant taking his eyes off the skies. Now that the nuns were privy to Seren's identity, it was but a matter of time before word spread to Stephen. He only hoped that, if Giles hadn't already found a way to disclose his recent nuptials to the king, he would be gone from London before the truth was revealed.

23

Avarice, envy, pride,
Three fatal sparks,
have set the hearts of all
On fire.
—*Dante Alighieri*

When thy father went a-hunting,
A spear on his shoulder, a club in his
    hand,
He called the nimble hounds,
'Giff, Gaff; catch, catch, fetch, fetch!'

Of course, as you must suspect, I have every intention of laying hands upon my grand-babes. I will bequeath them a gift—a lovely spell that will, in time, break their mother's heart, as she broke mine.

Or perhaps I should bind them—but nay, Elspeth would be relieved by this. She has never been at one with the Goddess.

So perhaps I should poison them in their cribs? That way, when she returns, she will find her sweet babes blue as the sea under which I was imprisoned— I search my cloak to be sure I have my herbs.

But, nay, killing them too swiftly would be boring. Elspeth would mourn them, never realizing her own mother had deprived her.

Nay, I decide. Better to curse them in their fortunes so she will weep blood tears for all their suffering. Even as I meant to bless Morfran, I will plague them.

Diverting myself with all the amusing possibilities, I seek my reliquary, allowing my senses to guide me. At long, long last, I am led to a women's solar, and here I am startled to find a small cauldron in the hearth.

"Elspeth," I exclaim, delighted. But of course, you would embrace your *dewinity* now that you've had a small taste.

I inhale the scent of her *spellcasting*. Power is, after all, an aphrodisiac. It weaves itself into your veins and then thrums into your heart, like a sweet but savage song.

I laugh to myself, endlessly amused.

Would that my daughter could know what I know...would that she could see the kingdom she has forsworn. Someday, before she closes her eyes in mortal slumber, I should show her all that she has forsaken.

The reliquary is near. I follow its scent—stronger and stronger nearer the floorboards, so I sink to my knees and crawl like a hound, sniffing along the old wood. Muscles taut with anticipation, I inhale deeply, exhilarated, because I sense that wherever my reliquary lies, there, too, I will find my *grimoire*.

Knocking on the floor, I discover a hollow where

the scent reeks strongest. Growling, I sink my nails into the grooves and pluck up the boards revealing a small compartment beneath, and here I discover the reliquary.

But not the *grimoire.*

My stomach plummets. My face contorts. *My Book isn't here.* There lies only a makeshift *grimoire* my daughters created in their ignorance. *Pah!*

It is all I can do not to lift it up and rip it to shreds, worthless as it must be. Anger, deep and dark roils from the depths of me.

How dare you defy me, daughter!

How dare you keep me from my Book of Books.

Calm yourself, I demand.

Calm yourself.

Could it be that Rosalynde took the *grimoire* with her? Nay, I cannot believe she would. Why would she carry the tome so far north, only to keep it?

Unless Elspeth did not, in truth, embrace the Craft? And in that case, perhaps she sent her sister away with the *grimoire* in hand? But nay...

My gaze travels across the room... to the hearth, where the cauldron sits, and I scowl as I pluck up the reliquary, grateful for its return. I pick up the book, and steal it to the hearth.

Inside the cauldron, I find traces of herbs. Rose petals for love... white sage for purification... amaranth for protection... asafetida to drive away demons —I laugh—byrony to amplify the strength of her brew. And there, too, I smell bits of copper, agate, malachite and amber, each to summon a guardian angel.

But that will not work, Elspeth.

Where *magik* dwells, angels do not—least ways,

not the sort you might think. *I am* the angel you would call. The Sylphkind are all eternal beings, bowing only to the Mother. All other gods are gods unto themselves. Angels, devils... we are all one, if only distinguished by the shade of our souls. Mine, as we have already determined... is black.

Rage is the color of my wings.

A glance down at the wood kindles a fire as I flip through the pages of my daughters' *grimoire*, finding the most detestably ordinary spells and concoctions.

Boring.

Drivel.

Waste.

I hurl the book into the flames, watching it burn only a moment before abandoning the solar to seek my grandchildren. They aren't difficult to find... Soft coos lead me to a room one flight up. The nursery is attached to the master's chamber, with whitewashed stone walls and pale-blue billowing drapes surrounding a lovely, ornate cradle.

Here, I discover the children... one asleep beneath sprigs of betony bound with rowan vines... the other peers up at me with those luminous eyes—eyes the color of Emry's.

Boys, I realize, and gasp in wonder. *Twins.* But not merely twins...

They are both painfully beautiful, but the fairest has a countenance the image of Taliesin's. His eyes are the changeable shade of cats-eye stones—a druid prince. Skin like pearls; nose, aquiline, like a Roman's; lips rosy as plums; brows tipped with hair so fair it could have been fine-spun gold silk. *A druid prince.*

The knowledge is both spine-chilling and glorious.

Born again... a prophet, a bard, a Merlin. He, who was promised... a shining torch to ward away darkness. Six hundred years Taliesin has been gone, his bright soul loosed about the world, like a butterfly without a perch.

The boy blinks, his beautiful lips curling into a smile, his fine-spun lashes brushing his soft, rose-petal cheeks, and he gives me a coo...

I cannot stop myself. I yearn to hold him. Beauty beguiles me. I long for the scent of his warm baby skin beneath my nostrils and I lift him up from the blanket's folds, careful not to wake the rufous-haired child. *A druid!* I marvel. A goddess-blessed druid, after so long. Emrys was the last, and before him... not since Taliesin. But this babe has something more than Emrys possessed... he has the soul of a Sylph shining from his eyes... pure and true. He will beguile when he speaks. He will command gods. He will...

"M'lady," intrudes a young maid, and I am enraged. Holding the child near to my breast, I spin about, forgetting my *glamour* and raising a hand to strike her down.

And, then... I stop myself, realizing she could prove useful. I will not return here, I know, for a trick of this sort can only be played once, and yet I will have need of eyes inside this demesne. Restraining myself, I soften my glance... such a pretty thing, with pale flaxen hair, a pert little nose and eyes as blue as my Elspeth's.

The young woman hesitates, clearly unsettled. Could it be she glimpsed my true self behind my *glamour*?

Or mayhap she simply despairs to see the look of fury on her mistresses' face.

I smile.

"M-my m-mother sent me to help," she says.

I crook a finger to summon her within. "Thank you, sweetling. Please, come in."

It does not matter if she suspects me now because my charm weaves its *magik* between us. Even against her will, she glides toward me, and I can smell her fear as I place my hand upon her arm, sliding it up, along the path of her dainty shoulder, and finally placing a finger beneath her sweet chin. I dig my nail into her virgin's flesh. "What is your name, my dear?"

"Ellyn."

"Ellyn," I whisper softly. "I weave the chains that hold you now, and to my will you shall bow." I lift a finger to touch her upon the brow, and say softly, "I need—" Completely at a loss, I wave a hand over the babe. "Whatever it is that babes must need. Fetch it down to the stables."

Fear has left her now. "Yay, mistress. Will you take both bairns?"

"Bairns?" I say, amused by her dialect. "Nay, I think not. I need only one—this one," I say. "What is his name?"

"Broc," she says, and tilts her head to inquire, "Shall I join you, mistress?"

"Oh, no... not today," I say. "I need you here, my pet." I turn with the child in my arms. "But, please, fret not. I will summon you before long, and in the meantime, please see my horse is prepared to ride."

"Yay, mistress," she says, and hurries to do my bidding.

"Oh, Ellyn..." She turns. "Please, do not speak of this to your mother."

"Yay, mistress, of course," she says, and I smile, holding my prize closer as she leaves.

"When thy father went a-hunting," I croon to the

child. "A spear on his shoulder, a club in his hand, He called the nimble hounds, 'Giff, Gaff; catch, catch, fetch, fetch!'" And I bounce the child, and laugh, and say again, "Giff, Gaff; catch, catch, fetch, fetch!"

24

The woods were tangled with undergrowth. Brambles strangled young saplings, lifting shoots to seek more prey. Pale green and concealing claws, they snagged at the length of Wilhelm's trews, nipped the hem of Seren's gown. Bendy and willful, vines clawed at the legs of their mounts, and on occasion finding purchase and drawing nicks of blood.

Wilhelm had never seen it so wild—overgrown and cruel with the will to prevail.

With nary a word of complaint, Seren endured the aggravation. He knew she must be relieved to be nearing the end of their journey and a heartfelt reunion with her sister.

The coursers, on the other hand, continued to complain, snorting and huffing in protest over the assault on their flesh, prancing with legs too high and stumbling over uneven ground. It was as though the path before them would impede their travels, driving them back to the road.

"Tis overgrown," Wilhelm grumbled, moving ahead and slashing at a thickening vines with his sword. "It must have rained aplenty since I left." But that in itself would be nothing new. Even during the driest of months they had plenty of rain in the north. Never in all his days had he ever encountered a forest so greedy and wild. It gave him a shiver at the back of his nape—not unlike that feeling he'd had on the morning he'd discovered Warkworth in ruins.

But, of course, it could simply be due the fact that he'd been so long traveling already—months if you counted the many weeks before discovering Seren in Dover. He'd been traveling so long, in truth, that at this point he hadn't the first inkling what was going on in London, nor even at Warkworth, and for all he knew, his brother could be locked away in a tower for treason. *Wasn't that what happened to men who forswore contracts with the king?*

He bloody well hoped Giles hadn't followed his hot-headed advice. It would serve no one at all for him to speak his true heart. But if he did, he hoped to God that Rosalynde would be prepared for the conse-quences. As it was, Wilhelm half anticipated returning to discover the castle under siege. It was the order of the day, so it seemed. Stephen was ever besieging one castle or another in pursuit of Matilda.

At the moment it was sunny, but while Seren's mood had vastly improved, Wilhelm's had taken a turn for the worst—mostly, because he realized that the very instant she was reunited with Rose, he was bound to be forgotten. For that alone he was glad to be traveling slower.

Taking a moment to calculate the distance, he reckoned that from Dover to Neasham it was a good ninety leagues, or more. From London to Neasham about seventy. From Neasham to Warkworth perhaps no more than twenty—a good two days' journey, little more, even with the overgrown brush. However, reluc-tance wasn't the only reason for his decision to avoid

the North Road. While it might have been easier traveling on the old Roman road, it was also well-traveled.
To make matters worse—at least for their purposes—
the entire thoroughfare, from London to Edinburgh,
was cleared of trees for a good ten to twenty meters on
either side of the road—a measure instituted by King
Henry as a defense against brigands. It only made
sense for the shires to keep it, though, at the instant, it
would be safer for Seren if they remained hidden.

Hacking at another thick vine, he cast her a glance,
wondering how she felt about Rosalynde and Giles.
Clearly, she'd been furious with him for keeping the
truth from her, but despite having said she would repudiate Giles, was she perhaps disappointed not to be
wedding an Earl? What woman wouldn't like to be
mistress of a great house?

Seren herself deserved to be lavished with riches
—riches Wilhelm could never afford.

Alas, that hadn't mattered when he'd passed that
dressmaker's booth in the market in Dover. He took
primal joy in the way she looked right now, in part because he had bought her that dress—blue camlet with
a matching ribbon. The soft material had caught his
eye, because it was only slightly bluer than the pale
color of her eyes. Unadorned though it might be, the
cloth, made from fine camel's wool, was imported
from the East. Soft as silk, the nap was tightly shorn to
give it a soft feel. Time and again, he sidled up beside
her, longing to reach out and snatch a feel of her
sleeve. Like her beautiful, radiant skin, he imagined it
to be soft to the touch... but if he breached that barrier
between them, he might regret it, and regret, alas, was
the concern of the day. But at least he needn't worry
whether Giles would regret repudiating Seren, not
when he loved her sister so deeply. The man was be-

sotted—as besotted as Wilhelm must be, although, once again, without reciprocation.

How could Seren possibly want him? He could offer the lady nothing. He was a soldier indebted to his brother, and he didn't even have a proper bower. He slept with the men-at-arms. So, then, what should he do? Bring her into his barracks and make love to her on a pallet in the company of an army of drooling *eegits*?

Nay.

But if only he had some future to share... *something.*

Wilhelm wasn't learned like Giles, but neither was he stupid. He sensed Seren held some affection for him, and he might better know what to do with that intuition if she were not so far removed from his station.

He sighed despondently, for no matter that he had a close relationship with his lord brother, he'd never dare ask for more than his father had been willing to give. The castle was as yet incomplete, but it didn't matter how grand it was supposed to be; there had never been a place for Wilhelm under its roof. In good time, he'd hoped to build himself a cottage, and mayhap keep a wife there, but even that was less than appealing. What was he going to do? Sleep apart from his bride in order to lead his brother's garrison? Slumber with his family and come running at the call of a horn? Watch his home burn from the ramparts if Eustace should happen to return?

Nay.

The thought alone was enough to put a viper's nest in his gut. Swinging his sword with a vengeance, he severed a thick, gnarly bramble, wondering if they should return to the road.

The deeper they traversed into the woods, the thicker the vines grew. And anyway, he did hope to encounter Giles traveling north. His brother was expected in London on the fifth of June. He and Seren departed Neasham around the eleventh. His brother's horse was a strong courser. He'd witnessed firsthand how the animal could tear up a road. On their journey south only a few months ago, they'd covered sixty miles in little more than a day. Ergo, even if he lingered in London another day or two after his audience with Stephen, it was still entirely possible that Giles could make the journey north in time to meet them en route to Warkworth. Moreover, even though Seren wouldn't complain, he could see the strain showing on her face. So, about midday, he led her back to the road.

Well-traveled as it might be, he fully anticipated encountering a pilgrim or two. What he didn't anticipate was the constant stream of traffic moving south. Weary and bedraggled, the men appeared as though they hadn't supped well in weeks. If there weren't so bloody many, he would have offered victuals from his satchel.

He gave Seren a meaningful glance, warning her without words to remain silent as he reached about and stole the reins from her hands, pulling her and her mare to the right side of his mount to better shield her. If there was a boon to be had for his size it was this: Most men dared not cross him.

And nevertheless, while these men might sooner pluck out their own eyes than tangle with the Hammer of Warkworth, none appeared to have much fear of him. They wore a look of desperation in their eyes that made him think they had naught to lose. But he wasn't worried for himself; dressed as he was in boiled leathers, he was far more prepared for a battle than they were, sad as it may be to say. These ragtag soldiers wore piecemeal armor: One wore a helmet, another chausses, no mail *sherte* or coif. They were equipped with weapons, to be sure, but none so much that would mete out any true damage, and even as he watched, one man took a gander at his blade—a fine, double-edged sword with a two-handed cruciform and pommel that once belonged to his father. Perhaps it should have gone to Giles, but Giles had returned from his travels with a weapon that far surpassed any that might be fashioned by their bladesmiths at Warkworth.

Raising a hand to his forehead in greeting, he said, "Well met."

"Hail sir," said a thin man, giving him a nod, assessing Wilhelm as he approached.

Compelled despite himself, Wilhelm reached back with his free hand to lift up the flap on his saddlebag, reaching in to see what he could find—a small round of cheese met his fingertips and he lifted it up, tossing it to the man. "God save ye," the traveler said, inclining his head.

"Well met," said another as they crossed paths, and Wilhelm dared to inquire. "Where to good man?"

"York, m'lord."

Wilhelm's brows lifted, and he let go of Seren's reins to turn his horse. "York?"

Turning in his saddle, the man's eyes lit with a fever of excitement. "Aye, m'lord. To join a siege with Duke Henry."

Wilhelm's brows collided. "Fitz Empress, at York?"

Eyeing the sigil on his breast, the man openly confessed, "David knighted him. They're taking York with the Earl of Chester."

Duke Henry was old enough to have been knighted by his own sire before his death, but Wilhelm was far more intrigued over the details of how the lad re-entered the realm so quietly. In due time, they were supposed to have used the port at Warkworth, but their arrival was still being discussed. In the eventuality it was approved, Duke Henry wasn't supposed to arrive until after the new proposal for ascension was discussed and accepted by the king. To Wilhelm's knowledge, that proposal—an agreement that Stephen could rule until his death, but cede the throne to Matilda's boy instead of his own son—hadn't met with resounding approval from the Vatican. A few of the Empress's "friends" believed she should be the one to wear her father's crown. To their way of thought, Duke Henry was scarcely a child, and he had too many years remaining before he would be ready to rule. "Under whose banner do you ride?" Wilhelm asked another man, as he trotted toward them.

"Rainald FitzRoy," said the soldier. "We've fresh come from council. More than half the northern barons will support David. I'm guessing you should be pleased enough to hear that news?" He tilted Wilhelm a meaningful nod, then put a hand to his forehead in salute. "Safe travels, m'lord. And if you should find yourself without the lady in tow, Duke Henry will welcome Warkworth's support."

Wilhelm nodded. "God be wi' ye, lad," he said, and gave Seren another meaningful glance. She arched one perfect brow, perhaps because he'd given her so much grief over assuming his title, and he'd let it slide for these men, but it served him well enough for these men to mistake him for Warkworth's lord. It was also quite telling these soldiers would speak so freely about rebellion. It was a testament to the growing unrest in England. People might not relish having a haughty woman on the throne, nor a beardless youth, but, it seemed they would prefer the boy to a hard-hearted despot—particularly one aligned to Morwen Pendragon. Stephen may not be guilty of tyranny, per se, but the man had one ass cheek off his throne, and he was already advocating for his son—*but, God's teeth, York?*

Clearly, to no avail, his brother had warned David not to take the diocese perforce. There was no way in hell Stephen would ever allow York to fall. If what these men claimed was true, it was a matter of time before Stephen drove his army north. If they came so far as York, Warkworth was no more than another thirty leagues north.

Grateful now that he'd avoided York en route to Neasham, he waited until the last of the cavalcade was out of sight before abandoning the road yet again, praying to God his brother was not embroiled at York. Their troubles would mount exponentially and God's bloody bones, he was growing weary of trouble.

SEREN DIDN'T QUESTION his decision.

Though she might still be vexed with him, she trusted Wilhelm without fail. It was clear to her that he was concerned for their wellbeing. Despite that Jack was no longer traveling with them and there were no signs of her mother's ravens, his mood had grown darker and darker by the mile. "Those were the Earl of Cornwall's men?" she ventured.

"Aye."

"So, it seems, Duke Henry aligns himself with David?

"So it seems."

"The Earl of Chester and the Earl of Cornwall are planning to take York?"

It was a bold move, Seren realized.

"Your guess is good as mine," Wilhelm said. "But I am not surprised. De Gernon has long been discontented, and Rainald is Matilda's half-brother."

"Yay, I know," said Seren, with a faint smile playing at the corners of her mouth. "Rainald is *my* brother as well."

Wilhelm's brows collided, as though only now perceiving this fact. But it was true; the Earl of Cornwall was as much Seren's kindred as he was Matilda's—obviously, so was Duke Henry. Perhaps it hadn't occurred to Wilhelm how many bastards her father had sired, or perhaps more significantly, how well he appointed them. But though her father had given little enough of his time, he had given *all* his children generous endowments, including Seren and her sisters. The simple fact that she couldn't claim her money was all due to her mother. And they were not alone in their complaint; even Matilda had been deprived of her due.

Ye gods! Duke Henry was at York. The significance of that was not lost to Seren. Tensions were escalating so quickly. And now, the simple fact that Duke Henry had joined this fight was momentous, because, in essence, it meant he, as the rightful king of England, would agree to cede York's archdiocese to Scotland, awarding the entire northern ecclesiastical power to David.

"How far from Warkworth lies York?"

"Thirty leagues, perhaps."

"Aldergh to York?"

"A little bit further. Closer to the border." He gave Seren a meaningful glance, correctly assuming her thoughts, because he said, "Your sister is safe there, and, in truth, I would venture to say that if tensions continue to escalate, Giles will send you both north to join Elspeth at Aldergh. I have never seen that fortress, but by all accounts 'tis inviolable."

Seren nodded, and for an instant—only the briefest instant—she suffered a pang of longing to return to York to meet her nephew. Whereas only a few months ago she mightn't have cared much about either Henry or Matilda, she longed now for some connection to her family. Or, perhaps it was something more like hope... something she now had a glimpse of thanks to Wilhelm. But, truly, with her sisters all scattered to the winds, and Arwyn... *gone*—she still could not conceive it—Seren had never felt more alone... except for Wilhelm. She glanced at him now, wishing she could smooth the worry lines from the corners of his mouth. It wasn't so much that she was no longer affronted by his lie of omission, but the darker his mood, the more inclined she was to try to lift it. "I must believe my father would support this," she said.

"Did you know him well?"

She peered up at a passing bluebird, watching it alight upon a low-lying bough. "Nay. I was only seven when he died."

"Still old enough to hold him in your thoughts," Wilhelm suggested.

"Oh, I do. But, as my mother was of the mind her *brats* should never be seen or heard, only Elspeth ever escaped this edict. My father came to know her better, perhaps because he and Morwen were... shall we say... newly entangled." Her cheeks burned with chagrin. "Elspeth was the first child Morwen bore him."

Wilhelm's dark eyes were warm, inviting her to tell him all her secrets. "So you were born in London?"

"I was. My sister was born at Blackwood. The rest of us in London." She sighed wistfully. "By the time I came along my father had very likely grown weary of so many…"

He lifted both brows. "Bastards?"

Seren laughed softly. "Aye, so see, we are not so different, you and me."

"I beg to differ," he said, and quieted as though to contemplate all that she'd told him.

For some reason it pleased her immensely to know he cared enough to know her history—as she longed to know his. "I don't know why, but I thought you were born in Wales," he said.

"Not I, though I was raised there. After my father died, I was sent to live with my sisters in the Vale of Ewyas—not very far from Blackwood."

"Why did you not return to Blackwood?"

Seren rolled her eyes. "Ah, well, that is a looong story. The short of it is that women cannot inherit lands in Wales. When my uncle died, Blackwood was forfeit to Gruffydd ap Rhys, the king of Dyfed. And, in order to keep the estate, my mother would have had to marry one of his sons. By then, Morwen and Henry were already…"

"Entangled?"

Seren nodded, her cheeks burning. "Elspeth was two, I suppose, and my mother was already in confinement with Rhiannon. At the time, Henry had a bit less tenuous influence over the Marcher lords."

He lifted his brows again. "Less than Stephen?"

Seren laughed softly. It was true. King Stephen had none at all. For the entire first year of his reign, he'd made some sore attempt to annex those lands, but it soon became quite apparent that the Welsh lords would never cede their lands or their kingships without a fight—one Stephen could ill afford, particularly when David was already seizing lands to the north, and Matilda was trying to rouse barons against him. But such was the power of destiny and the *ysbryd y byd* –*the spirit of the age.*

"At my mother's behest, my grandmamau appealed to Henry, so Henry agreed to allow her to keep Blackwood for her heirs, if only if she swore allegiance to him, not to Gruffydd ap Rhys, and only if my mother agreed to become a ward of his court. Later, when my grandmamau died, our lands were again forfeit, only this time to Henry."

"So, in reality, you came into this world as Henry's prisoner?"

Seren frowned over that plainspoken truth. "I suppose 'tis one way to look at it." Along with her mother, and her sisters, they were, indeed, all wards of her father's court. Still, Elspeth was indisputably Henry's favorite, even above his heirs—though not William, of course. William was always Henry's hope of hopes, and when he died, a part of her father died as well. He never quite took to Matilda. "I should say, we were far freer wandering my father's halls than we ever were at the priory."

"I see," he said.

And yet he couldn't see—not everything.

What would he think if he knew her mother had sent that mist to cripple the White Ship? Aye, it was true. It happened many, many moons before Seren was born, but Morwen oft bragged of the deed. In the blink of an eye, an entire generation was lost, and there were many who claimed it was the sinking of that vessel that doomed England to this anarchy. But Seren knew better. Rather, the cause of their woes was a greedy witch.

What more proof did they need?

With malice and forethought, her mother had sunk the White Ship, consigning their father's heir to the cold, black depths of the sea. Seren and her sisters also suspected that Stephen was privy to this treachery, and that, moreover, Morwen advised him to disembark the White Ship—which he did, of course, feigning some bellyache. He took another ship, sailing safely to England whilst so many of his cousins perished. And, if that were not tragedy enough, Morwen had murdered the man she'd claimed to love—the father of her daughters. And all the while she'd been poisoning Henry with potions, she'd been whispering venomous words into his nephew's ear, until Stephen of Blois was well-primed to steal his uncle's throne. Now she was poised to drive another king mad and replace him with a true despot, someone who took glee in the burning of castles and shedding of blood. Eustace, Count of Mortain, now Blois, was the worst thing that could happen to England, aside from her mother. Put the two of them together, and this would be England's doom.

Wilhelm moved ahead, whacking at another tangle of vines, and Seren fell silent, contemplating the day's news.

What did this mean for Elspeth? What could it mean for Warkworth? How did a siege at York fare for those remaining in the borderlands?

Gods forbid, what if David did, indeed, manage to take York? Warkworth would be left well north of David's southernmost lands. Would Giles be compelled to bend the knee to David? Would the Church intervene? And, if, in truth, it came to all-out war, would Matilda join her son at York?

She swallowed hard, thinking about Wilhelm.

He was made for war, and something about his demeanor gave her every impression he would be good at his job. His wide shoulders gave testament to a lifetime of training. But that scar on his face... it bespoke his vulnerability. How could she ever bear it if anything happened to her gentle giant?

She glanced at the sweet, beautiful man riding beside her, guarding her so jealously. When all was said and done, what would come of their affiliation? Was any sort of alliance between them even remotely possible?

She'd come to know him so well by now that she didn't like to think of parting ways. But, alas, Wilhelm Fitz Richard was only a bastard—as was she, though unlike Seren, he did not bear the blood of kings in his veins. Wilhelm probably feared he could not provide for her; little did he realize that she and her sisters had lived most of their lives in abject poverty, working hard for every morsel, and returning by night to a cottage with only a crude dirt floor. They shared a single bed together, and no one complained. If, in truth, he could wish her to be his bride, Seren believed she could be happy as the helpmate of a simple man.

Her belly fluttered over the shocking turn of her thoughts.

If Matilda or Henry should recover England, perhaps they would release her dowry? And, if they released her dowry, mayhap *she* could provide for Wilhelm? It was a fanciful notion, perhaps, but not entirely unreasonable. Amidst the Welsh people, there were many women who married simpler men, particularly in the case of an heiress. Since only men could inherit lands, a wealthy woman could, indeed, marry for love. Nor was every match made for gain.

Alas... what made her think Wilhelm had any desire for her at all? Even now his aura confused her.

Get yourself together, Seren. He is not for you, and neither must you win yourself a champion only because Rose and Ellie found one. Not every man desires you.

You're a witch, she chided herself. At least so far as most folks were concerned. No sane man would willingly tangle with Morwen Pendragon over any of her daughters, no matter how fair their countenance— and particularly not a man whose welfare depended upon the good will of his lord and brother.

Turn your heart, Seren.

Turn your heart from this folly, before 'tis too late.

And yet, she knew... she would defy reason to follow her heart. Only realizing how much she'd kept locked inside, she vowed to never again betray herself. And even as she thought it, her *witchwind* stirred yet again...

A breeze rifled the tree tops, scattering a host of sparrows from their perches. Poplar leaves tinkled in warning.

❧

IT WASN'T long after Lady Aldergh departed that Cora ascended the stairwell to check on the babes. She scolded her daughter for not having informed her at once that the mistress was leaving. Ellyn was not herself today. Only yesterday that girl would have wept blood-tears for having distressed her mother. Today... she seemed distracted.

It must be a boy, Cora reasoned. Ellyn was getting to be that age—sixteen, and more a woman than she would like to believe. With those lovely blue eyes and golden hair, she was naught at all like her father nor her mother. Cora herself was fair of skin, and pretty enough in her youth, but her hair was red, and her eyes, though blue, were never so bright as Ellyn's. Her daughter would make some good man a fine wife someday, and, she thought perhaps their mistress already had someone in mind—one of Lord Malcom's men-at-arms.

Thinking about that—about grandbabes bouncing on her own knee—she entered the nursery, feeling ill at ease. The air in the chamber felt strained. One of the babes lay whimpering, and she felt ashamed for leaving them so long unattended. "Ellyn," she railed. Her daughter was supposed to have traded her shift with another maid. These children were never to be left unattend—

Her heart flipped as she peered into the cradle. Swallowing a lump of bile that rose to strangle her, she stared in horror into the cradle. There was only *one* child here. Only wee Lachlan's anguished blue eyes peered up at her, his gaze entirely too knowing for a babe so young. But nay! Why would Elspeth take only one child, not the other?

Her heart pummeling her ribs in fear, she lifted Lachlan, and with the child in her arms, she bolted from the room into the hall. "Ellyn," she screamed. "Ellyn!" And then, sensing something terrible, she shouted for her steward husband. "Alwin!"

25

Wilhelm returned from the bushes to find Seren perched atop her mount, waiting patiently, though with her hands splayed in front of her as though she were examining something resting in her palms. For an instant, he hadn't any clue what she could be doing, but then, to his amazement, it appeared as though it were raining sideways—but only on her. Every drop of dew from the surrounding trees converged upon her hand, twinkling as they flew, catching sunlight like tiny gems.

A wondrous smile turned her lips. Clearly, she was pleased with the effort. "Did you see that?" she asked excitedly.

"I did," he confessed, adjusting his trews.

She turned her palm, spilling some of the liquid down the pad of her palm, into the bracken. She grinned. "Art thirsty?"

"It's all yours," Wilhelm said, because—God's teeth—as much as he would love to lap the salt from her flesh, if he dared any such thing, he might never stop. He would lick every inch of her beautiful body and more... and besides, the flagons were still full.

"I've been practicing," she said happily. "I can't wait to show Rosalynde. She can do better, but I have never quite accomplished this task so easily."

"I saw her do it once," Wilhelm confessed, as he hoisted himself into the saddle.

"Rhiannon taught us when we were young, but I was always too afraid to try."

"Of Ersinius?"

"Aye," she said. "Though, I don't know why. That man was more frightened of my mother than we were of him." She leaned forward to sip the remaining liquid from her palm, then shook her hand free. "I suppose I can thank Elspeth for putting the fear of the Goddess in me."

"Art certain you don't need to?" Wilhelm said, inclining his head toward the thicket from whence he'd come.

Seren shook her head, blushing. "Nay, I am fine."

Wilhelm didn't press. At any rate, he had no qualms at all over slowing the pace. So far as he was concerned, they could stop a thousand times or linger for days. At this point, every field they crossed, every burn, brought them one marker closer to Warkworth, and while Seren's mood grew more buoyant still with every mile they traversed, his grew more somber, and he needn't reflect overlong to know why...

He had waking dreams of taking Seren into his arms, kissing her soundly, then falling to his knees and professing his love. Regrettably, he was no wealthy lord to take such a beautiful bride. His only recompense would only ever be a pat on the shoulder for a job well done, and perhaps a thank you from Rosalynde and Seren. But his true reward—his only true reward—would be the memories he'd made along the journey north, most of them bittersweet:

He liked the way she laughed. He loved the way she smiled. He admired the allegiance she gave Jack. He loved how fearless she could be, and the courage she displayed.

Even now, he couldn't stop looking into her beautiful silver eyes. Forcing himself to tear his gaze away, he gave his mare a boot, and Seren followed without so much as touching her heel to the animal's flank, as though she'd compelled the beast, with no physical cues—if this be witchery, he supposed everyone should be that fortunate. There was nothing at all wicked about the skills this woman possessed, and, in fact, it seemed as natural as rain.

All the while they kept pace, she "practiced" again, and again, and Wilhelm fell back to observe. The sight of her was magical, and every time she summoned dew, she was encircled by a halo and rainbow. He didn't know how she was doing that—attracting water as a lodestone drew metal—but the sight was nevertheless breathtaking—never so much so as the sparkle in her eyes when she turned to find him watching and realized he wasn't judging.

Actually, Wilhelm might have liked to know how she was performing that trick; it would come in handy. But, for now, he was content enough to wonder, and he thought perhaps that if he lived to be a thousand, Seren would still be a mystery as well.

Over these past few days, they'd grown closer and closer, and the more he learned about her, the more questions he had. In truth, this was the first time in all Wilhelm's life that he'd found himself thinking of a woman as his friend—not merely the object of his desire. He liked conspiring with her, and he liked sharing meals. He loved their late-night discourse, whispering like youths over a flame with her eyes sparkling with gold.

Bored with the water trick, she turned and awarded Wilhelm with the most enthralling smile, and he moved forward again to ride like a puppy at her side—no doubt gazing at her like a besotted fool, but he didn't care. He longed for her to know what he felt in his heart, but was terrified to speak the words lest he break this wondrous spell. The very instant he confessed himself, it would become something less than innocent—a thing to be accepted or rebuked, and it was the latter possibility that roiled his gut.

Feeling like an old man before his time, he cast Seren another glance to find her inspecting the woodlands with all the enthusiasm of a child. He wished to God he could share her joy. Even more than her sister was, she was enchanted by fauna and flora, no matter how unremarkable, and even with all her troubles, she took joy in the smallest of things.

"Look," she said, pointing at the rich carpet of blue that grew along the path.

From April to May, the northern woods were filled with bellflowers, but not so thick as they grew near the Widow's Tower. "'Tis late in the year for those," he said, but when she lifted her gaze from the rich, blue mantle, her own silver eyes twinkled, and he found himself wishing those flowers could grace these woods all year long.

"I could fill my purse with the bounty of these woods," she exclaimed, pointing again, "There," she said. "Yarrow!" And again. "Wild carrots—but that is hemlock." She thrust a finger toward a tall, lacy flower as they trotted by. "You must take care with that one. 'Tis poisonous. It can very easily be mistaken. But," she expounded, "a proper herbalist may know how to use it, and it can be a very good sedative."

He would do anything to keep her talking... even inquire about things he mightn't normally care about. "I take it you must be a proper herbalist?"

She blushed again, the deep plum stain on her cheeks complimenting the wintry shade of her eyes. "Not so much as Elspeth, but I try."

God's truth, this woman was not at all what he'd supposed, and, if he could be honest with himself, after coming to know her sister, he'd suffered much trepidation over meeting Seren—why? Because, after meeting Rosalynde, he'd sorely envied Giles, and he'd realized even then that if Seren was half the woman her sister was, he might be lost.

And she was more.

And he was lost.

Seren Pendragon wasn't merely lovely. She was kind and sweet, and humble besides. Even her sister was far haughtier than she was, and if Seren's temper was ever riled, it was always over the welfare of others.

During their time together, Wilhelm had heard infinite praises for her sisters, and if Seren were to be believed, she was never the expert, always the student, learning diligently from her sisters—Elspeth who was eldest, Rhiannon who was wisest, Rosalynde, who was bravest, and Arwyn... well, understandably, she'd yet to speak much of Arwyn. Her eyes filled with tears when her thoughts returned to Dover. But, from all that Wilhelm could see, the woman traveling beside him had a giving heart, and having watched her with Jack—the gentle way she'd treated him, the sweet words she'd spoken to him—he found himself wishing she could be the mother of his babes.

And that was the entire crux of his mood—not

Giles, nor Warkworth, nor even York, or Matilda. It was Seren, and the indisputable way he was beginning to feel about her—*phfht, beginning?* Truth be told, he had fallen in love with the lady at first sight, and he'd envied his brother desperately. He'd gone into that hall at Westminster fully prepared to despise the woman, and he'd left with a pang in his heart that exacerbated his grief. That night, months ago, he and his brother had gone to some sad little tavern to commiserate over ale, and the entire time he'd sat there listening to Giles carry on about why he must wed Lady Seren—for the good of Warkworth, and no less the good of the realm—all he could think about was punching Giles in the throat.

It was not a feeling he was proud of, and he couldn't explain it to Giles. It was no wonder he'd leapt to the task the very instant Rosalynde asked him to find Seren, because, even then—months before he'd encountered her in Dover—he could think of little else. And now that he realized how worthy she was of respect he knew himself to be unworthy.

When most women of her station would have had naught but complaints over the bed he'd provided her each night—which was to say, none at all—Seren slept where she could and woke with a smile and 'good morn' fresh upon her lips, even despite her travails. Like Rosalynde, she was a soldier and he was proud of her for enduring the journey with so little complaint. If she was hungry, she ate what was provided. If she was thirsty, she drank what he drank, be it water from a brook, dew from a leaf, or stale *vin*. If she was cold, she made do with the blanket she was given. If she was hot, she spoke not a word in complaint.

As relieved as he was that their journey so far had

been uneventful, and that her winsome smile managed to ease any worry over danger, it was still there in the back of his head...

Morwen was still out there, somewhere; he felt her.

The air itself held a certain tension, as though every moment and every mile brought them closer to peril.

Distracting him from his brooding thoughts, Seren giggled. A butterfly had landed on her nose. But, instead of shooing the creature away, she endured it, wiggling her nose to alleviate an itch.

"How long will you suffer that bug?"

Seren smiled. "So long as it wishes to stay."

Wilhelm smirked, lifting his brow. "You'd better shoo it away. It will lay eggs on your snout, and then what?"

"Snout?" she asked, incensed by his description of her nose, and her laughter saved her from having to shoo the butterfly. It flew away, into the bellflowers.

"See what you did?"

"I do. I saved you from being the mother of pests," he said, and found himself eager to show her his favorite spot with a view of the sea. If she could smile so brightly over a glade full of bellflowers and a silly little butterfly, what else might she say or do over the sight of a thousand damselflies at dawn.

At low tide, Warkworth's beach was long, with sprawling white sand that stretched for miles. "Have you e'er seen the ocean?" he asked, and then suffered himself a fool. Because—God's teeth—of course she'd seen the ocean. He'd found her hiding aboard a ship en route to Calais. His cheeks burned like hot coals, and Seren must have realized his faux pas, because she giggled, then averted her gaze.

All told, Wilhelm was ill-equipped to have any form of courtly conversation. It was a struggle, to be sure—and more and more now that he was so painfully aware of himself in the lady's presence. Quite likely, Seren thought him an imbecile, because he certainly felt like one.

"But, of course, I knew you had," he dissembled. "'Tis only that the closer we come to Warkworth, the more eager I am to show you my home."

"I am eager as well," she confessed, and Wilhelm's heart tripped painfully. He wished to God he were brave enough to tell her how fond he was of her. "How long before we arrive?"

"Not long," he said. "If my guess is good, you'll be seeing your sister afore the sun sets on the morrow." And rather than twist his lips into a grimace, he forced a smile.

THEY HAD a veritable feast that night—blackberries, strawberries, pignuts and wild carrots, along with a good-sized trout Wilhelm caught by hand.

It was thrilling to watch—the swiftness with which he'd moved, the grace he'd displayed in the hunt.

And yet, now that the fish was prepared to be cooked, he was equally inept at building his fire, working stubbornly with his fire-steel, as he was inclined to do every time.

Alas, the flame refused to kindle, and Seren would have laughed if he weren't so disconcerted.

For some odd reason, it seemed to her that the ability to start a fire was strongly imbued into the makings of a man. It seemed to be a thing they *must* master in order to be considered a man, and in truth, she wondered idly if fathers ingrained this fear in their sons. It was something to think about... as she sat munching on a carrot. She wished she could do something to help. And because she wished it so desperately, even knowing her own limitations, she envisioned the tinder igniting, and suddenly, inexplicably, the wood exploded into flames, startling her as much as it did Wilhelm. Blinking, she held the carrot aloft, mouth agape as she stared at the blue flames.

He laughed. "My brows for a good flame," he said, and then turned to look at Seren with a question in his eyes. "I thought you couldn't do that?"

Seren's brows lifted in bewilderment, not only because the conflagration surprised her. It was a blue— as blue as the fire that took the Whitshed.

Witchfire.

"I-I didn't know I could," she said, a bit stunned.

Witchwind. Witchwater. Witchfire.

There was no doubt in her mind now that she was aligned to *aether,* but even so, these were *not* affinities that were common to *dewines*, not lest they be Goddess blessed and ordained, which she most certainly was not. Rhiannon was the one who should receive the gifts of a priestess, and nevertheless, she had never once seen even Rhiannon perform this sort of *magik*.

How was this possible?

Confused by the mystery, Seren shoved the remaining carrot into her mouth and then sat staring into the raging flame.

Truth be told, none of these abilities had ever manifested themselves before Arwyn's death. Could they somehow be connected to her sister's passing? Did Arwyn, somehow, convey her abilities to Seren? But nay... Arwyn had no *magik*. Barely at all. Much to her sister's dismay, she was *never* a proper student of the Craft.

So why here, why now?

Twilight passed, and night fell. Night sounds pervaded the air. Once their meal was done, Seren nibbled here and there at her victuals, studying the flames as they slowly cooled from blue to red and gold, casting a burnished light over their immediate surroundings.

For the love of night, so far as she knew, she was *not* a *dewine* priestess or she would have been groomed for this from birth. To be a Regnant, there were outward signs—the crossed amber-lit eyes, like Rhiannon's.

But even Rhiannon was not a priestess as yet. Simply because one had the potential did not mean one could ascend. One must study the Craft over a lifetime and eventually entreat the Mother Goddess. Only with the Mother's blessings could a priestess be ordained. And, even a fully ordained priestess might not necessarily have the power to manipulate the divine.

Witchwind, witchfire and *witchwater,* these were all divine elements, and so far as Seren knew, not even their grandmamau had had the power to conjure the extramundane. It was a skill that appeared only once in a thousand years. So why had these new powers manifested themselves to her so suddenly?

"Seren?" Blinking, Seren peered up at Wilhelm to find him watching her intently. His brows lifted. "You must be overtired," he said. "We should sleep and rise early."

Seren nodded, but what she really wished for at the instant was to speak to Rhiannon. Unfortunately, she could not *mindspeak* outside proximity, and, to

make matters worse, though she could feel her sisters
—Rosalynde and Elspeth—the *aether* was completely
devoid of Rhiannon's presence.

Wilhelm finished supping and rose, going straight
for the blankets, but despite the deepening night,
sleep was the furthest thing from Seren's mind.

26

"Here be your victuals."

The new warden lunged into Rhiannon's cell, seizing the morning's plate, still half full, and grousing as he shoved another plate onto her table to replace it.

"Tarry not," he demanded. "Hands bound or nay, I cannot be leaving plates all night long else ye'll be sleeping with rats." Muttering crossly beneath his breath, he turned his back to Rhiannon and rushed back out, though not before casting her a disgruntled glance.

He was new to the job, she knew—here only a week—but already he'd begun to show some pity, and that was the failure of her previous warden.

"She's vicious," she'd heard the steward say. "Show no mercy. And if you turn your back on that lady she'll skewer you with a fork. But if she doesn't kill you for showing weakness, I will."

Clearly, Cael d'Lucy was bored with her. He was gone to London now, leaving his cruel-hearted steward to oversee Blackwood's prison—a tower-full of Welsh insurgents, so far as Rhiannon could determine. If she could, she would free them all, but with the shackles she was wearing—a lovely gift from her mother—she was well and truly helpless. She couldn't kindle the fire in her brazier, couldn't summon a spoon. She couldn't spy on her sisters.

The shackles she wore effectively blocked *all magik* —how she didn't know, but she surmised it must be imbued with some sort of binding spell. Perhaps even the metal itself was inspired. Mercifully, her hands weren't fettered behind her back, but by now, her wrists were chafed enough from trying to free them that even the simple act of lifting a fork to her mouth pained her immensely.

Alas, no matter how tiny she tried to make her fists, they were well and duly bound. Even so, the shackles were fascinating. For all that it appeared they should be loose enough to slip off, they resisted. It was as though they could anticipate her intentions. So long as she needed freedom to perform perfunctory tasks—comb her hair or shovel food into her mouth— her hands remained loosely bound. On the other hand, the instant she tried to slip free of them, the metal appeared to expand, leaving no room at all, pinching her flesh till it threatened to cut off her blood supply. And nevertheless, she must persist, because she was lost without *magik*. There was little worse they could have done to her, except murder her sisters. They could have plucked out her eyes and Rhiannon wouldn't feel so inadequate. Only now she understood what it felt like to be ordinary—no sight, no *magik*, no ability at all. Frustrated, she examined the manacles again, holding them up to the light, hoping against hope to figure out how they worked.

As far as she could tell... they must be forged with

some type of alloy, though even as shiny as the metal appeared to be, they were far too unyielding to be pure. Most of the fused silver developed a patina, and she knew this because she and her sisters had been tasked with cleaning all the silver in the chapel at Llanthony. The purest pieces dented too easily, and therefore the majority of the candle holders at Llanthony were fused with another metal entirely. However, because Ersinius liked to have people believe his chapel was pristine, he'd made them clean the silver with a sour paste made of *vin aigre*. Whatever *this* was, it wasn't *that*. For even despite that these were ancient —she could tell by the etching—the silver was completely untarnished. And, if you looked closely, there was a small inscription on both wrist pieces, beside the keyholes. The rough edges of the engraving caught the light like small gems. She could scarcely make it out...

> Hic est Draco,
> Ex undis,
> Tenetur in argenteas
> A capite ad calcem, tace, et sile

Roughly translated, it meant, "Here be the dragon"—a true dragon? A Pendragon?

The witch Cerridwen was no dragon. Her sigil was the sigil of the house of Avalon, twin golden serpents entwined about the stem of a winged chalice. She was not directly aligned to Uther, only through the marriage of her granddaughter Yissachar. So, then, perhaps this was not a reference to a Pendragon by name, but rather a reference to the sea serpent, in which case, it could be Cerridwen. Many years after she was cast into exile, there were numerous accounts of her resurfacing as a sea dragon.

"Hic est Draco, ex undis," she whispered.

Here be the dragon from beneath the waves.

Indeed, these shackles must have been fashioned to keep her. But, if so, who could possibly have known she would return from her exile, and who had forged these manacles to bind her?

Bound in silver, from head to toe, silent and still, read the remainder of the inscription. Surely, this must be some sort of a binding spell. Written by whom?

Her grandmamau? Her father? Could Emrys have learned who Morwen was before she'd chanced to poison him? Was that why she killed him?

Or mayhap the engraving was inscribed by yet another hand? Someone who represented the Holy Church? Inexplicably—because these symbols were not used in the Craft—the inscription was bracketed by crosses.

Rhiannon pondered this mystery a while—a possible collaboration between the Goddess and the Church?

Was that even possible?

According to their grandmamau all gods were as one god, born of the same Great Mother. Their priestesses were not unlike Christian priests, who in their hearts and minds were merely closer to God. The tenets of the Holy Church were not so different from the teachings of the Mother Goddess, none so profound as this: Do good, harm none.

Dewines were not typically against the Holy Church, even though huntsmen had slaughtered their people for ages. When Taliesin became the Merlin of Britain—Myrddin in her own Welsh tongue—the

Holy Church had reviled him. Loathing his influence over the Emperor, and longing to besmirch his name —or worse, they began hunting his people in secret, using his own bard's tales to find and behead them or burn them at the stake.

These were the *faekind* and *dewinefolk* of legend— those who made their homes in the Summer Isles, even after the drowning of Avalon.

Deep in thought, considering possibilities, Rhiannon was scarcely aware that her gaoler had returned. Hers was typically the first and last cell he visited, and then he wouldn't come again till morning. To arrive here, it was a long climb from the courtyard.

Shivering, she scooted into the waning sunlight, lifting her face to the sun's last rays, as though, by sheer will alone, she could absorb its warmth. When the guard thrust his key into her lock, she opened her eyes, willing him without words to rekindle the fire in her brazier.

The man stared back at her, looking for an instant bemused, and she knew her exercise had proven futile.

"'Tis cold," she complained.

He ignored her, peering over at her untouched plate and shaking his head in disgust. He jerked the key back out of her lock, jiggling the bars to be sure they remained firm.

"My mum had blue eyes, too," he said conversationally. "But you won't live to see her age if you refuse to eat. And if'n ye cost me my job, as you did Berwyn's, I'll see you regret it, witch!"

Rhiannon simply wasn't hungry. She felt hopeless and lost. But suddenly it occurred to her what he'd said, and she cocked her head in surprise.

Blue?

But nay, she was born with amber eyes, and later, when she'd come to an age, one eye turned lazy. She'd suffered taunts for it most of her life. It wasn't until she'd learned precisely what her eyes meant that she'd found peace with the imperfection. From that day forward she'd devoted herself to studying the Craft, day and night, even defying her eldest sister when Elspeth forbade her. The guard turned to leave, still shaking his head. "Wait!" Rhiannon said, bounding up from the bed, though not to retrieve her plate. "Wait!" she demanded, and again, when it seemed he would leave. "Wait! Wait!"

"Quit yer prattling," the man said, but he refused to turn around.

"Please! Look at me," Rhiannon demanded. She shook the bars. "What color are my eyes?" Mayhap he simply hadn't looked closely enough the first time. He *must* be mistaken.

The guard turned with a frown. "Blue, I said!" And to confuse matters even more, he didn't bother to cross himself at the sight of her, as most people were wont to do—even Berwyn.

"Wait," she said when he made to leave again. "May I have that?" She pointed to the empty, metal plate in his hand. If she could polish it, she could glimpse her reflection.

"Nay," he said, his patience clearly at an end. "Ye got your own. Finish your supping then do what ye will with the plate." And then he left, abandoning Rhiannon to a quiet so pervasive that she could hear the scurrying of rats in the hall.

But it couldn't be.

It couldn't be.

She bounded over to the plate he'd left on her table, picking it up, wincing over the pain that stung her wrists, and flinging off the food, even knowing the consequences. She would go without supping tonight, and despite that, she was undeterred, rubbing the grease from her plate onto her dress, wiping it clean in hopes that she might spy something on the rust-covered surface. Once the plate was scrubbed enough, she rushed over to the waning rays of sunlight, peering into the makeshift mirror.

Blue, she saw. Blue eyes peering back at her. *Not amber. Not Crossed. Blue.*

Sweet, sweet Goddess, it was true; she had blue eyes!

With a bewildered shake of her head, Rhiannon dropped her hands, realizing that this was *only* possible if someone had put a *glamour* on her as a child— a *glamour* so powerful she couldn't even see through it herself. *But why?*

Crossed, amber eyes were the Mark of the Mother. It was a dominant trait for a Regnant priestess, but it alone didn't assure ascension; it must be a judgment by the Goddess. And yet, no Regnant so far as Rhiannon knew ever presided over a coven without the birthmark.

Moreover, only one priestess could preside at once, and only one gifted *dewine* was born to every generation. The Gift could not be passed along until the living Regnant died, or else she was renounced by the Goddess herself. Her father, Emrys, not her mother, had been the Promised One before her, but her father's gifts were never conferred, because he'd died many years before their grandmother. Therefore, Morgan Pendragon was the last Regnant to preside over a coven, and the Gift skipped a generation, as it sometimes did, because it was Goddess-granted. But though Rhiannon's ascension wasn't pre-ordained, she had prepared herself for the Mother's Gift for most of her life. She had been led to believe it was her destiny —only naturally, since Emry's was her father. But, if she was not born to be the Regnant... who was?

27

During the day, with the sun shining so brightly, and Wilhelm by her side, it was easier to forget her travails.

Now, in the wee hours of the morn, with Wilhelm fast asleep, Seren couldn't seem to slow the errant beating of her heart. Eyes open or closed, her traitorous thoughts flitted from one worry to the next. Her ears tuned into every sound in the forest: deer traipsing about, squirrels scrambling up trees, the uncanny bark of a fox in the middle of the night—all these things, though they'd seemed only natural before, now held a timbre of menace.

Somewhere out there, her mother was scheming.

Somewhere out there, Mordecai was lurking.

Somewhere out there, the king's soldiers were gathering for war...

Where are you, Rhiannon?

How she longed for her sister's counsel.

Rhiannon was the wisest *dewine* Seren knew. Even when they hadn't had access to a *grimoire* of their own, she had created one, filling it with experiments and illustrating it so beautifully. It never once mattered to her that Elspeth refused to convey their grandmamau's teachings; somehow, Rhiannon was born with the *knowing*, as though, with her dying breath, Morgan Pendragon had imbued her—and certainly, that must be true, because even before Rhi could talk, she'd understood things the rest of them did not. Betimes she even recalled things that transpired whilst she was in the womb.

For one, she vividly remembered the death of her twin... *Morien.* In her native tongue it meant 'born of the sea' and Seren often wondered what a sixth sister might have been like. One thing was certain: To this day, Rhiannon loathed Morwen for ingesting that potion to rid herself of her babes. Somehow, Rhiannon survived, much to Morwen's dismay. And perhaps to their father's dismay, as well, for no one ever quite knew how to deal with Rhiannon. For so long, no one understood why she'd seemed so possessed, betimes smacking her head fitfully against walls and wailing inconsolably. Only now, Seren understood... she understood, because the only thing keeping her from doing the same was the quiet strength of the man sleeping beside her.

So much as she envied Wilhelm's restful slumber, his smooth, easy breathing was a comfort to her, because it gave her reason to believe all would be well.

Certainly, if he'd sensed any danger, he would be as wide awake as she, and this was the first night since beginning their travels that he'd dared to rest so easily —now that they were in familiar territory.

Poor Rosalynde, she thought—*poor, Rose.* Her sister must be suffering as Rhiannon suffered—and perhaps more so, for while Rhiannon never had the chance to truly know her twin, Rosalynde and Arwyn had been inseparable. Arwyn had been her shadow, and though Rosalynde so oft lifted her into the light, Arwyn seemed perfectly content to bask in Rosalynde's glory. Sighing deeply, squeezing her eyes shut, she tried to remember Arwyn's face and tears pricked at her eyes because the image was already fading.

They'd spent nearly every waking day together for the majority of their lives, and with only weeks gone since Arwyn's death, already the finer details of her beautiful face were beginning to dim. It was this, perhaps, that bothered Seren most as the days marched quietly on, but she was equally troubled by the fact that, although her sisters must surely know Arwyn was gone, the *how* of it would be left up to her to explain. But there was nothing Seren could say to enlighten anyone, not even herself.

She'd failed Arwyn, that much was clear.

She'd left her alone, and somehow, the Whitshed burned. Later today, or mayhap tomorrow, she would face Rosalynde... and what should she say?

The answer to that continued to bedevil her, and whilst there was a short time in Wilhelm's company that she'd been able to block the tragedy of the Whitshed from her thoughts, now that she was closer to Warkworth, it was impossible to put aside all her questions. Goddess grant her peace, for she could find none on her own.

And then there was this: Despite that she longed to embrace Rose, the thought of arriving now left her feeling bereft, even as it filled her with elation. In the short time since she'd come to know Wilhelm, he'd become her strength as much as any of her sisters were. And yet, the instant they arrived, she would no longer be his concern. His job would be complete, and whatever bond they were forming... it would quickly unravel... fly away, like the windswept silk of a spider's web.

Shivering again, despondent over the thought, she huffed a weary sigh, pulling the covers higher over her ears and staring at Wilhelm's sleeping form across the fire.

His aura was dim at the moment, bordering on umber. Together with the soft glow from the fire, their immediate surroundings were awash with a coppery light. She watched intently as his chest rose and fell with his slumber, and reasoned that the past weeks must have taken a toll. Now, closer to home, he was bound to feel more relaxed. To the contrary, she was anxious, confused, happy, sad, frightened, exhilarated —so many conflicting feelings.

If only her situation weren't so dire, and the realm itself were not in peril... if only she didn't long so desperately to see her sisters... she would, indeed, find a way to delay their arrival. Dismayed, she turned onto her back, frustrated with the evening's course. If it wasn't one thing rattling about her brain, it was yet another—Goddess have mercy.

It was cold, she decided—thankfully not colder than it was in the Black Mountains. In fact, it was far colder there, and she wondered how her sister fared. They took her away that night without even a cloak to warm her. Doubtless their mother would not trouble herself to see to Rhiannon's welfare. Why would she now when she never had before?

Rhiannon, she called again. And was not surprised when the aether remained silent.

Are you there in that tower... like Creirwy?

Built on the edge of a steep cliff in the *Bannau Brycheiniog*—the Black Mountains of Wales, Blackwood's tower was said to rise so high as to be able to glimpse the duchies of Deheubarth, Powys and Morgannwg altogether—so high, in fact, that betimes the

Tower of the White Witch was dusted with snow, even whilst the ivy-tangled courtyard below was in full bloom. There was an old song about it. She hummed it softly, trying to remember the words...

> Blackwood, Blackwood, there she stays,
> Weaving a tale of Avalon drowned.
> Dancing forlorn in a white-crowned tower,
> Crooning to ghosts through the witching
>   hour.

> Blackwood, Blackwood, there she despairs
> Fore'er mourning her paradise lost.
> Keeping a vigil for ladies and lords,
> For dragons on deep, and dread Saxon
>   hordes.

> Blackwood, Blackwood, there she remains,
> All through the dark and the light of day.
> Eyes o' fire, and bright-silver mane.
> Summer to winter and summer again.

There were more verses... but Seren couldn't remember them all. Elspeth used to sing it now and again, though she couldn't remember if Elspeth learned that song from their grandmamau, or the maid, Isolde, who'd cared for them for a while in Henry's court. Her brows knit, because she had forgotten that lady. But for some reason her face re-emerged tonight from the depths of her memory.

Isolde... the very first woman to brush her hair... long before Elspeth was old enough to care for them. It was Isolde, in fact, who'd roused them from their beds on the night they'd learned their father's fate, and it was Isolde who'd escorted them to Llanthony in

Wales. But, for all that she'd claimed to love them, she'd handed them over to the priory, then stole away never to return. All lies, clearly.

For that matter, it was also through Isolde they'd learned about the Promised Land—the Summer Isle where *dewinefolk* lived free, without fear of persecution. It was now a drowned island, inhabited by lost souls. Perhaps all lies as well?

It could be, for it was also Isolde who told them the world was born in fire, and that it would end in fire. She'd also claimed herself a true maid of Avalon, and bade them to keep her secret. To this very day, so far as Seren knew, neither she, nor any of her sisters had ever betrayed her.

Curious how she'd blocked these memories... and curiouser yet that they'd returned to her as suddenly as had her affinity for the divine. She lay puzzling over that, when Wilhelm turned and whispered, "Art awake?"

The sound of his voice gave Seren a little shiver. "Aye," she said.

"Why?"

"I don't know. Mayhap, I am cold."

And it was true, though it was only partly true. There was too much on her mind... and too much in her heart... and, in truth, she could just as easily cast herself a warming spell.

He turned onto his side, peering over at her across the glowing embers, and was silent a long while, then said, "You can use my blanket."

"Oh, nay," she protested. "'Tis cold, Wilhelm, and I would not leave you..."

"Seren. I am not so noble as that. You may come lay beside me and we will double them together."

Seren's heart skipped a beat—as much for the

tender way he'd spoken her name as for this thing he'd proposed.

Share his blanket?

Whilst he lay beneath it?

"I will keep you warm," he said huskily, and then slid an arm out from beneath the blanket, inviting her over, and Seren swallowed with great difficulty. She held her breath until it grew painful. This was not an invitation to mate, but she was no cretin. She understood well enough what happened betwixt men and women when they lay in close proximity... what was more... she found herself longing for such things to happen betwixt them. *It was true.* It didn't matter that he was the bastard son of a lowly baron. Nor did it concern her at all that his brother was an executioner for the Church. If she lay beneath his blanket, she could not be held accountable for the mischief her hungry heart would rouse.

Uncertainty kept her still, but her heart urged her to get up and go to him. Sweet fates, she'd been confronted by men of all types, wanting this or that, but never in her life had any man wanted naught—and for that alone, she wanted Wilhelm all the more.

The fire between them burned lower, cooling with the long night, but the fire in her heart reignited.

"If you prefer, I can put more kindling on," he said. "But I loathe to do that now that we are so close. It would be a travesty if your mother discovered us when we are so close."

The night was black, with barely a star in the sky.

For days now there'd been no sign of her mother's ravens. It was all too easy to believe they were alone in this world—no one about for miles and miles. No one to see her weakness...

But she was a Daughter of Avalon; no matter what came of this night, she had nothing to be ashamed of.

Whatever happened was meant to be.

Exhaling, Seren let go of doubts, rising from her pallet. "Thank you," she said, and gathered up her blanket, then tiptoed over to where he lay.

WITH BATED BREATH, Wilhelm watched her steal over to his side of the fire. He'd been lying there for so long, trying in vain to sleep, acutely aware of every toss and turn she made, every huff, every sigh, and finally, when she began to hum so softly, so sweetly, his heart shattered.

Reveling in the thought of her lying close, he wasted no time peeling back the blanket, scooting over to allow her plenty of room. He'd folded his wool so that half lay on the bracken, the other half lay folded over him. Now, as he scooted over, shortening the half that covered him, he didn't care. He would sleep with a scrap to cover him so long as Seren lay here beside him. Vowing to hold her, naught more, he would carve this memory into his heart—her scent, her warmth, the silky softness of her skin—and take it with him to his grave.

Settling beside him, she threw her own wool over them both, and said again, "Thank you." And then she reached over to make certain his legs were covered before settling into the crook of his arm. The gesture was sweeter than he could bear. Not since his mother— God rest her soul—had any woman cared whether he would stay warm through the night. Wilhelm didn't know what to say. His throat grew tight, and it felt as though someone had shoved a wad of cloth down his gullet, and there it remained.

He should give her more of the blanket, no doubt. That was the reason she'd come over in the first place, but, the feel of her lying beside him fed his starved soul like a thirsty man stumbling from a desert. He couldn't think to respond. He couldn't in all his life remember a moment so bitterly sweet... nor any woman whose body fit so neatly against his own.

His heart thumped painfully, and his blood simmered like molten fire through his veins. She turned her bottom just a bit, so that it snuggled against the heat of his loins, and God save his rotten soul, he daren't move, nor speak—not even to warn her she was playing with fire... a fire that once ignited, would never again be put out.

It was more than he could bear. He put a hand plaintively to her hip, pushing her gently away. "Seren," he said.

"Nay," she protested, and then she turned to look him directly in the eyes, leaning so near to his mouth that, for a moment, they shared the same breath.

He could see her pale eyes shining through the darkness, brilliant and surreal.

"Seren?"

WHEREAS MOST GIRLS dreamt of having a husband and babes, Seren had always feared this would never be her destiny. She and her sisters each had dowries, but no advocates for their futures. They were subject to the whims of a king who bore them little love, and if aught at all, he was daunted by their blood—if not because of their father, then certainly because of their mother. Because of this, she had long feared that she and her sisters were destined to grow old together. Not for one instant had she had any affection from her father, nor any from her mother. Her grandmamau was long dead by the time she was born, her uncle Emrys, as well. Isolde had been kind to them, but despite that she was present when Seren was born, at this point, she was only a distant shadow from the past, a sweet old woman whose folk tales had kept them awake at night. As for Matilda and her sons, well, they shared a blood bond, no doubt, and clearly she had a hundred more kinsmen through her father alone. But Wilhelm was the first person aside from her sisters that she had ever felt close to.

Tomorrow their moment might be lost.

"Kiss me," she begged.

"Nay," he refused, but then he reached for her. "I dare not," he confessed, even as he placed two trembling fingers to her temple, sweeping hair from her face.

Auras were so tricky to read; so often Seren could see them as they existed for others, but for the first time in her life, she could read her own, in the arc of their auras combined. It glowed as bright as a flame... natural born, golden-hued and genuine. In that moment, frozen in time, she had a sense of something timeless... something... lasting... something pure.

There were times between times... times when the world itself ceased to breathe... only waiting for a new time to unfold. These were tween times, when the veil between worlds was at its thinnest and the *hud* was at its strongest. These were the golden hours from whence were born all possibilities and came all promises.

Moved to do so, Seren lifted her hand to Wilhelm's cheek, and even as she touched him, the trees sang, with leaves tinkling like bells. The cool wind kissed her warm skin, raising the small hairs of her flesh. It was, she believed, a whispered blessing from the Goddess.

"Kiss me," she dared again, and Wilhelm brushed another curl from her face. The feel of his warm hands gave her a shiver. "Art lovely," he whispered. "Too lovely for the likes of me... you were born for better things."

Seren shook her head adamantly. "I am not."

He smiled wistfully, his big fingers tentatively exploring her face. "You are beautiful," he argued. "Body and soul. I am a beast. Look at me, Seren. I am scarred inside and out."

"I see you," she said, and she did. And she wished he could see what she saw... the beauty and goodness in his eyes.

She could feel his hand trembling in the length of her hair, and she knew he struggled with desire. She had seen that look far too oft in men's eyes, but never before had she wondered how she could assuage it. She whispered, "You are beautiful to me, Wilhelm." And she reached up to brush a finger over the scar at his brow, tracing it across his lid, then down to his cheek. To her utter amazement it vanished beneath her fingertips. Amazed by the transformation, she peered at her hand, golden against the firelight, and then, encouraged, she took his whiskered face in both hands, and moved to kiss his brow, taking it as another sign from the Goddess. She was born to love this man.

He was her savior, but she might be his as well, and she sensed he was as alone in the world as she was. Wilhelm needed her as much as she needed him.

Taking a deep, fortifying breath, she dared to slide her fingers down to his breast, exploring the tightness of his leathers, stretched thin by the breadth of his chest. His hand covered hers at once, preventing any further exploration. "Seren," he said. "You must stop. I have naught to give you."

Their amalgamated auras burned brighter, until Seren could feel the heat of her own yearning slide though her like liquid flame, calling to her pagan self. Inhaling a shuddering breath, she tilted her woman's flower closer to the object of her desire, sensing instinctively that if he would only fill her, she could be complete. "Will you deny me?" she whispered breathlessly.

"As God is my witness, I would deny you naught I had the power to give it," he said, and once again, he brushed a strand of hair from her face, so gently that it might have been naught but a breath, and Seren shivered again, only this time not because she was cold. Nor was she tired. She was wide-awake, heart pounding in her ears.

"You have as much to give me as I have to give you," she argued, "and I willingly give all I have."

"Seren," he protested, only once more, but this time the certainty was gone from his voice. Seren felt his heart pounding so fiercely beneath her fingertips. After an audible swallow, he freed her hand, giving her leave to do as she pleased.

"My heart is mine to give," she said. "But I have no need to give it to you, Wilhelm. You have already stolen it."

His brows twitched with confusion, and Seren pressed instinctively closer, inhaling the intoxicating scent of his male flesh—a combination of leather, horse, sun, sweat... and something else... something that teased her in places she dared not confess.

Women were born with a certain intuition. She might not know precisely what should happen next, but she listened to the whisper in her heart... that voice from the Goddess that told her to tempt him a little more. "Speak no more," she said, brushing a finger over his lips, pressing the pad of her thumb gently against the curve of his mouth.

Wilhelm rewarded her with a lap of his tongue over her thumb and a low, throaty growl, and her heart tripped a few beats. At long last, he bent to kiss her, slowly, tentatively, as though he feared she would flee, and Seren's heart tumbled with joy as his tongue swept over her hot lips, tasting her, then dipping hungrily within to steal the nectar from her mouth. She moaned with desire, her body responding with a will not entirely her own. He answered in kind, and it was as though some baser instinct took over, their bodies entwining and writhing in a dance as old as time. Unbidden words came to her... from where, she hadn't any clue.

Freely choose, or choose to be free

"Yay," she said, as he slid down her body to suckle at her breast even through the fabric of her gown.

"Yay," she said again as the skimming of his lips and teeth nearly drove her to madness.

Eager for more, she reached down to lift up her gown. "I freely give myself to you," she said him, and then she was lost, because he growled again, deep in the back of his throat, like an animal possessed. He shifted to unfasten his trews, his movements deft, never taking his lips from her body... down, down, he slid, until he could press his tongue against the flower of her womanhood. And then, gone was the sweet man she had come to know, replaced with the beast he claimed to be—ravenous and formidable. Shrugging free of his trews, he covered her, and Seren abandoned herself to the moment. Somewhere amidst the chiming and tinkling of the leaves, she heard that voice again, ancient as time:

> Bound by destiny, to destiny bound,
> Another to one, one to another.

Throwing her head back and crying out in pleasure, Seren wrapped her legs about his waist, drawing him closer.

This is what she was made for.

Come daylight, she might think differently, but here and now, there was no greater purpose in life than this... to love Wilhelm Fitz Richard.

28

A messenger arrived from Aldergh during the wee hours of the morn, shouting as he approached.

"The babe," he screamed, leaping down from his mount and hurling himself at the iron-spiked oak, pounding furiously at the gate. "M'lady," he shouted. "The babe! Admit me! M'lady, the babe!"

"Gods bones, man! What the devil are ye wailing over?" inquired a guard from the ramparts. Peering up, the messenger stumbled to his knees, clasping together his hands, beseeching.

"Please," he begged. "I must see m'lady of Aldergh, please!" And then buried his face into his hand and wept inconsolably.

The guard hadn't the first inkling what the man was babbling over, but, clearly, he'd come a long way, looking worse for the wear, and sensing the exigency, he ordered the portcullis raised, and then sent a guard to wake the lady. Within moments, Lady Rosalynde emerged from her marquee in robes, along with her sister, and recognizing the man, the lady of Aldergh cried out in distress, and bolted into a run, falling to her knees beside the weeping man.

"Alwin," she cried. "Please! Speak!"

"Forgive me, m'lady," he said, tears shining in his eyes. "'Tis Broc," he said. "We thought it was you."

"Who?" Elspeth demanded. "Who! Please, tell me who!"

"You," the man cried. "It was *you*, m'lady! It was you!"

❦

A BLACKBIRD SANG in the treetop.

A damselfly whizzed past her nose.

Not that Seren wasn't already awake, or thrilled by the prospect of seeing her sister—perhaps even today —but she was loathed to end the moment. So far as she was concerned, the night should have lasted an eternity. Her lover's breath was warm on her nape, and there was a delicious ache between her legs—not one for which she had a true complaint.

Sheltered within Wilhelm's embrace, she daren't even stretch, for fear of waking him. She leaned back against him, and smiled joyfully when he nuzzled her sleepily.

Nude from the waist down, he was still clad in his *sherte*, but his leather gambeson had found its way into a bush, along with his trews and his boots.

She herself, remained fully dressed, but his hand was cupping her left breast, and her hair, disheveled from the night's pursuits, lay draped over her face, sticking to her lips.

Stirring lazily, she watched as a bee alit upon a nearby blossom, then changed its mind, buzzing away, only to settle on another.

Wilhelm stirred, every so oft, pecking lazily at her nape, nuzzling his whiskered chin against her tender skin, tickling the flesh of her neck. For the very first

time in so bloody long, everything was right with the
world, and Seren couldn't wait to share her joy with
Rosalynde. She was no longer a maiden, but what did
that matter? Should she have kept her virginity so her
mother could sell it to the highest bidder? Or so
Stephen could trade her for allegiances?

Nay. She was her own woman, no less so today
than she was yesterday.

Freely choose, or choose to be free, the Goddess had
ordained.

Well, she could choose both if she so wished, and
yet... deep, deep down, she knew she didn't want to be
without Wilhelm. If only he would allow her to try,
she would make him a good wife. How could such
tragedy lead to such overwhelming joy?

Fate was, indeed, a fickle thing. How was it possible she could lose her heart to the very brother of
her own betrothed?

It didn't matter.

Blinking back happy tears, she watched the fat bee
flit from blossom to blossom, suddenly joined by another. The two bees took turns with the stamens, and
she smiled contentedly, certain that even bees longed
for mates. It was a yearning that called from the
depths of one's soul.

In fact, she was so happy this morning that she
daren't acknowledge the whisper of a warning that
threatened to darken her mood. Nothing could spoil
this for her—nothing. If pain and suffering must exact
tolls, so must joy.

At long last, she felt Wilhelm's lashes flutter open.
"Art awake?" he asked gruffly, his voice hoarse with
sleep.

It was the most amazing sound Seren had ever
heard—more musical than lyres or harps, far more

delicious than tarts or *cryspes*, more pleasing than a swim in the brook on a bright summer day. "I am," she said, burrowing her bottom deeper into the roost of his body, lest he so much as consider rising.

In answer, his hand slid across her belly, hooking her between the legs, and pulling her firmly against his naked form. "Mmmh," he said. "I could wake this way for the rest of my days."

Seren blushed, her body responding to his touch just so easily. Even as he fondled her intimately, she felt the heat of her desire begin anew, and, for the first time since her sister's death—and so long before that—she felt a seed of true joy sprouting in her soul.

The truth was irrefutable: Wilhelm Fitz Richard was the love of her heart. She never, ever wished to abandon this glade. Even the bees and damselflies conspired to keep her, whizzing and buzzing a summer song to bewitch her.

"We cannot undo what we have done," he said, his breath hot against her lobe, giving her a shiver, and when she opened her mouth to agree—and to reassure him—he squeezed her gently, and said, "Shhh... I've more to say."

Seren nodded, very eager to hear it.

"I... I should have liked to have been a better man—"

She opened her mouth once more to speak and he squeezed her to silence her, and said, "I am not done."

But then, he fell silent a long, long moment and Seren could feel his lashes fluttering closed as he contemplated how best to continue—and yet, if only he would allow her to speak, she was so sure she could set him at ease.

He should not feel guilty for what she so willingly

pursued. She had known very well what would transpire the instant she lay down next to him.

She didn't regret it for an instant.

WILHELM SIGHED, hugging the woman whom destiny had placed into his arms—a woman of exquisite beauty, both inside and out. How, by the glory of God, he'd been so well favored, particularly at this trying time, he didn't know. But, here she was, and if she would allow it, he would attempt to provide for her in the way a good husband should provide for his wife. Alas, he didn't quite know how to put that into words, and he was heartily afraid she might deny him. After all, he had naught to offer, not even a proper bed.

They had been traveling together so long, it was perhaps to be expected they would cleave to one another, but in truth, he should have known better than to pursue anything at a time when she was bound to be so vulnerable.

Later, when they arrived at Warkworth, it was entirely possible she would regret everything... and if she did, Wilhelm would not stand in her way. He could never dare constrain her to a promise he'd exacted in a moment of passion. She was worthy of someone better than him, and... Christ almighty... the more he considered it, the more he knew he was speaking out of turn.

Something like regret soured his gut, diminishing his ardor and softening his cock against her bottom.

What the bloody hell was he thinking?

Disgusted with himself, he huffed a sigh, and said nothing of the sort he'd intended to say. "I am not worthy of you," he said, yanking the blanket up and over his lap, embarrassed now by his nudity, even despite that he'd never once suffered such an affliction in all his days.

Guilt colored his cheeks, and bloomed hotter when she spun to look at him with those haunting silver eyes—eyes that were somehow both happy and sad... and far too innocent.

He was older, besides—not that it mattered overmuch betwixt lords and their ladies, but one day, when his beard was gray and eyes were cloudy with age, and she was busy sweeping their crude, little hovel... she would look at him then, and truly, she could rue this day.

"God's teeth," he exclaimed. She was mourning her sister besides! What in God's name made him think this beauteous flower could ever be his to pluck and keep? "We should go," he said, and rising taking the blanket with him.

Seren's brows collided, and she hurried to fix her dress, her cheeks blooming as pink as a rose.

29

Appoint as a penalty life for life...
burn for burn, wound for wound, bruise for bruise.
—*Exodus 21:23-25*

L ife endures even in stone. Crystals bloom over
  time. Souls are not affixed only to dying flesh,
and there are places, like people, whose allure is as seductive as the glittering silk of a dew-dropped spider's
web.

Strangled with brambles, a tower looms before
me, sorrow clinging to the edifice like an acrid
perfume.

"Come," it whispers. *Wrap yourself in a cocoon of my
darkness.*

Like a stain of purpled blood oozing from a fes-
tering wound, a mantle of bellflowers lies untrampled
before it. But these bright, lavender blooms barely
conceal the stench of decay that clings to this bog-
ridden land.

Cradled within my arms, the child wails pitifully
—famished, I must suppose. But I am unmoved. He is

but a means to an end—mine or theirs. The simple fact that he bears such a striking resemblance to my brother and my once-born child is without merit, save that I know I cannot kill him with my own bare hands. His smile would stay my hand and his coos would twist my heart...

And yet, remembering another child I spared—a traitor born of my blood—anger spurs me forward. Continuing toward the waiting tower, bellflowers are crushed beneath my horse's hooves. But that is not enough: Before dismounting, I shrivel the blossoms with a turn of my hand, and in the blink of an eye, that which was alive, is now dead—a carpet of ash florets with smoking heads. Far more beauteous to me. Destruction. Blight. Desolation. Give me these, because they speak truth—not like the lies that pour from a lover's lips.

Answering my call, a congress of ravens alights atop the tower, familiar voices squawking in greeting. *My children, my loves, my ebony-winged champions.* Chortling in welcome, I make way to the tower to join them, staining the hem of my gown with ash as I walk.

Someday, I will rebuild my palace so men will be blinded by all that glitters. The land itself will be deluged in a darkness so deep that only my courtyard will brighten the endless night. In a flight of fancy, I envision plucking the sun from the sky, and the moon and the stars as well, swallowing them whole. Oh, yay, vengeance is *mine... I* shall repay.

When I am through, the realms of men will be inhabited by winged creatures, even as Avalon harbors lost souls. The *fae* will be no longer. Men will be no longer.

More birds arrive, until every branch of every tree

hangs low with the weight of my black-eyed, black-winged children.

Only pausing before I enter, I pluck a pin from my coif, transforming the bejeweled pin into a staff, with golden-eyed serpents. A simple feat. Not all spells require incantations, nor potions, nor brews. Some spells are performed by the will of the mind, no more, no less. To this end, I tap my sacred staff upon the ground, stirring ash into whispery plumes, then circle the tower, speaking familiar words:

> *Ye who would harm, ye who would maim,*
> *Proceed and face the same.*
>
> By all on high and law of three,
> This is my will, so mote it be.
>
> *Ye who would harm, ye who would maim,*
> *Proceed and face the same.*
>
> By all on high and law of three,
> This is my will, so mote it be...

Once the circle is complete, I transmute the staff once more into a coif pin and then return the adornment to my hair, before entering the ruins.

Like the exterior, the interior is decrepit, half walls with partial floors, a crumbling stone stairwell. I can see it was meant to be grand once upon a time—a belfry for a church, perhaps? The design is Roman, with rough and rubble walls and putlog holes to provide for wooden platform floors. There are remnants of the old wood, more than enough to burn. Clearly, someone has attempted to restore this place to no avail, erecting scaffolds to restore the floors.

I climb slowly, passing foyers and empty rooms, determining how best to use the edifice to my greatest advantage.

Old wood burns the same as new. I should rouse a fire they'll spy so far as York. Wouldn't that be delightful? I shall have an audience of thousands!

After all this time, the belfry is gone, but the roof is sturdy. Once I arrive, I lay down the child atop a small platform, weary of my burden, then wave a hand to bind him.

"Sweet boy," I purr. "It simply won't do if you fall." Removing a small pouch from my cloak, I set it, too, upon the platform beside the child, before unveiling the reliquary. I grin with pleasure at the sight of it—an intricately carved piece of metalwork, made from an alloy not presently known to mortal men.

"Oh, Mordecai," I say. "Sweet Mordecai." And I set the reliquary down on the platform as I remove the necklace bearing my athame. With its beautiful obsidian handle, it is an ancient blade, fashioned long, long before I laid eyes upon Avalon. The earth itself gave birth to this gem, and it was cut from the same alloy used in the creation of Caledfwlch. It glows in my presence, absorbing my soul's energy and reflecting it back. The Church has it all wrong. Caledfwlch does not glow in the presence of evil, nor does it do so in the presence of a *dewine*. This alloy only burns in the presence of a God.

Caw. Caw.

More ravens settle upon the crenels.

Caw. Caw.

Clearly, my daughters haven't had the wits to open the reliquary. It remains sealed.

Stupid, stupid girls.

It but needs the same care that must be taken with

the Book of Secrets—a drop of *dewine* blood and pretty words.

With a disdainful curl of my lip, I slash the blade across my palm, taking pleasure in the pain. And then, again, smiling, I turn my hand over the reliquary and speak sacred words.

> A drop of my blood to open or close,
> Speak now the song of ancient prose.
> Shackles be gone, Goddess reveal,
> The bonded soul my reliquary
>   conceals.

An explosion of smoke bursts from the artifact— so much smoke that it seems the vial should not have been able to contain it all. And once the smoke clears, I am faced with a man. "Hello, Mordecai," I say, greeting my old friend.

Mordecai inhales a life-affirming breath, and even as I admire the power of my *shadow magik*, his body reforms into solid flesh.

"Mistress," he says, finding his voice.

He gives a glance at the child, and I say, "There is work to be done, my friend. You will find a horse in the glade. Take it. Deliver a message to Warkworth for me." I hand him a slip of parchment. "Tell my daughters to bring *my* Book, and if they do, I will return the babe. If they refuse, I will kill him, and then return to destroy his brother."

"Aye, mistress, I'll fail you not," he says.

"See you do not. Next time... I will scatter your essence to the winds so you will never return."

"Aye, mistress," he says dutifully, without a trace of fear, and I know he will succeed. With a black-eyed glance toward the babe, he bounds for the stairs.

By now, more of my sweet children have arrived—my beautiful, dutiful children of darkness.

"*Dreiglo*," I say, and all about me, my ravens become soldiers, all clad in fine, black leather and bearing the sigil of my house—not Blackwood, Avalon—the twin golden serpents entwined about the stem of a winged chalice, my grail, my cauldron of cauldrons.

The babe is momentarily startled by the booted soldiers as they go, spilling down the stairs, like cockroaches.

Ignoring the child's wails, I peer over the crenels... at the circle I drew below, waiting for Mordecai to pass with all my soldiers. The instant they are clear of the circle, I whisper, "*Llosgi*." The circlet ignites.

No one may trespass now, lest they cross with my book. The Book of Secrets is the only passage they will have. If anyone steps through that fire, even so much as a toe, they will be consumed. I watch with glee as Mordecai finds my horse, mounting the beast. He puts a heel to the animal's flank, and I note he still bears a telltale tail, black as the darkest night. Pointed and pliant, like a serpent, it twines about the horse's tail as I settle to wait... after all, long after mortal flesh has withered to dust... here I will remain.

30

Worrying her hands, weeping at intervals, Elspeth paced the marquee all the while Rosalynde stood by, feeling helpless.

There were plans to be made; however, without knowing precisely what Morwen intended, it was impossible to respond accordingly. Already, they'd dispatched riders to find Malcom—wherever he could be —to inform him of his son's abduction. More messengers to Aldergh, only to be certain Elspeth's Lachlan is safe, as Alwin claims. As for the steward, the poor man, he is disconsolate. He has returned to Aldergh with an escort to ensure he arrives safely.

If, indeed, Morwen had Elspeth's babe, she must be somewhere nearby, but where?

Why would she take one child, not the other?

Did she plan to keep Broc?

But nay... this was not their mother's way. Morwen loathed children. Her own daughters were a testament to this fact. Even before Llanthony, she'd employed an army of maids to care for her children, and even whilst in the same room with them, she'd barely ever spared them a glance or a word. She was not a woman inclined to nurture, and she would never be a doting grandmother.

What did she want with that child?

"I should not have left," Elspeth sobbed. "I'm a dreadful mother. Malcom will never forgive me—gods forbid, I'll never forgive myself!"

Rosalynde hadn't the first inkling what to say under such dreadful circumstances, but it tormented her to hear her sister blaming herself.

"You did all you could, Elspeth. You warded that castle. You left the children in capable hands. You had no cause to believe our mother might infiltrate Aldergh."

Elspeth cast Rosalynde a dark look, her face twisting with anger. "I told you she is wily! I told you that nothing was safe from her—now, my sweet babe is gone!"

There was naught Rosalynde could say.

She knew her sister was beside herself with worry, and she wasn't herself. Much as Rose longed to calm her, she began to pace as well, worried beyond measure.

They sent another rider south to locate Giles. And yet another to King David, in hopes of enlisting the Scot's king's aid—one last time though it was doubtful David would ride to their rescue, when he had no hope of turning Warkworth's allegiance. And nevertheless, it was worth a try. Rosalynde was ill-prepared for war. Even after all these months, Warkworth was not ready. She was not a commander-in-chief, and what was more, she had no inkling of her mother's true powers or what her role should be in defeating her—but if only Rhiannon were present.

Rhiannon would know what to do.

Elspeth continued to pace disconsolately.

"If you wear yourself out, you will be of no use to your son."

"Quiet!" her sister snapped. "I cannot think for all your prattling."

Rosalynde frowned. She had said so little until now. Even so, she refrained from pointing that out, giving her sister leave to say or do as she would. It was not every day one lost a child. Morwen was not kind. Nor was she merciful.

Alas, hope was a luxury they did not have, and even so, hope was all they had. Foremost in Rosalynde's mind was the day they'd watched their mother strangle a poor maid who sat begging for her life.

"Lady Rosalynde," inquired Edmund, her steward, eyeing Elspeth sympathetically as he parted the tent to enter.

"What is it?"

His gaze was dark, sidling first to Elspeth, who barely acknowledged him, and then to Rosalynde. He gave her a nod, and she rose from her seat to follow him out the door. Poor Elspeth barely noticed.

"What is it?"

"We have a visitor," he said darkly.

"Did you bid them enter? Should we dare?"

He shook his head. "Nay, m'lady. I did not believe you would wish it."

"Who is it?" she asked, but even as she did, tendrils of fear rippled down her spine.

Edmund swallowed visibly, lifting his brows. "He calls himself Mordecai. He said you would know him."

Rosalynde's eyes widened. "Mordecai?" she asked. But nay, nay, they slew him back in the woods. Mordecai was her mother's Shadow Beast. "Art certain, Edmund?"

"Quite," he said, and then he handed her a slip of parchment. On it, lay scribbled eight terrifying words:

My Book for the child. Or he dies.

The parchment was unsigned, but it was not by Mordecai's hand the note was scribed. She knew her mother's script well enough to recognize it. The letters were etched so deeply into the parchment that it bespoke her fury. She wanted the Book, now, or she would kill the child. Rosalynde knew her mother well enough to know the consequences of defying her. But, deep in her heart of hearts she knew they needed the *grimoire* to defeat Morwen. And yet, if they kept the Book of Secrets, they would condemn the child. The babe would suffer the consequences. On the other hand, if they conceded the *grimoire*, Morwen would have one more powerful weapon at her disposal.

All hope of defeating her might be lost...

It was Edmund who gave voice to her deepest fear. "Even if you return the Book, there's no guarantee she will return the child unharmed."

Neither was Rosalynde certain anyone who faced Morwen would live to speak of it.

And still, there was no doubt in her mind: She could not live with herself if her decision brought about the death of her nephew. Nor would her sister ever agree to abandon her child. Rosalynde would not defy a mother's wish. So, it seemed they had no choice. *No choice at all.* Together, they must face that demon, come what may.

"Where is she?" Rosalynde asked.

"The Widow's Tower. In Holystone Wood, west of the nunnery. Even if you leave now, m'lady, you'll not arrive till the sun rises on the morrow."

Rosalynde nodded, her eyes stinging with unshed tears.

Mordecai.

White-hot fury coursed through her. "If that beast so much as attempts to enter my demesne, loose your arrows!"

"He is gone," said her steward.

Gone? Was he so certain they would concede the Book?

But of course, he was. They were dealing with Morwen, and Mordecai knew what they knew... she would kill that boy if they refused her. He was her mother's servant in every way, canny as she was.

"Gather a retinue," she demanded. "Find my sister a good set of leathers and a worthy sword. We ride at once." She turned on her heels to go inside to inform her sister.

"Lady Rosalynde," pleaded her steward. "You must wait until m'lord returns!"

"Nay, I'll not," she advised the man. And then she said it again, more to bolster her own resolve. "I will not!"

She was a *dewine*. A child of the Goddess. A daughter of Avalon. She would take the sword Giles gave her and put it to good use, and she would ride as the Queen of the Iceni once rode—with fury in her heart and vengeance in her soul.

❧

SEREN HAD GONE WILLINGLY into his arms, only because she'd believed Wilhelm held some measure of affection for her. How could she have been so wrong?

But nay, she was not wrong. He was a stubborn

fool, because it wasn't possible to feign what she'd spied in his eyes and felt by his touch. She had gone her entire life without falling prey to such temptation —not even when that handsome Thomas Becket came to visit with an endowment for their priory. She'd caught his eye, no doubt. But Seren had never even considered being alone with the man. He was pretty enough, and as most pretty young lords did, he'd coveted her body, but when the time came to speak from his heart, he hadn't had a word to say. What was more, he hadn't actually wished to hear a word from her, expounding endlessly about how a good woman should mind her father and her Church and tongue. She'd only wished she could turn him into a worm, not unlike what she wished to do to Wilhelm right now. Only, in her fury, she decided to take an example from her sister Rosalynde and speak her mind.

"Did I not please you?"

He didn't answer, and Seren insisted he address her. "Wilhelm!"

His cheeks bloomed—perhaps as brightly as hers —and he suddenly seemed to have great difficulty looking her in the face. In her anger, she gave her horse a heel and urged it forward, forcing Wilhelm to fully acknowledge her.

"You did please me," he said finally, scarcely looking at her. "More than you can imagine." But he spoke through his teeth, and she could see the knob rise in his throat.

Seren's eyes stung with unshed tears. Goddess save her; she could feel the same stirring in the *aether* that called to *witchwater*—but nay, she would not give Wilhelm the satisfaction of knowing how much he'd upset her.

"Seren," he said, shaking his head—but why? To deny her?

Already today, they'd come a long way without speaking. Only a good hour ago he'd confessed how near they were to Warkworth. Soon she would see her sister, and tomorrow he would scurry away, like a puppy with his tail between his legs. And then, her heart would bleed even more than it was bleeding already. What did he believe he was doing? Saving her from him? Or him from her?

Seren was desperate for him to address the issue.

"Why would you ruin everything? Do you regret what passed between us, because I do not. You're a foul-tempered man betimes, and you're a crude bore. You eat as though you'll never see another day, but I do not regret giving myself to you, Wilhelm Fitz Richard!"

He reined in his horse, looking at her with a tilt of his head and furrowed brows. Then, without a word, he slid down and came to her side, peering up at her with an intensity that unnerved her.

"Say it again," he demanded.

Seren winced. She had a terrible feeling that she'd pushed him to his limit and if she repeated her imputations, he might drag her off her mount and put her over his knee to spank her... and still, she dared—only softer this time, with a bit less anger. "You're a foul-tempered man, a crude bore, and you eat as though you'll never see another day—'tis all true, Wilhelm, but I don't care."

"Not that," he said with a frown. "All the rest."

"What rest?"

"Will you make me say it again myself, because if I do, it won't mean so much, Seren."

Suddenly, a smile tugged at Seren's mouth, realizing what it was that he wished for her to repeat, and for all that he was glaring at her so ferociously, she recognized the flare of hope in his warm, dark eyes. She lifted her chin, repeating, "I said... I do not regret giving myself to you."

"And have you? Because 'tis not your body I truly desire, delectable though it may be."

Lifting her chin, Seren answered his question with a question of her own. "Do you think me a wanton? Because I am not," she apprised him. "And if you dare imply 'tis so, I will box your ears."

He grinned, then tugging her down from the horse, pulling her into his arms. "I must advise you; I am no man to be trifled with. Nor do I relinquish my belongings once they are given, few enough that I possess."

He was holding her so jealously now that she could feel the length of his manhood stabbing her in the belly. The very feel of it stole her breath.

"I am no man's chattel," she apprised, though without heat. Because in truth, she feared she belonged to him as thoroughly as she could belong to any.

Shocking her, he reached down to lift up her dress in broad daylight, then slid a finger into her most private region and Seren startled over the warmth of it, shuddering with delight. Only this time, there was no tenderness in his touch, and he groaned deep back in the back of his throat when he found her damp. His eyes grew heavy-lidded and he walked her slowly backward to a nearby tree, gently putting her back against it, and looking her straight in the face.

WILHELM HAD HAD ENOUGH.

He'd let her blister his ears all morning long, calling him this name and that name, never truly understanding why he'd abandoned their discourse this morning.

He was in a quandary, because he had nothing to give her—naught that belonged to him. He only wished to save her from a fate she couldn't yet see. And still, she would prefer to accuse him of usury than to see what it was he was trying to do—spare her from a life with a man who could give naught but his heart.

Once again, with meaning, he reached down to lift up her gown—only let her think him crude; he didn't care. Simply because he'd bedded her, he would not constrain her to a fate she didn't want. If she denied him once they returned to Warkworth, he would fully support her and take their secret to the grave, but she should know once and for all that it was not some gentle lord she would tempt.

He desperately craved the taste of her on his lips, and the instant he found the bud of her woman's flower, he felt her knees buckle and caught her.

Undaunted, Wilhelm thrust a finger between her woman's lips, then lifted it to his mouth. His tongue lapped the taste of her from his fingers, and he groaned again, deep in his throat, savoring the delicious tang of his beautiful flower.

Watching him, Seren gasped aloud, her look akin to horror, and he narrowed his eyes, his lips curving wolfishly.

"This is what you court if you continue. I am not a courteous man, Seren. Nor am I gentle-born like Giles. I haven't the manners of a pretty lord, nor can I bestow upon you gold, or gowns. I am a crude bore, as you say." And only to drive home his point, he slid his finger back into his mouth and lapped it with relish, like a dog with a juicy bone, all the while never releasing her startled gaze. And when he was done, he asked, "Has any man ever tasted you this way? Ever?"

Wide eyed, Seren shook her head. She opened her mouth to speak, but he silenced her once again, dropping his hand down and lifting her skirt again, so his fingers could seek her soft curls. There, he drove his fingers into her mons, tugging gently. "I do not share," he said, with meaning, but there was no threat to his gesture. Rather he wanted her to remember everything he had done to her last night... all the liberties he'd taken, and he would do it all again, right now, in plain sight of God and anyone else who might wander by. Holding her firmly against the tree, he dropped to one knee, bowing beneath her gown, and then with relish, he lifted his tongue to press against her flower bud, as he'd longed to do from the instant he awoke with the taste of her upon his lips and her arse snuggled so intimately against his cock... and every second of every minute thereafter.

SEREN WHIMPERED WITH PLEASURE, her eyes glistening with unshed tears—not because she was sad, but because she longed to hold him this way forever.

Everything he was saying, everything he was doing... it was utterly shocking. Certainly, this was not the way a lord treated his lady, and yet, it was... so... so... very... delightful... and he was telling her true. He was not gentle born. She reveled in that fact, somehow knowing instinctively that no pretty lord would dare what he was doing.

"I do not share," he said again, the heat of his breath on her mons, as his tongue dove again into her body, suckling from her as a bee would the nectar from a flower. And then, she couldn't stop herself; she tangled her hands into his hair, and said, "You're a lout, Wilhelm."

In answer, he chuckled darkly against her curls, and slid his callused hands about her bottom, pressing her closer for the onslaught of his tongue, lapping and suckling in turn, and finally, he lifted himself, and dared to kiss her—right on the mouth!—sharing the most shocking taste on his lips...

It was outrageous, appalling, intemperate, delicious, disquieting, bewildering, brutish, crude...

"Say you are mine," he demanded.

Seren trembled. She could not find her voice to speak, but she nodded anyway, and he growled with satisfaction, somehow managing to unlace his trews and dropping them to the ground as she delighted in the finger that danced so boldly inside her body. And then, once again, he was bare from the waist down—without any shame—his trews tangled about his ankles. And, with a guttural moan, he angled his hips down, and up, impaling her where she stood, and Seren gasped with delight, drunk with pleasure as he filled her with soft, silky heat. Her head fell backward against the tree, and she let him have his way, lifting her beneath the knees, and guiding her legs about his waist. He held her firmly against the tree, stroking her body from within, and this time, there was naught gentle about their loving. It was hungry and greedy, and when Wilhelm was done, he looked at her with a grin on his face, and said, "I hope you enjoy gruel; that's all I've got to feed you."

It wasn't true, Seren knew.

He was, indeed, a lout, because he'd already provided far more for her than she'd ever had in all her life. But what he hadn't done this time was satisfy her completely. Even their loving last night had left her with a glimpse of something... something maddening... something that promised... more. She tilted her hips again to tease him and said dreamily, "I am still hungry," and to that, his grin widened, and, inconceivably, he hardened. Again.

As Seren offered her neck to be ravaged, waiting to be fulfilled, the wind lifted, swirling leaves.

31

I t was the worst possible turn of events.

Giles was gone. Wilhelm hadn't been seen in months. Warkworth was vulnerable, and Rosalynde hadn't any choice but to empty their garrison. Perforce, she would leave a few good men to defend the castle, but there was nothing more critical than the battle she faced right now, and she was ill prepared to wage it.

To make matters worse, somehow Mordecai had survived the ordeal in the woodlot, and she knew he would be there, fighting by her mother's side. The very thought of facing that creature alone put a tremor in her belly.

So much depended on the outcome.

It had been months now since she'd last met her mother and so much had transpired since that day. She'd known very well that Morwen would never take the loss of her *grimoire* lightly, and that she would stop at naught to see it returned. Even so, she'd never once considered that her mother would endanger an innocent child.

Anticipating the battle to come, she dressed herself in the chainmail her husband had given her—

hauberk, chausses, tunic and gauntlets. She offered Elspeth a suit of boiled leather, as well as a mail coif, knowing her own armor would never fit. Elspeth was shorter than she was, but the babes had put a bit of weight on her and the chainmail wouldn't stretch. Alas, she would have preferred to see Elspeth better protected. She was a mother, after all, and had another babe at home to return to, but because she was a mother, there was no way Rosalynde could ever hope to keep a sword from her hand.

Besides, Elspeth was the eldest of her sisters. As such, there was little chance of telling her sister what to do. Elspeth was hard-headed. She was also furious, and at the instant, Rose pitied anyone who stepped in her sister's way.

Once they were armored and well-armed, the sight of Elspeth left Rosalynde awed. With her red-gold hair, and her bright blue eyes glinting with vengeance, she reminded Rosalynde of their mother. Save for the color of their hair and eyes, Elspeth and Morwen shared the same features. She had never quite noticed the startling resemblance before now, and it was no wonder Elspeth's servants had beckoned her inside. That's the only way Morwen could have trespassed against Elspeth's warding spell. She would have had to have been invited, and for that alone, though he didn't fully understand, Alwin was despondent.

About an hour after Mordecai departed, they received a message via homing pigeon: Even now, David and his men were traveling south to York. Malcom was said to be among them, but Giles was not.

Considering the circumstances, communicating by pigeons was not at all propitious, but there was so little time to waste. With all due haste, they'd dispatched yet another bird, with the intent of informing

Malcom of their travails. As of yet, they'd received no response, but neither had they anticipated hearing before their departure, nor could they wait. Rosalynde only hoped that with fifty good men, they would have some small chance against Morwen. If luck be theirs today, Eustace would not be with her in Holystone Wood, and she would not have his army by her side. Alas, even if she did, there was no way to avoid the conflict.

My Book for the child. Or he dies.

The very sight of those words had left Rosalynde sick to her belly. Sensing how important the Book of Secrets was to her mother's plans, she preferred not to hand it over, but again, they had no choice. Unfortunately, even if they managed to successfully negotiate for the return of the child, Morwen would still have won, because she was sure to use that *grimoire* to ensure their doom in the end. These were troubling times, and they could use all the help they could get. In light of this, while awaiting word from Edmund that the warriors were prepared to ride, she and Elspeth slipped into her marquee, joining hands in prayer.

"Mother Goddess hear our plea," Rosalynde whispered. "Dark be the hour, but you hold the key."

Elspeth joined her refrain. "Guide us now in your light, from darkness we flee. By all on high and law of three, What be your will, so mote it be."

There was no more to be said.

Their fate was in the hands of the Goddess, and England itself would rise or fall according to the outcome.

Tears sprang to Elspeth's blue eyes, and Rosalynde's eyes stung. Even together, they were ill-equipped to face their mother. Where, for the love of night, was Rhiannon?

THEY RODE OUT BEFORE DUSK, a company clad in silver, led by the Pendragon sisters, armor winking against a waning sun. They had but thirty miles to go—twenty as crows flew, but they were not crows. They rode swiftly, but no matter how swift the pace, it was impossible—as Edmund predicted—to arrive at the Widow's Tower before sunrise.

The ruins were not approachable by road. They must circle around peat bogs said to be greedy enough to swallow a man whole, and then re-enter Holystone Wood through the Lady's Walk. From there, it was another league or two traipsing over dry land.

A well-equipped cavalcade of fifty, they traveled all night long, and at long last, when the tower appeared on the horizon, the sun was beginning to rise, still sweltering enough to boil flesh in the confines of Rosalynde's helm.

With a gasp of distress, she drew off the helm, shoving back the coif to consider the battlefield and the best course of action...

The tower itself where Morwen was said to be keeping the babe was not so impressive, save that it was impossible to believe such an edifice had remained standing for so many decades, much less centuries. The structure seemed ancient as Avalon, surrounded by a mantle of black ash—as though the entire premises had suffered a fire.

A cacophony of bird cries filled the air. Nearly every tree within a half-a-mile radius was laden with shrieking birds.

Worse, Morwen had lit a circlet of blue fire to keep her enemies from the tower—*witchfire*, no doubt. Barred by that fire, it was only possible to breach by air, and the last time Rosalynde looked, she didn't have wings to fly, and neither did Elspeth.

But that wasn't what gave Rosalynde the greatest pause; it was that army of black-clad soldiers standing outside the circlet's perimeter, three rows deep—hundreds at the ready to do her mother's bidding. Her fifty-odd soldiers were no match for this army, not even with the help of witchery, and even the simple boon that Mordecai was nowhere to be seen was only small comfort.

Fear prickling her flesh, she stood watching from the shelter of the woods, wishing to the Goddess that they had more men. So, it seemed, they'd underestimated Morwen.

Yet again.

"God's teeth," exclaimed Edmund, bringing his mount forward to advise Rosalynde. "She has an army of mercenaries."

"Nay..." Rosalynde said. "They are not mercenaries."

She swallowed convulsively, recognizing the sigil. She had never once laid eyes upon that seal in person —at least never emblazoned upon armor—but Rhiannon had illustrated it so oft that the image was etched upon her mind. It was also writ upon many of the pages in the *grimoire*.

"Those... are..."

Elspeth shook her head quickly, warning Rosalynde without words to remain silent, because these were no common soldiers. No matter that their husbands had accepted them and their legacy, most men were still unprepared to know their *dewine* secrets.

Loyal steward though he might be, Edmund was but a simple man who'd served the old lord of Warkworth —a mortal man with mortal expectations. He was unprepared for the truth. Sweet fates, neither Rosalynde nor Elspeth were prepared themselves. But there was no denying what their eyes revealed... these men they would face wore the sigil of the house of Avalon—the twin golden serpents entwined about the stem of a winged chalice... the sacred cauldron some would call the Holy Grail.

But how... how was this possible?

Avalon, and *all* its denizens was long vanished from this realm. Now, who was Morwen Pendragon to claim them?

The question sent a frisson of fear down Rosalynde's spine. Elspeth's, too. Their bellflower gazes mirrored the same questions. The answers brought a new fear: Clearly, there was much they did not know about their mother. She had forces beyond their knowing at her beck and call. And nevertheless, her eldest sister remained stoic, prepared to do battle for the return of her son.

So, too, was Rosalynde.

It would serve no one for either of them to fall to their knees in despair. But what now? She swallowed a growing lump of fear, turning to regard her loyal steward.

"Remember your lessons," he said grimly. "You can do it, m'lady. Stay in the saddle, boots in the stirrups. Maintain the advantage of height. Swing wide, but not so wide you cannot reclaim your sword. 'Tis heavy and will wont to fly. Use both hands. I will guard your back."

Rosalynde gave the elder man a nod, grateful for his vote of confidence, and, more, his willingness to

fight beside her, and still... she was paralyzed with indecision, hot tears pricking her eyes.

Goddess help her, even if she issued the command, they could advance no further than the circlet.
She had never had an encounter with *witchfire*, but
she knew it to be deadly. The very instant the intense
blue flame ignited, it was impossible to extinguish,
even with water. In fact, according to legend, Taliesin
taught the Greeks to create a similar conflagration
from naphtha and quicklime. Greek Fire, they'd called
it, and like *witchfire*, it ignited on contact with water.
Whatsoever it touched—with even the tiniest spark—
burned until consumed. Though, unlike *witchfire*,
Greek Fire was an invention of the natural world and
could be extinguished with some effort. Both burned
with that same intense blue flame, but if the circlet
had been born of Greek Fire, by now, it would have
spread into the surrounding woodlands. Nay, this fire
was not naturally made. Rosalynde had no doubt in
her mind... it was *witchfire*, and she hadn't any clue
how to fight it.

But even if they could find some way into the circlet, they would first have to battle their way through
Morwen's black-clad soldiers—all of them afoot,
though armed to the teeth. Their armor shone black
as raven's wings.

The surrounding woods were rife with dragonflies
and midge flies. The stink of molder and mire filled
the air. A smoldering miasma wove itself through the
aether—so thick in places that Rosalynde's *dewine*
eyes could see it clearly.

"What is this place? she asked.

Edmund frowned. "The only thing I know for
certes is that the tower is cursed. Moons ago a lord
dared claim this land. They found his bride prone be-

neath the tower. Every year, the meadow surrounding it springs to life with her favored flower. And every year, the bellflowers creep further and further afield, as though she would still claim these lands in the name of her lord. No sane man will ever again claim these lands. Not even King Henry would count it among his Royal Forests."

It was a queer place... overgrown with brambles all choking the trunks of nearby trees. Lichen and moss grew, but not only on the north side, on the south side as well—as though the very laws of nature were circumvented here.

The place was made stranger still by the profusion of birds squawking and gawking from the branches.

Shivering, Rosalynde peered again at her sister. Elspeth's lips quivered, but Rosalynde restrained herself from reaching out to comfort her.

They had both heard of places like these—portals to the Nether Realm, like fairy glens. They were inexplicably perceptible when you stumbled across one, because the hairs of the nape stood at end, and the air held an unnatural chill. And yet, here, the sun shone brightly, glittering off bits of what appeared to be coal.

"How far lies York?" she asked.

"More than twenty leagues."

Rosalynde's shoulders fell with resignation. It was not possible to send another messenger to see if Malcom had received their message. And while it was certainly possible to travel the distance from York in a single day, it didn't seem possible for Malcom to plead his case to David, then travel all the way back in time to meet them here.

Still, she prayed. To any god or goddess who would listen.

In the meantime... fighting their way into the

tower didn't appear to be a wise option... therefore, they must negotiate... and pray to the Goddess their mother would honor her part in the bargain.

Swallowing another knot of fear that rose to choke her, Rosalynde fingered the pommel of her sword. Even at this distance, it had begun to hum in response to her mother's proximity. "You have the Book?" she asked Elspeth.

Elspeth nodded, flicking a glance at her sword. "It's glowing," she said softly.

Rosalynde gave a single nod. "Is there aught at all in that book to aid us?"

Elspeth shook her head.

Desperate for something, anything, Rosalynde asked, "You spoke words at Aldergh without knowing them beforehand... can you do it again?"

Elspeth shook her head. "I only spoke what the Goddess told me, but I do not hear her now."

The sisters turned their gazes to the tower, each whispering silent prayers to the Goddess, knowing full well that her intervention was not a given. The Goddess worked in mysterious ways, bending only where it served the spirit of the age. Such as it was, one lone child might not merit the altering of fate—not even for *dewinefolk*.

Soft and haunting, a melody drifted from the tower... rising in crescendo until it reached their ears... a familiar song... an echo of their youth...

> When thy father went a-hunting,
> A spear on his shoulder, a club in his
>   hand,
> He called the nimble hounds,
> 'Giff, Gaff; catch, catch, fetch, fetch!'

The tune lifted on the fetid breeze, impossibly loud, and nevertheless quiet as the scurry of a mouse.

"She's here," said Elspeth, shuddering. And even as she uttered the words, Morwen's dark-clad army shifted in formation, parting to form a path to the circlet.

Heart pounding with fear, Rosalynde waited to see what Elspeth would do. It was her child; the decision must be hers.

Lifting her head, Elspeth pushed back her shoulders, accepting their mother's invitation. Her sword hissed as she withdrew it from her scabbard and rode forth, eyes bright with vengeance—bright and blue as the fire girding the tower—leaving Rosalynde to follow.

THE PATH GREW NARROW NOW, with wild carrots growing thickly beside a meandering trail. By now, Seren's bottom ached, so did her legs. She felt like a court jester who'd turned summersaults for the king. By the blessed cauldron, she never knew there were so many ways to have relations; Wilhelm must have learned every one as thoroughly as he had the use of his sword—not only the one in his scabbard. The very thought made her cheeks bloom again, but she sighed contentedly.

"How far did you say we must ride?"

With a lazy grin, Wilhelm asked, "Art complaining already?"

Seren laughed softly. "Nay, I am not." She eyed him meaningfully. "I would but know. Thanks to you, yesterday's pursuits have left me... disadvantaged."

He chuckled low, the rich sound of his laughter

lifting her spirits as few things could do, considering the circumstances.

Soon enough, she would face Rosalynde, and what could she possibly say to make amends? Even after contemplating the Whitshed night after night, she hadn't the first inkling what had happened back in that harbor. Mulling it over again and again, she recounted the day as meticulously as she could. She'd gone to see a courier with Jack. They didn't linger going there or back. Forsooth, she wasn't even gone very long. By the time she'd returned, that ship was already consumed.

"Art thinking of your sister?"

"I am," Seren confessed. As of yet, over the course of these past few weeks, they'd barely spoken of the ordeal.

"There was little you could have done differently," he suggested. "Except perish with her... would you have it that way, instead?"

Seren shook her head. "Nay," she said. "I would not."

Not the least for which she would never have known Wilhelm. She cast a glance at the man she had begun to think of as her Goddess-given champion, watching him as he ripped off a length of dried corned-beef—a gift from the sisters at Neasham.

"Thank you," she said, again. "Were it not for you, 'tis certain I would have been returned to my mother's keeping."

His lips curved ruefully, as though he felt guilty over the events of these past few days, and she only meant to reassure him. "Wilhelm... if I had a thousand lives to lose, I would entrust them each to you."

His dark eyes twinkled with black humor. "Aye,

well, you have but the one," he advised, and averted his gaze.

Seren sensed that, no matter how many times she spoke to the contrary, he would blame himself for stealing her maidenhead. And, in truth, there would be consequences to pay for this, but Wilhelm stole nothing. Furthermore, she would never regret it—not even if she lived to be a thousand.

She frowned then, remembering that *dewinefolk* were hardier and lived longer than most. Her grand-mamau was seventy when she died more than twenty-two years ago. Her forbear, Yissachar, was said to have lived to be two-hundred and twenty. Morwen? Goddess only knew. Would she grow old enough to watch the man she loved die in her arms? It was a sobering thought, but however long she lived, Seren could never regret loving him, and she vowed to be a better mother than Morwen was—and suddenly, she found herself grinning, peering up at Wilhelm, realizing, only for the first time since their consummation, that she could, indeed, be carrying his child. She put a hand to her belly in wonder.

Oh, sweet Arwyn, she said silently, shifting from a high note to a heartrending low.

Would that you could know him.

Wishing with all her might that she did not feel such intense joy over an occasion that was born by her sister's tragedy, she peered up into the sky, and it was then her eye caught a formation of birds in the distance... black birds... ravens... thick as smoke...

The tiny hairs on her nape prickled.

Only once before had she seen them fly like that, mimicking the ebb and flow of smoke... as though reveling in the burning. Another mass of birds swooped in, then another... all of them diving into nearby trees,

and the closer Wilhelm and Seren rode in that direction, the louder their squawks.

Seren could tell by Wilhelm's expression that he'd
spied the birds as well. "Morwen," he said with a note
of trepidation, and Seren's eyes returned to the skies.

THERE WAS nothing in the natural world that could
draw so many ravens all together.

Unwilling to leave Seren behind and unwilling to
ride ahead, Wilhelm led them through the woods,
along the Lady's Walk.

Alone, he might have been far more inclined to
take chances; but he was not prepared to endanger the
woman he loved. Aye, it was true, he loved her. Now
that he understood something about his own true
heart, he realized he'd never loved Lady Ayleth at all.
That was affection, and perhaps lust, but not at all the
same sort of longing he felt for Seren.

Now, the possibility that her mother was near
filled him with dread down to his bones, because, this
time he realized beyond a shadow of doubt, if he lost
the love of his heart, he would never endure another
day without her.

He would perish with grief.

The Lady's Walk was said to have been forged in
the first days of Christianity by the lady of Rothbury.
Nearby there was a small pool where St. Ninian was
said to have baptized Christians. Her husband meant
to build a church to claim these ancient lands in the
name of his faith. He managed to construct no more
than a bell tower when his wife's body was found limp
by the door. Now, even when the woods grew thick
enough to throttle the trees, the Lady's Walk always
remained passable. By far, it was the easiest pass to

Warkworth, up until you reached the meadow with the tower. From there, they must return to the lower bogs, but they were not the first to traverse this path over the past few days. He spied the evidence cast at their feet—hoof prints made by fifty or more horses.

Following the path with some trepidation, they emerged near the tower. And there, in the meadow, he spotted the glitter of chainmail. Dismounting, thinking to leave Seren only an instant whilst he assessed the situation, he froze, recognizing the sigil of his house.

These were Warkworth's soldiers.

Swallowing with trepidation, he recognized his brother's wife at once, her glorious red-gold mane unbound, and his brother's glowing sword in her hand. Before he could speak to warn Seren, she, too, slid from her mount and rushed toward the clearing.

"Rose," she shouted. "Ellie! Rose!"

32

After everything she had endured—after losing Arwyn—nothing in this Goddess-given world could keep Seren from her sisters. Never had she been so relieved to see two people in all her life. She would know them from leagues away.

"Rose," she called, her eyes stinging with unshed tears. "Rose!" Only belatedly, she realized something was terribly wrong.

These were not all her sisters' soldiers. Armed in black, some stood staring, like statues. They did not even acknowledge her when she approached.

"Seren!" exclaimed Elspeth, sliding from her mount, and coming to embrace her, eyes red-rimmed and feverish, as though she'd been weeping for days. Her cheeks were high with color—anger, Seren realized.

Bright, burning anger.

Rosalynde, too, alit from her mount, only after re-sheathing her sword. She cast her arms out in greeting, but the reunion was short lived. Explanations were hurried: Their mother awaited inside that tower with Elspeth's child. In trade for the boy, she wanted the Book of Secrets. Rosalynde herself had brought fifty armed soldiers—but altogether they were not enough to challenge Morwen's army, so she'd commanded them to stand down and stay back.

Seren's eyes widened with fright as her gaze alit upon the *grimoire* in Elspeth's hand—that ancient tome Rosalynde herself risked her life to steal. Even despite the risk of returning it, they intended now to return it, except that the circlet of *witchfire* was impassible. Though none of Morwen's dark soldiers had so much as moved to prevent them from attempting, the sisters each understood the danger of attempting it.

"How did you find us?" asked Rose.

"The birds," said Wilhelm. Rosalynde met his gaze, and the two embraced as a rich, peal of laughter resounded from the tower.

"Oh, my," said Morwen, excitedly. She was holding Elspeth's babe in her arms. "How fortuitous!"

The hiss of metal stole through the glade as Rosalynde unsheathed her sword. "Give us that child!"

Morwen ignored the threat. "'Tis too bad Rhiannon and Arwyn cannot join you." She chortled again, clearly amused. And then, before anyone could respond, she dangled the child out by his arms. The baby began to wail, kicking his legs in fright, and Elspeth gasped.

"My book for your beastly child," she demanded. "Bring it to me now or I will cast him into the flames and you will watch him burn to his bones, like your grandmamau."

"Nay," Elspeth begged. "Please!"

Unmoved, Morwen laughed, and Rosalynde put a hand to her sister's arm. "Stay strong, Elspeth. We will get him back."

"Alas," Morwen continued. "So much as I enjoy our reunions, I must fly away, and since I do not trust a single one of you deceiving bitches, if I must choose one to bring me that book, I choose Seren." Her black eyes glittered like tourmalines as she hoisted up the wailing child and returned him to the cradle of her arms. "Only *one* may pass with *my* Book. The book is your passage. But for one," she repeated. "If two dare attempt the crossing, the second will burn."

Wide-eyed, Seren peered again at her sisters.

Rosalynde said, "She believes you to be most malleable, Seren."

Of course. Whatever her mother demanded, Seren always did, if only to keep the peace. She was, indeed, the most biddable of her sisters. Only Morwen hadn't any clue what she had endured since Dover, nor what she'd learned since Arwyn's passing—nor could Rosalynde or Elspeth possibly understand. Only there wasn't time to explain. "I will go," she said, holding a trembling hand out for the book.

Neither of her sisters dared argue. Tears slid down Elspeth's cheeks as she nodded, offering Seren the Book, her eyes glinting with gratitude.

"Nay!" said Wilhelm, with a voice like thunder. "I'll not allow this!"

Prepared to argue, Seren turned to face him, but he surprised her by seizing the *grimoire* from her hand, then bolting toward the circlet.

"Nay, Wilhelm," she screamed. "Nay, stop!"

Still as stones, Morwen's soldiers did not prevent him from passing and Seren held her breath as he slipped through the circlet, unharmed. She watched with bated breath as he marched toward the tower's entrance, and nearly fell to her knees in despair.

Sweet fates!

She would have gone after him, but Rosalynde

and Elspeth held her back. "Let him go," Rose demanded. "Let him go!"

"Nay," cried Seren. "Nay… she'll kill him!"

"'Tis too late," said Elspeth.

Indeed, it was.

Too late.

With the book in his hand, and without a backward glance, Wilhelm vanished into the tower… and just at that instant an arrow flew from the tree-line, passing through the circlet, embedding itself into the arch above the door.

Gasping in horror, Seren turned to find Morwen's ravens shrieking, taking flight from the boughs of nearby trees.

Thinking it was her men, Rosalynde commanded them. "Stand down, stand down!" she said. "Stand down!"

But the arrows kept coming—one whizzed past Seren's temple. She avoided it only because she turned to look at the tower entrance.

Too late.

Morwen's army sprang to life, drawing weapons. Only it was not Warkworth's men loosing arrows. An army of mail-clad soldiers poured into the clearing from the woods. They came mounted, bearing David's golden lion standard. It was David of Scotia, and realizing they had reinforcements, Rosalynde shouted, "To me! To me!"

Warkworth's soldiers gave a united war cry and rushed into the fray.

Her heart beating with fear, Seren was left with no weapon at all, confused, surrounded by tramping hooves, flying missiles, and swords.

33

It was all Wilhelm could do not to piss himself as he sprinted through the roaring wall of blue flames. He didn't give himself time to think about the consequences—nor his fear.

Not Warkworth the morning after the burning, nor Ayleth, with her twisted burnt body. Not the reek of smoke, nor the stench of scorched flesh.

In his wake, he left the sounds of battle—the clash of metal and shouts of "To me! To me!"

God save them, he thought. *God save them all.*

If not for the child, he didn't care what happened to him, but there was no way in bloody hell he would let Seren face her mother. Clutching the book in his hand, he bolted up the stairs, losing his footing twice before realizing he must ascend as close to the wall as possible.

Even then, the stones could scarcely bear his weight.

The tower was ancient, fallen to decay, the stone stairs crumbled beneath the heel of his boots.

Sunlight sluiced through the roof, pouring into the interior, highlighting the dust motes he stirred; the more he disturbed, the more it billowed like smoke—

and that was nearly his undoing. His heart pounded painfully as images of Warkworth once again accosted him—Lady Ayleth, with her skin charred and peeling away, her limbs twisted from the fall into the *motte*; his father, his brother and sister, burnt skin sliding off bones. The reek of death stank the air, caked into the hairs of his nostrils... even now, the remembered stench made his stomach roil.

Keep going, he commanded himself. *Keep going.*
For Seren, and her sisters.
Keep going, he commanded himself. *Keep going.*
For his father and his brother and sisters.
Keep going, he commanded himself. *Keep going.*

God help him; if he'd taken another instant to consider his actions, he might never have crossed that circlet of fire.

Even now, he imagined the stench of his own burning flesh, felt the heat of it eating through muscle and bone, and the smell revolted him.

Keep going, he commanded himself. *Keep going.*

It was all his imagination. His skin wasn't afire. Nothing was burning—nothing but that circlet. Somehow, the book itself was like an amulet. His clothes were untouched. He was whole. His clothes were untouched. *You are whole. Keep going,* he commanded himself. *Keep going.*

It was true; little in life frightened Wilhelm so much as fire, but more than fire, the thought of Seren meeting the same fate as Lady Ayleth.

His nape prickled with fear, but he had no regrets —not even now as his legs faltered over the strain of the climb.

Mindful of the book in his hand, he lost his footing again. He stumbled and fell near the top of the tower, nearly dropping the book. Hanging by one hand, he grunted in pain. A lesser man would have fallen, but he had more weight on his body than most, and the strain was unbearable. *Keep going,* he commanded himself. *Keep going.*

Somehow, he managed, with blood-stained nails, to claw his way back up and continue up the stairs. *Keep going,* he commanded himself. *Keep going.*

Sweating and exhausted, he felt Morwen's presence before her saw her—that same feeling he'd had on the day after the burning—a darkness that unsettled him to his marrow.

Keep going, he commanded himself. *Keep going.*

His boots found purchase where they could, and with his free hand, he groped at the stone, pulling himself up the last few feet, wondering how in creation she'd mounted this stairwell with a babe in her arms.

Keep going, he commanded himself. *Keep going.*

Laughter resounded from the rooftop—hideous peals of raucous laughter, and suddenly she began to sing, her voice, sweet as a siren, bouncing off stone— bouncing and bouncing, so it felt as though she sang to him. *Keep going,* he commanded himself. *Keep going.*

Her voice came from his right, from his left...

> When thy father went a-hunting,
> A spear on his shoulder, a club in his
>   hand,
> He called the hounds,
> 'Giff, Gaff; catch, catch, fetch, fetch!'

She was evil incarnate, he thought. How could she croon to that child whilst the world burned around her? *Keep going,* he commanded himself. *Keep going.*

At long last, he scaled the final steps and faced her,

and it was impossible not to stand in her presence and not feel terror. She loomed larger than life, somehow peering down at him, though he stood taller than most men. The look on her face was both gleeful and disdainful at once, and when she spoke, he could feel the rumble of stone.

"The arrogance of men," she said in greeting. "Wilhelm, Oh, dearest Wilhelm. Did you truly believe you would defeat me when my daughters cannot? You are no more than a toad!"

Wilhelm's brain focused on the cacophony surrounding them—the ceaseless shrieks of birds, the battle cries ringing in the distance, the clang of steel against steel. Morwen must have guessed at this thoughts, for she smiled. "Alas, you may have suffered your worst fears for naught." She bounced the babe in her arms, greedily eyeing the tome in his hand. It grew heavy as solid steel in his hand.

"Intemperance will be the undoing of men—you are rash and thoughtless," she declared. "But I shall, indeed, give you the child, and you may descend to find yourself surrounded by carnage—not unlike the day you returned to find Warkworth in ash." She smiled thinly. "Of course, you know, I did linger that day," she confessed. "As you must have sensed. I felt you," she admitted. "I spoke to you—and, oh, how I reveled in your pain. I had a bird's view, if you please." And she laughed again, still bouncing the babe.

It was all Wilhelm could do not to rush at her and pummel her face as he would a man's. Fury mounted inside him, overtaking his fear. "Take the book!" he demanded, thrusting it out to her, refusing to give her the satisfaction of reliving his worst nightmare. "Give me the child," he said. "Or, by God, I will strangle you with my own hands."

He might try it anyway, he thought, though he knew beyond a shadow of doubt this woman was not of this world. If he opted for vengeance, he and the child would both die.

She laughed in response to his threat, and then, it happened like a dream... She leaned forward, her body fluid, spilling the child into his arms, somehow seizing the book at the same time. It was an impossible feat that left him blinking in confusion. "Fool," she whispered in his ear, and the single word was filled with glee.

She drew the book to her breast and closed her eyes victoriously as he heard a sudden explosion below, the roar climbing higher and higher. One glance down revealed more of that bright blue flame wending its way upward, burning the tower from below.

Wilhelm stood, frozen. God help him, there was nowhere to go. Without the child in his arms he might have taken a chance, diving into the flames, but he would never risk the babe... and yet, if he stood here doing nothing, they would both perish. "We had a bargain," he screamed.

The witch answered with a slow, conniving grin. "So we did," she said, and without another word, she transformed herself before his eyes into a creature not unlike the one he'd spied in the woodlot south of Whittlewood and Salcey. Leaving only plumes of smoke, she burst from the tower with a peal of laughter, taking the book with her and leaving Wilhelm alone with the child.

34

To Seren's dismay, the circlet began to spread inward, as though the tower itself had inhaled the flames. It burned so brightly the entire glade lit with that strange blue light. "Nay," she screamed. "Nay, oh nay!"

With the battle raging all about her, she rushed toward the circlet. "Rhiannon," she screamed. "Goddess, please! Help me! Somebody, help, please!"

No one came. No one answered.

Her sisters, astride their steeds, wielded their weapons against Morwen's army. Rosalynde moved through the melee with her glowing sword drawn, striking down everyone in her path. Her steward remained at her back, dispatching all she missed. Elspeth too had been swept into the fray, fighting for her life, swinging her blade and shouting words that came to naught.

> By the power of earth, fire, air and
>   water, my Goddess, I beg protection.
> By the power of earth, fire, air and
>   water, my Goddess, I beg protection.

Seren whirled again to face the tower. She had no weapon in her possession—nothing—but her fury raised a storm that shook her mother's birds from nearby trees. With cries of protest, the birds launched into the swirling wind, into the fray, pecking furiously at the heads of allied soldiers.

Crying out in fear as they came for her, with their beady eyes and bloodied beaks, Seren peered at the tower through blood-stained hands, praying to anyone who would listen.

Bring him back.

Goddess, please, keep the child safe.

Even as she watched, something black erupted from the tower, roiling like smoke, unfurling wings as it soared skyward.

As suddenly as the battle was engaged, it stopped.

Morwen's soldiers vanished.

It happened so swiftly no one could be sure what transpired. Like their master, her soldiers *shapeshifted*, then took wing, pursuing their dark angel. But the tower itself was still aflame, burning so brightly that the stone glowed like the metal of Rosalynde's sword. Second by second, the flames licked higher, higher, tendrils reaching out through each window it passed, spreading so swiftly Seren hadn't time to think, only feel...

"Nay," she screamed. "Nay!"

Morwen had betrayed them. She had fled with the Book, leaving the love of her heart to be consumed by *witchfire*.

Wilhelm would not survive it.

The babe would not survive it.

Her throat thickened with emotion. The first tear came unbidden, and with it, came a single drop of rain. Another tear, and another drop, and within an instant, came the deluge. Only Seren understood what it was... and she knew because it was not the first time.

Witchwater—witchwater, pure and true. *Witchwater* to put out the *witchfire*.

"Wilhelm," she sobbed, and in speaking his name, she only wept harder. The wind rose, gripping trees, as dark clouds swept over the clearing, converging over the tower—black as night, only with a silver lining that shone as bright as the sun. Every soldier... every man bearing witness... re-sheathed his weapon. Bloodied, and battle weary, they stared with mouths agape as little by little the glittering rain began to extinguish the fire, putting it out, lick by lick by lick.

Seren fell to her knees, her fingers grasping at sodden ash. She was only vaguely aware that Rosalynde and Elspeth had come rushing to her side—Elspeth only waiting for the circlet to vanish, so she could rush into the tower to find her child.

Rosalynde whispered with a note of awe, "Witchwater."

Indeed, it was.

Indeed, it was.

Indeed, it was.

Turning up her palm to catch the glittering droplets, Seren wept and the storm raged harder, washing away the coat of ash from her palm.

"True love's tears will save the newborn prophet," Rose whispered softly, but Seren hadn't any clue what her sister was talking about. She didn't care about prophets or prophecies. At the instant, she didn't care about anything at all except Wilhelm and the babe. He came marching out of the tower and Seren's grief turned at once to joy.

Elspeth's babe was cradled in his arms. The child wailed as Seren wailed, flailing his arms about.

Elspeth rushed to greet them, her arms reaching desperately for her child.

Swallowing her relief, Seren's heart hammered like thunder. Her eyes inspected Wilhelm greedily—his dirty, sooty, red-flushed face, his arms and legs in one piece. His beautiful dark eyes met hers and clung to her, even as Elspeth embraced her baby, stealing him away.

He was alive.

His eyes only for her, Wilhelm strode to Seren, arms open wide. He caught her in an embrace, kissing her soundly. She clung to him, tasting the salt of her own tears. "I love you," he said, tearing his mouth away, and she wept. "I love you more than life, Seren. Be my wife!"

Without question, Wilhelm Fitz Richard, bastard son of Richard de Vere had risked his life for her. He'd faced her mother so she wouldn't have to. His love burned brighter than any *witchfire*. The truth was plain for everyone to see. In that instant, as he waited for Seren to speak, it seemed that the very breath of the world waited as well.

The babe was alive.

Wilhelm was alive.

Morwen and her soldiers were gone.

The fire was doused.

"Yay," she whispered. "I will marry you." And she kissed him again, as every man and woman in the glade erupted with huzzahs. Even surrounded by the carnage of battle, the sight of two lovers kissing lit the glade with another fire entirely... the light and flame of hope and love.

Seren and Wilhelm were wed at Warkworth on a summer morn, with Rosalynde and Elspeth and their entire families in attendance. The ceremony was modest, presided over by a Church priest, with vows spoken again in private to honor the Mother Goddess.

Jack was delivered to Warkworth and spent a month with Seren and Wilhelm before boarding a ship to Normandy. Escorted by an emissary of the Church, he returned to his mother in Calais, vowing to return to England when he was old enough to avenge his father.

No word ever arrived about Rhiannon. No matter how oft they entreated the king for news, Stephen refused to answer their pleas. They only knew she was still alive because Giles had a spy in Stephen's court. But nobody anywhere knew where Morwen had gone, and the longer her absence, the more Seren feared she was out there... scheming.

Four years had gone by since the Battle at the Widow's Tower, four years to the date. Having split his army to ride to Elspeth's defense, David mac Maíl Choluim forfeited York, and during the Battle at the

Tower, King Stephen slipped into the city of York to
fortify its garrison, forcing David to withdraw his remaining troops. His debt to Elspeth was paid in full.

As for Stephen, his Queen Consort was dead—
perished of a fever at Hedingham last year. Now, he sat
alone upon his stolen throne, and despite having
saved York, the bishopric did not go to Stephen's
choice. However, there was a new Pope now, and
Stephen would see his nephew reappointed. While it
was possible he would succeed in that endeavor, the
new Pope still refused to consecrate Eustace. But the
Empress Matilda was no longer the favored candidate
for succession. As the true and rightful heir to England's throne, by virtue of his father and his grandfather, the Vatican would see twenty-year-old Duke
Henry crowned instead, and they would employ any
means to see it done, including engage the Papal
Guard. Once again, tensions were escalating.

Early this past January, Duke Henry returned to
England with a modest army, taking the king's castle
at Malmesbury.

In retribution, Stephen intensified his long-run-
ning siege of Wallingford. Now, even as Rosalynde,
Seren and Elspeth sat conversing in Warkworth's solar,
Stephen's own brother, Henry of Blois and the Archbishop of Canterbury were aligning forces to broker a
treaty for peace. Giles himself rode south to help with
the negotiations and Malcom rode west with David to
quell unrest in his northern shires.

Fortunately, the castle at Warkworth was complete
and fully girded—so much so that Malcom had
brought his wife and three children to await his
return.

At any rate, they gathered at Warkworth every year
on this precise date to hold a memorial for Arwyn.

The timing was perfect, and Wilhelm, for all that he was bastard-born, was now Warkworth's warden, with a place at his brother's side. Dressed as befitted a lord, he came sauntering into the solar, stopped to give Elspeth's twins a tip for swordplay, then went straight for his wife, with the sole purpose of offering his lady a kiss—on the lips, no less. Shockingly crude, with little decorum, but everybody already knew he was bastard-born. He left again without a word, though not before casting the sisters a backward glance, and a wink.

"That man is besotted," said Rosalynde, smiling, resting a hand on her increasing belly.

"Entirely," said Elspeth. "I wager he'll return within the hour for another."

The sisters all laughed, and Rosalynde said, "Alas, Elspeth, it seems we two are widows and Seren is the only one with a living husband."

Seren smiled. "Malcom and Giles will return soon," she consoled her sisters. And yet, she knew well enough that "soon" would never be "soon enough" for her sisters. Certainly, if the case were reversed, it would not be soon enough for her. She was eternally grateful Wilhelm's duties kept him at home.

"Broc!" rebuked Elspeth. "Do not strike your brother!"

"Mother, please! We are learning to be proper warriors," said Broc, who was too young, at five, to handle his wooden sword. And nevertheless, he tried. The make-do weapon swayed as he held it aloft, and his brother held a curled fist upside his own head. "Uncle Wilhelm said we should practice," Broc explained, his pale brows colliding. "See, he's already recovered."

Chin stiff, and brows furrowed, Lachlan nodded in support of his elder, twin brother and rose.

"Of course, you must practice," agreed Elspeth.

"But must you be so violent? And please, do not play here in the solar," she demanded. "You will wake your sister."

The boys shared a meaningful glance, then darted from the room together; only Broc stopped to peer back at them as the wee babe threw up her hands in fright and began to wail. Broc grinned then, and vanished into the hall.

"What a terror!" said Seren. "Defiant to his soul!"

Rosalynde asked, "Did he wake her apurpose?"

Elspeth shrugged, wearied by her son's antics. "Who knows? He reminds me so much of Rhiannon," she said. "Draw a line in the sand and forbid him to cross it, and he'll wait until you're watching to do it— with a grin, no less." She sighed. "Alas, everything reminds me of Rhiannon."

Elspeth settled her babe, rocking the small, wooden cradle that had been gifted to Rosalynde for the coming babe. "I long to know how she fares. Surely, someone somewhere must know..."

Seren's sisters were both blessed with new babes, though Rosalynde's was yet unborn. Lachlan and Broc had welcomed their little sister with gleeful smiles, and despite that Broc seemed to like to harry his mother, he adored young Arwyn more than words could say. His admiration was in his eyes for all to see.

Seren, on the other hand, had yet to conceive, but not for lack of trying. She knew in her heart it must be because the Goddess had something more in store for her... what this could be, she didn't know. But... it was a feeling she had.

Frowning, her thoughts returning to Rhiannon, she turned to look out the window, and started at the sight of a lone black bird sitting on the sill—a plain old crow, not a raven, but, before she could remark on it, a knock sounded upon the solar door. "My lady," said a handmaid. "There's an auld woman here to see you."

Seren blinked, peering back at the window to find the bird gone.

"Says her name is Isolde."

"Isolde!"

All three sisters spoke at once, but Seren was up before Elspeth could snatch her child from the cradle. Dropping her needlework, she rushed for the door, trusting that Rosalynde and Elspeth would follow.

Neither she nor her sisters had seen that woman in a score of years, and the last time Seren so much as thought of her was the night before Wilhelm asked her to marry him.

They found her seated alone at one of the lower tables in the great hall, kicking her toes against the rushes. She rose to greet them when they approached and sat again without being asked to, almost as though she couldn't find purchase on her tired old feet. Seren peered down to find her legs spindly and twisted, not unlike that of a bird's.

"Isolde," she said warmly, leaning to embrace the woman where she sat. It didn't matter that they hadn't seen her in so many years; Seren remembered her kindness. As her sisters greeted her as well, then chatted, she ordered sustenance for their guest, and as they waited, Isolde apprised them of the reason for her visit. She'd come to advise them, somehow knowing they would all be in residence at Warkworth.

"Gird your loins," she warned, crooking a finger at Seren. "The time has come! Even now, the king's son has begun the end-time prophecy. *She* will return, and only *Caledfwlch* will stop her." She leaned forward now, looking Seren straight in the eyes, emphasizing with great meaning. "Only *you* can imbue that sword."

Seren's hand lifted to her breast in confusion.

The old woman nodded. "Sweet Seren... by now you must realize your sister is not the Promised One."

Seren felt herself grow dizzy over the woman's words.

"When you were a babe," Isolde explained. "Not more than two, I knew what you would become, and I bound and *glamoured* you."

Seren peered up at Elspeth, standing close with the child on her hip, brow furrowed.

"A trick of the eyes," the old woman continued, brushing a hand through the air as though to remove a veil.

Elspeth's mouth gaped open. So, too, did Rosalynde's, for in the wake of Isolde's hand flourish, Seren was changed.

"Sweet fates!" Rosalynde said, with as much confusion as Seren felt. "Your eyes... they are..." The woman waved her hand again, and her eyes were again blue.

"How is that possible?" demanded Elspeth of the crone. "Rhiannon is the one whose *magik* was strongest. I don't understand."

"Indeed, Rhiannon's *magik* is powerful," agreed Isolde. "Though not because she is Goddess-blessed. Rather, she is blessed by your grandmamau with the *hud* powerful enough for two." She held up two bony fingers. "I knew your mother would keep the Promised One close, only to kill her if she manifested the power of the divine, so I *glamoured* Rhiannon's eyes as well."

Rosalynde narrowed her eyes. "So what you're saying is that you endangered my sister's life by altering the color of her eyes, only to keep my mother from knowing who the true Regnant should be?"

The old woman sighed. "Alas, 'tis true." She straightened her back. "And what would you have had me do? Allow her to murder the one-true Regnant? Do you believe I am the only one to have contrived such sacrifices?" she asked, and then answered her own question. "But nay." She addressed each of the sisters in turn. "Rhiannon, too, contrived, so did Arwyn."

"The fire," Seren whispered, somehow understanding what the old woman was saying.

"Aye," the lady confessed, turning again to Seren, spearing her with ice-blue eyes. "She had a visit that morning, and your sister sacrificed herself so you could remain free. *You* will be the Regnant, Seren."

Gasps of surprise followed her announcement, but neither Seren nor her sisters could form questions, so shocking was the proclamation.

"You were aptly named," said Isolde. "In our tongue, as you must know, Seren means star, and little did your mother realize that the "star" she gave birth to was the Regnant she should fear—you and only you, and if not you, then no other in this day and age. But now you must earn your laurels."

Somehow, though the old woman's words offered more questions than answers, Seren understood... Everything she already knew confirmed it; everything she didn't know came rushing forth, like a torrent.

Since that day at the Widow's Tower, she and Rose and Elspeth had many times pondered her newfound abilities. None of them could find any reason to explain them.

It was her *witchwater* that put out the *witchfire* at the Widow's Tower, and no other means could have doused it.

"I don't understand," said Elspeth.

The old woman ignored her two sisters, speaking only to Seren now. "You must find your true self, Seren. Only then will you have answers. Find yourself, then imbue *Caledfwlch* with the power of the divine."

Her gaze moved to Rosalynde, and she said, pointing a finger quite vehemently. "That sword is no longer yours to wield. Give it to your sister. When the time arrives, only she will know who to give it to."

The old woman then smiled cannily, peering up at Elspeth, and said, "There are mysteries in life we are not meant to know, Elspeth Pendragon." She wagged a finger. "You guard your boys. 'Tis not over, and it will not be over until the Queen of Avalon is restored to her throne. But the sea will not keep her."

"You speak in riddles!" Elspeth said, annoyed. "What—"

"Hush, Elspeth. Remember the sigil on the livery of Morwen's soldiers?" Elspeth nodded, and Seren said, "Let the woman talk."

The old woman gave Seren a grateful nod, and then continued, "I was her student before she understood she was my teacher. Only now you must realize... she is no daughter to Morgan. She is the witch Goddess who sought the prophet's doom. It was your own mother, the child, who summoned the Lady from the Lake, and your uncle Emrys who opened the door."

"How?" asked Rose.

"Blood *magik*," the woman hissed, and she placed a finger to her lips. "Blood *magik* so hideous I dare not speak it. But the how of it you must not long to know. Only know this, Daughters of Avalon; once she realizes her mistake, she will return for that child. He is her doom."

The woman then narrowed her ice-blue eyes on

Elspeth. "He'll not be the one to close her eyes, but once she is vanquished, it is *he* who holds the key to keep her from the realms of men."

"My son?" asked Elspeth.

"The fair one," Isolde said with a nod. "He is the Merlin reborn, and if you doubt me, see for yourself; he bears the birthmark at his—"

"Nape," said Elspeth. The woman nodded. The birthmark had been covered since he grew his first wisps of hair.

"The divine symbol of life, the mark of the quintessence, which binds all elements before it."

"My son?" Elspeth whispered again, but this time her voice held a note of wonder. "You must call him Emrys henceforth, for by naming him by his true name, you imbue him with the legacy he is born to fulfill."

"Emrys," whispered Elspeth.

"It means immortal," explained the old woman.

"And is he?" Elspeth asked.

The old woman smiled. "Alas, my dear, there are mysteries in life we are not meant to know..."

Outside, in the courtyard, the boys could be heard shouting, "To me! To me!" —a call to arms.

To this day, Seren could not hear those words without some trepidation. But boys were meant to be boys, and no one could stay the hand of fate.

"Gird your loins," the old woman said again, with fervor, and then came a five-year-old's wail. Seren, Rosalynde and Elspeth all ran into the courtyard to see what had happened, leaving the old woman seated at their table.

"Broc!" said Elspeth. Lachlan was kneeling before his twin brother, who was now the one seated on his rump, red-faced and pouting, a black and blue knot the size of a buckle on his forehead.

"He told me to do it," said Lachlan, looking ashamed. He held his toy sword aloft, showing his mother the true culprit. Elspeth seized both wooden swords from her sons—first Broc, then Lachlan—and the boys looked perfectly contrite. She commanded both to apologize before everything erupted into chaos. A horn sounded—heralding a rider's approach. Leaving the boys where they sat, the sisters all ran to see who it might be.

It was Malcom Scott who rode in through the open gate, accompanied by his father and two men. He sought his wife's gaze at once, sliding down from his horse, taking his steps as leaps until he held Elspeth in his arms. "God's bones! I've missed you," she said. He kissed Elspeth soundly, embracing her still.

"Papa, papa," screamed the boys, and Malcom released his wife only to scoop up both children into his arms.

"You are early," said Elspeth, her cheeks aflame, and her eyes filled with warmth at the sight of her husband holding his sons.

He grinned. "Or late, depending on the state of one's belly. Mine demands supper."

"My boy was always a hungry beast," said Malcom's father, and Seren laughed, along with her sisters, taking the MacKinnon by the arm.

"Wilhelm will be so pleased to see you, and you have arrived just in time to meet our guest—a woman who raised us since birth. You can prod her to your heart's content for all our secrets," Seren said, and Elspeth shook her head.

"I fear he hasn't the heart to hear more," Elspeth jested. And nevertheless, Seren proceeded to tell him all about Isolde—all that she could remember, at any rate, and everything the old woman had told them. Unfortunately, by the time they returned to the hall, she was gone.

No one saw her leave. No one knew where she'd gone to. Apparently, she'd never said a word to anyone. Nor did she exit through the front gates, or she would have passed right by them. She was simply there one instant; the next she was gone. Only Seren could still feel her presence...

She peered up into the rafters, spying a blackbird perched up high. The bird cocked its black head, peering down at them, and Seren smiled.

"Where is she?" asked Elspeth.

"Gone," said Seren. "But something tells me she'll be about."

She winked at her sister, finally understanding what she must do. After all, what else was there to do in the presence of hungry men, except feed them? Tomorrow would bring more strife, but the moment was sweet enough for a feast. She reached for the chatelaine's keys at her belt, leaving her sisters to chatter with the men whilst she considered the contents of their larder... and as she walked into the courtyard, the blackbird flittered to her shoulder... whispering into her ear.

A HEARTFELT THANK YOU!

Thank you from the bottom of my heart for reading Fire Song. There are millions of titles out there, and I'm honored you decided to read one of mine.

If you enjoyed this book, please consider posting a review. Reviews help other readers discover our books and I sincerely appreciate every single one, no matter how long or short.

Would you like to know when my next book is available? Sign up for my newsletter and follow me on social media:

Facebook: facebook.com/tanyaannecrosby
Twitter at @tanyaannecrosby
Instagram at tanyaannecrosby

Also, please follow me on BookBub to be notified of deals and new releases.

Let's hang out! I have a Facebook group:

Tanya's Book Tribe

I'm also a member of the Jewels of Historical Romance. I hope you'll visit our Facebook group, the Jewels Salon. Read on for links to our Fabulous Firsts collections, two six book anthologies featuring starters for our most beloved series—each set is just 99c!

Thank you again for reading and for your support.

Tanya Anne Crosby

NEXT IN THE DAUGHTERS OF AVALON SERIES...

RHIANNON

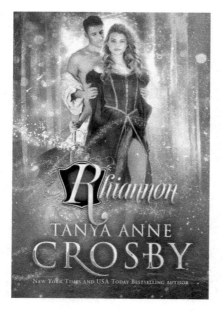

Coming 2020

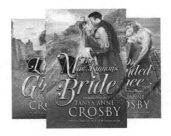

DAUGHTERS OF AVALON

Rhiannon

ALSO BY TANYA ANNE CROSBY

DAUGHTERS OF AVALON

The King's Favorite

The Holly & the Ivy

A Winter's Rose

Fire Song

Rhiannon

THE PRINCE & THE IMPOSTOR

Seduced by a Prince

A Crown for a Lady

THE HIGHLAND BRIDES

The MacKinnon's Bride

Lyon's Gift

On Bended Knee

Lion Heart

Highland Song

MacKinnon's Hope

GUARDIANS OF THE STONE

Once Upon a Highland Legend

Highland Fire

Highland Steel

Highland Storm

Maiden of the Mist

ABOUT THE AUTHOR

 Tanya Anne Crosby is the New York Times and USA Today bestselling author of thirty novels. She has been featured in magazines, such as People, Romantic Times and Publisher's Weekly, and her books have been translated into eight languages. Her first novel was published in 1992 by Avon Books, where Tanya was hailed as "one of Avon's fastest rising stars." Her fourth book was chosen to launch the company's Avon Romantic Treasure imprint.

Known for stories charged with emotion and humor and filled with flawed characters Tanya is an award-winning author, journalist, and editor, and her novels have garnered reader praise and glowing critical reviews. She and her writer husband split their time between Charleston, SC, where she was raised, and northern Michigan, where the couple make their home.

For more information
Website
Email
Newsletter

CPSIA information can be obtained
at www.ICGtesting.com
Printed in the USA
BVHW041804300621
610839BV00006B/118